LARRY COLLINS'

MAZE

"COLLINS' STORY IS THE STUFF OF HEAD-LINES. . . ."

—*The Oregonian*

"In a Frederick Forsyth way, Collins layers on the technical detail. . . . A complex rabbits' warren of plots and subplots . . . *MAZE* is a big-engined thriller that motors along nicely. . . . There's plenty here to please. . . ."

—*Kirkus Reviews*

"One of the earmarks of a Larry Collins book is the meticulous research that goes into it. . . . From *MAZE*, his latest tome, it is apparent that Mr. Collins still does his homework. . . . THIS IS GOOD, ENTERTAINING STUFF. . . ."

—*Baltimore Sun*

"A TALE OF INTRIGUE THAT VAULTS ALONG AT A BREAKNECK PACE . . ."

—*Boston Herald*

"FAR BETTER THAN JOHN LE CARRÉ."

—Hal Youngblood,
"Nighttime Detroit," WJR-AM

(more . . .)

Books by Larry Collins

Fall from Grace
Maze

LARRY COLLINS

MAZE

POCKET BOOKS

New York   London   Toronto   Sydney   Tokyo   Singapore

This book is a work of fiction. Names, characters, places and incidents are either the product of the author's imagination or are used fictitiously. Any resemblance to actual events or locales or persons, living or dead, is entirely coincidental.

POCKET BOOKS, a division of Simon & Schuster Inc.
1230 Avenue of the Americas, New York, NY 10020

ISBN: 0-671-70822-8

First Pocket Books printing November 1990

10 9 8 7 6 5 4 3 2 1

POCKET and colophon are registered trademarks of
Simon & Schuster Inc.

Cover illustration by David Mann

Printed in the U.S.A.

FOR MY FATHER

CONTENTS

CONTENTS

PART 1

"HOW IN HELL
DID SHE DO IT?"

T wo hundred fathoms down in the Atlantic depths, 317 nautical miles southeast of Greenland, the USS *Boston* tiptoed through the ocean's perpetual night at four knots. She was an SSN-688 Los Angeles Class attack boat, among the latest and the best of the U.S. Navy's hunter/killer submarines. In his command position in the submarine's attack center, her captain followed her painfully slow progress on the green spiderweb of his dead reckoning tracer monitor.

As she had been for hours, *Boston* was running a steadily diminishing series of concentric circles around a position at the center of the display identified as Area Bravo. Currently, she was running the circumference of a circle sixty miles in diameter. That *Boston* should even be in the area at all was in contradiction of one of the most fundamental principles of the submarine service. Every operations order on every boat in the Atlantic Submarine Fleet made it clear that Area Bravo was virgin territory, an absolute no-go area. Area Bravo was the sanctuary, the private patch of water of another U.S. submarine, the *Ohio*, a Trident missile boat twice the size of the *Boston*.

Yet *Boston* had been ordered to invade the heart of *Ohio*'s lair while she was returning to New London from special operations by an urgent "immediate execution" order from COMSUBLANT. The computer-generated code name of her mission was Seashell. Studying it, the *Boston*'s captain had felt a shiver of concern.

His assignment was to stalk the waters around *Ohio* "to determine whether or not *Ohio* was under surveillance without her knowledge by potential enemy forces."

If that was the case, it would be a disaster with incalculable consequences. The *Ohio* and the other missile-bearing subs in the U.S. Underseas Fleet were the heart of U.S. nuclear deterrence policy, the one nuclear weapon no disarmament treaty would ever discard. Neutralize *Ohio* and her missile-bearing sister subs, and the whole concept of U.S. nuclear deterrence was in jeopardy. At the limit, the United States could then be at the mercy of the Kremlin.

And if, unknown to *Ohio,* a Soviet hunter/killer submarine lurked somewhere in that black nautical envelope, *Ohio* would be neutralized. A Soviet missile could destroy her in seconds, long before she could execute her retaliatory mission.

The captain of the *Boston* knew *Ohio* would either be hovering motionless or moving at two knots in lazy figure eights around the precise geographic center of Area Bravo. Nineteen hundred and thirty-four fathoms below the surface of the center of Area Bravo was a conjugate-point cavity in the ocean floor identified in the restricted submarine services charts as C9357. Years ago, Navy convoys trailing sonar arrays had scanned every square foot of the ocean floor. The resulting mass of data, translated into specific configurations by Cray computers, had given the Navy a library of charts of the ocean's floor as precise, as reliable, as any topographical map of the earth's surface.

Once a day, *Ohio*'s secure 3D sonar system confirmed her position over the center of cavity C9357. In the event of a Soviet nuclear missile launch on the United States, even if every navigational satellite had been blown out of space and her own inertial navigation system was out of order, *Ohio* could get a positive geographical fix of her location by firing a sonar ping into the center of cavity C9357. By matching his missile's guidance system to the position provided by his sonar ping, *Ohio*'s captain could launch his missiles at targets deep in the heartland of the Soviet Union knowing they would impact with an accuracy of no more than three hundred yards from target center. It was that ability that made *Ohio* such a vital part of U.S. nuclear deterrence policy.

Ohio's fundamental task, therefore, was to live by the submariner's motto "Run Silent, Run Deep." Her job was to lurk in her underseas envelope absolutely undetected by enemy subs. At his current distance, thirty nautical miles from the heart of Area Bravo, the *Boston* had no sonar contact with *Ohio*. Nor, he knew, could *Ohio* have picked up his presence out here tiptoeing along his circle.

"Sonar," said the captain. "Attack center. Anything?"

"Negative, Captain," came the reply as it had since the operation had begun.

The captain stood up, stretched, finished his sixth cup of coffee of the day, and decided to go below to the sonar room.

The sonar room was the nerve center of a modern nuclear submarine, the area where its eyes and ears, its abilities to pierce the black, dimensionless walls around it, were focused. Its heart was a wheel eight inches in diameter which, guided by the sonarman on watch, rotated its way through the eight-foot-tall tubular hydrophones of the sub's sonar array. Each hydrophone focused on two degrees of the 360-degree circle surrounding the submarine—although, since her baffles were dead, there were always two silent arcs on any given bearing. The sonarman could sweep the seas surrounding *Boston* by moving through his hydrophones in a regular pattern; he could pursue just one noise by fixing on one hydrophone and its two-degree arc; he could leap back and forth between two different sonar contacts on opposite sides of the sub. Now, as the *Boston* was running a search mode, the sonarman moved slowly from hydrophone to hydrophone, listening intently to each sector before flicking his wheel on to the next hydrophone and a new bearing.

Boston's senior sonarman was an E9, a master chief petty officer named Santucci from Marblehead, Massachusetts. Santucci had spent seventeen years of his life in submarines listening to the symphony of the sea. He was a master of his craft. His ears could distinguish in a few tens of milliseconds between the low bloops of a porpoise or a dolphin, the peep of a humpbacked whale or the shriller tweet of a great white, the honk of a blowing seal or the crackle of a bed of snapping shrimps. Normally, Santucci did not stand sonar watches. When *Boston* was at battle stations, however, or on a special mission such as this one, no one could keep him from his monitor.

"Anything?" asked the captain as he stepped into the sonar room.

"Nothing out there, Captain," Santucci answered, "except a pair of humpbacks moving through our starboard quarter."

The captain nodded. Santucci's second and his recorder, earphones clamped to their heads, sat on either side of their chief. Above the wheel was a digitalized clock, its figures reading out in hundredths of a second. Below it was the ship's Cray computer, an exquisitely programmed multimillion-dollar plaything. Straddling it were a pair of UNQ7 recorders. Their ten-inch reels of tape registered every sound picked up by the *Boston*'s hydrophones and played them into the Cray.

The discordant note for which Santucci's sensitive ears listened was any sound that man, not nature, had brought to the depths. Ultimately, what Santucci and his hydrophones were after was the noise signature of a submarine, the acoustical fingerprint, the genetic patterning that made each submarine moving under the ocean's surface unique in its species.

Popular lore held that that fingerprint came from the noise given off by the submarine's propeller blades as it drove the boat through the waters. In fact, it was the summation of a complex series of noises of which the propeller noise was only one element.

As Santucci and the captain knew, those precious signatures had been obtained by other U.S. submarines at considerable peril, often lying on the ocean floor inside Soviet territorial waters off Murmansk and Vladivostok.

From their hiding places, they "shot" Soviet submarines moving in and out of port with BQR6 passive sonar arrays. They recorded the passing sub's noises from three angles: port, starboard, and stern. What came back was a range of sound: the hum of the air-conditioning unit and the refrigeration unit, the steady beat of the generators, the whir of the turbines, the sound of the water pumps returning condensed steam back to the sub's nuclear reactor. Some sub's air-conditioning units might be closer to the hull by a few inches, modifying the sound they produced. A generator might have its own quirky "kerplonk" as some automobile engines will have a special sound of their own.

The summation of those sounds was a composite noise level that made up the sub's noise signature. And there on Santucci's Cray computer were stored the noise signatures of every submarine the Soviets possessed, waiting for his hydrophones to deliver the few characteristic sounds that would reveal to *Boston* not just the presence of a Soviet submarine but also exactly which submarine it was, what armament she carried, and the precise nature of the threat she might—or might not—pose to *Boston*.

"I'm going to my stateroom to catch up on some paperwork," the captain told Santucci. "If you get anything, call me on the secure line."

Exactly twenty minutes later, Santucci sat upright in his chair, listening. His recorder and his second stared at him. Neither man had heard anything on the earphones. Santucci punched his monitor and rewound the tape on one of the UNQ7 recorders. Half a dozen times he listened and relistened to the last seconds recorded by the number-nineteen hydrophone. Finally, his second heard the almost inaudible thump that had caught Santucci's ears. He looked at him quizzically.

"The only thing I know is that ain't no fish," Santucci mumbled. "I think I'll invite the captain's attention to that."

He pushed the buzzer on his direct line to the captain's stateroom. "Captain," he said, "I have something I'd like you to listen to."

The captain was there in seconds. He picked up a set of earphones.

"We read this on a bearing of two seven three," Santucci told him as he played the tape of the sound that had caught his attention. The captain listened to it half a dozen times.

"What do you think?" he asked Santucci.

"I only know one thing, sir—it's not a normal sea noise."

"Is there anything on that bearing now?"

"Nothing."

Both men listened intently to the hydrophone scanning bearing 273. There was nothing but a wall of silence.

"I have a crazy idea, sir," Santucci said.

"What's that?" asked the captain, who knew Santucci's ideas were rarely crazy.

"Maybe, just maybe, somebody blew an ejection chute out there and one of the weights bumped on the way out." Submarines have to eject their accumulated waste periodically through special chutes like torpedo tubes. The waste is packed in bags weighted with bits of scrap metal to be sure they sink. "I'd like permission to close on that bearing, sir."

The captain reflected for a second. That would mean breaking out of his search mode. "Okay," he said, and reached for the intercom. "Con, this is the captain. Come left to bearing two seven three."

The maneuver swung *Boston*'s bow to the direction from which Santucci's noise had come. It put the boat's most sensitive hydrophones right on that bearing. For over an hour, *Boston* crept along the bearing, her hydrophones picking up absolutely nothing but the silence of the sea. The captain had begun to debate how much longer he could allow himself to maintain their course and whether he should return to his normal search pattern when Santucci stiffened.

"Sir," he said, "I have a definite contact this bearing."

The captain grabbed his earphones. After a moment, he too heard the sound that had alerted Santucci, a faint humming noise.

"I think we've got a submerged submarine," Santucci said. He reached forward and started the UNQ7's digital processor feeding into his Cray computer. At the same time, the captain buzzed the con. "Con, this is the captain," he said. "Reduce speed to two knots. Rig for ultra-quiet. Man the phones."

Because *Boston* was closing on the contact bow first, she was coming in on her quietest posture; still, the captain wanted to take no chances of alerting the contact of his presence.

"The contact's not moving," Santucci said. "I have no propulsion noises."

All four men in the sonar room now had their eyes focused on the Cray, into which the UNQ7s were relaying the sounds picked up by the sonar array. Suddenly a chain of gray-green letters flashed onto the display screen.

```
INITIAL CLASSIFICATION NOVEMBER
CLASS SUBMARINE HULL NUMBER AS YET
UNDETERMINED REQUIRE FURTHER INPUT
FOR POSITIVE IDENTIFICATION.
```

A November was the Navy's designation for one of the USSR's best nuclear hunter/killer subs.

"Holy shit!" breathed the captain. "I would never have believed it! Con, all stop."

Now the sonar room was silent as each man listened intently to the hydrophone noises being fed into his earphones. Santucci was the first to speak. "I'm getting the reactor coolant pump noises," he whispered.

"Any sign he's made us?" the captain asked.

Santucci shook his head. "We're picking up sounds of only one generator." Had the Russian been using two generators it would probably mean he had gone to battle stations because his sonar had detected *Boston*'s presence.

The computer screen began to blink again.

"We got a match," Santucci said as a new line of text came flashing onto the screen:

POSITIVE IDENTIFICATION NOVEMBER
CLASS SUBMARINE HULL NUMBER S174.

The captain pressed the buzzer. "Con," he ordered, "this is the captain. We've got a definite November off our bow. We're in his baffles. Back down very cautiously until you've put five thousand more yards between us."

As the *Boston* tiptoed undetected back out of the November's sonar range, the captain and the sonar crew watched the display, horrified and fascinated by what they were seeing. The Soviet hunter/killer submarine was in its turn edging its way around position C9357, the center of Area Bravo, clearly shadowing the moves of the *Ohio*, ready, should she be ordered to do so, to destroy the American sub in minutes.

"So much for nuclear retaliation," *Boston*'s captain mused. "Get the communications officer down here."

"Encrypt this and send it to SUBLANT by shot method," he instructed the communications officer. "Positive ID November Class Hull Number S174 holding position fifteen thousand yards bearing zero nine zero from *Ohio*'s position C nine three five seven stop appears to be shadowing *Ohio* stop no indication *Ohio* has detected her presence stop await further orders."

"That's going to shake up SUBLANT," Santucci said.

"Not half as much as it's already shaken me up." The captain sighed. "How in God's name did SUBLANT ever get the idea a Russian boat could be out there riding *Ohio*'s coattails?"

Art Bennington stared balefully into his bathroom mirror. He did not much like what he saw there. His eye sockets were puffed and lined from the fitful sleep that cursed his existence these days. The flesh under his chin was beginning to sag a bit just as the skin below his cheekbones was taking on the appearance of an unstretched drum. Maybe a face-lift, he thought on days like this, but then how the hell would he afford that on what the CIA paid him? Face-lifts were for real estate developers and di-

vorce lawyers. His hair, okay, his hair was still so thick
he could barely get a comb through it, but it was getting
grayer by the day, and, given the state of his nerves and
intestines, it seemed to produce enough dandruff each
day to fuel a snow-making machine up at Stowe. The
contours of his nose had been rearranged so many times
back in the days when football was played without face
masks that it had left him looking, as a girlfriend from
Smith had once remarked, "so ugly you're almost cute."

What was it they said, Bennington thought—after fifty
your sins start to show on your face? Christ, if he only
had a few more sins, good, meaty carnal ones, whose
memories could console him when he looked into his mirror on mornings like this.

He padded back into his bedroom and flicked on CNN.
That was as much a part of his waking routine as brushing
his teeth, and, good behavioral scientist that he was, he
knew his reason for turning it on was not a compulsive
need to find out what was happening in the world, but
simply to bring the sound of human voices to this unutterably dreary two-bedroom flat on the wrong side of
Route 123 in Vienna, Virginia, a few miles from downtown Washington, D.C.

As the screen flickered on, he noticed the ruby power
light on the tape recorder by his bedside table was still
on. He rewound the tape and switched off the recorder.
What a godsend she had been, that hypnotherapist up at
Tysons Corner. That she had been able to get him to kick
his two-pack-a-day cigarette habit in two half-hour sessions was not a surprise.

After all, his own years of research at the CIA had
given him a fairly accurate perception of what hypnosis
could and could not do. Where she had been invaluable
had been in helping him calm the obsessive rage left by
his divorce, the bitter, protracted court struggle, and the
devastating legal judgment that had come out of it. He
could actually think of Terri from time to time now without sinking into an instant black rage. She was over on
Wendover Court in Carriage Hill on the fashionable,
western side of Route 123, in a spacious red brick colo-

nial. He'd bought it for $275,000 in 1973, putting every dollar he had been able to save into the down payment and saddling himself with a twenty-year eight-percent mortgage at the Arlington Trust Company. It was worth close to a million now, but not to him. His wife's divorce lawyer, a bull dike bitch nicknamed the Great White Shark who worked out her hatred of men by nailing them to her golden crosses in the divorce court, had seen to that. She'd persuaded the judge who'd heard their case to award it to Terri, his ex-wife, so she could live there with her latest lover, a wimp from Hill & Knowlton four years her junior. He labeled himself, with the pomposity of his calling, a public relations counselor; in fact, he peddled the snake oil of any Arab or Asiatic dictator with enough cash to pay his fees.

Art shook his head. These, as the hypnotherapist would have told him, were not thoughts on which to begin building a successful day. He knew that, of course. After all, he had devoted his life to studying the strange and fragile proceedings of the human psyche. And yet, when he'd found himself drowning in a sea of his own midlife frustrations, he'd had to find someone else to tell him what was self-evident. He'd considered going down to Personnel and signing up for one of those let-it-all-hang-out series of sessions with an Agency shrink, but that was not what you would call a career-enhancing move for senior officers of the CIA. No one knew better than Bennington did the little alarm bells something like that set jingling in the system.

When he'd realized she'd succeeded in getting him to stop smoking, he'd said to himself, why not use her instead of a shrink? It was a way to keep his problems private, and from his behavioral work he knew deep-state hypnotherapy was often an effective tool for dealing with obsessive behavior. And in his case, it had been.

On that, he padded into the living room for the vigorous physical workout that had been embedded in his daily routine since he'd joined the Agency. Then, sweating profusely, he returned to the bathroom, checked his weight, and threw himself a second glance in the mirror.

He weighed 197, just ten pounds over the weight at which he'd played blocking back and linebacker on Charlie Caldwell's Princeton single-wing teams in the early fifties, back in the days before sixty-minute football players had become a memory and the national media still recognized the existence of Ivy League football. The vista in the mirror from the neck down was considerably more reassuring than the earlier view from the neck up had been. His regular exercise had left him with a heavy, well-muscled upper body, clearly defined biceps and broad forearms, and, okay, a spread around the waist, but less of a spread than enfolded the waists of some of his Agency subordinates twenty years younger than he was.

His improved spirits lasted until he sat down to his breakfast. A brown sludge of bran flakes and blue-tinged no-fat milk waited sullen, soggy, and wonderfully unappetizing on his plate. God, he thought, remember when breakfast was a meal it was actually a pleasure to eat: scrambled eggs and bacon and a couple of toasted English, golden curls of melted butter circling through the dark brown indentations of the muffins?

He'd reached an age at which life was a series of constraints and "no" seemed the most active word in his daily vocabulary. No butter, no eggs, no thick rare steaks. Cholesterol. No chocolate mousse cake, no pecan pie with vanilla ice cream. Triglycerides. Forget those roaring-hot Mexican dinners that could turn a Margarita to steam in your intestines. One of those would set the hemorrhoids off for days. No dry martinis so cold the first sip could bite your tongue; no Johnnie Walker Black, dark and brooding on the rocks with a twist. Try a lemon Perrier instead and spare your liver. Smoke cigarettes and you risked being beaten to death by a horde of ecologists long before the cancer struck. No sex; AIDS. Christ, he thought, forcing a last spoonful of this dreadful high-fiber breakfast medicine into his mouth, what do they leave you when you pass fifty?

At least, he told himself, scraping off his breakfast dishes, divorce had turned him into a regular pearl of domesticity. This latest bachelor abode of his was a rented flat in the Park Terrace Apartments, a three-story development built in an L with four entries and two identical apartments set onto each floor of the four entries. It was the kind of place that was done up with such mind-boggling sameness that if you came home drunk, you risked winding up in bed with a neighbor, not out of lechery but by mistake. His apartment had a ten-foot-square terrace which afforded Bennington an unbeatable view into the living rooms of those neighbors, an assortment of used-car salesmen, computer programmers, and pizza-parlor managers, all of whom he'd scrupulously avoided meeting. That was partly out of snobbery, partly out of the restrictive sense of friendship service in the CIA engenders.

Time, he realized, to get out his twenty-five-year-old Hawes & Curtis Savile Row blazer. It was practically his uniform, and he still treasured the memory of the day he'd ordered it. It was in the early sixties when Allen Dulles's OSS boys still dominated the CIA and everything British was beautiful. It was also a time, he reflected, when being an officer of the Central Intelligence Agency was a matter of pride, a calling people might admire and even envy. D'Arcy Watt, his MI6 counterpart, had taken him by Hawes & Curtis after a lunch at White's and introduced him to old Mr. Winterbotham, who, Watt had confided, was the tailor of Prince Philip and Dicky Mountbatten. A CIA officer's salary in the early sixties permitted the occasional luxury of a blazer like that or half a dozen Turnbull & Asser shirts. Now when you needed a new shirt, you waited for the Washington's Birthday sales at K mart.

Well, Bennington told himself, it wasn't that bad. Not quite. He was in the Senior Intelligence Service, an SIS4, just two grades below the sixes, the deputy directors, of whom there were only four. He was making $72,000 a year after more than thirty-five years' service to the country. That was the top salary the government paid its career ambassadors, its four-star generals, the directors of its National Institutes of Health. Seventy-two K a year and the chance to get into a dogfight for the bone of a twenty-thousand-dollar bonus every two or three years to supplement the ten that automatically came to Agency hotshots like Bennington.

Shearson Lehman Hutton and Goldman Sachs paid kids out of the Harvard Business School more than that in entry-level salaries, and what contribution did they make to the national welfare? They put together mergers and takeovers to throw steelworkers in Youngstown and factory hands in Peoria out of work.

On this spring morning, he reflected, his net liabilities consisted of a $1,615-a-month mortgage payment on a house that was no longer his, and his assets were composed of his CIA retirement and disability plan, $23,275 in assorted shares in his brokerage account at Thomson McKinnon, and $13,750 in CIA Credit Union Savings. That was it. That was all he had to show for thirty-five years of service in one of the most elite services, if not the most, of the U.S. government.

Still, no one had forced him to join the CIA. He could remember the day he'd been recruited as though it were yesterday. He'd just come off a twenty-four-hour stint toward the end of his internship at Columbia Presbyterian. There had been a call from Dr. Pinckney Arledge, his professor of neurology. The professor had a friend up from Washington who was interested in bright young neurologists with a complementary knowledge of pharmacology. Flattered, Bennington had gone out to breakfast with the visitor at Dom's Sub and Pizza, a student hangout across Columbus Avenue. It had taken about three sips of coffee and a bite of scrambled eggs to understand the guy was from the CIA. The guy knew he knew, too, but nothing was said. Bennington, the visitor reminded him, was looking at his obligatory two years of military service, delivering babies at Camp Gordon or checking for hernias out at Fort Riley, Kansas. Not a very broadening experience from a medical point of view.

He had an alternative to suggest, the visitor told Bennington, one in which he would be working in his field, the brain, performing services of a high and valued order to the nation. He would receive a captain's commission and a captain's pay, but he would never have to look at the inside of an Army barracks or put on a uniform.

Bennington had jumped at the chance. To substantiate his CIA cover, he was assigned to a nonexistent U.S. Army medical liaison unit at a nonexistent office with a phone that rang in the Pentagon. His CIA career began, in fact, in an organization so tiny, so secretly held, so esoteric its name did not even appear on the most secret of the CIA's organizational charts. It was a branch of the Technical Services Division of the old DDP, the Deputy Directorate of Plans, clandestine services. The division's job was to furnish the clandestine operators with state-of-the-art tools of their trade, everything from silent blowguns to briefcases with secret compartments so carefully concealed they were virtually searchproof.

On his first day on the job, the man who'd recruited him drove Bennington to lunch at a small inn twenty miles into the Virginia countryside. Sipping a dry martini, he laid on Bennington a burden of knowledge which changed the course of his life.

The top echelons of the U.S. government, up to and including President Eisenhower, were convinced there was tangible evidence the Soviets and the Red Chinese had developed techniques to alter human behavior, techniques the United States neither understood nor possessed. The evidence was everywhere: in the drugged appearance of show trial victims like Cardinal Mindszenty in Hungary and brainwashed American prisoners in Korea. The job of their tiny unit was to determine how that could be done: how an individual's behavior could be modified by covert means. The implications of success or failure were enormous. At stake might be the nation's very survival itself.

"This is a rough game," his new boss had warned. "What we're talking about here, for want of a better word, is malevolent medicine. For defensive, not offensive purposes, of course. But there's still no getting away from one reality—what we're doing is looking at unconventional and unacceptable applications of science."

The code names for the multitude of projects the branch handled were as innocent as the projects were disturbing. There was Bluebird, the "search for individuals with high extrasensory-perception abilities to see if their abilities can be applied to the practical problems of intelligence." There was the search for a drug that could be slipped into a hesitant defector's drink and for ten minutes would give him the balls he needed to make the break and get his feet wet. Years had been spent trying to find a way to soup up the rate of metabolism at which alcohol is absorbed into the bloodstream. What a blessing that would have been for CIA agents who had to stay up all night drinking a potential defector through his doubts or debriefing a nervous agent in some anonymous safe house. Could they find a drug that would induce temporary amnesia to make an agent interrogation-proof? To make an individual more susceptible to hypnosis? To make a hostile foreign leader, a Nasser of Egypt, for example, rambling and incoherent at a mass public meeting in order to humiliate or disgrace him?

There had been studies on the effects of implanting electrodes into animals' brains. They'd located a "sweet spot" in the brain of the rat which, when electrically stimulated, produced a sensation of intense euphoria. Place an electrode into that "sweet spot" so it could pick up a tiny electric charge from a bar over the rat's cage, and the rat would do nothing but flick his electrode against the bar. He wouldn't eat, he wouldn't drink, he couldn't be sexually tempted. He would do nothing but go on hitting that bar until he died—a happy but nonetheless very dead rat.

They had placed an electrode in the brain of a pigeon and guided the bird to the window ledge of a KGB safe house in Paris's Sixteenth Arrondissement with radio signals. Once there, the bird had planted a miniature radio transmitter the size of a dice cube on the ledge. For months it had transmitted conversations inside the room to a nearby CIA listening post.

Their most remarkable success had come with a donkey into whose brain they had implanted an antenna, a receiver, and an amplifier. It picked up a tiny five-microamp signal which it transmitted through the hypothalamus of the donkey's brain to give him a shot of euphoria. They had sent the donkey up a two-thousand-foot mountain in New Mexico and brought him down again to the spot from which he'd left with the Pavlovian technique of rewards and punishments, a jolt of happiness when he was on course, silence when he strayed from his path.

Later, much later, when that bastard Frank Church and his Senate committee had savaged the CIA, Bennington had been one of the sacrificial lambs tossed out of CIA headquarters to appease Church's retroactive morality and his towering ambition to be President of the United States. Church had turned him into a kind of Dr. Strangelove and tarred him with the Agency's LSD experiments, work they'd in fact carried out on the orders of the White House. And, of course, work that represented barely five percent of the activities they were studying in their search for ways to modify human behavior.

Bennington checked his image in the mirror. Not bad, he thought, when you think of all the years of wear and tear on the old machine. He was a touch vain about how he looked, which was perhaps a good thing. A little vanity would probably do more for his appearance than those face-lifts he couldn't afford and didn't want anyhow.

He touched his pockets to be sure he had everything he needed. Dr. Strangelove, he thought angrily. His memories of those days always made his blood boil. Well, that title, those initials M.D. after his name, not even Church or a congressional committee could deny him—despite the fact he'd never practiced medicine or hung up a shingle. You might regret that once in a while watching your neighborhood neurosurgeon humming down the George Washington Parkway in his steel-gray Mercedes, chatting on his cellular phone with his money manager or dealing with his condos in Telluride or Lyford Cay. Life turned on the hinges of choice. He'd made his when they came to him after his two years of military

MAZE

service with the Agency were up and asked him to stay on, to give up his ambition to be a great neurosurgeon.

What they offered in return was an opportunity to spend his life at the forefront of one of science's most challenging, most important areas of research; to have access to the best minds, the best technologies involved in that area; to command financial resources beyond those of which most medical foundations could ever dream.

Like most of life, it was a trade-off. He might never set foot on Lyford Cay, but he was the chief of the Behavioral Sciences Division of the Deputy Directorate for Science and Technology of the CIA, with 350 employees under his orders and a budget of $75 million at his command. His charge was that most mysterious, arcane, challenging and important of problems, human behavior in all its ramifications. He might drive a fifteen-year-old Volvo a divorce judge had considerately left him after taking his house away; he was at the outer edge of the envelope, out where the most important and vital scientific developments of his lifetime were taking place. That was, after all, what had gotten him into the CIA, what had kept him there through the tribulations of the seventies, and why, despite these black tides that occasionally churned up inside him, he was still there on this spring morning.

He started out the door. He was about to lock it behind him when he stopped. He went back in, took the black cellophane bag out of his garbage can, knotted it up, and retraced his steps. Art Bennington might be the chief of the Behavioral Sciences Division of the world's most important intelligence agency, but he still had to take out his own garbage.

The intelligence officer of the U.S. Navy's Atlantic Submarine Fleet, carrying a blue Top Secret folder with diagonal red and black slashes across its upper-right-hand corner, walked up to the desk of the admiral commanding the fleet in Norfolk, Virginia. The admiral didn't even look up from the fleet status report he was studying. "What is it?" he asked impatiently.

"The latest reports on Project Seashell are in, sir," the officer, a lieutenant commander, replied.

The admiral's head came up from his report with a snap. The full and not altogether welcome force of his attention was brought to bear on his intelligence officer. "So what are they?"

"Very similar to the ones we've had in the past, sir. Eleven of the coordinates the CIA gave us turned up nothing except dead water. But the twelfth was a disaster. *Boston* found a November riding herd on *Ohio*."

"What?" The admiral's bushy eyebrows shot up. "I don't believe it!"

"And what's worse, *Ohio* didn't even know he was out there."

The admiral slapped the table with his palm. "Where the hell is the Agency getting those coordinates from?"

"I don't know, sir. The Agency isn't letting on. If I had to make a guess, I'd say they've got a new asset buried somewhere in the Soviet naval establishment and they're trying to evaluate how good his information is."

"How many coordinates have they given us?"

"Seashell's been under way for seven weeks, sir. Eighty-four coordinates. This is the third one that's proved out."

"That's really strange. How can that spy of theirs be wrong so often and then, bang, hit the nail on the head?"

"I don't know, sir. It's very puzzling."

The admiral paused for a moment. "Tell Operations to bring *Ohio* back to Norfolk and program her for a new sanctuary. Why the hell didn't she pick that November up?"

"It must be one of the boats they've equipped with those new Toshiba blades."

"Damn the Japanese! Alert every boomer we've got at sea to the possibility they've got a Soviet sub walking on their heels."

"Yes, sir."

"And when you send that data back to Langley, tell them for God's sake to keep it coming."

Glancing up at the white concrete spans that soared like a pair of wings over the main entrance of the Central Intelligence Agency, Art Bennington couldn't help imagining a grotesque prehistoric bird mired somehow in the Virginia countryside. Like half the guys marching to work in the Agency this morning, he thought. Their forward progress was accomplished under the lifeless bronze gaze of the Agency's patron saint, Nathan Hale, whose statue, erected on Allen Dulles's orders, stood watch right beside the building's main entrance. With the British tyrant's noose draped gracefully around his neck, Hale's lips seemed poised to utter that deathless phrase "My only regret is that I have but one life to give for my country."

A noble sentiment, Bennington always liked to point out, and one that would be rendered even nobler were there not so much historical reason to doubt Hale had ever uttered it. Entering the broad marble lobby, Bennington was confronted by the second Agency artifact which provided him a regular source of delight, the inscription from Saint John chiseled over the entrance: "And the truth shall make you free."

Every time he saw it, it reminded him of the words at the entrance to the Spanish Ministry of Information during Franco's reign: "Our mission is to convey the truth to the Spanish people." Beneath that stirring phrase was a mural apparently representing what, for the Franco regime, was the perfect depiction of how truth should be conveyed. It showed the Angel Gabriel announcing the Immaculate Conception to the Virgin Mary.

That, it had always seemed to Bennington, was a pretty good summation of the regard in which intelligence agencies, his own included, held the truth. He pulled his plastic ID card from his wallet and fitted it into the slot of one of the subwaylike turnstiles guarding the employees' entrance. The card's most fetching characteristic was that nowhere did it mention the CIA. A stranger finding it might think it opened the gate to some executive parking lot or perhaps gave its bearer access to the cash he'd accumulated in his Christmas Savings Club.

As the card hit the slot, a small computer screen on the turnstile's face lit up. Bennington punched his four-digit, two-letter personal code onto the keyboard below it, and the turnstile snapped open, allowing him to pass. The system was supposed to represent the state of the art in high-tech security surveillance. It also, it had occurred to Bennington and a number of others, provided Big Brother with a precise accounting of the daily movements of a group of men and women who would have risen as one in angry protest at even the suggestion that they should punch a time clock.

Bennington's office was in the C wing of the fifth floor, the area which housed the key divisions of the Deputy Directorate for Science and Technology. Like any huge bureaucracy, the Agency had its subtle distinctions and unofficial pecking order. The glamour guys, the ones the directors liked to unwrap every so often for a show-and-tell downtown, were in the Deputy Directorate for Operations, the clandestine-affairs side of the house. Surface one of them for a meeting and people tended to get turned on, projects authorized, budgets passed. The intellectuals, headed by a group of senior employees referred to as the College of Cardinals, were in Research and Analysis, the directorate responsible for the National Estimates and the "World Today" summary placed each morning on the President's desk. Elitists tended to gather in James Jesus Angleton's old division, Counterintelligence. They didn't loom large or have the extrovert personalities of the covert guys, but they were convinced that theirs was the most important job the Agency offered.

The off-the-wall guys, the mavericks with the creative minds, were in Bennington's directorate, the S&T. It had been that way from the beginning. Washington government bureaucracies, whether at the Pentagon or the Bureau of Indian Affairs, rewarded people who learned to cover their ass, didn't make mistakes, and were impervious to the notion of taking a chance. That had never been the Agency's attitude. Here the top levels of management were ready to entertain, at least, any far-out idea, no matter how flaky it might seem at first look. Originality of thought would never get you laughed out of court at Langley. The Agency prided itself on its willingness to take chances—although, as Bennington had learned to his regret, top management wasn't always there to hold your hand if your risk-taking led you to a mistake. Still, Bennington presided over a division as far out as any in the Agency, a tribute to the fact that the CIA, like the Church of Rome, had a talent for accommodation, a readiness to order its values to the beat of necessity's drummer if the occasion demanded.

Bennington knew that as he walked the halls of this building there was always somebody somewhere pointing to him, nudging an Agency neophyte and whispering: "Look, there goes old Doc Bennington, the guy that got burned to a crisp by the Church Committee in the seventies over all that LSD stuff, remember?" Or, were the nudger's political convictions of a different order, the whisper might be: "Look, there's old Doc Bennington, the guy who told Colby to stuff it."

In any event, Bennington had long ago accepted his role as the Peck's Bad Boy of the CIA, the redeemed sinner the top brass liked to finger for young officers as an example of the Agency's willingness to reclaim and rehabilitate its prodigal sons.

"Hello, little treasure," he said, opening the door to his office suite. His words were addressed to his intelligence assistant, a clever and devoted Vassar graduate in her mid-forties for whom the Agency was now probably the only marital partner she would ever know. Secretaries at the Agency were never referred to as such. "Intelligence assistants" was the term, and it was an appropriate one. Many were privy to more Agency secrets than the director.

"My!" she said. "We're in a good mood this morning, aren't we?"

"Are you kidding?" Bennington answered, tossing his *Washington Post* onto the top of a filing cabinet. "I can't remember the last time I was in a good mood coming to work in this nuthouse."

Ann Stoddard, the intelligence assistant, followed him into his office, clutching a folder in her hands. "Let's see if I can." She tilted her chin toward the ceiling as though some moving finger might have written the answer to his question there. "The day Bill Colby got the ax?"

Bennington emitted a sound which could have been construed with equal justification as a grunt or a laugh, and reached for the folder she carried. It contained his "overnights," urgent cables from any of his project officers or news of any startling developments in the areas that were the concern of the Behavioral Sciences Division. Their charge was patrolling the scientific frontiers of any field relating to the human mind: how it functioned, how it could be studied, how it determined behavior, how behavior might be influenced, modified, controlled. Probably no area in which the Agency worked was filled with more uncertainties, legal minefields, and traps. Occasionally, Bennington's people worked and talked directly with the scientists involved. More often, they dealt with those scientists at second hand, through cover organizations, designed to conceal the Agency's interest in the subject.

They had worked with neurologists in Michigan employing radio waves that could be passed through an individual's brain, then read by remote means on the way back out. The idea was to develop a device by which a man's emotional mood could be read without his knowledge. A negotiator sitting across from him at a bargaining table could then be given an indication of what his rival's feelings were, a huge negotiating edge. In another project, his division had developed earphones which could be slipped, for example, into an Iberia 747 taking Fidel Castro from Havana to Madrid on a visit. If the Cuban put them on to watch a movie, he would leave behind to be recovered later by the Agency a representation of his cardiovascular functions as complete as that the best electrocardiogram could provide.

Bennington's people had produced a device which fit into a television set and could monitor, from across the room while an individual enjoyed *L.A. Law,* his blood pressure, his heartbeat, and his pulse rate, all potential indicators of his emotional state. That wasn't all. Suppose Yassir Arafat decided to visit the UN and the device was secreted into his television set in his hotel room? When the chairman came home at night and switched on his TV to watch Ted Koppel, not only could that device be employed to record all his vital signs, it could transmit an undetectable electromagnetic wave which would affect his emotions by altering his heartbeat: speed it up to give him a sensation of stress and anxiety; slow it down to induce lethargy.

Ultimately, Bennington's subordinates feared, a device similar to theirs would be developed which could kill someone from across the room by stopping his heart with a very finely tuned microwave, employing not massive amounts of power but extremely precise frequencies. Nothing would indicate the victim had died of anything other than a heart attack.

Then there was the lady in California. She was experimenting with the ability of extremely low frequency electromagnetic waves, similar to those the Navy used to communicate with its nuclear submarines, to influence emotions. "Give me money and three months," she'd told one of his subordinates, "and I'll affect the behavior of eighty percent of the people in this town." She was referring to her community in the Bay Area. "And they won't even know it. Make them happy—or at least they'll think they're happy. Or aggressive."

That obviously was the kind of suggestion the Agency wouldn't touch with a bargepole, not after the Church Committee. Furthermore, to some the lady's ideas were tinged with quackery. She liked to talk, for example, of an "aphrodisiac frequency" she'd discovered down around 9.41 hertz. Turn it on a gentleman, she joked, and he'd be ready for action all night. Because of such suggestions, conventional scientists tended to throw up their hands at the mention of her name. Nonetheless, Bennington liked to remind them, the lady had a Ph.D. diploma in nuclear physics from Cal Tech hanging on her office wall. Cal Tech didn't pass out documents like that along with the laundry chits, and many of science's great advances had been made by men and women who flew in the face of the conventional scientific wisdom of their day. Nothing, Bennington liked to declare, endangered scientific progress as much as a closed mind. Hanging on the wall behind his desk was what was for Bennington the perfect illustration of the perils of the closed mind. It was a framed quote uttered by Admiral William Leahy, President Roosevelt's naval adviser in World War II:

"The atomic bomb project is the dumbest thing this country has ever done. It will never go off and I say that as an expert on explosives."

The world toward which they were drifting—as measured in the slow movement of those overnight cables— was, Bennington thought, mysterious, perplexing, sometimes terrifying. Progress in the study of the brain alone had been increasing almost exponentially with each passing year of the eighties. New technologies were opening up possibilities of exploring it that were undreamed of a decade ago, inconceivable when he was in medical school. All sorts of questions were now being raised on how it might be affected by magnetic fields, by electromagnetic waves, how its electrochemical processes really worked, how they could be influenced from outside the brain. Some of his division's work in these areas, Bennington joked, was so highly classified even the classification was classified.

He was ready to turn to his overnights when his deputy, Pete Bancroft, a forty-two-year-old Ph.D. from Carnegie Tech, walked into his office. Bancroft closed the door and leaned against it, his arms folded across his chest. He was in a state of considerable nervous agitation. "Art," he said, "you're just not going to believe what I've got here."

"Pete, I left my belief system down in the parking lot. Up here, I don't believe, I evaluate."

"She's done it again."

"Who's done what again?"

"That woman, that psychic up in New York, Ann Robbins. The Project Seashell reports just came in from Norfolk. They're absolutely unbelievable. Not only did she give you the exact location of the submarine again but the damn thing was sitting right on the *Ohio,* one of our Trident boats, and the *Ohio* didn't even know it. The Navy's going bananas."

"What about the others?"

"Nothing. Absolutely nothing. Here's the stuff." He passed a telex to Bennington.

"You talk about your belief system, Art," he said as Bennington glanced through the telex. "I mean, I can't handle this. This makes three times out of seven she's located a sub, in all those thousands of square miles of ocean out there, for God's sake. You know what the statisticians downstairs told me? The probability she could have done that by chance is twenty-seven million to one." The incredulity in his deputy's voice seemed to underline each figure as he pronounced it. "How in God's name is it possible, Art? How could she have done it?"

"My boy, if you and I could answer that question, they'd give us a Nobel Prize—even after the Swedes found out we were working for the CIA."

Bennington got up and walked to his window. It looked down on a freshly mowed field sloping off to a grove of birch and flowering dogwood partially concealing the scar of the electrified fence surrounding the Agency. Project Seashell. Ann Robbins. Seashell was a low-priority, low-budget project of the division, another reflection of the CIA's four-decade-old interest in probing the mysteries of ESP, extrasensory perception. They'd selected twelve psychics, seven men and five women, reputed to be the best in the country for a ten-week program. None of them, of course, had any idea they were working with the CIA. They'd been led to believe they were engaged in an experimental Navy project. Each week, each of them was given the photograph of a Soviet submarine and its captain, then asked to indicate where in the immensity of the oceans the sub was.

To any normal, rational person, the whole thing would have seemed like a ludicrous exercise, a perfect example of how the government throws the taxpayer's money right out the window. Were it not for one thing—just over a decade ago, the Agency had discovered someone with an uncanny ability to do exactly what this program asked its twelve psychics to do. Since then, they'd been looking for someone equally gifted. At last, thanks to Seashell, they had apparently found one.

"There are three more passes left to be made in the program, right?" Bennington asked his deputy.

"Yup."

"Well, let's go ahead with them just as we've planned. The one thing we don't want to do is make waves. Be sure they're keeping their mouths shut down in Norfolk."

"That's no problem. They're convinced we've got a new mole in the Kremlin."

"Can you see the look on the chief of naval operations' face if he ever found out where this stuff is coming from?" Bennington laughed.

"One day, Doc, you'll have to tell him."

"No I won't."

"You won't? How come?"

What he liked to refer to as his smile of Christian forbearance creased Bennington's face. "Pete, surely a smart guy like you never thought the reason we were running this little project of ours was to develop a new way for the Navy to find Soviet submarines?"

"It had struck me as a remote possibility, yes."

"No way. The U.S. Navy would never, never, never rely on a psychic's word even if she'd found the sub ninety-nine times out of a hundred. And they're right."

"So why did we run the exercise, then?"

"For ourselves. To find someone who can do these

things, find submarines, whatever, a fairly good percentage of the time.''

"Well, it looks like maybe you got her," Bancroft acknowledged, giving his head a kind of spastic toss as though to dislodge from it thoughts which had no business being in the mind of a Carnegie Tech Ph.D. "But I gotta tell you I feel like the guy who said, 'I won't believe this stuff even if it's true.' What are you going to do with her?''

Bennington started back to his desk. "Turn her into a guinea pig, if she'll let us. Get her into a laboratory where we can really monitor her closely." He returned to his chair with a thud. Bennington didn't sit in chairs; he dropped into them with an abruptness that could cause a hostess to pale or an antique dealer to have a cardiac arrest. "We've developed so many new techniques, so many new technologies, for peering into the brain in the last decade. Maybe, just maybe, one of them can give us some hint, some faint clue, some glimmer of what the hell is happening in there when a woman like this does these things.''

"And you think this Ann Robbins will go along with that?''

"Ah, Ann Robbins!" At the name, a smile, a real smile, burst across the crags of Bennington's face. When they'd launched Project Seashell, he'd made himself Ann Robbins's scientific case officer. He hadn't even laid eyes on her at the time. It was simply a way of writing off the pleasures of a weekly visit to Manhattan on Uncle Sugar. That first day he'd rung her apartment doorbell, he'd been expecting your layman's version of a psychic: an old crone with crooked fingers, a voice as soft as a fishmonger's, an urbanized gypsy with the sex appeal of yesterday's newspaper.

He found a short, auburn-haired woman just past forty with the lithe, muscled body of a teenage gymnast. She was wearing a tubular black dress in one of those stretch materials that emphasized the roundness of her buttocks and each gentle curve of her thighs. There was only one thing that would make you think of a gypsy in Ann Robbins, her eyes. They were dark and constantly animated and seemed to possess some strange power to compel him to look into them. "Come drown in me," they seemed to whisper.

"Well, when we wind this thing up in three weeks, I'll just have to come clean with her. Tell her who we really are and see if I can't convince her to come down and work with us."

His visits to Ann Robbins, in his incarnation as Captain Eldon Tyler, U.S. Navy, had become the high points of his working weeks.

"I'll tell you one thing, Peter my boy. Taking Ms. Robbins out to dinner on Uncle Sam's money to persuade her to come to work for us is going to be one of the most pleasurable assignments our employers have handed to me in some time."

Ann Robbins traced a pink lipstick tube along her well-fleshed lips, then pressed them together to perfect her handiwork. She checked the result in her mirror while with a free hand she smoothed a few wayward hairs back into the pageboy bob that enclosed her face. Démodé, perhaps, but it was a cut that had always set off her features well. After all, she thought, there comes a time when a girl has to learn to make a few trade-offs, give up a little in fashion to gain a little in the end result. She smiled at her image in the mirror. Not bad, she thought, not bad at all.

Assured, she strode into the living room to give the apartment a final check. With her usual obsessiveness, she verified the alignment of each of the statues in her bookcase, her dancing Shiva, her cuddly Ganesh, the Elephant God, her Hanuman, the Monkey God with its pert gold-plated nose, the Buddha a Tibetan monk had pressed on her in Darjeeling when she'd studied meditation there a decade ago. Most of her visitors assumed she had chosen those icons of the East for their artistic value. That was not the case. It was rather because Ann realized people had prayed to them, venerated them, for generations, centuries perhaps. That knowledge, she felt, bound her in some special mystic communion both to the objects and to those who had once addressed their hopes and fears to them.

For a few minutes, she played with her flowers, the bouquet of mauve chrysanthemums and the half-dozen pink roses she'd bought from a street vendor down by the Gulf & Western building yesterday. She glanced out the window and down 71st Street to the trees of Central Park. The sky was cobalt-blue. It was one of those electrifying days when just to be alive and in New York was a special blessing.

Captain Tyler, she thought, should be here any minute. The table, the bridge table covered with a purple cloth at which she received her clients, was ready for him. On the bookcase just beside it were a row of crystals, a blue-and-rose quartz, a black onyx, and an obsidian, talismans of the New Age. In fact, Ann had no use for them whatsoever. They were, she was convinced, the magic wands a whole new wave of quacks and charlatans employed to dupe their gullible clients.

Still, she was shrewd enough to have them around, because their presence reassured many of her clients—and it was, after all, the need for reassurance that brought people through her front door. She often thought she was, these days, a mixture of psychiatrist, priest, social worker, and what her cards said she was, a psychic counselor.

That was not at all the destiny she'd had in mind when she'd left her job as a copywriter at Benton & Bowles to become a professional psychic. Then she had imagined herself as a kind of psychic games player, using these strange and terrifying gifts she occasionally seemed to possess to confront challenges and riddles like those on which she had first begun to use them two decades ago, police work.

It had not worked out that way, of course. As her word-of-mouth reputation had spread through the city, she had become a kind of society bauble, the chic *Women's Wear Daily* psychic the ladies in mink coats stopped in to see on their way home from lunch at La Grenouille or the Côte Basque. Theirs was not the overt quest for a dark and handsome stranger that sent their less fortunate sisters into those dingy rooms on 46th Street where so-called gypsy ladies read tarot cards for twenty dollars a go; still, that concern was never far from the surface of their conversations, either.

As a result, she had become, Ann felt, a kind of verbal vending machine dispensing emotional support for women like herself slipping toward the uncertain shores of middle life—except that the machine worked on hundred-dollar bills, not coins. That, strangely, was the heart of the problem. Ann had never tried to understand the nature of these puzzling insights which could, on occasion, overwhelm her, nor did she really wish to understand them. Such knowledge, if it somehow was obtainable, might be more than she could handle. What she did know, however, was that you couldn't summon up these things six or seven times a day, turn them on and off like a water faucet at the prompting of a hundred-dollar bill. And so, with most of this heavy, semicelebrity clientele of hers, what Ann was really doing, she knew, was employing the psychological insights she'd picked up in fifteen years of sitting in this living room. She would watch for the flicker in a client's eye, the revealing twist of a ring or a tightening of the hand, then set off to mine the vein her alert senses had revealed.

And every so often it would happen. Something really would come gushing out, and once again, the legend of Ann Robbins would go flashing around the East Side and a new covey of clients would be flushed out of their high rises. As Ann was the first to admit, the steady flow of hundred-dollar bills they produced, most of them well beyond the reach of the IRS, paid a girl's rent. They also, unfortunately, tended to overwhelm the far less well paid assignments such as police work, whose appeal had originally lured Ann to her calling.

Psychics, as no one knew better than Ann, were employed by law enforcement officials far more frequently than the public realized or law enforcement was prepared to acknowledge. Evidence developed by psychics could not, of course, be introduced into a courtroom. Employing a psychic, many police officers felt, could jeopardize a prosecution's case. As a result, when police officials called on her, it was usually with a plea for her discretion and a very limited budget. In cases in which a psychic such as Ann turned up information that appeared convincing, the usual police tactic was to employ it in a confrontation with a suspect. Sometimes that could jar him into the confession that would convert him into a long-term guest of the New York State penal system—without the suspect or his lawyer being aware that the information had been generated by a psychic.

Ann's name, along with those of a dozen of her fellow psychics scattered around the country, was also on a Rolodex in the office of a congressional staffer in the Russell Senate Office Building in Washington who served as an informal liaison between the psychic community and the government agencies that wished to use their services. To Ann's certain knowledge, the Pentagon, the FBI, the Secret Service, and the National Security Council had all at one time or another employed psychics, with varying degrees of success.

She herself had been one of three psychics flown by the Pentagon to Italy at Caspar Weinberger's behest to see if they could help the Italian police locate General James Dozier when he'd been kidnapped by the Red Brigades. Her trip had served as a perfect illustration of the problems and shortcomings of psychic assistance in police work. One of her colleagues had reported that Dozier was being held in a room next to a kitchen in which someone was cooking pasta. That was not a particularly helpful insight in Italy. Between them, the trio had generated certain scraps of information for the Italian police about which they had been fairly confident: that Dozier was being held on the second floor of an apartment building; that the door to the apartment was green; that there were great crowds of people on the main floor of the building. One of the trio drew a sketch of the scene he claimed was below Dozier's window: a little piazza with a fountain at its center and benches ringing its flanks.

None of that information had the specificity required to be of any use to the police. They located Dozier by conventional police work. But when they found him, he was indeed in an apartment with a green door, on the second floor of a building on Via Pin de Monte in a flat above a supermarket and overlooking a little square very similar to the one Ann's associate had described.

Other psychics, Ann knew, had been used successfully by the Pentagon to locate a Soviet Tu-95 Backfire bomber lost in Africa before the Russians could find it and an A-6 Intruder that had crashed into a remote corner of the Shenandoah Mountains. During the Iranian hostage crisis, one of her colleagues, Keith Harary, had been secretly employed by the National Security Council in an effort to try to get some indication of where and how inside the U.S. embassy in Tehran the hostages were being held.

Captain Tyler, Ann felt certain, had located her through the Pentagon contacts with whom she'd worked in Italy. She loved the challenges he regularly set at her feet. It was a kind of game for her, a child's game, and somehow it had always seemed to Ann that her most successful psychic experiences came as the result of a kind of sophisticated game playing.

The thought of the captain sent her scurrying to the kitchen to set water boiling for tea. The doorbell rang before she was finished.

As always, the captain was in civilian clothes. He had on a dark blue blazer and gray flannel slacks and a Brooks Brothers blue button-down shirt whose collars belled out like flaring nostrils. He was a big man with heavy shoulders, and it almost seemed her doorway was too small to accommodate his bulk.

As she hung up his coat, she looked up at him and laughed. What amused her about the captain was the gap between his two front teeth. "I told you you should get that gap in your teeth fixed. I see whole armies of women in your future once it's gone."

Art Bennington considered winking at her, then thought better of it. The rogue's smile would do, he decided. That gap between his teeth, which always seemed to get some remark out of her, was a trademark of his. "Hey, if I didn't have that, I couldn't think. I mean, where would I put my tongue when I want to turn the machine on?"

He followed her movements with an interest that was distinctly unprofessional as she led the way into her living room. She was wearing a beige wraparound skirt that stretched taut over that bewitching firm behind of hers and a white satin blouse which had offered just a provocative hint of the white lace bra beneath it.

She left him sprawling on her couch, carefully studying her living room, while she went to get the tea tray. One thing had always fascinated him on his visits to Ann Robbins, besides Ann Robbins herself: her apparent obsession with the colors pink and purple. "Boy," he said, "you certainly seem to have a thing for purple and pink."

"It's not that," she replied, setting the tea on the table before him. "Colors have meaning. At least they do for people like me. Pink is the color of universal love. Unlike red or scarlet, which is the color of passion. Physical passion, but anger, rage, too. Purple is the color of healing. So I chose to surround myself with colors that mean something to me."

"No passionate reds?"

Ann laughed. "They're in another room."

"Ah!" Bennington arched one eyebrow into a devil's peak, a trick he'd learned as a teenager. It was meant to make clear the interest Captain Eldon Tyler, USN, might have in further exploring these premises. "Tell me," he said, "I've been told psychics, particularly female psychics, have very strong feelings. Do you think that's true of you?"

Ann had settled onto the couch beside him, her legs tucked under her buttocks so she faced him. The beige skirt folded above her knee. She'd kicked off her shoes, and it was all Bennington could do to keep from sliding a hand onto one of her beckoning thighs. "Yes, I think that's true. But at the same time we tend to be wary of emotional involvement.''

Her perfume, Art noted, was musky, Oriental. Jasmine, probably. Her long scarlet fingernails seemed to spin like the spokes of a pinwheel from her fingertips as she talked. "Yes, I can certainly see how you'd be wary of your clients becoming emotionally dependent on you.''

"And others as well.'' Ann smiled.

"Men, for instance?''

"Oh, certainly. Many women psychics I know tend to be drawn to rather mystic relations. Did you ever hear of Eileen Garrett?''

"Of course.'' Garrett had been perhaps the best-known American female psychic of her day.

"She was like that. She sought out almost anonymous relationships. She liked men she could pick up as though they were little hurt birds, comfort for a while, then sort of throw from the nest to fly off on their own.''

"Well now.'' Here was a little ground worth testing, at least. "Let me see if I can do my imitation of a robin with a broken wing.''

Bennington's words drew a tinkling peal of laughter from Ann Robbins. "My dear Captain Tyler, if there is one thing you most certainly do not resemble it's a hurt little bird.''

The bemused sparkle in her eye conveyed one pleasant bit of news to Bennington: hurt little birds were not this lady psychic's cup of tea. Just wait until I can shuck this disguise, he thought. He reached down and snapped open his attaché case. "I suppose we'd better get on with our own work.''

He stood up and withdrew a huge map of the Atlantic Ocean from his attaché case. Carefully, he opened it onto her table, its folds falling over the edges of her purple cloth. Then he returned to his case and drew out two pictures. The first was of a submarine. It was one of the Soviet Union's new titanium-hulled Typhoon Class fast attack submarines with a squat bow and a profile in the water that vaguely resembled that of a bloated dolphin.

Painted on its sail, its protruding tower, was the number S92, by which the vessel was known to its foes in the U.S. Navy.

The second photograph was of an unsmiling Soviet naval officer, two rows of ribbons pinned to his dark blue tunic. He was Commander Vladimir Besznovskii, the captain of the S92.

When he had set both photographs on the table and Ann had taken her seat, Bennington pointed to the Skagerrak, the narrow strait of water running from Göteborg in Sweden to the tip of Denmark's Jutland Peninsula. Beneath those waters ran a chain of NATO sonar devices strung like pearls on an electric cable. "The sub's last sighting was here twenty-four days ago at four thirty-three P.M. New York time."

He then returned to the sofa and settled, as quietly and unobtrusively as he could, into his seat. He had been through this ceremony several times, of course, and the routine varied little. Ann sat at her table, hands folded on the map, staring straight ahead as if meditating. She appeared oblivious to his presence. What she was doing, she had explained to him on an earlier visit, was trying to effect a change of focus, to defocus from the objective world around her and her own mental images of it and then to allow whatever it was that was supposed to happen to happen.

She could sit there like that for forty minutes and suddenly, as though she were coming out of a hypnotist's trance, announce that nothing had happened. Sometimes, in less than five minutes, she would finger some spot in those vast and trackless seas and proclaim with an absolute certainty that that was where the Soviet submarine was lurking.

Today, Bennington guessed as the time slipped by and half an hour passed, was going to be another fruitless occasion. He had, in fact, resigned himself to it when Ann Robbins stirred. She was paler, and Bennington could see glistening beads of sweat at her temples and below her nostrils. Her finger struck at an anonymous patch of blue sea southeast of the Azores. "Here," she announced.

Bennington got up and carefully noted the latitude and longitude coordinates of the spot she had fingered, then he registered the spot on the map itself with his pen.

Ann rose and started to stretch. Her breathing, her visitor noted, was shallower and slightly more rapid than usual.

"I do wish you could let me know if any of this is working," she said. "I think it would help me."

"I know," Bennington answered, "but you've got to realize we're in some very sensitive areas here. I'm afraid I simply can't tell you. Remember, for God's sake please don't tell anybody about my visits. Just imagine the circus we'd have in the press if it got around that the Navy is using psychics to hunt Russian submarines. And," he added as a final warning, "you never know. There might be some people out there who may resent your helping us."

He gathered up the maps and photographs and returned them to his attaché case. Then he placed four hundred-dollar bills on the table.

"I enjoyed it—as I always do," he said, taking her hand. And I'm really going to enjoy taking you out to dinner when this little charade is over, he thought. She gave his hand a brief but unmistakable squeeze. Maybe, Bennington told himself, she reads minds as well as finding Russian submarines.

Outside her apartment, Bennington paused and looked up and down 71st Street. It was deserted. He checked the cars parked along the block within his range of vision. They were, as far as he could see, empty. Casually, he strolled over to Central Park West and headed downtown. He did his "throw the tail" bit. It was just for routine, of course. Finally at 54th he hailed a cab and headed down to the CIA's New York regional office at United Nations Plaza.

. . .

Instead of taking the Dolley Madison and heading down to CIA headquarters in Langley as he usually did, Bennington got on the Capital Beltway South, then turned up 395 toward Alexandria. It seemed like a month, not forty-eight hours, since his visit to New York and Ann Robbins. His destination was a three-story steel-framed building of green tinted glass at 2640 Huntington Avenue, a model of the kind of office complex that had sprung up with the fecundity of crabgrass in a suburban lawn around Washington in the last two decades. Inevitably, they tended to house a breed of entrepreneurs referred to as Beltway Bandits, specialists in feeding in the taxpayer's troughs.

Electrobiological Research Associates in Suite 200 on the second floor had all the earmarks of a perfect representative of the species. The company brochures on the waiting-room table described it as "a Virginia corporation founded in 1966" devoted to "the study of the effects of electromagnetic force fields on biological systems" and the search for consequent "practical applications in educational enhancements, medicine, cancer therapy, and the behavioral sciences." A very close observer might, however, have noticed the extra thickness of the door to Suite 200 and been struck by the fact it was the sole entry to the half-dozen rooms in the corporation's office suite.

Electrobiological Research Associates was, in fact, a CIA dummy, one of over a dozen such satellites of Bennington's Behavioral Sciences Division. He had a lab on the Maryland shore ostensibly studying radar systems which he employed as a cover for certain animal experiments. He ran institutions similar to this one across the Potomac in Georgetown, in Palo Alto, California, in El Paso, Texas, in Framingham, Massachusetts—everywhere that the nation's high-tech industries flourished.

For his major, multimillion-dollar projects, Bennington could go into black, classified research at the great national laboratories, Lawrence Livermore in California and Sandia and Los Alamos in New Mexico. For smaller, highly sensitive projects, covers like Electrobiological

Research Associates were his preferred way of operating. Every employee of the corporation from the receptionist and the secretaries to the senior scientific staff was a covert employee of the CIA. That gave its operation a high degree of security.

He settled into the spare office kept for his visits, and after a secretary brought him a cup of coffee he went to the electronic safe in his office wall. From it he extracted a one-page memo that, in a sense, would set the agenda for his morning meeting. Its cover bore the usual Agency seal and Top Secret label. It read:

```
            OPERATION SLEEPING BEAUTY
Purpose: To study the theoretical
         possibilities of the
         offensive use of
         artificially generated
         extremely low frequency
         electromagnetic fields in
         the following:

         1. Hostage Situations

         —Employing a field to effect
           perceptual distortion in
           the hostage takers,
           diminishing their threshold
           of awareness, rendering
           them less capable of
           effective defense or
           impairing their judgment.
         —Temporarily incapacitating
           the hostage takers to
           expedite hostage rescue by
           friendly forces.

         2. Terrorist Situations

         —Disrupting a terrorist's
           heart rhythm at a distance.
```

-Effecting perceptual
distortion as in (1) or
disrupting the terrorist's
brain's information—
processing capacity.
-Incapacitating the
terrorist either
permanently or temporarily.

3. Control of Hostile Crowds

-Effecting mass perceptual
distortion.
-Disrupting physiological
processes in some or all of
the people in the crowd.

This, Bennington knew, was the doorway to the twenty-first century. Despite Ronald Reagan and his Star Wars, the conflicts of the future were not going to be waged in the infinity of outer space. They were going to be waged right here on earth with weapons far more deadly than lasers and space stations. Genetic engineering. Electromagnetic emanations and weapons like the ones Buck Rogers used in the 1930s comic strips. They were the real menace. And they'd be used not in the limitlessness of space but inside the neurons of man's brain.

Dear God, he thought, if it ever got out to the press that the Agency was even contemplating weapons that could scramble a man's thought processes or fry his brain cells with electromagnetic radiation, the savaging they would get would make the Church Committee hearings look like a little old ladies' garden party. This time they wouldn't just rip out his balls, they'd dice and quarter them.

And yet he knew there were few areas of research in which the Soviets had shown more interest in the past decade than this.

The secretary's knock interrupted his meditation.

"The professor's here," she said. "They're all waiting in the conference room."

Bennington walked across the hall. He greeted the three young CIA scientists his front employed and the professor, Austin Kilbourn, a neurophysiologist at the University of Calgary who was in to report on the results of some contract research he'd been doing. He was an intense, rather gaunt man in his late thirties with the kind of quirky brilliance that always appealed to Bennington.

When they'd gotten through the routine coffee chit-chat, the professor took over. He'd already fired up the videotape machine and set up two schematic drawings, one of a human brain, one of a rat's brain, on an easel.

"Okay," he said, "the challenge you guys threw up was: Is it possible to develop some kind of exotic electromagnetic weaponry that could be employed, for example, against a rampaging mob that will basically make the members of the mob a lot less enthusiastic about rioting? Or that could be used to disable terrorists in, say, a hostage situation?

"I've gone back to some remarkable work done by José Delgado with fighting bulls when he was a professor of physiology at Yale. Delgado was studying cats, monkeys, chimpanzees, and later, fighting bulls in Spain to find the areas in the brain which could either increase or decrease aggressiveness in a species. In Spain, he anesthetized the bulls and implanted an electrode in the depths of the animals' brains. Their terminal sockets were anchored to the skull and connected to micro-miniaturized stimulators which Delgado could activate with a radio signal."

Kilbourn rubbed his hands in satisfaction. "They turned the bull loose into an arena with a matador. He tore after the matador like he was going to kill him. Then, from ten yards away, Delgado sent a radio signal that stimulated the area in the bull's brain that inhibited his aggression. Pow! The bull turned into a pussycat. The matador could go over and caress him and he just stood there.

"Delgado turned the signal off, and pow, he was back

in action, ready to kill again." He paused. "The implications of that are extraordinary. Aggression has also been inhibited in humans by electrodes planted in the brain for therapeutic or diagnostic purposes."

Bennington's three young CIA scientists sat up as though they'd just been jabbed with cattle prods.

"But that's not all." Like most professors, Kilbourn liked to save the juiciest morsels for last. "Delgado was convinced you could produce those same effects without actually implanting the electrodes in the animal's brain. You could do it, he claimed, by zapping him with a very precisely pulsed electromagnetic field. And he did it with other animals. He was able to get fighting fish to stop fighting by exposing them to an electromagnetic field. He took monkeys and put them under different fields. One would go to sleep, the other would fly into a rage, depending on the signal he was sending them."

Kilbourn got up and walked to his easel. He stood there an instant, thumping a collapsible pointer against his palm.

"What we have here," Kilbourn began, "is a schematic diagram of the human brain. Here, in the postramus at the very back of the brain where the spinal cord opens, we have a lot of our mast cells, the cells that contain histamine." He looked at his little audience. "You've all, I'm sure, taken antihistamines when you've had a cold. That's because histamine tends to clog you up. Produce mucus.

"Now what's interesting is that the area around the mast cells can also trigger nausea. Dump a shot of histamine in there by manipulating those mast cells and you are going to feel instantly rotten. You'll be vomiting your guts out in minutes. And you can bet you're going to lose any interest you have in aggressive behavior in one hell of a hurry. So the question we asked ourselves was this: Is there some way to tickle those mast cells electromagnetically from a distance? Expose them to an electromagnetic field from *outside* the human organism that will cause them to order histamine dumped into a man's body's system and get him violently ill?"

One of Bennington's aides emitted a low whistle. Kilbourn looked at him and slowly nodded his head. "Some of the implications of this are pretty hairy."

He turned back to his easel. "There is no human organ better shielded against electromagnetic radiation than the brain. Whether by accident or design, the bone of the skull serves as a remarkably effective barrier against most of the electromagnetic emanations we're exposed to in our modern world." Another bemused smile crossed the scientist's face. "Interesting, isn't it, when you think that the skull evolved long before man had the vaguest notion of what electricity was.

"Anyway," Kilbourn noted, getting back to his subject, "what this means is, the electromagnetic fields most apt to get through the skull's barrier are ELF fields—extremely low frequency fields—because they have such high penetrating power. We know," he continued, pointing back to his easel, "that mast cells are in basically the same location in the brain of a rat as they are in the human brain. If the effect we're looking for could be produced in a laboratory with rats, then, we reasoned we could feel relatively certain that, with enough experience, we could produce the same effect in humans."

Kilbourn switched on the videotape player. The TV screen lit up. A cage full of rats appeared on the screen, a dozen scurrying, nibbling, loathsome little creatures. In the upper-right-hand corner of the screen, a red light glowed on.

"We've just started exposing them to a field of an intensity of 0.5–3 tesla at half a hertz," Kilbourn said.

For a few minutes nothing happened. Then, almost as if on command, the rats began to tumble to the floor of the cage. Some just lay there inert; others writhed in evident agony. Within seconds, all of them were clearly ill.

"Sweet Jesus," gasped Bennington. His three deputies were too stunned to talk.

"And you're suggesting that what you just did to those rats you could do to humans, with this same technology?" Bennington asked.

Kilbourn leaned against the office wall, again stroking the palm of his hand with his pointer. "Yes," he replied. "Sure it's a big step between what you can do in a lab and what you can do out in the real world. But if you want to look at the possibility of an electromagnetic weapon you could use to control hostile mobs or employ in certain kinds of terrorist situations, this is the way to go. The beauty of this is that it's reversible. It's not like having a hole punched in your body by a bullet."

"Okay," said Bennington, "let's take a hypothetical situation. We've got a Pan Am 747 that's been hijacked by half a dozen Palestinian crazies with a couple of hundred people on board sitting on the runway up at JFK in New York. Could you see this technique being used in a case like that?"

"I could. The idea would be to bathe that 747 in an electromagnetic field of a very precise order to get everybody on board—terrorists, hostages, crew—instantly, violently sick, so your SWAT teams could move in unopposed."

"How big is this machine that's putting out the signal going to be?"

"The intensity of this signal diminishes as the cube of the distance from your power source. So if you're working across the room, it's pretty easy. Get out to two or three hundred yards and you're talking a device you could put in the back of a Marriott catering truck and park it out there at night where the terrorists couldn't see it. Then turn it on to take them out when your SWAT teams were ready to move."

"And that electromagnetic field is going to be able to penetrate the skin, the fuselage, of the 747?"

"Oh absolutely. No question."

"And these terrorists in there, they're not going to spot anything funny when you turn that generator on?"

"Of course not. That field is completely undetectable by ordinary human senses. You couldn't pick up its presence any more than you can pick up all the radio and TV signals that are floating around you in the air of this room right now."

"Suppose," said Bennington, "we have a nice little old lady there in the plane with cardiovascular problems. If she gets violently ill, isn't there a risk she's going to have a cardiac seizure?"

"Yes," Kilbourn acknowledged, "that's always a danger."

"How about the side effects of being exposed to that electromagnetic field?" Bennington asked. "Do we know if that's going to affect things like hormonal balances, cell structures, Christ knows what?"

"Right now, we don't," Kilbourn acknowledged. "Given the intensity of the field and the time those people on the 747 would be exposed to it, my guess is that any such effects would be temporary and negligible. But you'd have to do some experimental work to get the answers to your question."

"On humans?"

"Doing it on ants won't get you the answers you're looking for."

Kilbourn returned to his place at the conference table, obviously wrapping up his presentation. "Look," he said, "if you're willing to pursue the research, I can certainly foresee the day when you'd develop a generator to produce those fields that you could station, for example, in embassies in potentially hostile areas. Say a mob comes charging down the street at your embassy in Tehran. The marines wheel this thing to the window, turn it on, and depending on what the geographics in front of the embassy looked like, you'd wind up with five thousand Iranians puking on the pavement instead of being inside the building taking hostages."

"Ah." Bennington smiled. "That is a gratifying image."

They went through the usual farewell rituals and he escorted Kilbourn to the door, then returned to his colleagues.

"Well," he said, "that little lecture would make you sit up and think, wouldn't it?"

The case officer on the project, a physicist from MIT, cleared his throat. "We've been hearing for some time

46

from scientists about how these extremely low frequency fields affect the central nervous system, producing behavioral changes, modifying cells, stuff like that. Most of these guys are from outside the scientific mainstream. The mainstream community tends to reject this out of hand. After all, classic theory says a six-foot man cannot be an antenna that's going to pick up an electromagnetic wave thousands of miles long. Those extremely low frequencies have wave lengths of that order.''

"Yup," Bennington agreed, "but I remember when the idea of particle-beam weapons first got floated, every scientist in the government community kicked it in the head. Never work. It took some quirky fellows on the outside who said, 'Hey, it's far out, but who knows?' Now we've got a big Star Wars program going on particle beams and there are people saying the Russians have been working on them for years. Could this be the same thing?''

"That's my concern," declared another of Bennington's young scientists. "You all know we have soft intelligence saying the Russians have made a major breakthrough in this domain. Okay, again this is an area of controversy. But we know for a fact the Russians are conducting extensive research into electromagnetic weaponry.''

Dear Lord, thought Bennington, it's a time warp. We're back in the fifties, I'm a young buck, and we're worrying ourselves sick about the Russians finding some secret gimmick to use LSD to modify behavior. "Gentlemen," he said, "you're forgetting one thing. Kilbourn's talking rats. We're talking people. And we can't get from one to the other without some human experimentation. Which is about the biggest single no-no this government of ours has.''

"You mean," said the young man who'd been concerned about the Russians, "we don't try to advance on what Kilbourn's given us?''

"I mean Mrs. Bennington's little boy is not going up to the director's office and say, 'Hi, Judge. We'd like authorization to recruit about fifty GIs down at Fort Benning for a little experiment in how electromagnetic fields of a certain nature affect people. Get them sick to their stomachs if we possibly can, in the national interest.' What do I say when the Judge asks: 'Will there be any side effects to this?' 'Uh, sir, that's a very good question, and in fact that's just one of the interesting things we'll be finding out'?''

"Well," his assistant pressed, "what do we do with this in that case?"

"We make a little risk-benefit assessment. What we have here is a fundamentally unproven, questionable technology which reeks of highly negative publicity. Are the risks involved in pursuing it worth running?"

"I gather, Doctor," his assistant said, his voice a fine blend of regret and sarcasm, "you think they're not."

"I think," Bennington said with a sigh, "we stick some absolutely inoffensive label on this, bury it at the bottom of the biggest stack of paper we can find, and hope to Christ no investigator for a congressional oversight committee ever finds it."

Despite his apparently firm decision, Bennington continued to agonize over the question of what to do with Kilbourn's research all the way back to Langley. It seemed clear there was no way to advance the project without getting into human experimentation, and just mention that phrase and your career was in jeopardy—particularly if your name was Arthur Holt Bennington.

He was still mulling over the problem when he walked into his office on the sixth floor of the Agency's headquarters.

"The New York regional office just called. They want you to call back. It's urgent," his assistant announced.

He went to his desk and punched New York up on his WATS line. "Bennington," he announced. "You wanted me?"

At New York's message, he slumped in his chair as though he'd just taken a hit to his solar plexus. "My God!" he gasped. He looked at his watch. "I'm coming up on the two-o'clock Eastern shuttle." He slammed his phone into the cradle.

"Ann!" he yelled. "Get me a car to go to National Airport right away. And call the FBI liaison office. Tell them I want someone from the Bureau to meet me at La Guardia."

It was death's special signature, an odor which, once smelled, was never forgotten. Nineteen years in the department, thirteen of them carrying the detective's gold shield, had left their layer of protective calluses on Tim McQueen's soul; still, one breath of that sweetly rancid smell and all the sordid memories accumulated in two decades of New York police work could come sweeping back over him.

They were with him now as he leaned against the wall of the woman's apartment, his arms folded across his chest, studying her body crumpled inside its little island of yellow crime-scene tape. He seemed to be studying the corpse with a kind of bemused clinical detachment, about as indifferent to the subject matter as a mechanic pondering a defective carburetor might be. That was not true. McQueen was a good cop, and, like all good cops, he yielded up a tiny bit of his soul to each of the lifeless figures that constituted the raw material of a homicide cop's calling.

This victim, McQueen guessed, was in her early forties. She was lying there on her apartment floor, folded up in a dark sea of her own dried blood, her joints unhinged in that curious fashion of the violently dead, a little bit like a Cabbage Patch doll some kid has pinched and twisted out of shape. She was wearing a purple jacket over what had been a pink silk blouse until the guy had started to cut her up, and a tight purple skirt. She wasn't wearing any jewelry; that had probably gone out the front door with the perp.

Studying her clothing, her apartment, McQueen guessed she was some kind of former Village bohemian migrated up to the West Side thanks to a little middle-aged affluence. On the wall opposite McQueen was a painting of one of those Egyptian pyramids with a big eye at its center staring out at him. In the cluttered bookcase lining one wall of the living room were half a dozen statues of Hindu gods and goddesses, the kind that had snakes for a hairdo and dorks down to their knee joints.

The super, who'd found her two hours ago and called the precinct, said she was a psychic, one of those upmarket fortune-tellers that peer into a crystal ball for a hundred bucks an hour to tell some woman whether her husband is screwing around or not. McQueen sighed. The forensics guys were, as usual, taking their time doing their thing, getting the dimensions down, taking the measurements, shooting up a storm with their crime-scene-unit videocameras. In the old days when McQueen came onto the force, it was just black-and-white stills. Today it was color photography and the newest thing, a VHS video machine. Get iced in New York now, McQueen mused, and they make a home movie out of you.

McQueen thumbed through the pad in his hand in which he'd been jotting down his notes. The victim's name was Ann Robbins. One of the neighbors had complained about the smell and called the super. He'd called the Two O, the 20th Precinct, which had sent up the car with the rookie cop at the door looking pasty-faced and swallowing hard now as he tried to play Kojak in front of his first sliced-up stiff.

The lady's keys were still dangling from the lock on the front door where the super said he'd found them when he came up to check out the smell. He was a black, a big teddy bear of a guy who didn't seem to be too much into work, so McQueen could believe him when he said he hadn't been up to the fourth floor in a week. The guy upstairs, on the top floor, the one who'd called the super, was seventy-three, said he never used the stairs, always took the elevator, which meant, McQueen thought, those keys could have been there in the door for a week and who's to know?

Except for the one giveaway that brought the whole thing together. Just inside the front door, its contents spilling out onto the floor, was a brown grocery bag. McQueen had gone through it piece by piece, noting down its contents: three Stouffer Lean Cuisine frozen TV dinners, two grapefruits, a bar of Camay soap, and a box of Ben & Jerry's New York Fudge ice cream. Ann Robbins had come alive for McQueen when he saw that. That ice cream had probably been the last indulgence of a pretty lady trying to lose a pound or two. Now it was just a sticky brown stain on a dead woman's floor.

At the bottom of the bag, McQueen had found what he was looking for: a cash receipt from Paik's Grocery around the corner on Columbus Avenue between 71st and 72nd. It gave the time and the day the clerk had rung up the sale. That slip of paper confirmed what McQueen's nostrils had told him when he stepped into the apartment: the woman had been dead for about forty-eight hours.

Her wallet, ripped apart, was on the floor beside her body. You would take a bet there hadn't been much money in there. Ladies living alone on the West Side were streetwise today. Never carry anything important in your pocketbook. A few dollars, mugging money. Let them make their score and push off. Except some of the guys out there today, they don't push off.

That, McQueen thought, is what you would figure happened here. Some guy, some junkie out to score a nickel bag of heroin, a little crack, buzzes himself in downstairs. Delivery. Her building, 22 West 71st Street between Central Park West and Columbus, was one of those old, narrow five-story brownstones. No security. He disappears into the shadows and waits for someone to come home. Along comes Ann Robbins with her grocery bag. He sees she gets off at the fourth floor, and while she's playing with her keys, he glides up the stairwell in his fifty-five-dollar Reeboks. Boom, as soon as she opens the door, he hits it with his shoulder, knocks her inside, and kicks the door shut so the super can't hear her scream, which is unlikely anyway since he's probably downstairs with *The Gong Show* going full blast on his box. She gives him the wallet but it's not full enough so he starts to cut her to make her tell him where her stash is. A real horseshit case that was going to wind up as just another sixty-one with "Perpetrator Unknown" written across the top when they closed the case file.

"Okay, you guys," the forensics sergeant said, snapping his camera shut. "We're finished. She's all yours."

The medical examiner rose from the victim's couch, gloved himself, and knelt down beside the body. For a few seconds he studied the woman's body the way an infantry major might study a piece of hostile terrain. Getting the time of death right would be vital in this case, because if it coincided with the cash receipt McQueen had picked out of the shopping bag, the detective would have at least one solid base on which to anchor an investigation.

He tweaked the woman's jaws, then probed the muscles of her neck. Both were as hard as wooden planking. He played a light at her cloudy eyeballs, then touched them with his fingertip. There was no elasticity left; they were like marbles.

"Yeah," he grunted to McQueen, "forty-eight hours is probably going to be about right. I'm going to roll her over and look for lividity." The ME beckoned to the rookie patrolman who'd been the first officer to respond. They were preparing to turn the body when the doorbell rang.

McQueen moved to open the door. "Customer coming up to get a fortune cookie."

In front of him was the last person he would have expected to find ringing this particular doorbell—Kenny Cook, the deputy director of the Federal Bureau of Investigation for the City of New York. Behind him was a man McQueen didn't recognize, a big guy about fifty swinging the shoulders of an old linebacker. He was wearing one of those very expensive and very tweedy English sport coats, the kind with the suede patches on the elbows the history professors up at Columbia University like to wear. Cook was, as always, the fashionplate in a blue shirt with white collar and white cuffs, a camel's-hair overcoat, belted behind, casually draped over his shoulders. His dress was a bit of a legend in the city.

McQueen waved them in. "Jesus, Kenny," he said, "you look more like a wise guy than most of the wise guys I know. J. Edgar could see you now, he'd be doing cartwheels in his coffin."

"Ah," replied the FBI man, "our deceased leader never did have a sense of dress, did he? I think he bought his suits straight off the pipe at Sears Roebuck. I was driving downtown listening to Detective Two for entertainment when I heard your call letter and learned you were here. My friend"—he nodded to the man behind him—"is a visiting Washington criminologist. He's spending half a million dollars of the taxpayers' money doing a study on emerging patterns of violence in urban crime for the Bureau. One of those three-hundred-page masterpieces that will have all the academics drooling in glee and be worth sweet fuck-all to those of us who are supposed to be doing something about urban crime. I thought you might give him a little direct exposure to the subject."

"No problem," replied McQueen. Visiting firemen on a case were no big deal. "Just don't touch anything," he told the visitor. "Otherwise we'll have to print you and run you through for elimination prints."

"Winthrop," Art Bennington answered, extending his hand. "Stanley Winthrop."

"So," said Cook, "what have we got here?"

"What we have here," McQueen answered, "is a real piece of horseshit. A push-in. An open-and-shut case. Some spade junkie—"

Cook coughed. McQueen got the warning. These Washington guys were up to their armpits in civil rights.

"Some junkie looking to make a score. Maybe he follows her back from the grocery store or maybe he's in the shadows out there in the hall when she comes home. He jumps her, shoves her inside, and it's twenty-questions time. Maybe he's too excited, kills her by mistake. More likely once he's got her dough, he figures, what the hell, she can make me in a lineup, so he decides to finish her off."

"Anything seem to be missing?" Bennington felt a desperate need to say something, to do something that might force his mind and his vision away from the horror before him. This stench of putrefying flesh, the sight of the gaping wounds in that lithe body he'd fantasized clasping to his, those eyes, the glistening eyes that had so enthralled him seventy-two hours ago, now just dark marbles: he wanted to retch or to weep. Or both. And yet he had somehow to remain impassive before Cook and this New York cop.

"Naw," said McQueen, pointing to the bookcase where the TV, the videocassette player, the compact disk machine sat untouched. "It's a straight cut-and-run. That's how these guys operate—bang, bang, in and out. Grab the cash and scram. Nobody makes you. Go out the front door with a television in your arms and the neighbors start to get curious, you know what I mean?"

On the floor the ME was probing under the victim's armpits with his fingertips.

"What's he doing?" Bennington asked.

"Checking for body temperature," McQueen said.

"Like that? With his fingers? Without a thermometer?"

"Hey," snarled the ME, "this isn't *Miami Vice*. Thermometers are for television cops."

Bennington had inadvertently touched on a point of pride of the Office of the Chief Medical Examiner of New York City. MEs in New York, unlike those in many major cities, always register body temperature at a crime scene by touch.

The ME got up. "I've got to darken the room," he announced, "so I can go over her with the Wood's light."

"Checking for semen," McQueen explained, "see if the guy banged her too."

"Oh God!" This time Bennington couldn't hold his emotions in check. Maybe, he told himself, they'll put it down to the reactions of a nervous layman. "You mean he raped her, too?" He felt his muscles tightening. If he could have had the heroin addict who'd done this, he would have been capable of killing him, of ripping his testicles from his body with his bare hands.

Bennington feigned an interest in the bookcase while the ME ran the Wood's light over Ann Robbins's clothes, then lifted her skirt and probed her lower body, looking for the telltale fluorescing of light that would reveal the presence of semen.

"No," he said, "I don't think he banged her. Just cut her. We'll double-check when we have her on the table tomorrow."

He put aside the lantern, and while the patrolman opened the curtains and turned the lights back on, the ME picked up Ann Robbins's hands one by one. Almost tenderly, he turned them slowly in his own, studying her palms. Bennington couldn't help seeing their scarlet fingernails dancing before him, thinking how he had fantasized about those nails skimming their way along his own skin. The ME drew each hand close to his face to scrutinize the fingernails, then unbuttoned the sleeves of her blouse and looked at her forearms.

"No defensive wounds," he announced. "Whoever the bastard was, she didn't try to fight back."

"Probably scared shitless," McQueen observed. "What's a nice lady like that supposed to do with some wired-up junkie with a knife in his hand?"

As McQueen was talking, the ME slipped two plastic bags over Ann Robbins's hands. Tomorrow at the morgue they would study her fingernails for any scrap of flesh or hair she might have scratched from her killer's face or body before dying.

"What do you figure for probable cause?" McQueen asked him.

The ME sighed and returned his gaze to Ann Robbins's mutilated body. "Wheel of Fortune," he said. "Take your choice. I've counted nine cuts. Any of them could have been fatal. I'm going to put it down to multiple lacerations until we have a look at her tomorrow."

"Excuse me," Bennington said, "but what are your chances of solving a crime like this?"

"You want an honest answer, Mr. Winthrop?" McQueen replied.

Bennington nodded.

"Lousy. I've ordered a canvass of the neighborhood for tonight. Knock on doors. Did anybody see anything? Somebody following her home? Some guy coming out of the door downstairs in a big hurry? Whatever. We'll have the Anti-Crime Unit turn the heat up on the street a few degrees. Shake up the assholes over on Columbus Avenue a bit. Any of the dealers hear anything? Maybe the guy bragged to somebody how he iced a lady down on 71st."

"You see, Stanley," Cook, the FBI man, said, "in this urban crime scene you're so interested in, if we are going to get a conviction in a crime like this, it will almost certainly come as the result of a little deal. A few months down the line the DEA or the NYPD will have a dealer in custody. The gentleman will be looking at ten to fifteen years as our guest. He'll call us in and say, 'Look, if we can get this thing down to possession'—which is a misdemeanor—'maybe I can help you find who did the lady on 71st Street six months ago.' And he snitches. If his information is good, we swap a drug dealer for a killer."

Bennington had seen enough. What a miserable, rotten place this city was. Why had that drug-crazed junkie had to pick on her? Why couldn't he have found some other victim for his mindless, irrational violence? What a shame, what a miserable fucking shame.

"Well," Bennington said, extending his hand, "we don't want to be in your way any longer. You have more important things to do than talk to us, I know."

"No bother, Mr. Winthrop," McQueen said. He looked down at the mutilated body that had been the cause of their meeting. "I tell you, you talk about your urban crime. I don't know what this goddam city is coming to."

Downstairs, Cook and Bennington paused a moment to look down West 71st Street. It was a quiet, peaceful-seeming place. Marjorie Morningstar territory, the breeding ground of Jewish American Princesses from the thirties to the fifties, now beginning to dance to the beat of a Latin drummer. You could see the harbingers down at the corner of Columbus Avenue: Victor's Cafe 71— Cuban Cuisine, Los Ranchos, La Fortuna.

"So," Bennington said to his FBI escort, "what do you think?"

"I'll tell you, Stanley, McQueen's a good cop," Cook replied. "I think he's got it about right. This place looks peaceful enough, but there are some bad blocks around here. Eighty-third between Columbus and Amsterdam crawls with junkies. So do 87th and 88th around Broadway. By the way," he added with a smile, "your people got you up here in a hurry."

"They read the New York police wire in our United Nations Plaza office," his guest said. "Incidentally, while I wouldn't want anyone"—Bennington glanced at Cook to underscore his point—"to be aware of my organization's interest, I'd appreciate it if you could very informally keep abreast of the investigation for me. If anything comes up, I'd like to know. It's a kind of personal thing, you know?"

He took a plain white card from his pocket and wrote a number on it. "You can get me at this number during the day." Then he looked at his watch. "Well," he sighed, "I can just make the next shuttle. Christ, what a cruel business that was."

"Stanley." The quality of Cook's compassion had been too long strained by the violence of the city. "This is a cruel place."

Upstairs in Ann Robbins's apartment, McQueen performed the last official act prescribed by the rigid protocols of murder in Manhattan: he wired a UF95 tag to Ann Robbins's left toe and called for the morgue wagon that would deliver her body to one of the 126 refrigerated compartments in the morgue of the Office of the Chief Medical Examiner of the City of New York.

It had been almost two months now since these biweekly sessions had become anchors embedded in the routine of Art Bennington's existence. How grateful he was for them. They were life buoys steadily drawing him back to sanity's shores from out of the black, bitter tides that had threatened to engulf him after his divorce. "There won't be a day for the rest of your life when you won't think about it," one of his friends, an emotional cripple of the divorce wars, had warned him.

Well, his friend had been wrong. Thanks to these hypnotherapy sessions, he was actually reaching the point where the painful memories of those months were becoming ghosts he could confront and live with. In a certain way, the very fact he could have felt so attracted to that poor murdered psychic, Ann Robbins, could be put down as one of the benefits of those sessions. He turned off the Leesburg Pike onto Chaucer Lane. All the streets in the new development where the hypnotherapist had her office were named after writers: Hemingway Drive, Poe Road, Chaucer Lane. Another example of the terminal cuteness you found everywhere in the Virginia suburbs these days.

Her office was located, naturally, in what was called a "professional building," the kind of place in which you'd expect to find your standard assortment of chiropodists, osteopaths, orthodontists, and second-rate suburban dentists. Throw in two computer consultants, an Association of Retired Postal Employees, and a hypnotherapist and it was pretty much what you had here.

Divorce, Bennington thought, as he pointed his Volvo into one of the building's white-lined visitors parking slots. It's the great American contribution to the social mores of the latter half of the twentieth century. Imagine, we've managed to industrialize the destruction of the family. The same wonderful people who brought you the automotive assembly line now bring you the altar-to-courtroom marriage, each step along the way made almost effortless through careful planning.

At least he could almost laugh now when he thought back to that day when he'd come home to find his clothes, his books, and a clutch of his personal belongings dumped on the front lawn: a yard sale for a worn-out marriage. A terse note from Terri and a court order evicting him from his home obtained by the Great White Shark crowned the summit of his pile of junk like an explorer's flag atop Mount Everest.

What a nightmare the next weeks had been. Every night seemed to last forty-eight hours. First there was the sheer physical anguish, the ache in his bowels for his lost wife. No other form of withdrawal could be so excruciatingly painful. Then there was the rising bitterness as he'd seen his financial crucifixion being artfully maneuvered by the Great White Shark. She'd managed to turn Terri into a woman he didn't even know anymore. He'd had no alternative but to go out and get his own fast-lane divorce lawyer. Two hundred and fifty bucks an hour the guy had charged—imagine, the most expensive hourly consultant's fee in the U.S. capital, and for what? A divorce lawyer.

The whole thing had cost him $45,000 and cast him into a life of lower-middle-class poverty. He'd moved into a seedy Pennsylvania Avenue hotel that was kind of a halfway house for middle-aged guys tossed out of their homes by their wives. The Woggery, they called it, because its only other occupants seemed to be Middle Eastern exiles. From there he'd gone to a cellar studio billed as an "English basement flat" in the arch hyperbole of the real estate lady who'd found it for him. The only thing English about it was that it was damp and cold. Its windows offered a breathtaking view of passing feet. Fortunately, since it was in Georgetown, occasionally a pair of those feet were worth watching.

How great it was to have so much of that behind him now. He could actually get out of his car and notice again the perfume of a freshly mowed lawn in the air, appreciate the flash of scarlet and gold on the wings of a Baltimore oriole drifting overhead.

He walked up the four flights to Nina Wolfe's office

suite. The waiting room was sparse: three chairs, a round table, and thumbed copies of *The Reader's Digest, U.S. News & World Report, Better Homes and Gardens*. There were no diplomas with gothic scrolling on the walls; hypnotism was a talent that was not taught in schools or institutions. It was handed on individually, from teacher to student, practitioner to neophyte.

Hypnotism also happened to be a subject about which Bennington knew a great deal. The CIA had looked into the whole subject in exhaustive detail in the late fifties and early sixties. They'd played with the notion of post-hypnotic suggestion, the *Manchurian Candidate* stuff, programming a guy to assassinate somebody on a prede-signed signal. That was bullshit, pure fiction. Their major thrust had become finding the perfect interrogation tech-nique, the infallible tool that could rip the most precious secret from a prisoner without his consent. Hypnotism, they had learned, could not do that. To get someone to reveal something he shouldn't reveal under hypnotism was an exceedingly difficult challenge.

"Good morning!" Nina Wolfe came out of her office with her previous client, a clearly overweight woman. Smokers and overeaters made up over half her clientele.

"How's the oil business?" she asked as the woman left. Bennington had told her his name was Art Booth and he was a lobbyist for Exxon.

"Could be better. Texas crude is off again."

"That's too bad—I think."

"Not for you. Gas will be cheaper."

Nina Wolfe was in her late thirties. She had fluffy red hair, freckles, and attractive green eyes. She was given to wearing mannish coats and skirts like the gray pin-stripe number she had on this morning. Probably, Bennington surmised, to discourage the emotional dependence that could develop so easily in the hypno-therapist-client situation.

"Are you using the tapes I gave you?"

"Every night. Better than Mother's Irish lullabies."

"And you're sleeping well?"

"Better."

They walked into her office. The curtains were drawn to mute the light. Bennington took off his coat and hung it on the coat tree in the office corner. Then he loosened his tie, unbuttoned his shirt cuffs, and stretched out gratefully on the leather lounge chair she reserved for her patients.

Classical hypnosis, the kind Nina Wolfe practiced, involved three stages of trance, each deeper than the one preceding it. The first, which she employed for people who wanted to give up smoking or stop eating, was really not a trance at all but a state of deep relaxation. The second brought the patient to a stage at which he retained his sense of feeling but had little sense of pain. He would be aware of a pinprick but not wince at it. A heightened sense of memory and an acceptance of posthypnotic suggestion characterized this stage.

The third stage produced a trance so complete that patients were fully anesthetized. People with deadly allergies to conventional anesthetics underwent major surgery in third-stage trances: cesareans, breast implants, thyroidectomies, even battlefield amputations in World War I.

Only one person in four or five, however, could be put into a third-stage trance. Art Bennington happened to be one of them. It was essential to his therapy, because only in the third stage could the hypnotist achieve "regression." Regression was a voyage into the client's past life —in Bennington's case, his marriage. What was involved was a kind of play-acting with the hypnotherapist assuming different roles, friend, mother, father, boss, to spur the client's memory. The aim was to find in that exploration of the past explanations for the client's problems, to discover positive feelings, attitudes on which to anchor a therapy of posthypnotic suggestion.

Nina Wolfe picked up a silver bulb on a stalk. It looked like a shiny mushroom. "Now watch this," she commanded. "Your eyes are getting tired. Your eyelids are getting heavy." Her voice took on a metronomic beat. Bennington's unconscious was already conditioned to it, because it was the same steady tone of voice she used on the tapes he listened to at night.

Imperceptibly, she lowered the bulb so that Bennington's eyelids were in fact lowering to follow it, reinforcing the suggestive process of her words. "Your eyes are heavy. You are sleepy. . . . Now I will start to count backward from twenty to one. When I say one, your eyes will close completely and you will go to sleep. . . . Nineteen . . . your eyes are closing . . . eighteen . . ."

Bennington was deep into his trance by the time she reached nine.

Nina Wolfe contemplated him for a moment, sensing the pattern of his regular, slow breathing. "You are sleeping now. Sleeping deeply now. You can hear only my words." Her voice caressed his unconsciousness with a silken hand. She took a pair of pointed calipers and pinched his wrist. There was no reaction. He was gone.

"Take me back to a time now, a time when you were happy. Take me to your third wedding anniversary. Be there. Be there now," she commanded.

"Terri was mad."

"Why?"

"I'd been away in Europe working. She's mad."

"What are you doing? What are you saying to her? Be there."

"She was . . . I . . ." Bennington mumbled a second. "I am in the front hall. I have the porcelain vase I brought back from Berlin."

Nina Wolfe smiled. His shift in verb tense from past to present was the clue. He was in full regression. She could now search for those positive feelings, memories, which she would then try to embed into his unconscious mind with her posthypnotic suggestions.

Their session lasted just over an hour. When he came out of the trance, Bennington felt wonderful. It was like waking up from a deep, refreshing afternoon nap. He stretched and yawned.

"You're progressing well." Nina Wolfe smiled as he put on his coat and took his billfold out of its pocket.

"With another session or two, I think we can consider your course finished."

No outpost of New York's city government ever seems to be without one—those red-heart decals proclaiming, "I love NY." They show up in some unlikely locations, such as the holding cells of a precinct station house or the cashier's cages at the Parking Violations Bureau. Nowhere, however, do they appear more out of place than they do on the walls of the Office of the Chief Medical Examiner of the City of New York, a low building fronted with blue glazed brick at the corner of First Avenue and 30th Street situated, appropriately enough, between two of the city's great medical facilities, Bellevue Hospital and the NYU Medical Center. To the refrigerated compartments in the building's cellars are delivered each year the city's two thousand or so homicide victims; all suicides; all DOAs at Manhattan's hospitals; and every citizen whose demise has not been attended by a physician, whether it's Nelson Rockefeller, a bag lady plucked stiff from a subway grate on a January night, or an unidentified corpse, ankles planted in cement overshoes, fished out of the East River.

That building was the last way station in the life of Ann Robbins. At nine-thirty on the morning following the discovery of her body, Dr. Mordechai Herzog, the young associate medical examiner who'd made the preliminary examination of her corpse, presented the case of Ann Robbins to the chief medical examiner's daily autopsy caseload conference. Ann Robbins was a number now, case M89-1376, the identification her file would carry with it on its long, tortuous, and almost certainly fruitless passage through New York City's criminal justice system in the quest for her killer.

As usual, the chief medical examiner presided over the conference. The chief was a short man in his mid-sixties who looked like the kind of nice Jewish family doctor who still made house calls in Scarsdale. He was, in fact, a tough battle-scarred veteran of his trade who could reduce any of the half-dozen young associate MEs gathered around his table to jelly with a few well-chosen words. There was little in the file of case M89-1376, however, that was likely to tax the abilities of Dr. Mordechai Herzog, the chief, or anyone else in the Chief Medical Examiner's Office. The case was assigned to the eleven-o'clock autopsy without discussion or question.

By tradition, autopsies begin in New York at eleven in the morning every day except Sunday and run through until midafternoon. The schedule was developed, according to legend, in the days when detectives were required to attend their homicide victims' autopsies, a procedure which generally left the detectives with little desire for a lunch hour.

The autopsy room, in the cellar of the CME's office, consisted of ten metal autopsy tables, on wheels like gurneys. By tradition, table one was reserved for the chief. None of the cases on the docket today, however, was of sufficient importance to merit his attention. Instead, as the autopsies began, he paced up and down the room like an anatomy professor overseeing the dissections of a group of medical students.

The first, and least unsavory, task of Herzog's autopsy was to undress Ann Robbins's corpse. He marked each piece of clothing as he removed it with his and her initials, then sealed everything into a container which would become a part of the chain of evidence in the event anyone should ever stand trial for her murder.

Next, he removed the bags he'd placed on her hands the day before, took off each of her fingernails, and placed them in separate containers for microscopic examination in the laboratory. Herzog did not order X-rays. They were usually reserved for firearm homicides. At the foot of his table, he checked a row of bottles, red, green, blue, yellow, white, black, which would shortly be filled with specimens of Ann Robbins's blood, urine, bile, intestines, liver, and kidneys. The toxicology lab would examine them for any traces of drugs in her body before her death.

Then he pressed a foot switch to activate the microphone of the Sony tape recorder suspended above the center of his table and began to dictate his autopsy protocol, the document that would serve as Ann Robbins's epitaph in the bureaucratic archives of New York City.

"The body is that of a well-developed, well-nourished white female measuring five foot six inches in length, weighing approximately a hundred and twenty pounds, and appearing the stated age of forty years old."

Carefully, he described each of the knife wounds on her body, giving as precisely as possible its location, width, and depth and an indication of the organs it had penetrated. Then he took a whirring saw and began his autopsy with a standard Y-shaped incision running from shoulder to shoulder down to the midchest, then straight down to the pubic bone.

The procedure was long, slow, and painstaking. Herzog was, as always, exhausted when he had finished. With the exception of a minimal amount of internal hemorrhaging, there was nothing to set this autopsy apart from any of hundreds of similar autopsies Herzog had performed in five years in the Chief Medical Examiner's Office. Pulling off his gloves, he dictated the final paragraph of his protocol: "Cause of death: Multiple stab wounds (nine) of chest, abdomen, back, lungs, and liver. Homicide."

"What's that?" It was the chief. Ann Robbins's body was on her stomach, and the chief's finger indicated a black-and-blue mark roughly the size and shape of a very small button inside the back of her left knee joint just above her calf. Without waiting for an answer, the chief poked at the spot. The pressure of his finger stretched the skin, revealing, at the center of the circle, a black dot.

"Give me a hand lens." With the lens, he leaned over and peered intently at the black-and-blue spot.

"Looks like a needle," he said. "Any of you ever hear of a junkie shooting up behind the knee?"

By now, two other assistant medical examiners who'd finished their own autopsies were gathered around Herzog's table. They all shook their heads.

"Still," grunted the chief, "in this city, who's to know? You get toxicology on her yet?"

Herzog shook his head.

"Get it."

Herzog went to the phone and was back in minutes. Toxicology did a standard screen for narcotics, alcohol, and knockout drugs.

"Negative, Chief," Herzog said.

"Any anomalies in your autopsy?" asked the chief.

"No. Except," said Herzog almost as an afterthought, "minimal internal hemorrhaging."

The chief considered the implications of that a moment. "Get the crime-scene photographs," he ordered.

By the time an aide brought the photos down, the group around Herzog's table had expanded to half a dozen, all fascinated now to observe the chief in action. He took the photos and studied them carefully, one by one. He was looking for what was known in his calling as Indian-club spurts, a characteristic pattern of staining made by fresh blood when it bursts from a newly inflicted knife wound. Most frequently, they were found on the surface of the skin adjacent to the wound.

"You see any Indian clubs here?"

Herzog and the other MEs studied the photos in turn. The chief had a point. There were, in fact, no Indian-club patterns on Ann Robbins's body.

"Something is screwy," declared the chief. "Give me a scalpel. I want to look in there for a track."

With the blade, he cut below the black-and-blue spot into the flesh under the bruise, looking for the characteristic entry track of a hypodermic needle.

He found a track. It was, however, slightly larger than that usually associated with a hypodermic needle, and it had penetrated just over an inch and a half, farther than the ordinary heroin injection.

He put down his blade and stood before Ann Robbins's corpse thinking. This strange track, no Indian-club spurts, very little internal hemorrhaging. He looked at the assistant MEs gathered around him like interns hanging on a professor's diagnosis.

"Okay," he said, "suppose she was already dead when she was cut?"

Access to the Executive Dining Room of the CIA was one of the privileges that went with Art Bennington's rank of SIS4, Senior Intelligence Service, Four. It was a tasteful, clublike place located in the rarefied atmosphere of the seventh floor. The predominant color was mauve, the lighting was muted, and the walls were decorated with CIA house art: the oil paintings of little-known modern American painters whose principal artistic merit was the relatively low price of their canvases. Seating was open, an idea inspired by those London men's clubs like White's and Buck's so esteemed by the Agency's founding fathers.

It was a distinct improvement over the two push-a-tray cafeterias downstairs where Bennington had eaten lunch throughout most of his Agency career. Up here you were served by waitresses and ordered your meal from what was usually a very appetizing menu card.

The waitress, who knew both Bennington and his habits, brought him a Sprite along with the day's menu. No liquor was served in the dining room, which explained why, although just over one hundred CIA officers were entitled to use it, the forty-place dining room was rarely full. Bennington was debating between the corned beef hash Duke Zeibert and the Caesar salad when the waitress returned. "A call for you, sir," she whispered.

It was Ann Stoddard down in his office. "A Mr. Cook from the FBI in New York wants to speak to you urgently." It took Bennington just an instant to place the name.

"Okay," he said. "I'll come down and take the call there."

"Ah, Stanley Winthrop," Cook said when Bennington had gotten through to him. "I gather your secretary's a new employee."

"Why do you say that?"

"She seemed to hesitate a bit when I gave her your name."

Bennington suppressed a laugh. He was trying to think of a clever reply when he realized Cook didn't expect one.

"You recall that psychic lady, Ann Robbins, whose death prompted your recent visit? The one who was iced by a junkie of unknown ethnic origins?"

"I sure do."

"We have a tradition here in some of our best Mafia families. You just place an icepick in a friend's ear and give the knob of the pick a good hard whack. Your friend is suddenly very dead. Clean a little blood out of his ear and no coroner is ever going to spot what happened. Cause of death will inevitably be put down to cardiac arrest."

Why in hell is he telling me all this? Bennington wondered. Cook, he had understood in New York, was one of those guys who couldn't talk in a straight line. For whatever reason, he liked to converse in circumlocutions.

"We have a somewhat analogous situation with your Miss Robbins."

"How is that?"

"Forty-eight hours ago, the chief medical examiner up here, who is a very clever fellow, sent us a sample of her blood and asked us to send it down to the Center for Communicable Diseases in Atlanta for an immunological screening. He had apparently begun to have some doubts about the cause of her death."

Bennington sat up.

"His toxicology lab is only equipped to deal with the detection of drugs or things like knockout drops. They can't pick up sophisticated poisons. To do that, you've got to be able to screen for antibodies. Find out if the body's immune system was reacting to a foreign substance injected into the bloodstream."

The CIA man could feel his stomach knotting. "Yeah, yeah, Cook, I know all that. Get on with it."

"I have Atlanta's report here on my desk. Do you remember that Bulgarian who got zinged behind the leg in London with a little dart full of ricin poison? Markov was his name, I believe.''

"I sure as hell do," Bennington said.

"Atlanta found ricin antibodies in Ann Robbins's bloodstream. She wasn't killed by a junkie, my friend. She was killed by some of your East Bloc friends, then cut up after she was dead to make you think she'd been iced by a junkie.''

"Christ!" Bennington paled. Ricin was the signature of Department V, the executive-action department, the "wet" department, of the KGB.

"Has that report gone over to the New York police yet?" he asked Cook.

"Not yet."

"If we give it to them, we might as well give it to the press, no? We'll have a headline in the *Post* tomorrow shrieking, 'KGB Kills City Psychic.' ''

"Yes. That, I think, is a very logical supposition, Stanley.''

"Listen, Cook." Bennington tried out his sternest division-leader tone. "I would like to ask you, in the interest of national security, to sit on that report. Just tell the police Atlanta's reports all came back negative.''

There was a long and clearly embarrassed silence at the other end of the phone.

"Okay," Cook sighed finally. "I think maybe I can do that. But if I do, I've got to have two things to cover my ass, Stanley.''

"What are they?"

"What the hell is your real name and title?''

PART 2

"DON'T EXPLAIN THE DIFFICULTIES. DO IT."

I t had been over half an hour since engineer Vladimir Sorubnov had seen another vehicle on this lonely stretch of highway cutting its way across the southern corner of the Qara Qum, a vast desert area the size of California nestled in Turkmenistan, the southernmost republic of the Soviet Union. Before his headlights, the road seemed to fade away to an infinitely distant horizon, flat, straight, lifeless, and forlorn. The moon had not risen yet, and the warm night enveloping his car was as dark as the "Black Sands" from which the Qara Qum took its name.

Engineer Sorubnov was not native to this part of the Soviet Union, and he did not like it. He was a Byelorussian from Minsk, far to the northwest. His heart was irrevocably fixed in those colder climes, and more of his day than he would care to acknowledge was spent scheming for a way to get a transfer back to Minsk, or even better, Moscow. Sorubnov and his wife, Elena, had moved to Ashkhabad twelve years ago, as soon as he'd received his degree as a hydroelectric engineer at the Minsk Teknikon. Their move was part of a carefully orchestrated program to shift population from the USSR's European republics out here to the Asian republics, to counterbalance the overwhelmingly Asiatic, Moslem populations of the eastern republics with an injection of better-educated and harder-working—and more loyal—Russians from the west.

The lure had been the usual: better job, better housing, better pay. And in that the party had kept faith with Sorubnov and his wife. This car with which he inspected installations on the 495-mile-long Qara Qum irrigation canal was proof of that. So, too, was the new four-room apartment he had just been assigned in a new block built by the Hydroelectric Workers Cooperative in Ashkhabad. What Sorubnov could not abide was the Turkomans, the Moslem people among whom he'd been plunged. He was suspicious of them. He distrusted them. He found them frightening, threatening, even dangerous. They spoke their own language in preference to Russian. They looked different, thought differently, ate differently, even, for all he knew, made love differently.

And they made no secret of their hostility toward the European Russians in their midst. Sorubnov's children were constantly being beaten up by packs of Turkoman children on their way home from school. After twelve years in Ashkhabad, Sorubnov and his wife did not have a single Turkoman friend. All their social acquaintances were European Russian. So, too, were their neighbors. For all practical purposes, they lived in a ghetto surrounded by an alien people who looked on them as foreigners and colonialists.

His thoughts had so wandered with the monotony of his drive that for a second he did not see the figure gesticulating wildly at his car from the road up ahead. Behind him an uptorn tree, one of a glade planted by the Hydroelectric Authority, lay stretched across the highway. Christ! thought Sorubnov, skidding to a stop. It must have been one of the sudden windstorms that were always surging over the Qara Qum.

The man leaned into his car window. Sorubnov knew immediately from his knitted cap and his vile garlic breath that he was a native. *"Gospodin,"* the man said, employing the old prerevolutionary form of address, "a storm blew down the tree. Can you help me move it?"

"Of course the damn thing was blown down," Sorubnov grumbled as he got out of the car. "Did you think it fell down by itself?"

He was so impatient to get back to his wife and children that it did not strike him as curious that there was no apparent transportation nearby to account for the man's presence. Nor did he notice the second figure emerge from the shadows behind his car and start circling toward him. He did not hear a footstep or the rustle of the man's loose belted cloak. In fact, he was not aware the man was there until a strong left forearm had whipped around his neck, snapping his chin backward and driving his skull up against his assailant's shoulders. In his terror, Sorubnov saw the distant glimmer of the stars against the night sky. He tried to shout, but his mouth was jammed shut. Then he saw the glimmering of the knife, a large, curved Afghan warrior's dagger, as it ripped through the air on its journey to his throat. There was a terrible burst of pain as the blade plunged deep into his flesh and then, in one continuous move, swept from one side of his neck to the other.

His assassin released him, and he fell to the ground. He tried to shout, but the knife thrust that had severed his carotid arteries had ripped apart his vocal cords as well. All that emerged was a hollow gurgling sound. Sorubnov's eyes, terrorized and uncomprehending, tried to focus on his killers.

He felt a pair of strong hands rip open his belt and jerk his trousers to his knees. The bastards are robbing me, he thought. With a sudden burst of horror, he felt a set of strong fingers grasp his sexual organ, and he realized robbery was not his assailant's aim. This time, the pain of the knife's thrust was multiplied by the dying man's revulsion. In his fast-fading consciousness, Sorubnov understood. This, his friends who'd served in the Afghan war had told him, was what the Mujahedeen did to their Red Army wounded. But why, why to him?

His last sight as life and consciousness drained from his being was of his killer holding his sexual organs over his mouth, ready to plunge them into the orifice which his hands had just pried open. Behind him, the man who'd stopped Sorubnov's car finished dabbing the green crescent of Islam on the Moskvitch's windshield with a spray of green paint.

"Come," he whispered to the killer.

The killer wiped his knife on his victim's jacket, then sheathed it. Like jackals, the two loped off into the darkness.

ALMA-ATA,
KAZAKHSTAN REPUBLIC, USSR

Athousand miles from Vladimir Sorubnov's corpse, in Alma-Ata, the capital of the Soviet Republic of Kazakhstan, a pair of young men in black leather jackets and faded blue jeans, their hair teased out in an unsuccessful but determined imitation of London punks, ghosted their way down the alley of fir trees leading to the monument at the heart of Brezhnev Square. One of them carried a canvas bag, the kind many Russians used to carry their lunch to work. It wasn't lunchtime, however, it was one in the morning.

The top of the sack contained, nonetheless, a stack of sandwiches. The two approached the monument. It constituted a massive bronze hammer and sickle enclosed in a wreath fixed to a wall of highly polished marble symbolizing the undying fraternal unity of the republics of the USSR. As they reached it, the young man carrying the sack put his hand inside, threw the sandwiches to the ground, and pulled out a can of green spray paint. He handed the sack to his partner and started to deface the wall beside the monument with the green crescent of Islam.

As he did, his partner took half a kilo of plastic explosive from the sack. He wedged it into the base of the monument just above the bronze scroll with the letters KCCP for Kazakh Soviet Socialist Republic. He took out his preset firing needle, twisted it to start its countdown, and worked the pin into the slab of plastic.

"Ready?" he whispered.

His companion nodded, and they strolled off out of the square.

Each time Art Bennington walked down the hallway of
the seventh, executive, floor of the Central Intelligence
Agency, it reminded him of one of those up-market psychiatric institutes in New England, the kind to which the
wealthy sent their drunks to dry out and their mentally
sick to waste away in unembarrassing anonymity. The
walls and ceiling of the tunnel-like corridor were a lifeless, antiseptic white; the floor was laid in institutional
green linoleum of a kind which had proved remarkably
resistant to every effort to put polish on it. Bennington
half expected to hear the squeak of a nurse's rubber soles
on the floor behind him and a female voice snickering,
"We found scotch in old Mr. Van Dyke's hot-water bottle again this morning."

Bennington hurried into the reception room of his boss,
the deputy director for science and technology. "He's
waiting for you," his assistant said. "Go right in."

The DD/S&T, John Sprague, was ten years Art's junior, but their relations were close and comfortable.
"We've got a problem," Bennington announced as he
strode into the room. "A big problem. You remember
that lady psychic in New York I told you about?"

"The one that was murdered by a dope addict?"

"Right—or rather wrong. She wasn't killed by a drug
addict. She was liquidated by the KGB."

"Holy shit!" The DD almost tumbled from his chair.
For the KGB to kill an American citizen on American
soil was an act so rare it was almost unheard-of. "Hold
on," he said, pressing on his intercom. "Get Frank in
here right away, and no calls, except the director," he
ordered his assistant. Frank Pozner was S&T's internal
security officer.

"Take it from the top," the DD ordered as Pozner
joined them. "Remind me exactly what our relation with
this woman was."

"We were using her in a thing called Project Seashell.
Do you remember it?"

"Only vaguely." The S&T directorate's seven operating divisions were running over three hundred research projects, and Sprague could not possibly keep abreast of them all.

"It's part of our ongoing study of what we call paranormal phenomena," Bennington said.

"The ESP stuff?"

"In a sense, yes. We took twelve of the top psychics in the country, the ones with the best track records with police work, the FBI, the Secret Service."

"You mean those guys are into this stuff?" Pozner interjected.

"Sure. Although they'll swear to you on their firstborn's head they don't know what the word 'psychic' means if you put the question to them in public." Bennington described Project Seashell's use of psychics to try to locate Soviet submarines.

"Far out." It was the security officer again, and the tone of his voice was not exactly vibrant with admiration for Bennington's project. He had laid the security net over Seashell, but until this moment he'd had no idea what the operation was intended to do.

"Listen, the Navy's getting desperate because of those new propellers the Russians have got thanks to our Japanese friends. They'll try anything. Anyway, up until last week, we'd asked each of them seven times to try to find a sub for us." He paused. "Eleven of those people turned up nothing at all. All seven times, seventy-seven times in all. Not even vaguely close. Miss Robbins, on the other hand, gave us the exact location of the sub within twenty nautical miles three times out of seven."

"I don't believe it!" exclaimed Pozner.

"Neither, in a certain sense, do I, but there it is."

Bennington then reviewed for Pozner everything he knew about Ann Robbins's murder.

The DD followed him intently. "For the moment, put aside the details of how she was killed. Why now? Was there something significant in the timing? Do they have some major aggressive move in mind that made it important to eliminate her and her ability to spot their subs right now?"

"I've looked at that," Bennington said. "The first thing I did when I heard this was go downstairs to the Pit." The Pit was the CIA's basement war room, manned by a staff of technicians twenty-four hours a day. "It's as peaceful out there as a Sunday-morning prayer service in Iowa. The Soviet armed forces are in their lowest readiness posture. There's no unusual traffic flow between any of their command posts anywhere in the world. NSA's busted a whole series of their alert codes and not a single one's been broadcast."

"The satellites? Poland?"

"Nothing. Anywhere. The whole thrust of Soviet foreign policy in the last eight months has been nonaggressive."

"That could change."

"Sure it could. But I tell you, John, I just feel in my bones that their motivation in killing her was scientific and long-term."

The DD stroked his chin. "Such as?"

"There's something both of you guys should be aware of." Bennington sighed. "It happened before you came aboard, Frank, and"—he glanced at the DD—"you were probably never aware of it, John. It has a very direct bearing on why we're even into this Project Seashell business.

"Back in the early and middle seventies, we funded a program out at the Stanford Research Institute. The heavy hitters out there were as skittish about our involvement as debutantes in a whorehouse, so we kept at arm's length, but these guys weren't your state-of-the-art California flakos. They were first-class people. They were looking at something they called 'remote viewing.' Do certain people have an ability to access, by some mental process we don't understand, information they shouldn't be able to access by normal sensory means?"

"Could you just put that into simple English I could understand?" Pozner smiled.

"Sure. They'd take two experimenters. One stays here in this room. One goes off, a mile away, then he's told to go to a certain location. The Kennedy Center, let's say.

An hour later he's there thinking about what he's seeing and the guy back here in the room tries to describe where he is.''

"Black magic."

"If you want to call it that. Now, they got a lot of garbage. But every so often they'd come up with some remarkable stuff, particularly with one guy, a man called Pat Price. So the Agency sent me out there to have a look, check out the validity of their scientific techniques.

"We spent an afternoon in their lab doing one thing and another. Some of it was impressive, but I wasn't convinced, because I hadn't had total control over any of it. So I said, look, tomorrow morning I'd like to set up a little experiment of my own.

"Well, the SRI guys were nervous, but Price said, 'Sure, why not?' He was anything but your long-haired guru. He was a Mormon from Salt Lake. He'd been a pilot in World War II, a gold miner up in Alaska, ran a coal-mining company for a while, then settled in Burbank, California, where he even spent a few months as a police commissioner.

"I pick them up the next morning and take them to a small airport. I'd already made arrangements to do a run in a glider, which is a hobby of mine. 'Okay,' I said, 'I'm going up, and exactly thirty minutes from now, I'll make some notes on a piece of paper and you see if you can figure out what they are.' One thing was sure: there was no way in hell Price was going to see my hand moving when I made my notes.

"So I went up a couple of thousand feet, ten-thirty came, and I took out my notepad. The glider had an altimeter and it had a serial number, seven or eight figures so small you could hardly see them. I wrote down the last three, seven four three. Then I thought, Christ knows why, of Winnie the Pooh. So I sketched a teddy bear. Except instead of a smiling face, I gave him a frown. Then I folded the paper up and put it back into my pocket.

"When I got down, Price handed me his notepad. He'd written three numbers on it: three seven four. 'I kept seeing these numbers, but they weren't in order. Then I got the image of a teddy bear, but the damnedest thing is, he was crying. I started to sketch him, and I could see the beginning of a design below the numbers—and then this other figure started swinging back and forth across the teddy bear's face and I began to get sick to my stomach and had to stop.'

" 'Another figure?' I asked.

" 'Something like this,' Price said, and he took his pad back and started to sketch.

"Now, I was wearing a blue turtleneck under a shirt like the one I have on now. He draws a design. I look at it and nearly pass out. I was wearing an Egyptian amulet under my turtleneck my wife had given me. It had a unique design to it. I knew for a fact that there was no moment that morning when Price could have seen that amulet. None. And yet the sketch he handed me was a perfect drawing of the damn thing.

"Now, that's not very scientific, but it did make me sit up and think a bit. We decided to bring him in-house so the SRI people wouldn't be aware of what we were doing and we could keep his work exclusively to ourselves. He liked to work with geographic coordinates, so one day we gave him the numbers for a place out in West Virginia, a place I'd never even seen. It's NSA, the Big Ear facility that monitors satellite communications. So secret even a CIA clearance won't get you inside.

" 'West Virginia,' Price said after a couple of minutes. 'Near a crossroads with a Getty gasoline station. There's a steel door built into the side of a mountain that rolls up and a flagpole to the right. An elevator that goes down a shaft a couple of hundred feet. Now there's another locked door. It gives onto a room.' He describes the room. 'There's a Picasso drawing on the wall,' he says, 'some kind of stick figure of a bullfighter. There's a desk, another flag, a filing cabinet.' He even reads off some of the labels on the drawers of the filing cabinet. Then he takes a notepad and sketches the site.

"I go back and hand all my notes and his sketch over to the guy who'd set up the experiment. He sends them to the NSA and asks them to check it out. The next day I've got three NSA security guys in my office fuming with rage. The sketch checks out, the description checks out, the labels on the filing cabinet check out, even the goddam Picasso checks out. 'Pull another stunt like this,' they tell me, 'and we'll have you up before the White House.' "

The DD looked at Bennington with a quizzical regard. "Have you got all this down in what we like to describe around here as due and proper form?"

"Everything's down in the vaults. Anyway, the last point. We decided we'd try him out on Soviet submarines just the way we were doing with this Ann Robbins. One Saturday morning I was with him in that Holiday Inn in Rosslyn. I gave him the usual stuff, a picture of a sub and its captain. He stews around for a while, apparently not getting anywhere. Finally, he looks at me with this puzzled expression.

" 'Hey,' he says, 'there's something strange going on here. Some of this sub's missile tubes are empty.'

" 'Okay,' I said, 'but where is it?'

"So he goes back into his state of meditation or whatever it was he did and finally sites a spot for me in the Atlantic about a hundred miles south of Bermuda. I went back to Langley and called the coordinates down to my contact at COMSUBLANT at Norfolk. Now I didn't know this, but at the exact same time I was sitting in that Holiday Inn motel room with Price, there was a Navy helicopter overflying the sub he was supposed to locate. The sub was cruising about a hundred yards below the surface, and at that depth, a helicopter can pick up the gamma rays its missiles emit and follow him. I'd marked the time Price had come up with his coordinates in my notebook, and the chopper had its ongoing log. Price was sixty-three miles away from the sub's true position when he gave me his coordinates, which, if you consider the size of the Atlantic Ocean, isn't bad.

"But this is what blew us away: the helicopter's gamma-ray detector showed that three of the sub's missile tubes were empty."

The DD whistled.

"What happened to your Mr. Price?" Pozner asked.

"He's dead," Bennington replied. "The poor guy, we discovered, had a terrible cardiovascular system, and we tried to get him to have a bypass. He didn't want to hear about it.

"One day in 1976 he was out in Las Vegas with a friend. They were going to see if they could use Pat to locate abandoned gold mines with reserves you could go in and exploit. After dinner, Pat gets into bed and suddenly he sits up like a jack-in-the-box. Massive cardiac arrest. The friend calls the hotel switchboard for an ambulance and they rush him to the hospital, but Price is DOA. The young resident is going through the standard resuscitation drill just for the books when a guy Pat's friend has never seen before comes rushing in with Pat's medical records. 'Hey, my friend was a cardiac,' he shouts and gives the doctors the records.

"The resident takes one look and he has all the evidence he needs as to why Pat has died. So he signs out the corpse without an autopsy despite the fact that under Nevada law an autopsy is supposed to be performed whenever you have an unattended death. The body's flown to California and his wife arranges a cremation, which is what Pat wanted. She was the only person who knew he was working with the CIA, and she called me to tell me he'd died.

"I fly out to LA and get there just in time for the ceremony. We're waiting to go in when the guy who was with Pat when he died tells me about the stranger who showed up at the hospital with his papers. What do I do? Stop the cremation and demand an autopsy? On the authority of the CIA? The one thing we wanted to do was keep the psychic program and our whole association with Price secret.

"I knew about his cardiovascular problems, so I decided to do nothing. But there's always been that unsettling question hanging over his death: who was that guy who showed up at the hospital with his papers?"

"Sure," Pozner said, "but it could easily have been

the assistant manager of the hotel, who would have been assigned as a routine thing to secure his room. Finds the papers and rushes off to the hospital after you.''

"That's how I rationalized it myself at the time." Bennington ran a set of nervous fingers through his hair, dislodging a fine trickle of dandruff. "And I've believed it until just now. You know, in all the years I've been looking into these paranormal phenomena for the Agency, I've found only two people who convinced me they really had the ability to do these things.''

He looked at Pozner and Sprague as though he somehow expected them to provide him the answers his own mind didn't yet have. "Pat Price was the first. He's dead. Ann Robbins was the second. Now she's dead. Christ knows if Price really died of a heart attack or not. But the KGB sure as hell killed Ann Robbins. Why? And how in God's name did they learn that of all the people we were working with, he was the only one who ever fingered a submarine for us?''

For forty-five minutes, the two figures had been moving with slow, stealthy steps up the nearly dried-out riverbed. They advanced down the middle of its course, the stream's lazy trickle rising halfway between their ankles and their knees. To the north was the great black swath of the Qara Qum, which they'd just left. To the south, beyond three parallel ridgelines, was the Soviet-Afghan frontier. Before them, a crescent moon ebbed down to the horizon.

The lead man stopped. He was wearing a loose, rough shepherd's cloak, its folds girded by a leather strap into which he'd fitted the curved blade of his Afghan warrior's dagger. For a moment he scrutinized the walls of night around him. He had hunter's eyes, deep-set, fixed in a constant half-squint to sharpen the focus of their vision. In the spring, with his white goshawks, he used those eyes to forage the rougher lands to the north for game, rabbit, fox, ferret. In the colder weather, they followed the soaring flight of the eagles in search of wolves. He reached into his cloak and drew out a small object he raised to his lips. It gave out a shrill squeal, somewhat like a cicada's call.

Out of the darkness came a similar sound. The hunter returned his whistle to the folds of his cloak and started forward, moving to the sound. Three minutes later, he and his companion were at the entrance of a cave cut into the rise of land above the riverbed, a dense screen of underbrush concealing its entrance.

"*El Hamdu il'Allah*—Praise God," a voice whispered out of the darkness.

"It has been done, *el Hamdu il'Allah,*" answered the hunter.

The two men advanced into the cave. When they'd entered, the man inside lowered a rough cloth, camouflaged with sprigs and branches, over its entrance and lit a candle. Then the trio formed into a rough circle around the candle, sitting on their haunches, their legs folded beneath them. For a moment, they rested like that, the two new arrivals catching their breath after their tense and hurried trip. When they had, the cave dweller extended his hands, palms up, to the center of their circle. Slowly, he drew them upward, mumbling as he did an almost inaudible chant. His palms finally reached shoulder height, then turned upward to the roof of the cave in the gesture of a man releasing a pigeon skyward. As his chant faded, the two others extended their arms and began a similar invocation of their own.

The three were members of one of the oldest, most disciplined and rigorously secret societies in the world, the Qadiri *tariqa,* one of the three major Sufi brotherhoods. Those patterned, ritual gestures they performed traced their origins back through seven and a half centuries to the Baghdad of the caliphs, to Islam's golden era of conquest and conversion.

The cave dweller was a *murshid,* a master. Each of the two men who, a few hours earlier, had murdered Vladimir Sorubnov on his lonely roadside was a *murid,* an adept, recently accepted into the brotherhood after a long, rigorous period of indoctrination, interrogation, and examination. The mystic initiation ritual which each had recently accomplished bound them for life to the brotherhood. Theirs would be an existence of discipline, of obedience to their *murshid*. Above all, a sacred bond of secrecy had been laid upon them, a bond even more imposing and rigorous than the Mafia's bloody code of *omertà*, silence. Through the seven and a half centuries of its history, the brotherhood had sought to lead its followers along its mystic *tariqa*, or path, to Allah, the One, the Merciful, the Compassionate.

But it had also fulfilled another, far more temporal mission. Together with the Naqshbandi, the other major Sufi brotherhood of the Soviet Union, the Qadiri had for centuries been the fomentors and the focus of Islamic resistance to Russian conquest, be it by czars or commissars, in the Caucasus, the Middle Volga regions, on the sprawling steppes of Central Asia. From the Imam Manzur to Sheikh Uzun Haji, who fought the Red Army in the twenties, admission to their pantheon of heroes demanded one virtue: resistance to the Russian unbeliever.

When his two disciples had finished their rite, the master sat back on his heels and smiled. He was an Afghan, a former member of the Mujahedeen, in the ranks of the Party of Islam of Gulbuddin Hekmatyar. Before the Russian invasion had changed his life, the master had studied history at Kabul University. Since then, terrorism and counterterrorism had been the focus of his mind.

He paused so that his words would bear the emphasis they deserved. "Why, may you ask, this man? Why not another?

"It does not matter who, that is the answer. The death of this man tonight will sow fear in the hearts of ten thousand Russians. The death of the next man will start them scheming how they can leave and go home to Leningrad, to Moscow. This is how our Algerian brothers struck at the French. How once in Africa the Mau Mau terrorized the lonely English farmers."

"They will strike back hard," warned the hunter.

"Good," said the master. "That is what we want them to do. Let them send their tanks and police militia here.

They will brutalize the people. And for every one they brutalize, we will have a hundred converts to the struggle. That is how the others struggled against the colonialists in Indonesia, in Africa, in the Near East. They are the last colonialists. They, too, shall fall in their turn.''

Outside, the first pale indication of dawn had lightened the corners of the cave's cover. The master blew out the candle. "I go now," he said. "Tomorrow, I return to our brothers in Afghanistan. In two weeks I shall be with you and, *inch' Allah,* we will do God's holy work again.''

He rose. His two disciples accomplished a ritual bow.

"You will know I am here by the usual sign," he said. Then he disappeared into the fading night.

It was a few minutes past eight. As he did almost every morning, Ivan Sergeivich Feodorov stood by the ten-foot-high window panels of his third-floor office, a cup of scalding-hot tea in his hand, contemplating the panorama of awakening life in the square below his feet. From the Dzerzhinskaya subway exit, a gray stream of men and women flowed toward the six pedestrian gates of his nine-story headquarters despite the fact their official working day did not begin for almost an hour. Such zeal was almost unheard of in the Soviet Union. As Feodorov well knew, it was inspired not by devotion to the organization over which he presided, but by one of the privileges service in its ranks conferred. In the basement of this building, a massive cafeteria provided Feodorov's employees each morning with a breakfast of fresh fruit, milk, eggs, bacon, and sausages; a feast such as the average Muscovite could count himself fortunate to sample two or three times a year.

On the square, facing him, as though somehow asserting a claim to Feodorov's fealty at this morning ritual, was a soaring bronze statue of the man who had founded his organization with twenty-three employees and a teenage girl secretary, Feliks—"Iron Feliks"—Dzerzhinsky. The patterned gray facade from which Feodorov looked out onto Dzerzhinsky Square was the Moscow "Center" of spy lore and legend, the headquarters of the Komitet Gosudarstvennoy Bezopasnosti, the KGB, the Committee for State Security of the Soviet Union.

"We stand for organized terror," Feliks Dzerzhinsky had proclaimed when he founded the Cheka, the organization from which the KGB was descended. Seldom in history has an institution fulfilled quite so completely the dream of its founding father. A whole generation of Russian mothers had terrified their children into obedience with the threat "Iron Feliks will get you if you don't do what you're told." Even on this spring day, Russians still scornfully referred to members of the KGB as Chekists.

Thousands of Russians had died in the basements below Feodorov's feet, most with a bullet to the base of the neck, many after their strength and spirit had been wasted by hours of brutal torture. They were only symbols of the millions of victims of purges, of show trials, of forced collectivizations, of population transfers herded by the KGB and its predecessors onto the sacrificial altars of socialism. The mass brutality they represented, however, bore little real resemblance to the KGB controlled by Ivan Sergeivich Feodorov this spring day. The instrument of "merciless mass terror" created by Dzerzhinsky at Lenin's behest had been transformed into an organization whose terror was selective, scientific, and reasoned. The blunt ax was sheathed. The modern KGB was a scalpel: sharp, swift, and precise, but no less deadly for that.

The hate-filled revolutionary zealots and the barely literate thugs of Chekist legend were gone. The ranks of Feodorov's KGB and particularly those that served it outside the USSR were filled with highly educated, intelligent, dedicated men and women. As the CIA had worked the campuses of Yale, Harvard, Princeton, Georgetown, and Stanford for promising candidates in the fifties and sixties, so the KGB had culled the pick of the litter, the best and the brightest from the Soviet Union's top academic institutions, in the seventies and eighties.

Even more subtle had been the shift in the role discharged by the KGB within the Soviet power structure. Its original function, as defined by its Chekist motto, was to serve as "the sword and shield of the party." In particular, it was to provide a control on the Red Army or any other potential source of power that might challenge the supremacy of the party.

Now, however, it was often the Praetorian guard that controlled Caesar and his cohorts, and the shield provided by the KGB was as much a constraint as it was a safeguard for the party. The Politburo of the Communist Party of the USSR, Muscovites joked in private, might be more aptly described as the Politburo of the KGB. Five of the voting members of the Politburo, including Mikhail Gorbachev and Eduard Shevardnadze, were either officials of the KGB or its protégés.

Let the outside world imagine the power center of the Soviet Union was behind the high Kremlin walls two blocks from Feodorov's office. He believed it was right here inside the forbidding precincts of "the House that Feliks built." Feodorov strolled over the priceless Bokhara and Kashgai carpets to his desk. Just as the KGB over which he presided was totally different from the KGB of legend, so Feodorov was cut from a different pattern from the gray and stolid men who had preceded him in this office. He was tall and lean, with the muscled upper body of an athlete, which, in his youth, he had been. A Universal weight tree imported from the United States graced his private suite behind his office. He used it and the sauna next to it almost daily.

His black hair was just beginning to show a few strands of gray. It was always immaculately combed and trimmed. His Georgian ancestry on his mother's side had gifted him with a dark complexion and quick black eyes which bespoke an excitable temperament and a more than casual interest in women. A widower—his wife had died of cancer almost a decade ago—he provided the Moscow gossips with a steady source of conversation about his amorous activities.

This morning he was wearing a double-breasted navy-blue wool-and-fiber suit made for him by Brioni in Rome.

Each year, the Italian sent a tailor to Moscow to update his measurements and offer him a selection of cloth swatches from which to choose the half-dozen suits that would later be delivered to Moscow by diplomatic pouch.

Waiting on his desk for his perusal as they did every morning were two piles of the KGB's overnight intelligence summaries, the distillation of the KGB's reporting from around the world. The first, inside a red leather folder, dealt with the world beyond the borders of the Soviet Union and its satellite empire. The second dealt with potential dissident or subversive action inside the USSR, for the KGB, unlike the intelligence organizations of the United States, France, and Great Britain, concerned itself with all possible threats to the USSR, both internal and external.

He studied first the international folder. It contained two copies, one of which he would keep. The other, once approved by Feodorov, would be hand-delivered by KGB courier to Mikhail Gorbachev's Kremlin office. The inconsistent and sometimes perplexing behavior of the new U.S. President continued to puzzle Feodorov as it did Gorbachev. The President, the report noted, had left a state dinner for the visiting Mexican President for almost fifteen minutes without explanation. The Washington KGB *rezident* noted no crisis that would have justified his absence.

Feodorov took his pen. "Sec Gen CP," he wrote. "Our Scientific Directorate has prepared an in-depth psychological profile of the new President to provide some indication of his potential weaknesses/vulnerabilities. The profile will also investigate his health. I expect it on my desk shortly."

As Feodorov well knew, the evolution of the KGB could be perceived in the paragraph he had just written. Two decades earlier, no one at Moscow Center would even have heard of a psychological profile, much less have been ready to consider its possibilities as a potential tool of Soviet policy. That he could have written those words today was thanks to the man who had been Feodorov's patron for twenty years, the architect of the transformation of the KGB, Yuri Vladimirovich Andropov.

No one else, Feodorov firmly believed, had influenced and changed the USSR as Andropov had. Two decades before Gorbachev, he had understood the still-unuttered truth: Marxist-Leninist ideology was dead. In fact, Yuri Vladimirovich had about as much use for Marxist-Leninist ideology as an apostate might have for canon law. The only ideology Yuri Vladimirovich understood was power: the power of one man over another, of a clique of officers over an army, of a cabal of leaders over a mass, of an elite over a nation, of a nation over an empire. How to seize power, how to keep it, how to use it to manipulate men and events—it was the study of that, not *Das Kapital,* that had absorbed Andropov.

Internationally, he had quickly understood why the KGB's sources of espionage had run dry: the day of the Kim Philbys, the George Blakes, the Klaus Fuchs, the Rosenbergs, of those ideologues burning with their missionary zeal to remake the world, was past. To penetrate the citadels of Western power now, he had proclaimed, the KGB must attack the capitalists' Achilles' heel, greed. Recruit spies with money, not moral precepts. Give them what they needed to buy their Porsches, to keep their expensive girlfriends, to travel their Western playgrounds first-class. Just how right his analysis had been, Feodorov's rivals at the FBI and the CIA had discovered in the 1980s.

Feodorov had first crossed Andropov's path in Kiev in February 1968, less than a year after Andropov had taken over the KGB. Before Andropov, the visits of the head of the KGB to his outstations had been conducted with the formality of a royal progress. The protocol of such trips changed radically under the new chairman. On the evening of his visits, Andropov always reserved a private dining room in a local hotel. There, around a banquet table covered with bottles of vodka and fine Georgian wines, he gathered the station's senior staff for an informal get-together.

Feodorov was the adjutant of the KGB's Kiev chief

that night. A social scientist with degrees in sociology and behavioral psychology, he had been recruited by the KGB after serving five years as a paid KGB informer, first as a graduate student at Kiev University, then as a young member of its psychology faculty. His recruitment bonus, he liked to recall, had been the promise of two new suits and a pair of shoes a year.

Dissidence was the subject they were discussing.

"Dissidence," Andropov declared, "is like a brushfire on the steppes. Stamp on it as soon as it starts and you can put it out in seconds, with your feet. But let it catch a wind and it will turn into a blaze that will burn for days and immobilize a regiment of firefighters.

"Unfortunately, our legal system makes it difficult to deal as quickly as we should with dissidence. Investigations, interrogations, the trial before our dissidents are on their way to labor camps—all that requires time, and time focuses attention on our dissident. What results? More dissidents."

To the horror of his colleagues around the table, Feodorov broke the respectful silence that followed the chairman's words. His was a breach of protocol so enormous that he might just as well, one of his friends later joked, have stood up and pissed in the chairman's wineglass.

"Yuri Vladimirovich," he said, "there might be a better way."

"If there is, I, for one, would like to know it."

"Instead of bringing our dissidents into court, suppose we bring them before a psychiatrist? He examines them, finds their behavior characteristic of an unbalanced mental state, and commits them to an institution for treatment. There's no trial, no appeal, no publicity, no sentence. The dissident is confined as long as we choose to keep him confined. Instead of making him a martyr, we make him an inmate of a mental institution. Mental patients don't lead revolutions."

No one spoke when Feodorov had finished. The silence was so complete it was almost physically painful. Andropov sat rigid at the head of the table, his only movement the slow undulation of his eyelids behind his thick eyeglasses. Feodorov had begun to redden in regret for his impetuousness and his shattered career when Andropov picked up the vodka bottle in front of him. He stretched across the table and filled Feodorov's glass, then added a few drops to his own.

"Do you know Moscow?" he said, raising his glass.

"No sir."

"I think you will like it. I'm taking you back to the Center with me to put your suggestion into operation."

Six months later, Feodorov was firmly established at the Center as one of Andropov's "Iron Young Men." When he took over the psychiatric program, the KGB operated two mental institutions, both of them for the study and treatment of the criminally insane. By the time he'd finished, there were thirty-three such institutions around the USSR; their combined staffs numbered in the hundreds and their inmates in the thousands. Those institutes also provided an elite corps of neurologists, brain surgeons, behavioral scientists, and psychiatrists with the laboratories in which to advance their sciences. Drug therapies, experimental brain surgery, studies of the brain's workings, new techniques to measure its functioning, the impact of electromagnetic fields on behavior —there was almost no aspect of mind research that was not being studied in one of the thirty-three institutes. After all, since the day of Pavlov and his animal experiments, the study of behavior had been a special concern of Russian science.

Feodorov's fascination with the mind embraced another tradition as old, almost, as the Russian steppes—a fascination with the possibility of psychic phenomena. He opened a major research center in the USSR's Science City of Novosibirsk to study the whole subject. After all, if such phenomena really did exist, he reasoned, the implications for the KGB were incalculable.

Strangely, it was probably Feodorov's willingness to entertain the possibility, at least, of these phenomena's existence that had put him in line for the chairmanship of the KGB. As Leonid Brezhnev lay dying of a multiplicity of ailments he found his most constant relief and comfort not among the members of the USSR's prestigious medical establishment, but from a faith healer, a dark-haired young woman from Tbilisi named Dzhuna Davitashvili. Some emanation of bioenergy apparently flowed from the young woman's fingertips, because on numerous occasions her skills seemed to bring the dying Secretary General back from death's doorstep. Indeed, a whole coterie of Soviet intellectuals, scientists, and artists availed themselves of her services.

Prolonging Brezhnev's life struggle did not convenience Andropov. His accession to the throne was prepared. Delay only postponed the moment when the ultimate power in the USSR would be in his hands. And so one afternoon in October 1982 he had summoned Feodorov here to this third-floor office at the Center.

Normally, Andropov was a kind of Slavic Charles de Gaulle in his dealings with his subordinates, all aloofness and austerity. On this occasion, however, he exuded warmth and cordiality. He was seated in one of his richly brocaded armchairs and waved Feodorov onto the sofa beside him. His office housekeeper brought tea from his private kitchen. As soon as she was out of earshot, Andropov turned to Feodorov.

"This young lady healer who has been attending the Secretary General," he said. "Do you know her?"

"Yes. When Leonid Ilyich first employed her services, I called her in. To emphasize that we counted on her to keep in complete confidence the fact she was seeing the Secretary General."

Andropov sipped his tea, thinking. "Do you really believe there is anything to this healing power of hers?"

"Scientifically, I can't answer that question. We've tried in our institutes to see if there is any measurable form of energy, heat, an electric current or whatever, that passes between the healer and a patient. There is an indication that something is going on, but just what it is we have never been able to determine."

"I've met her," Andropov admitted. "I think she's a Rasputin in skirts."

"She seems to have done the Secretary General considerable good."

"Do you think so? I think not. In any event, she does no good to the USSR. She's become a dangerous liability."

"Why do you say that?"

"Can you imagine the consequences if this got to the Western press? The Secretary General of the Communist Party of the Soviet Union being treated by a faith healer, by a glorified witch doctor? That would make a mockery of everything Marxist-Leninism stands for before the world."

Feodorov said nothing.

"I want you to get her back to Tbilisi for a while. Do it without anyone becoming aware we were responsible or why we sent her away."

"Her absence may be a very painful shock for the Secretary General."

"Leonid Ilyich has devoted his lifetime to the service of our party and our nation. This will be a last sacrifice which I am sure he will wish to make for them both."

Feodorov felt a chill in the small of his back. It struck him as extremely unlikely that Leonid Ilyich would willingly sacrifice his faith healer's ministrations for the party, for the state, or for any other reason. She'd become the umbilical cord holding him to life. Remove her and he would surely die. This was an invitation to a socialist regicide from the crown prince. "I'll see that it's done," he said.

Within hours, Dzhuna Davitashvili had been bundled out of Moscow. As Feodorov had foreseen, her absence had a devastating effect on Brezhnev. Like a child deprived of his security blanket, he withered without the treatments of his faith healer. In less than a month he was dead.

Feodorov's swift compliance had, as he had foreseen, cemented his bond with Andropov. Two years later, when Yuri Vladimirovich lay dying—of kidney failure compounded by two bullets fired into him by the wife of the interior minister he'd arrested for corruption—Feodorov and his predecessor, Viktor Chebrikov, were the only leaders allowed by his bedside. Their presence in his death chamber had confirmed them as heirs to the leadership of the KGB.

Now, as he studied the second of his daily intelligence summaries, the one dealing with the Soviet domestic situation, the teachings of his patron were very much on Feodorov's mind. Andropov was a student of history—real history, not Marx's wishful thinking. Nothing was more vital to the survival of the Soviet state, he had held, than its empire, that array of peoples, Balts, Ukrainians, Georgians, Tartars, Moslems, Turkomans, Uzbeks, girding the Russian heart with their protective layers of humanity. History taught that either Moscow would rule them or they would rule Moscow. The first imperative for the Soviet state, therefore, was to maintain a firm, centrally directed control over those disparate elements of empire. And here on the first page of his intelligence summary was a flashing red light warning that, for the first time, the empire's central control was under physical attack.

The night before, in over two dozen locations in the Moslem Soviet republics, in cities from Alma-Ata to Tashkent to Dunshanke to Samarkand, terrorist bombs had exploded. In each instance, the terrorists had left behind their signature, a green Islamic crescent splashed on a wall, a window, or a building. Their targets had included monuments, Communist Party and Komsomol headquarters, the offices of Tass, *Pravda,* and *Izvestia*—in short, any symbol of Moscow's rule or the party's ideology.

Furthermore, three Soviet subjects, all male, all citizens of one of the Russian republics who'd moved to the Moslem areas of the USSR, had been brutally murdered. Their killers, too, had left behind the green crescent signature and had mutilated their victims in the same grisly fashion as Afghan mujahedeen had savaged Red Army soldiers unfortunate enough to be taken alive in the Afghan war.

Three murders and two dozen bombings in one night,

across hundreds of square miles of Soviet territory: it was clearly a concerted, rigorously coordinated terrorist campaign, an overt challenge to Soviet rule. It had broken out without warning, without any indication, any whisper from a KGB informer anywhere in the Moslem republics. That was a failure on the part of the KGB that would not go unnoticed or uncriticized.

Feodorov pushed back his chair and reflected for a few moments. This was where the real menace to Soviet society lay, not in Washington, not in the Atlantic Alliance. It was right here in the vast and vulnerable underbelly of the Soviet empire, running from the shores of the Caspian Sea to the gates of Sinkiang. Fifty million Moslems lay inside that arc, almost a quarter of the USSR's population today, God knew how many tomorrow. One Soviet in three, some population experts predicted.

The Red Army's humiliating withdrawal from Afghanistan had thrown fuel on the flames. Nightly, clandestine radio stations in Iran and Afghanistan poured their vile streams of hate and vitriol into the ether, preaching their dogmas of religion and revolution. Mujahedeen slipped across the borders, itinerant prophets of Jihad.

Stalin's answer, ruthless oppression with the Red Army, was no longer viable. It was the KGB that would have to respond to the challenge. But how?

He slumped in his chair and squeezed his eyes shut as though somehow that gesture would force his thoughts inward, enhancing his ability to concentrate on the problem before him. Suddenly, Xenia Petrovna's memorandum came back to him, the one dealing with the psychic lady in New York the CIA had been using. What was it she said? That her studies with psychics on behalf of the KGB had brought her very close to a technology that might be employed to modify an individual's behavior at a distance—without his being aware of what was happening to him.

He stood up and walked back to the window overlooking Dzerzhinsky Square. The idea that had begun to germinate in his mind would have been worthy of that wonderfully devious bastard perched on his marble pedestal. It was subtle, dangerous, filled with imponderables and unresolved problems. But if it could be made to work, its symmetry was more exquisite than that of a perfect algebraic formulation. It would be the Americans, not his fellow Soviets, who would solve his problem for him.

He took his pen in hand. "Sec Gen CP," he noted. "I intend to convene immediately a meeting of the Fifth Chief Directorate and the senior KGB representatives in the Moslem republics to review all aspects of this situation." The directorate had been set up by Andropov in 1970 to suppress intellectual dissent, halt the rise of religious practice, and annihilate nationalism in the ethnic republics. "I will apprise you of the results."

Feodorov glanced at his gold Rolex. His principal subordinates should be at their desks by now. He turned to one of his newest Western toys: a Sony multimonitor closed-circuit TV system that linked him to his ten senior deputies. Most of them were out at the KGB's modern office complex just off the Moscow Beltway. He activated the circuit to the head of Department V, his "wet affairs" department. The deputy knew, without being told, why Feodorov was calling.

"He's back," his face said from the screen on the wall. "He came back last night on Aeroflot from Paris."

"Good. And there's been nothing to indicate any connection to us in New York?"

"Absolutely nothing. Just one brief story in *The New York Times* which accepted the idea it was done by a drug addict."

"And there's nothing to indicate any suspicion has fallen on the illegal who provided us the information?"

"Nothing. Nor should there be. The illegal only communicated twice, each time directly to us with a Spetosk transmitter. The first time was to give us the man's name, which, of course, led us to his file at Central Registry. And then the information you decided to act on."

"Excellent. Please congratulate your man on my behalf and see that he's properly compensated." Feodorov chuckled softly as he watched his deputy's face on the monitor. "Indeed, his work reminds me of a saying that used to be heard frequently in this house, an old Chekist saying."

"Which one, Ivan Sergeivich?"

"Anyone can commit a murder; it takes an artist to commit a suicide."

The President of the United States stared up at the ceiling through the shadows of his darkened bedroom. The illuminated dials of the clock on his bedside console indicated it was only six-fifteen. Beside him he could hear the rhythmic breathing of his wife, sleeping soundly. He, however, was far too excited to waste his hours on sleep. He was hungry for the dawn, anxious as he had been every morning since his inauguration, to face the challenge of a new day. It was the adrenaline surge, the excitement, the sheer exultation that came with the discharge of the awesome responsibilities of the most powerful office in the world. The instant his eyes blinked open now, he was awake, alert, his mind already beginning to spin its way through the myriad problems each day brought him.

That he should even be lying there in the presidential bedchamber was regarded by a large number of both his political friends and his foes as something of a political miracle. He had spent the better part of life being the good subordinate, the loyal number two. Chairman of the Republican National Committee in the early seventies, then ambassador to NATO, he'd been appointed Secretary of Commerce in his predecessor's first term, White House Chief of Staff in his second. He had, in fact, assembled the perfect résumé for an appointive office. Never, however, until he had stepped forth into a snowy Iowa primary had he run for elective office.

Yet against the odds, the polls, and the collective wisdom of most of the Washington press corps, he had won. He had won by exhibiting the plodding, relentless determination that had characterized almost every stage of his life. His ambition was more inculcated than natural, motivated as much by a sense of *noblesse oblige* as by political hunger, by a desire to fulfill his family's place in the scheme of things rather than a prince's lust for power. His slow, inexorable march from a huge deficit in the polls in June to a stunning electoral triumph in November had surprised almost everybody except the President himself. Still, his foes and intimates should have known better. No one would ever get rich by betting against the determination of the newly elected leader of the United States.

That was part of both the legacy and the burden left him by his father. His father had been the very stereotype of the stern New England patriarch who could trace his family's lineage to the *Mayflower*. He was an austere, domineering man who brooked no dissent from his five children and no backsliding from the high standards he set for them. The senior partner in the Wall Street law firm of Knight, Ridgeway & Polk, his father had demanded two things of his daughter and four sons: service and loyalty. His concept of service was that long transmitted by patrician New England families to sons delivered by birth from the unseeming need to make money—service to the nation, to the community, to the less favored.

It had been an almost idyllic *Town & Country* upbringing, the big house in Darien, the apartment on Park Avenue, summers in Maine, Greenwich Country Day, Hotchkiss and Yale. Indeed, only one secret stain had marred it. The father had been a heavy drinker and a violent man when drunk. His drunken wrath had fallen most frequently on his eldest child and only daughter, the President-to-be's soulmate. Pampered, somewhat spoiled, and intimidated by his powerful father, the boy had been tormented almost beyond bearing by his inability to save his beloved sister from their father's blows. Time and the Institute for the Living in Hartford had ultimately resolved the father's problem. The family closed ranks and pretended it had never happened, making sure the knowledge of the patriarch's failing stayed inside the family circle. The President bore its secret scars on his soul.

He had left Yale after his sophomore year during the Korean War to join the Navy. He took flight training, flew sixty-two carrier missions against North Korea, was shot down, and came home wearing the Navy Cross. When he'd graduated from Harvard Law School, he'd stunned his father by refusing to join the family law firm. He went instead to Denver, Colorado, borrowed against his trust fund to buy a Coca-Cola franchise, and set out on his own.

By the time he was thirty-five, he'd put together a modest fortune. He sold everything to enter politics and take up his birth-imposed burden of service by joining the Republican State Committee. Guided by two precepts, "Do the right thing" and "Be a good soldier," he'd launched himself on the road that had carried him to the presidential bedchamber.

He glanced to his right toward the great windows looking out on the Ellipse and across Constitution Avenue toward the Washington Monument. Edges of light slid like slowly moving glaciers out from under the heavy brocade curtains that screened the window. He decided to get up and tiptoe across the Oval Sitting Room out onto the Truman Balcony to watch for a few moments as the spring sunlight offered his capital the fresh paint of a new day.

It happened the instant he started to stand up. The floor seemed to tilt madly as though an earthquake had struck. The window before him swayed slightly. His eyes perceived it in a kind of double vision, like the refracted images of a cubist painting. He squeezed them shut, and his head began to reel. He was overwhelmed with nausea. It was the same attack that had seized him in the Oval Office, at lunch with his wife, at the state dinner for the President of Mexico. But this attack was far worse than the others. He felt himself beginning to fall and slumped to his knees. His hands grabbed the edge of the bed as they might a life raft on a stormy sea.

Slowly, the attack subsided. The President pressed his

face into the side of his bed, trying to force a pattern back into his being. For the first time since he had been shot down near the end of his tour of duty in the Korean War, he was confronted with his own mortality. It was a brain tumor. What else could it be? The reading he'd done since the last attack had made that clear. He pulled himself back into bed and lay there staring up once again at the ceiling. How could God be so cruel? God had allowed him to achieve this goal toward which his entire life had been a pilgrimage, and now that at last he had realized it, He was going to snatch it away from him. He was going to die. Or worse, end his life as an uncomprehending vegetable. He trembled in fear. He had told no one of his attacks, not even his wife, but he could no longer conceal them. He would have to call Admiral Peter White, the chief of internal medicine at Bethesda, who'd been named his physician.

His wife stirred. Her hand poked sleepily toward his chest. He took it in his, drew it to his lips, and, choking back a sob, kissed it in despair and tenderness.

A young man in his late twenties wearing a blue blazer, gray flannel slacks, and a rep striped tie greeted Art Bennington and his two companions at the door to the executive suite of the director of the CIA. He looked as if he'd stepped out of an *Esquire* "Back to the Campus" ad except for the plastic ID card and key card hung around his neck on a beaded metal chain. The key card, Bennington knew, was to the director's elevator. It linked this office to an underground parking area to which visitors whose identity had to be kept secret could be driven, then whisked up to the director's suite.

A blue blazer showed them to a small sitting room. Bennington noted with an approving smile that there was barely a ripple in his blazer's folds to indicate the presence of his .38 service revolver. Another blue blazer appeared in seconds to offer them coffee while they waited for the director. Still a third blue blazer, Bennington observed, was standing guard at the elevator entrance. I wonder, he thought, does Brooks Brothers give the Agency's Internal Security Division a quantity discount?

A blue blazer interrupted his musings. "Gentlemen," he announced, "the director's ready."

The director was standing behind his long mahogany desk, winding up a phone call, as Bennington, John Sprague, and Frank Pozner walked in. To the left, on the wall behind him, was a large sepia portrait of the CIA's spiritual father, Wild Bill Donovan, in his open-necked brigadier general's uniform. The obligatory bank of pictures of the director with Jimmy Carter, Ronald Reagan, and their successor at the White House lined the wall behind the desk. He replaced his receiver in his telephone console, a wood-paneled box of space-age wizardry so complex each incoming director had to spend half a working day learning how to operate it.

The director, or the Judge as his subordinates called him, waved them to his oval conference table at the far end of the room. Meetings with Allen Dulles, Bennington remembered, always opened with a little gracious chit-chat: "How's the daughter up at Vassar?" Dick Helms liked a quick joke, Casey a few tidbits of capital gossip.

Not the Judge. He was a taut, intense man who wanted to go to the heart of the matter immediately.

"Basically, sir, this is the situation," John Sprague, the DD for Science and Technology, said as soon as they'd sat down. He sketched quickly the account of Ann Robbins's death, the KGB's involvement in her murder. "Art, give the director a full run-down on the project and what we think is the possible significance of this."

Bennington reviewed the psychic's work and her striking success rate, sketched out the details of Pat Price's activities and death, and concluded with the Pit's judgment that there was no indication of imminent Soviet hostilities that would appear to have motivated the murder.

"You feel justified in your conclusion it was the KGB, Doctor," the director asked. "We're not rushing to judgment here?"

"Judge," Bennington replied, "who else uses ricin?

Not the Mafia. She was killed by a technique and a poison that has been employed only three times that we have been aware of and each time by the KGB or a KGB-sponsored service.''

"Okay, how do we deal with the murder investigation? Do we want to inform that deputy director of the FBI office up in New York that we've got a problem in respect to this incident and we'd like them to monitor the investigation for us as discreetly as possible?''

"Why? We already know who killed her. What are the New York cops going to come up with that's going to help us—a blond man with Slavic features was observed loitering around her apartment? These KGB guys don't leave footprints. The killers are already back at the Center having their vodka and caviar.''

"Has this information from Atlanta on the ricin been passed on to the New York police?''

"No.''

"Why not? Do you intend to let the New York police go stumbling around in the dark while we sit down here aware of who killed her and how?''

Oh-oh, thought Bennington. Here we go. The Judge had come to the CIA from law enforcement. There was a joke in the corridors that all federal statutes were equal in his eyes, that he tended to lump overtime parking on government property into the same category as espionage for a foreign power. Educating new directors in the ways of intelligence was always a problem for the Agency's old boys. Some, like Stan Turner, never learned. You couldn't teach him because he was always up on his bridge posturing, speaking in parables. As far as Bennington was concerned, the jury was still out on the Judge. Well, he mused, let me give it to him between the eyes and see if he blinks.

"What we should be concerned with here, Judge, is not letting this goddam thing become a media issue, making the front page of the *New York Post* three days running and letting our involvement with the psychic community hang out for the world to see. After all, the KGB knows who killed her. The only thing they don't know is that we know they did it. Why tell them? Forget the investigation.''

The director's cold gray eyes fixed Bennington with a stare he figured was about as warm and welcoming as you might expect the mayor of Tel Aviv to offer, say, Yassir Arafat. Is it because I'm being my surly, sarcastic self, he wondered, or is it that he's read the "Eyes Only Future Directors" note Bill Colby dictated so all his successors would know what an evil SOB I am?

"And let the New York police run around in circles for days?" the Judge continued.

"Judge, you know how much time the New York cops are going to give this case? The time it takes to write 'Perpetrator Unknown' on her file and stuff it onto their stack of unresolved homicides.''

"That may be so," the Judge conceded begrudgingly. "Although I must tell you this is the kind of short-circuiting of legal procedures the Agency got into under my predecessor and I don't want to see on my watch.'' The director let Bennington and his two other subordinates mull over that a moment.

"I certainly understand your concerns, sir.'' A little toadying might, it struck Bennington, warm the atmosphere. "But I think you should know that this psychic research has a tremendous humiliation factor attached to it as far as the Agency is concerned. There are a lot of people in Congress, in the administration, right here in this building, who think this stuff should be classified Top Stupid and not Top Secret. Just let Jack Anderson or *The Washington Post* tear into the story that the CIA's using psychics to find Russian submarines and you'll have Senator Proxmire downstairs in the lobby passing out the Golden Fleece awards.'' And you, Bennington thought, will be the first to get one.

"Mr. Director, I have to agree with Art.'' It was Pozner from Internal Security. "Letting this go public, even for the most praiseworthy of reasons, is only going to make an already serious situation even worse. The first thing we've got to concern ourselves with is how in hell did the KGB know that of the twelve psychics Art's people were running in this program, this woman up in New York was the only one who ever came up with anything? At the best, this means we're faced with a grave indiscretion somewhere, and at the worst, with a KGB penetration of the Agency."

"Well, what do you propose to do about it?"

"We'll have to run file checks, internal audits, and polygraphs on everybody in the Agency who was involved in the program from day one."

"All right," the Judge concurred, "get on with it as hard and as fast as you can. Go intra-agency. Make sure you touch bases with the relevant people at the NSA and the FBI.

"Now." He leaned back in his chair. "Let's look at why they killed her. It's a goddam unusual thing."

"It is," Bennington agreed. "Almost unheard-of. But the way they did it was so good they had every reason to believe we'd never pick up on it. And we wouldn't have, if New York didn't have an incredibly sharp chief medical examiner."

"And why would they use the ricin?" the Judge asked. "Isn't that leaving their fingerprint on the thing?"

Bennington shrugged. "Convenience, I suppose. They have timed, injectable capsules of the stuff coated in a plastic that dissolves at body temperature. They're so accurate they could fix her death within an hour. Besides, as I said, I think they never thought we'd find it. After all, there's no standard autopsy procedure used anywhere in the world that can detect it. The stuff decomposes into proteins that are usually found in the body."

The director reflected a moment, then appeared to accept Bennington's reasoning. "Still," he said, "they had to have one hell of a good reason for doing it. What could it have been?"

Bennington leaned his heavy upper body forward. His fists were heavy and menacing, formed from the kind of hands you'd expect to find on a bricklayer, not a man who had once aspired to be a neurosurgeon.

"There are a couple of dimensions here. First of all, of course, the obvious one. Sometimes those explanations are the best. We have a tendency in this building to breathe on these things so hard, we turn a dog's turd into Chicken Little. Maybe the Soviets attach enough importance to keeping those new Toshiba-bladed submarines of theirs immune to our detection systems that if they discovered she was hitting on them, they'd, well, kill her.''

"Yes." The Judge nodded. "There's a certain compelling logic in that, all right. After all, if they didn't kill her because of the submarines, then why did they kill her?"

"Quite frankly, I don't know," Bennington replied. "I can only guess. Suppose they wanted to back us away from this whole psychic-research area? Suppose they were afraid we might stumble on something they've already discovered and they're trying to protect?" As he spoke, Bennington could visualize again the mutilated body of Ann Robbins lying at his feet, the grotesque image of the medical examiner peering at her scarlet fingernails. "Suppose they were concerned she might lead us into some areas they're aware of but we don't yet know exist?''

"Such as what?"

Bennington stood up, stretched a second on his tiptoes, then began to pace the area around the conference table. "We know the Soviet Union is heavily involved in every aspect of mind research, whether it's in this ESP area we were in here, or in the more fundamental area of brain studies. Their goal is to develop an ability to control or modify human behavior by remote means—to affect a human being or a group of people at a distance without their being aware they are being manipulated.''

The Judge digested Bennington's words with the hesitation of a man taking his first tentative bite of an unfamiliar dish. Clearly, the perspectives Bennington had raised were not to his liking. "You really believe such a thing could happen?"

"My beliefs don't matter, but I think it's possible, yes. The fact is they're attempting to develop this capability. Their efforts take two forms. They're heavy into studying RF, radio-frequency weapons. Precisely controlled antipersonnel weapons that fire beams of electromagnetic energy like a focused laser beam. Their target would be the human nervous system and especially the brain. We know they've had small, portable RF weapons effective at a kilometer since 1985. They're also looking at a 'brain bomb'—so are we, incidentally. The idea is to produce massive amounts of microwaves that would stun the brains of every human being in the bomb's impact area. But that's for the Pentagon. Our concern in the CIA is what they might develop to modify the behavior of individual human beings.''

Bennington paused in his pacing and turned to face the Judge. "They hold this very, very close. One thing we do know, however, is that they're concentrating on how extremely low frequency electromagnetic fields might affect human behavior.''

"Can they?''

"Our scientific establishment has always said no, those frequencies can't affect human beings for one simple reason: their waves are both nonthermal and nonionizing. Therefore, no heat, no effect. It's as simple as ABC.''

The Judge nodded. Bennington wasn't certain whether the gesture reflected an understanding of his words or the layman's reluctance to dispute a scientist.

"Except that it's not that simple. When the Navy wanted to plant its antenna farms for the Sanguine/Seafarer Project up in Wisconsin and northern Michigan to talk to their submarines, the good folk up there got upset. They began to say, 'Hey, this stuff may give us cancer or something.' ''

Bennington laughed. "The Navy trotted out their usual panel of well-tamed establishment scientists who proceeded to pee on the whole idea. Listen to them and you'd think this stuff was actually good for you. Well, some of our less-well-tamed scientists are also interested in this stuff, and what they're finding out is very, very scary. We now know these extremely low frequency fields can affect human cells in a test tube. Believe me, if an unequivocal correlation is ever established between those fields and human behavior, we're going to be faced with something that makes splitting the atom pale in comparison."

"I'm surprised I haven't seen any of this." The Judge shifted nervously in his chair. The inquisitor's tone with which he'd opened the meeting had disappeared.

"It's not something anyone in the government is anxious to publicize. We don't want to uncork an uproar that's going to jeopardize our ability to communicate with our submarines." Bennington resumed pacing the floor. "The Russians' research into psychic phenomena is based on the theory that the explanation for how this stuff works is going to involve these extremely low frequency waves."

"Why, for God's sake?"

"Three reasons. First, these waves are incredibly long. Second, they can penetrate just about anything. They penetrate water to great depths, which is why we use them with our submarines. They also can get through the bone of the skull which protects the brain. Third, and most important, we know that the dominant frequencies on which the human brain operates are down there in this extremely low frequency range. So are the brains of every mammal and fish that we've ever been able to study. Sharks, whales, and certain insects can communicate with each other over distances and at speeds which defy explanation in any normal, sensory way. We don't know much about how they do it. Are they somehow using these extremely low frequency channels? Is it possible man once had the same capacity before he developed better sensory channels of communication?"

"And every so often, someone like the lady up in New York somehow finds this ability lying dormant in her and uses it?" asked the Judge.

"That's the theory."

The Judge laughed. "Dr. Bennington, we old country lawyers have a saying." The Judge was tugging the nub of his chin with his thumb and forefinger, getting into what Bennington assumed was his cracker-barrel sage mode. "Facts convince juries; theories just confuse them."

"Unfortunately, Judge, I can't help the jury here. In science, unlike the law, theories are often all we have to work with."

The Judge got up and strolled over to one of the huge window panels looking down on the formal drive to his headquarters. He stared moodily out of the window for a few seconds while his three subordinates watched in respectful silence. "Three times out of seven, you say, she got the sub? In all those hundreds of thousands of miles of ocean? I've just got to tell you that in my gut, I don't believe it. There's got to be a trick somewhere. It's quite frankly incredible."

"I agree," Bennington said. "I find it incredible, too. Just as I found some of the things Pat Price did for us incredible."

"Look, Dr. Bennington, you've had more experience with this than anybody in the Agency. Tell me as a man, not as a CIA officer—do you really believe in this psychic stuff?"

Bennington arched, then dropped his deltoids like a boxer flexing his shoulders waiting for the summons of the bell. Twenty years ago, a question like that from the director would have set his alarms jangling, his mind to scanning the horizon for a potential trap. Not anymore. Dissembling was an art form for which he had lost his taste. "I was a skeptic when I got into this thirty years ago, and I'm still a skeptic, but I've seen enough along the way to shock me into keeping a very open mind. I believe that, yes, something is going on out there that is beyond our ability to understand or explain."

The Judge seemed to wither a bit digesting his words, as though they were not quite what he had hoped to hear from a man of Bennington's background. He walked back across the room, sat down, put his black loafers onto the oval conference table, and bestowed on Bennington what was known in the Agency as his "Missouri mule, show me" look.

"Well, how do you explain what she did, then? How the hell did she pinpoint the location of those submarines? If, in fact, she really did."

It was Bennington's turn to meditate a moment. "There's only one honest answer to your question, Judge. We don't have any goddam idea how she did it. If you want theories, I can give you those. But hard, scientific explanations? The Agency's been looking for them for forty years and we still haven't found any."

Bennington raised his arms as though to capture in his gesture the frustration of those years of fruitless research. "Let me give you a little parable. Suppose you and I took a portable television set down to the Amazonian jungle and we turned it on for a bunch of primitive Indians that had never been out of the bush. Now, in terms of their own society they'd be pretty shrewd people —able to hunt, kill, survive in very difficult natural conditions. You ask them to explain how that TV works. They'd think awhile and probably come up with the idea there were some little people in there doing all that. The idea that the air around them was filled with silent, invisible electromagnetic emanations, that those emanations just touched the little metal knob on the antenna and were drawn down into those silicon chips and turned into a picture on the screen, is so far beyond anything their social environment has prepared them for that not only could they not comprehend it, they couldn't even imagine it."

"So when it comes to understanding these psychic phenomena of yours, we're all a bunch of Amazonian primitives—is that what I'm supposed to get from that?"

What you're supposed to get from that, Bennington thought, is a little bit of humility, although I've never known a director of the CIA who was much into humility. "Well, the point of the parable is, I suppose, that just because we can't understand or even imagine a phenomenon doesn't mean that phenomenon doesn't exist. The more we learn about the physical world around us, the more we know we don't know, and what we don't know seems to get more impressive as each day goes by. I mean, we know we live in a world framed by four dimensions, time, height, width, and length, right?"

"So I was taught."

"Well, some of the smartest minds around today will tell you that if you believe that, you're like those people who used to believe the earth was flat. They say we live in a universe of six, seven, ten, God knows how many dimensions. Or that we've got a fifth, a sixth force out there. Or that Einstein had it all wrong when he said nothing travels faster than the speed of light."

"I take it what you're suggesting is that if modern science can accommodate stuff as far out as those notions, then it can somehow find a place to squeeze in your lady who finds submarines?"

"More or less."

"Just exactly what have we learned from our own work with this?"

"We've turned up the evidence that these things really do happen. I feel there's no doubt about that. What has driven us nuts is trying to find out why. Or finding some way to replicate these things on anything even remotely like a regular basis. The very best people, such as this woman was, will blow your mind away once in fifteen, twenty times. But the rest is pure garbage. But if it ever works, if we could ever make the breakthrough, the intelligence implications are enormous."

The Judge stood up, indicating their meeting was over. "Frankly, I just don't know why we waste time, resources, and money on all this." He looked at Sprague, his DD/S&T. "Review every program we're running in this area. You'd better have damn solid grounds for every red cent of the taxpayers' money you put into it.

"You," he said to Pozner, "get on with your investigation. And Doctor"—he shot Bennington a withering glare—"try to come up with some better explanation of why they killed your lady psychic."

"Sure thing, Judge." Bennington sighed as he unwound from his chair with an aging athlete's stiffness. "Not to worry. If there's anything to my crackpot notions, our friends at the KGB will find some way to let us know about it soon enough anyway."

• • •

"No matter how much you feed a wolf, he keeps looking back to the forest."

Employing old proverbs to shore up a debating point was for the Russians as firmly established a tradition as penning *haiku* in times of stress or sadness was for the Japanese. It showed, among other things, that the employer of the proverbs was *kulturnyy*, cultured. Ivan Sergeivich Feodorov, the chairman of the KGB, therefore made a point of using them frequently in argument and conversation. It not only underscored the fact he was cultured—which he was—but also set him clearly apart from the men who had preceded him into his office. "The problem we face is, just how do we keep our wolf from heading back to the forest?"

The "wolf" of his proverb was the Moslem populations of the USSR, the "forest" militant, fundamentalist Islam luring them from all along the nation's southern borders. Feodorov posed his query to the eight men gathered around his table with what was meant to be his most disarming smile. All of them held the rank of general in the KGB. Most were older than Feodorov, representatives of the generation of men drawn into the Organs, the KGB, before the Andropov revolution. Six were KGB director generals in the USSR's Moslem republics: Azerbaijan, Turkmenistan, Kazakhstan, Uzbekistan, Kirghizia, and Tadzhikistan. The other two were the director and the deputy director of the KGB's Fifth Directorate, which was responsible for repressing dissidence and stamping out nationalism and ethnic loyalties in the Soviet empire. Feodorov had summoned them all to Moscow to study the crisis in the Moslem republics heralded by the outburst of terrorist actions noted three days ago in his morning intelligence summary.

"Break the wolf's goddam legs," growled Vladimir Viktorovich Pektel, the KGB's director in Tadzhikistan. "That'll keep him out of the forest all right."

A rumble of laughter seconded his suggestion. Two of his fellow KGB directors in neighboring republics raised their vodka glasses to Pektel in an approving salute, a clear indication of the feelings of most of the men at

Feodorov's table. The chairman had invited them to dinner in his private dining room to provide an informal setting for their discussion. He picked a Cuban cigar from the humidor one of his waiters had set in the clutter of dishes on the banquet table.

"To break our wolf's legs, Vladimir Viktorovich, we would need a Stalin," he declared, lighting his cigar, then driving away the gray cloud of smoke blossoming about his head. "Our Secretary General is a man of many fine qualities. But a Stalin he is not."

A derisive little snicker rippled through their dining chamber, the barometer of the limited regard in which most senior officers of the KGB held Mikhail Gorbachev and his reforms.

Feodorov smiled through his cigar smoke at his subordinates. In one sense they summed up better than anything else could the dilemma the USSR faced in its six Moslem republics. All of them were Slavs. Not a single one of them had so much as an ounce of blood of any of the Soviet's Moslem peoples in his veins. Yet they were the policemen, rulers—jailers, some of the people whose lives they administered would contend—of the USSR's Moslem population. You were as likely to find a non-Slavic face in a KGB office in those Moslem republics as you would be to find a Moslem with a yarmulke on his head praying at the Wailing Wall in Jerusalem. So complete was the Slavicization of the KGB in the Moslem republics that even the *dezhurnyi,* the KGB's female watchdogs who handed out the keys on each floor of a hotel, were non-Moslems.

The only roles Moslems filled in the republics' security apparatus were those nobody but a Moslem could fill—informers or penetration agents assigned to infiltrate Moslem dissident organizations. And that, as Feodorov had recently had the opportunity to note, was not a task they carried out with much success. There were no Moslems assigned to the KGB border forces which patrolled the immense frontier separating the Soviet Union's Moslems from their fellow Moslems in Iran, Afghanistan, Pakistan, and China. The highest-ranking Moslem in the

Red Army was a colonel. Moslem conscripts inevitably found themselves in supply or infantry battalions, about as far from modern weaponry as it was possible to get while still carrying an arm. The only exceptions were the special Ministry of the Interior troops employed to maintain public order. In those battalions, Moslems served in the Baltic and Russian republics. They could, after all, be counted on to shoot Russians with the greatest pleasure.

"Ivan Sergeivich." It was the director of the Fifth Directorate, the senior man present, an officer who had spent fifteen years as the KGB's chief representative in Uzbekistan, the most populous of the Moslem republics. He was well past seventy, a prototype of the old-school KGB officer Feodorov was trying to phase out of the organization. He still effected those stiff, ill-cut double-breasted suits Khrushchev had worn, the kind that moved like a tent caught in a high wind if the wearer shrugged his shoulders. Years ago, during the repression of the thirties when he'd mastered the Chekist's trade, a prisoner had bitten off his right forefinger at the knuckle. The action had cost the prisoner his life and bestowed on the chief the nickname he'd carried ever since in the Organs—"Four Fingers." He waved the stump of his forefinger at the gathering. "May I first offer an overview of the situation as we see it in the Fifth Directorate?"

Feodorov blessed his initiative with a nod.

"We face an open challenge to our rule. They have dropped the mask, those peoples. Their loyalty is not to Moscow. It never was. It is not to Marx. It never was. It is to Mohammed."

"Exactly," echoed his deputy. "Those people down there all pretend they're atheists. All our party members, the most senior officers of the party, even members of our own Presidium. And do you know where they wind up?"

He gave a harsh laugh, momentarily choking off his answer to his question.

"In a Moslem cemetery!"

"The problem is a historical one," Four Fingers noted, taking back the floor. He might not be an intellectual, but he knew the principles of sound socialist analysis. "There has never been the slightest enthusiasm for the revolution, for Marxist-Leninism, for our socialistic experiment, among the Moslem population."

"Revolutionary zeal, we must admit," Feodorov commented with the suggestion of a grin, "is rarely inspired by the tip of a saber or the snout of a gun. Our revolution was made in Leningrad by European Russians, then imposed on the Moslems by force. There wasn't a Moslem within a thousand miles of the Winter Palace in 1917."

"Josef Vissarionovich," said Pektel, the KGB's Tadzhikstan boss, employing Stalin's patronymic, "had the right answer in the 1930s." He was referring to what the Moslems called the Decade of Repression from 1928 to 1939 when Moslem clerics, intellectuals, community leaders, anyone suspected of opposition to Moscow, were murdered or carted off to Siberia. Islam was as rigorously repressed as the Russian Orthodox faith had been repressed in the north. The number of mosques functioning in the vast Moslem areas tumbled from twenty-six thousand to barely five hundred.

"One of the results of that," Feodorov said, enjoying playing the devil's advocate, "was that hundreds of thousands of Moslems rushed to join the Fascists when Hitler invaded in 1941, didn't they?"

"The bastards!" Four Fingers raged. The massive defection of Soviet Moslems to Hitler's banner remained one of the sorest points in relations between Moscow and the Moslem republics, between the Russian peoples of the north and assorted Moslem peoples of the south. In truth, it was only the most recent manifestation of the long and troubled relations between the two fundamentally dissimilar peoples. With Spain and Greece, Russia shared the historical distinction of having been one of the three major European nations to live under Moslem rule.

Feodorov glanced at the map he'd ordered set alongside their dining table. After four decades of the Arab-Israeli conflict, most people tended to place the center of gravity of the Islamic world on the Arabian Peninsula. Most people were wrong. The center of gravity of the

Moslem world was inside the Soviet Union, somewhere along the great Asian steppes between Anatolia and Sinkiang. Just because Uzbeks in Uzbekistan or Turkomans in Tashkent did not burn with indignation over the plight of the Palestinians, they were no less Moslem for that.

"The root of the problem is Mikhail Sergeivich's *glasnost*," declared Arkadi Sokolov, the KGB representative in the turbulent and troubled Republic of Turkmenistan, bordering Iran and Afghanistan. "It's one thing to let the playwrights, the artists, the intellectuals here in Moscow prattle away about all their little problems. It's another to allow these nationalist leaders free rein. You saw what happened in Estonia and Latvia. And down in Nagorno-Karabakh. But that is nothing, just a match in the night compared to the firestorm all this free speech has unleashed on us with these Moslems."

"Are you suggesting I go to Mikhail Sergeivich and tell him to please forget about his *glasnost?* To let us return to the Brezhnev days when we could arrest somebody for looking cross-eyed at Lenin's tomb?" Feodorov asked.

Sokolov threw up his hands. "Piss in a windstorm and you'll get wet." He laughed. "We wouldn't want that to happen to you, Ivan Sergeivich."

The chairman of the KGB joined in his subordinates' laughter, pretending as he did to flick a few drops of liquid from his Brioni suit. "Still, you're right. This *glasnost* business was a terrible error. And then, of course, there was our defeat in Afghanistan."

"Thanks to Afghanistan," Sokolov continued, "I now have a tidal wave of venom, of hate, of anti-Soviet propaganda pouring across my borders every night."

He was referring to the clandestine broadcasting transmitters now located all along the Afghan-Soviet border. Set up and operated by different Mujahedeen groups, they provided the Moslems of the USSR with a nightly incitation to violence and rebellion in their own languages and dialects, those they shared with their brothers to the south.

"Before the war, the Afghan government would never have dared to do such a thing. Now those bastards down there do it with impunity because they think we won't send the Red Army back in."

"Can't you jam them?"

"We try, but they keep switching their locations on us."

"It's become a plague," added the KGB director in Azerbaijan. "Against us, there are eighteen stations in Iran broadcasting in Turkoman alone. And every other language you can think of. Radio Tabriz, Radio Golden, Radio Urushi. Those CIA stations in Munich are a joke compared to these people."

"The broadcasts are just the beginning of the problem," echoed Sokolov. "It's the Khomeini system. Each broadcast gets reproduced on cassettes. They pass them out in the bazaar like pistachio nuts the next day. They're a plague of locusts eating up a field of wheat. Except they're eating up the minds of our people."

"People in my republic never paid attention to these Moslem feasts," said the Azerbaijan chief. "They didn't know what to do, how and when to fast, how to slaughter sheep. Not anymore. This year, thanks to those damn radio stations, half of the republic—can you believe that, half of our population—made the Ramadan fast! They slaughtered millions of sheep for Bairam exactly the way those radios told them to."

"Fifty percent of your people following the fast?" It was a statistic Feodorov had never heard, perhaps because no one had wanted to give it to him. "What are you becoming down there—Saudi Arabia?"

His subordinates grimaced and plowed on. "They're very shrewd. They slant the broadcasts toward the young, because, whether we like it or not, there is a tremendous appetite for this kind of information among our youth. We have to drive them into the Young Pioneers and the Komsomol with clubs, but they can spend hours every day soaking up this drivel about the glory of Islam, great Moslem warriors, all the battles they've won for Allah. Which, of course, is just another way of telling them they can defeat the Red Army."

"Ivan Sergeivich." Four Fingers had little patience

with careful exposés. "Who gives a shit if the mullahs tell people how to kill sheep? What those radios preach every night is violence and the Jihad. 'The Russians are colonialists. Western colonialists exploiting you. Marxism, Communism are all foreign, alien doctrines they're trying to impose on you. We're pan-Islamic brothers. Throw the Russians out with blood and fire.' That's what those bastards are preaching—not how to say your prayers before you go to bed at night.

"And that's just the beginning." His explosion had yet to run its course. "There's the disastrous fact that we've allowed our borders with Afghanistan and Iran to become sieves. People are slipping back and forth across the border by the hundreds every night. Pamphlets, leaflets, Korans, cassettes are inundating us. We know pamphlets produced in Kabul are in Samarkand two weeks later. We've clocked them."

"I've fired seven senior officers in the border security forces in the last two months," Feodorov fumed. "Haven't you noticed any improvement in the situation?"

"None."

"Then I'll fire another seven until I get someone down there who can control the problem."

"Ivan Sergeivich," declared the KGB man from Azerbaijan, "the trouble is the people on both sides of the borders have decided they're brothers now. They're all involved in the traffic. They guide border passers to illegal crossings where they know our patrols are light. They hide them. They give them false ID. Those people all look alike. They speak the same language. You can't tell them apart. You need an electric barrier, a minefield, something like the Berlin Wall if you want to keep the frontier closed."

"Wonderful!" Feodorov proclaimed. "Can you imagine how our Western enemies will feast on that? Two thousand miles of an electrified, booby-trapped frontier to celebrate *glasnost!*"

"The border, those damned radios, sure they're terrible problems," growled Four Fingers, waving the stump of his right forefinger at the table again, "but we still haven't gotten to the heart of this whole damn mess, those Sufi brotherhoods! They're the people behind these bombings and killings."

An echoing rumble all along the table endorsed his words.

"They claim they follow their *tariqa,* their path, leading to God," declared Four Fingers, each word weighted with scorn. "Believe me, it is not to God their path is leading. It is to revolution. They are fanatical anti-Soviet, antisocialist reactionaries. Their only goal is to destroy our socialist system. They're more disciplined than the party. They're more secretive than the party.

"How many of you have ever, just once, succeeded in penetrating a Sufi cell in your republics? Or developing a Sufi informer?" asked Four Fingers of the generals at the table.

He glared at each of the six KGB officers in turn. His only reply was an embarrassed silence.

"The fact is," admitted Sokolov, "it is they who are penetrating us. They're in the administration, the police, the party hierarchy. I even suspect we may have some in the Organs."

"What's your current estimate of their membership?" Feodorov asked.

"We can only guess," Sokolov replied. "No one joins the Sufis. Their recruiting is on a master-to-disciple basis. You have to be asked. It's one of the reasons it's been impossible to penetrate them the way we penetrated the Jewish and dissident groups. I'd guess they number at least a quarter of a million, maybe more."

"It's the quality, the secrecy of the brotherhoods that counts, Ivan Sergeivich," avowed Four Fingers. "Regular little Bolshevik-like revolutionaries is how they see themselves. They're everywhere and nowhere. We can see their hands but never their faces. If only we had some idea who their leaders were, we could pay them a midnight visit and offer them a trip to a colder climate. They're out to destabilize Central Asia, and they're getting closer and closer with each month that goes by. Now with this terror campaign of theirs they're out in the open. It's a revolt against our rule and nothing less."

"So what do you propose we do?" Feodorov asked the head of his Fifth Directorate.

"Stage a provocation. Somewhere in Tadzhikistan. The situation is worse there, because the frontier with Afghanistan is so close. Use it as an excuse to bring in the Red Army. Stamp out this pestilence with the one thing those Moslems understand—force."

"Stamp out whom?" Feodorov asked. His tone was soft and deliberately unprovocative. "How? You've just admitted we have no idea who these people are."

The head of the Fifth Directorate was silent. Feodorov's question implied a delicacy in employing repressive force Four Fingers was not accustomed to in chairmen of the KGB.

"The first rule of terrorism is to provoke a massive overreaction in the authority against which the terrorism is directed, isn't it?" Feodorov continued. "Create sympathy for the terrorists. Give a justification to what they've done by your overreaction."

The eight officers around the table looked at their chairman in silence. It was not that they questioned the wisdom of the axiom he had just stated. They didn't. It was simply that they had never thought it applied to their own domestic problems.

"With this *glasnost* of the Secretary General's, we'll have as many television reporters as troops in Tadzhikistan, all of them running around asking people if it hurt when they got hit on the head with a club. The world will compare us to the South Africans and the Israelis, which will not, I think, please our Secretary General beyond measure."

"Then send the Red Army back into Afghanistan," Four Fingers barked, slapping the table with the palm of his hand. "Wipe out the villages where those broadcasts are coming from. Don't leave a stone on stone. That will shut them up."

"After their last visit to Afghanistan, my friend, it's difficult enough to convince our Red Army generals to stage a parade for the Moslems of Tashkent or Alma-Ata, to say nothing of paying a return visit to a country they're very anxious to forget. The situation is urgent, I agree with you all on that." Feodorov gave a thoughtful puff to his cigar to allow himself a moment to switch the focus of the discussion. "The solution, however, requires something new, something subtle. Ideally, something unseen."

"Tell me, Yuri Vassilievich," Feodorov said, turning toward the KGB chief for Kazakhstan, "what do the people in your republic think about the Americans?"

"The Americans!" Four Fingers exploded. "What the hell do they have to do with this mess?"

Feodorov ignored him, keeping his gaze fixed on his Kazakhstan chief. The man shrugged. "To be truthful, the Kazakhs seem to hold the Americans in a certain regard. When we had those riots in Alma-Ata in 1986, Kazakh Communists were hunting down Russians in the street, imagine, party members beating up Russians, and shouting, 'Throw the Russians out. The Americans are with us.' "

"Exactly," said Feodorov. "These Moslems prefer the devil they don't know to the devil they know. And they all are very much aware of how the Americans helped the mujahedeen in Afghanistan, aren't they?"

There was a mumble of assent around the table.

"But when their Navy shot down that Iranian Airbus in the Persian Gulf?"

Every man at the table stirred. Three of them started to answer at the same time. "They were shocked, outraged," said the KGB chief from Kazakhstan.

"The worst thing the Americans could have done," Sokolov of Turkmenistan echoed. "The people couldn't believe they'd do such a thing."

Feodorov poured himself a tumbler full of vodka from the bottle encased in ice in the bucket beside his place. On this occasion, he did not propose a toast to his subordinates before tossing off half of it in one gulp. He wanted fuel for his thoughts, not fellowship.

"Or, from our standpoint, it was the best thing the Americans could have done, no?"

"Absolutely," Sokolov said. "There is a real sense of Moslem solidarity with these people. Offend one, you offend them all. Kill one, you make a hundred enemies." The others at the table voiced their rapid and vocal assent to his words.

"And suppose the Americans did something so vile, so outrageous, to, say, the Iranians, and we were able to tar them as Moslem-hating racists? Set up ourselves as the only superpower the Moslems can count on, as the Moslem world's one true champion? You remember how proud our Moslems were in 1956 when Khrushchev threatened the French and English with rockets during the Suez War? Suppose America's action allowed us to revive those feelings? Would that choke off this surge of dissidence in our Moslem republics?"

"I think it would depend to a great degree on what the American action was," answered Sokolov. The others seemed instinctively to defer to him. "If it was serious, I think, yes, it would have an effect. It wouldn't change their long-term aspirations. But it certainly could modify the situation we're facing right now, that is very possible."

"I wish you'd tell us what the hell you're getting at with this American stuff," growled Four Fingers. "I just don't see what the hell they've got to do with it."

"I'm trying to think of a way to get the Americans to do for us what the Red Army won't—or can't—do. To save our Secretary General from some of the unfortunate consequences of his *glasnost* policy."

"Well, Ivan Sergeivich," the old Chekist said, his voice a harmonium, its bellows fueled by a night's worth of vodka and tobacco. "You're a clever young man. Always have been. I can't imagine what it is you have in mind. But let me tell you this—we're going to have an explosion in those republics. It may come tomorrow. It may come the day after tomorrow. It may come the day after the day after tomorrow. But unless you do something and do something fast, that explosion will come as sure as a horny bull will stick his dick into the first hole he sees." Four Fingers grimaced. "One of my old proverbs, Ivan Sergeivich," he said.

Ivan Sergeivich Feodorov's adjutant, a KGB major in his mid-thirties, laid three identical folders in their pale blue KGB binders on his desk. Each bore the security label *SOVERSHENNO SEKRETNO*—"Completely Secret"—and the additional classification *'v RUKI LICHNO ISF*—"personally to the hands of ISF," Ivan Sergeivich Feodorov. That meant that once these three texts, the only copies of the document available, had been signed off by Feodorov and consigned to the Central Registry, only the personal authority of the chairman of the KGB could secure their release. They contained the material Feodorov had anxiously been awaiting all afternoon—the just-completed psychological profile and personality assessment of the new President of the United States.

"Is the doctor here?" Feodorov asked.

"Yes, sir."

"Have him wait while I study this."

Feodorov picked up the profile. He knew that the Western intelligence agencies were convinced the KGB had little use for psychological or psychoanalytical studies. This they ascribed, erroneously, to the Russian aversion to Freudian psychoanalytic theory. It had always struck Feodorov as curious that they should do so in view of their knowledge of the KGB's intense interest in studying the workings of the brain and the paranormal. However, it was an aspect of Western ignorance he intended to encourage. That accounted for the papers' high classification. Let the West remain ignorant of the fact that the KGB had introduced psychology into its armory of weapons, Feodorov reasoned.

It had done so, of course, largely because of its knowledge of how effectively the CIA had employed psychological profiles in guiding John F. Kennedy in his dealings with Nikita Khrushchev in the Cuban Missile Crisis and later in handling France's prickly leader, Charles de

Gaulle. The Agency had also used them with distinct success to target potential defectors inside the KGB's own ranks.

It was Andropov who had cast aside the constraints of Marxist dogma and ordered the KGB to start preparing psychological profiles of key world figures. The Organs' subsequent profiles of Jimmy Carter and Ronald Reagan had provided the Soviet leadership with invaluable insights into each man's probable behavior in a crisis. Carter's indecisive handling of the Iran hostage problem had been predicted in his profile. In Reagan's case, the psychologists had detected under the President's image a man who would be exceedingly cautious in the use of force unless he was certain of immediate and overwhelming success.

And now the study of the new U.S. President was ready at last. The decision to prepare studies on both nominees had been taken right after the nominating conventions in the summer of 1988. The *rezidentura* in Washington had first subscribed to every databank in the United States, accumulating masses of computer printouts on both men. They contained virtually every word that had ever been written about either candidate. That harvest was delivered to a battery of psychologists in Moscow. They broke it down, studied it, analyzed it, to develop a long series of checklists, which were in turn sent to the *rezidentury* in Washington and at the United Nations. Dozens of KGB agents were then tasked to interview people who'd known each of the nominees: old schoolteachers, early lovers, military bunkmates, friends from college, fraternity brothers, boyhood pals. To do that, they had used a variety of covers, but by far the most successful, Feodorov was amused to note, was that of an FBI agent doing some sort of security background check. It was amazing what a polite young KGB officer employing impeccable English and forged FBI identification could extract from an unsuspecting American.

Feodorov picked up the document and began to study it. It ran to just over twenty pages of text with appendices and an annex for relevant material obtained after the text had been completed. As he did with documents of such importance, Feodorov read slowly, going back over critical passages two or three times until he was certain he had understood and digested them.

Today, his reading was carried out with particular care. If he was going to take the tremendous gamble shaping up in his mind to resolve the threat of a revolution in the USSR's Moslem republics, he must first find certain psychological vulnerabilities he could use against the President in these pages.

When he'd finished, he sat up and rubbed his eyes. He'd found in the profile just what his work as a behavioral psychologist had led him to suspect. There was a quiet, rigorously controlled intensity to this President's character, and particularly to his capacity for anger. He was not a man who banged his fist on the table, shouted, or slammed doors. But he had a temper. His anger was controlled, targeted. That was encouraging.

Further, it was a dictum of behavioral psychology that no individual "owns" his or her own identity. It belongs to the environment that produced the individual. Two elements in the President's environment had leaped off the pages at Feodorov. One he had suspected. The other was a complete surprise.

The first concerned the President's relationship with his father. Popular mythology in the American press had it that the President had adored his patrician, distinguished father, the very model of the old New England paterfamilias.

Wrong. The father had been a stern, inflexible disciplinarian, a man who had tolerated no questioning of his paternal authority. Relations between father and son had been stormy and often bitter. The father was a big man, his body hardened by years of active exercise as an amateur boxer. No one ever intimidated him physically, and he had never hesitated to use force to beat his sons into line.

It was the second revelation, however, that had riveted Feodorov's attention. In his middle years, the father had been an alcoholic. The fact was the family's most carefully suppressed secret. During his drunken rages, he had inevitably turned his anger not on his wife or his sons, but on his daughter, now a concert pianist, two years the President's senior. The President as a young boy had adored his sister more than any other human being on earth. From the time he was six until he was about to enter his teens, she had been his dearest friend, the receptacle of his most intimate secrets, his only true counselor.

Yet, week after week, as a frail child he had had to watch his drunken father beat and abuse his beloved sister, while he, young and weak, had had to stand by helpless, screaming out his rage and impotence. Often in those unhappy childhood years, he'd revealed later to a college friend, he had wept himself to sleep with the bitter tears prompted by his inability to do anything to protect his sister from his father's drunken rampages. You didn't need a doctorate in behavioral psychology from Kiev University to sense the smoldering psychological fires an experience like that would leave within a man.

Feodorov jabbed at the intercom to his front-office secretariat. "Send in the doctor," he ordered. The doctor was the report's author, Professor Lev Timosheyev. He was a Jew, one of the few in the employ of the KGB, but there was no doubt in anyone's mind about where his loyalties lay. He was a third-generation Communist. His Temple Mount was only half a mile from Dzerzhinsky Square behind the walls of the Kremlin.

Feodorov congratulated him on his report as he settled into the chair in front of his desk. "Now," he said, "I'd like to review a number of things with you."

The professor respectfully inclined his head. He was a gaunt man in his late fifties, his skin pale, his hair a thinning thicket of gray strands striking out toward each point of the compass.

"How do you suppose this man's anger will manifest itself in a crisis? Under great and sudden stress?"

The professor contemplated his elongated, bony fingers for an instant. "What we are dealing with here is an extremely self-centered, ambitious individual. He's used that self-centeredness, his ambition, in a constructive way, and it's paid off. He fought his way into the White House with dogged, relentless determination. So in a crisis, he's a man who will fall back on his reactions, his own instincts. He'll make a show of consulting his advisers, but he'll be listening to his own inner voices, not theirs."

Feodorov encouraged the professor to continue with a smile.

"I'd also say he's logic-type-compartmented. Once he makes a decision on how to act, it's likely to be set in concrete. He's not much of a believer in compromise, despite that image of the great pragmatist he tried to create during his campaign."

Feodorov reflected on his words, then turned a few pages in the report until he found the paragraph he was looking for.

"This business about the father always beating up the sister in his drunken rampages."

"Devastating," commented the professor. "The central traumatic experience of his life."

"How do you see it affecting him now?"

"Very substantially. Out of that experience has come a stern, retributive frame of mind. The avenging hand of God. You see that all through his career. One of his subordinates makes the slightest moral slip, ticketed for drunken driving. Borrows a hundred dollars from petty cash. He throws the book at him. No mercy. No compassion. When he finds someone he thinks deserves punishment, he overreacts. That built-up, suppressed aggression of his pours out."

Virtually the portrait of the man he needed, Feodorov thought.

"When he was a young boy and his father was regularly beating his sister, he wanted to fight the father, didn't he? But physically he couldn't. He had to suppress his rage. Now he's in a position where he has almost infinite power at his disposal to give vent to his rage." Feodorov paused, then asked, "Would he be apt to use it?"

"He might. He is clearly a man who is suppressing a capacity for exaggerated aggressive behavior. He's learned satisfactory ways of sublimating his aggressive impulses. Look how he's always out jogging, playing tennis. Extreme kinds of physical activity can help sublimate aggression. Eisenhower was full of anger. That's why he was always out on the golf course, working his anger out on a little golf ball. You can assume this man is repressing a tendency to aggressive behavior. It's not a question of whether it's there or not. The question is, what will precipitate it?"

Feodorov stood up and walked to the long windows looking down on Dzerzhinsky Square. That was the question: how do you precipitate it? Clearly, the opportunity was there. The psychological pattern was as good as he could possibly hope for. He picked up the report and leafed through the appendices and annex. For a moment or two, he stared moodily at the professor. It was not his frail form that Feodorov saw sitting before him, however. It was the image of the President of the United States, jaunty and full of self-confidence.

"Excellent work," he said. "Better, I think, than even your studies on Carter and Reagan. I shall take it personally to the Secretary General. And I will be sure that he is aware to whom praise is due for a job well done."

Shortly after noon the following day, Ivan Sergeivich Feodorov's black Zil limousine, virtually a carbon copy of the stretch Cadillacs that ferry rock stars around New York and Beverly Hills, flashed along the green lane of Ulyanovskaya Ulitza at ninety miles an hour. The car was yet another manifestation of the marriage between power and privilege in the USSR. It was one of just over a score of such vehicles in the Soviet Union, each hand-crafted, each reserved for the exclusive use of a member of the Politburo or a very senior Soviet official.

From the leather upholstery of the car's rear seat, the chairman of the KGB peered through bulletproof windows at the gray-uniformed militiamen saluting his passage with their *pozhaluista* sticks, "please sticks," the shiny white batons they used to control traffic. Not that that was an onerous task in Moscow. Russians rarely question authority. There were only two kinds of people, Feodorov mused, that you'd be apt to find standing patiently on a corner waiting for the sanction of a green light before venturing to cross the street, Russians and Germans.

Feodorov's destination this afternoon was a community some forty kilometers from the Kremlin called Zhukovskii after the hero of the USSR's victory in World War II. It was one of several such satellite communities encircling the capital, conveniently close to central Moscow but just outside the twenty-five-mile limit to which foreign visitors were confined. It was home to the Institute of Flight Testing, several army institutes, and, for the last three years, the institution which was Feodorov's proudest creation in the period before he took over leadership of the KGB, the Institute for the Study of Human Neurophysiology. On the institute's sprawling 235-acre site, Feodorov had assembled under one central direction all of the USSR's key mind and brain research facilities. It included the best scientists from the Leningrad Brain Institute, the Serbsky Institute for Forensic Psychiatry in Moscow, in which a generation of Soviet dissidents had been confined, and the Parapsychological Research Laboratories of Novosibirsk. The grounds also sheltered a three-hundred-bed psychiatric center for the criminally insane, whose inmates provided the scientists and researchers of Feodorov's institute with the laboratory animals they needed for their experiments. To equip the institute, Feodorov's planners had had access to virtually unlimited funds. As a consequence there was almost no technology, no piece of medical equipment relating to the study of the brain, which could not be found on the grounds of the institute.

The institute's proudest and most important possession, however, was not some marvel of sophisticated medical technology. It was a human being, its director. A presiding member of the Soviet Academy of Medical

Sciences, the holder of the Order of Lenin, and a Gold Star Hero of Socialist Labor, the director was the foremost student of the human brain in the USSR and, as far as Feodorov was concerned, in the world.

Most surprisingly, however, the director was a woman, a forty-two-year-old, stunningly attractive woman named Colonel Dr. Xenia Petrovna Sherbatov. When Russian women are blessed with beauty, Feodorov thought—and his KGB activities had led him to travel in one guise or another throughout most of the globe—they are the most beautiful women in the world. The colonel doctor did more than just fall into that category; she led it.

Her beauty was not, however, the consequence of a worker/peasant heritage enhanced by the blessings of state socialism. The colonel doctor was descended from one of the proudest branches of the czarist aristocracy. Her grandfather had been the second son of Duke Nikolai Sherbatov, scion of the immense landowning family from Kiev. He was the most brilliant neurologist of his generation in Russia, a peer and contemporary of the great Pavlov. An intellectual rebel against both his family's privileged existence and czarist society, he had been an early and enthusiastic convert to the Bolshevik Revolution. While the rest of his family had fled to Turkey with the Grand Duchess Tatania, he'd remained behind to offer his talents to the New Russia. His reward was an institute in Kiev in which to pursue his work, a position in the Directorate of the Academy of Medical Sciences, and a state funeral to which Stalin had sent a personal representative on his death in 1929.

The colonel doctor's father had continued the family tradition, becoming a brain surgeon. From 1942 to 1945 he was the chief brain surgeon of the Red Army, and thousands of Soviet soldiers owed their life to his talented fingers and his unflagging devotion to their salvation. Exhausted by those three years, he died shortly after Xenia Petrovna's birth. She, however, had determined to follow in the footsteps of her father and grandfather. She graduated from medical school in Moscow at nineteen, completed her residency at twenty-one, and was running her grandfather's Institute for the Study of the Human Brain in Kiev by the time she was thirty, an accomplishment virtually unheard of in the USSR.

Brilliant. Uncompromising. Temperamental. Those were the three traits Feodorov most frequently associated with his colonel doctor. In a field overwhelmingly dominated by men, her brilliance set her apart, a notch above her colleagues. In some ways it seemed a pity to Feodorov that for the last decade her research had been under the exclusive control of the KGB, which kept her work from getting the international recognition it deserved.

As for her temperament, she was to the depths of her soul a Slav. That the Slavic zest for emotional excess was an essential ingredient in her makeup was attested to by three husbands and reports on enough lovers to fill several pages of her KGB file. Life with the colonel doctor was clearly an emotional roller coaster, a wild ride that alternated dizzying exaltation with equally dizzying despair. Xenia Petrovna, Feodorov was certain, was one of those Russian women who plunged into a love affair as much for the anticipated sadness of the affair's conclusion as for the exhilaration of its beginning.

At the moment, however, it was the colonel doctor's undisputed intellectual brilliance that concerned Feodorov. For perhaps the twentieth time in the past seventy-two hours, he picked up her recent memorandum. Its three typewritten pages had served as a death warrant for the female psychic in New York. That no longer interested Feodorov, however. What had excited him was the promise inherent in its pages, the grail Soviet brain science had sought for so long and which had eluded so many talented scientists: a way to modify human behavior through remote means.

Once again, he turned to the passage that had intrigued him:

Our work with psychics in the USSR far surpasses in quantity and quality the research the Americans have done. It has conclusively established that psychics, no matter how gifted they may be, cannot perform tasks such as locating submarines with the degree of consistency needed to justify their use in military and intelligence tasks. No psychic has ever demonstrated that ability.

The opportunity this woman represents to the CIA and the danger she poses to us lies not in her work with submarines but in the further use to which the CIA may put her. We assume that the CIA's goal in working with her is the same as ours has been in our work with psychics: to learn how and why psychic phenomena occur. This work can only be pursued with the cooperation of a very, very gifted psychic such as this woman appears to be.

As you are aware, our research into psychic phenomena is predicated on the assumption that these phenomena are made possible by extremely low frequency (ELF) electromagnetic waves. This thesis is a result of the evidence produced in 1976 in studies done on our sailors at the Submarine Communications Center in Gomel; personnel exposed to these waves were subject to increased tension, irritability, and various other nervous disorders. Those studies conclusively established that these ELF waves affect human organisms and specifically the central nervous system.

Our scientists then undertook a major research program to study the possibility that these fields might explain psychic phenomena. Thus far they have not been able to demonstrate that the thought processes of the brain can directly produce an effect on those waves. They have, however, discovered that the inverse is true, that ELF waves can and do influence the workings of the human mind. By employing an ELF modulation of a high frequency radio signal, our researchers have discovered that it is possible to bypass the normal sensory mechanisms of certain of the brain's organisms and to influence the brain directly.

The implications of that are staggering. It brings

within our grasp our long-standing goal of finding a way to influence human behavior at a distance by remote means. It would be tragic if the CIA, working on the same basis with this psychic, were to match our progress.

Feodorov folded the memorandum and glanced out his tinted window. They'd left the streets of Moscow behind, and suburbia in the capital was a short-lived thing. The transition from cityscape into countryside was accomplished with the abruptness of a tropical sunset. Each time he made this trip, Feodorov marveled at the immutability of the Russian landscape, at how impervious the countryside had been to the dream of socialist change. These wood-frame houses, these strained, gray faces, these villages still mired in mud, were pages out of Tolstoy. He loved it. These were the vistas that inspired the emotional excess of his Slavic soul: the groves of slender birches, the fir trees in their majestic solitude, this undulating landscape stretching on forever, in its melancholy immensity. At moments like this, there was only one enduring reality for Feodorov: Russia, the *Rodina*, the motherland and the empire that served and protected her. And that was why he was driving to Zhukovskii this afternoon: to find a way to save that empire from at least one of the threats menacing it.

Colonel Xenia Petrovna Sherbatov was waiting to greet him at the institute's main entrance. She could take the most banal of garments, a white laboratory smock, and make it look like a Paris *haute couture* creation, Ivan Sergeivich Feodorov thought. He followed her figure as she advanced along the highly polished corridor of her institute with an attentiveness the chairman of the KGB normally reserved for subjects of a rather different magnitude.

The whispered crackling of the smock's starched folds and the aloof yet suggestive manner in which they wrapped her hips and thighs were remarkably provocative.

The colonel doctor was unusually tall for a Russian woman, an attribute she had chosen to underline this afternoon by wearing high black leather heels. A glance at them told Feodorov one thing: they were not Russian. They were undoubtedly an offering brought back from the West by one of her lovers. The figure rising above them was lean, full-fleshed but muscular; the kind of body that was often found in a woman her age in the West but in the Soviet Union was rare.

Her eyes were pale green suffused with just a hint of yellow. They had an intriguing upward slant, as though one of her Sherbatov forebears had had a long and fruitful period in the East. Her high, arching cheekbones were as Slavic as her brooding temper. Her lips curled in sensual splendor along a wide mouth. This afternoon her hair was knotted into a bun behind her neck, a concession to the hygienic rules of the institute. Flick away a few pins, give a toss to her head, and that hair would tumble in ash-blond waves to the collar of her smock.

Xenia Petrovna led the way to the institute's main conference chamber, a coldly sterile room laid out and furnished by a team of Finnish designers whose work was much admired in the ruling circles of the USSR. More traditionally Russian, bottles of sulfurous mineral water waited at each place set at the table with a complement of writing pads and pens. Feodorov moved to his place at the head of the table and gestured to them to sit down.

"Sudarynya," he said, smiling down the table at Xenia Petrovna. It was an old, prerevolutionary form of greeting—"madam"—for which the Soviet ruling circles had developed a sudden and surprising taste. *Tovarishch*—"Comrade"—was employed about as frequently in the corridors of the Kremlin as it was in the White House. "You have good news for me, I believe?"

"We hope so."

The colonel doctor bestowed a tight little smile on Feodorov. She tended, he had noted, to ration out her smiles as a teacher might, offering them to her diligent pupils as a reward for work well done. "It concerns, as I told you, our program to develop an infallible lie detector."

"I'm sure you can appreciate, Xenia Petrovna, the immense advantage such a device would give us in our work."

Her smile turned playful. "Yes, I think I can. Now, I must warn you we do not yet have that perfect machine you're looking for, although we are getting close. But we do have something which is infallible under certain conditions. We felt that you should be made aware of its existence because it may be of use to you now."

"I appreciate your thoughtfulness."

Xenia Petrovna activated a button on a control panel beside her seat. It dimmed the conference-room lights, and at the same time, four photos of a human brain appeared on a screen. "The technology involves a new and quite revolutionary way of studying the brain and how it functions. The brain, as perhaps you are aware, is the most complex piece of machinery on this planet. To begin with, its cerebral cortices contain fifteen billion nerve cells, or neurons." Xenia Petrovna rose and strode to her display panel. "Each of our minds holds more cells than our planet does people. Each cell is an intricate mini-laboratory, almost constantly functioning."

"Ah, yes," Feodorov declared brightly, "like a computer."

Xenia Petrovna stopped in full stride. "The comparison between the brain and a computer is one many people make. It is quite wrong." Imprecision of thought was not something she held in high regard.

Feodorov was startled. People prepared to contradict the head of the KGB were not exactly legion in Moscow. On the other hand, those words were a measure of the woman's great self-confidence; he liked that.

"Nothing in the brain happens faster than a thousandth of a second. Comparing that to the speed with which modern computers process information is like comparing the speed of a man walking to that of a Ferrari. However, each of the brain's neurons can be compared, perhaps, to a computer's central processing unit. Most computers have one. A very few have five or six. The brain has fifteen billion. That gives it a parallel-processing capacity that is so much greater than that of any computer man has even dreamed of that we cannot begin to comprehend it."

"I stand corrected, *sudarynya*." Feodorov smiled. "I will be more wary of facile comparisons in the future."

This time there was more warmth in the regard she bestowed on him. "Now," she continued, "we know that everything a human being experiences from happiness to aggression to speech to motion is related to a pattern of electrical and chemical events in the brain. You cannot raise your little finger, have a thought or a feeling, listen to a note of music or sense cold, without an electrochemical action in your brain."

Xenia Petrovna pushed a button on a hand-held control panel. One of the pictures on the screen was replaced with a photograph of a man with his head shaved and hooked to a complex of wires, each running into a sensor fixed to his skull.

"For three-quarters of a century, the only tool we have had to study and measure the electric currents associated with each of those actions was the EEG, the electroencephalograph. The one we're employing in this illustration has thirty-two sensing points, which is about as sophisticated as we can get. Yet even with this level of sophistication, the EEG is a very unsatisfactory tool." The colonel doctor stabbed at the diagram of the brain in profile with a pointer. "It cannot detect electrical activity in the brain for more than a few centimeters beneath the skull. That means that this entire area of the brain"—and now her pointer swept over the center of the diagram— "the limbic system, the guts from which our emotions spring, is an undiscovered planet as far as the EEG is concerned. The EEG simply cannot pick up an electrical impulse from the nerve cells here, because by the time that impulse reaches the skull it is so weak it cannot penetrate the bone, and as a result we get no signal."

"And what are the consequences of that?" Feodorov asked.

"This is the area where all our most fundamental emotions are centered—love, hate, fear, hunger, lust, aggression. To try to understand how the brain works without being able to study how this area functions is like trying to understand how a car's engine works without lifting up the hood."

"In other words, we are blind when it comes to understanding how the things that really matter in the brain work?" As he said those words, Feodorov was thinking, If we can't understand the brain, how can we possibly influence it?

"Until now," Xenia Petrovna answered. "But that is about to change."

Feodorov stiffened.

"By the most fundamental law of nature, every electric pulse in the brain creates both an electrical field and a magnetic field. Unlike the electrical field, the magnetic field is not diminished in strength by the bone of the skull. It comes out intact from the center, the heart of the brain. The limbic system I just pointed out. It's been there since man has existed, waiting for us to find a way to measure it."

"Well, why haven't we measured it, then?" Feodorov asked. "I know from my own studies years ago that we have ample ways to measure magnetic fields."

"Because it's so unbelievably weak. It's one billionth of the earth's natural magnetic field, the field we're standing in right now, the one that makes the needle on a compass swing north. Trying to capture it was like standing in the middle of Olympic Stadium and trying to understand the words a three-year-old girl was whispering to her father in the top row of seats—while a hundred thousand people were cheering a Red Army goal. Impossible."

Feodorov was about to interject a thought, but he checked himself. Clearly, the colonel doctor had reached a critical point in her exposition.

She paused for dramatic effect, then continued, "Today, at last, we can begin to hear those words that child is whispering. We are beginning to peer into the depths of our brains.''

She walked slowly back to her seat, each click of her heels underlining what she had just said. ''This is the device that allows us to do that. It is called a magnetoencephalograph. The Americans think that they are far ahead of us in this technology. They are wrong.''

Again, she flicked her control panel. This time what looked to Feodorov like a very modern black leather dentist's chair appeared on the screen. Clearly it was designed to be used with the patient—if that was the term —in a semireclining position as though he were in a sleeperette in the first-class cabin of a Western airliner. At its head was a helmetlike device that reminded him of the instrument women employed at the hairdresser while they were having a permanent wave. Above it was a white metal cylinder slightly larger than the oxygen tank underwater divers strap to their backs.

''This is the very latest model of a magnetoencephalograph. Inside that helmet are two hundred and sixty-five coils of indium wire the size of a shirt-collar button distributed over a surface sixty centimeters square. The tube to which the helmet is linked contains a reservoir of liquid helium, which cools the indium so that it becomes superconducting. What this device does is allow us to study the whole brain simultaneously by reading the magnetic fields it is giving off. Instead of giving us a series of snapshots of the brain the way a scanner does, it gives us a movie, a three-dimensional motion picture of the brain in action. This is going to open to us the door to the deepest mysteries of the human psyche.''

She again flicked her control panel. The profile of a head appeared.

''Here is a computer-enhanced portrait of what happened as this subject listened to Stravinsky's *Firebird*.''

To Feodorov's amazement, a whole chain of little red pinheads began to dance their way through an area of the man's brain no larger than a kopek.

''Those beads of light show us what groups of cells are reacting to the music's auditory stimuli, where they're located, and the sequence in which they're responding. We can freeze-frame those movements to match each note of the suite with the group of cells which register it."

She clicked her panel again. "We have just told this patient to clench and unclench his right fist."

A new chain of light began to move through another, distinctly different area of the brain.

Xenia Petrovna clicked her remote control yet again. "Now we have immersed the man's left hand in ice-cold water."

Again a new and different pattern of lights blossomed on the screen.

"The implications of this are staggering," Feodorov said. "I'm very impressed."

Xenia Petrovna offered Feodorov another of those patronizing smiles of hers. "One of the most fascinating things we have discovered working with the magnetoencephalograph is that the brain anticipates a reaction or a gesture before you actually have that reaction or make that gesture. With this, we can see that you are going to raise your little finger a millisecond before you in fact raise it. If your senses are stimulated, if you hear a familiar sound, smell a familiar odor, see a face or a sight that you've recognized, the fact that you've recognized it is recorded in your brain. It doesn't matter if you deny it. There's a record stamped there in your brain of the fact that you have recognized it. This machine allows us to read that record."

Xenia Petrovna stood up and smoothed the folds of her smock. She even managed to radiate sensuality in a gesture as mundane as that.

"I've arranged a little demonstration for you of just how it works," she announced. "I've selected two of our inmates whose skills as liars, I can assure you, are comparable to the dancing skills of the Bolshoi's prima ballerina. They're going to try to lie to my machine."

A throaty, malicious laugh sprang from her throat. "I can assure you they wouldn't be able to lie to this machine if their lives depended on it."

With their hair shaved down to a fine gray stubble, their features frozen into sullen stares, the two inmates chosen by Xenia Petrovna to demonstrate her new technology for the chairman of the KGB resembled a pair of unruly Red Army recruits who'd just been informed they were on their way to a disciplinary battalion in Siberia.

"The one on the left," she whispered to Ivan Sergeivich Feodorov, "is a psychotic. He's subject to uncontrollable rages—killed four people in a drunken rampage in Kiev six months ago. He was sentenced to death, but we decided to save him from the firing squad and bring him up here." She gave Feodorov a tight little smile. "To help us advance the cause of socialist medicine.

"His companion"—she indicated the second inmate, a dark little man who, Feodorov thought, resembled a ferret searching for a hole in which to hide—"is a Georgian from Tbilisi. He's spent more time in the courtroom than most of our judges have."

"On what sort of charges?"

"Every form of petty crime against the state you can imagine—theft, black marketing, receiving stolen goods, fraud."

"And he, too, decided to come up here to advance the cause of our science?"

"Indeed. He found the prospect considerably more attractive than spending the rest of his life in Siberia, which happened to be the only alternative open to him."

The doctor led Feodorov away from the two inmates into a room that Feodorov thought could easily have been mistaken for a sauna. The walls, ceiling, and floor were paneled in ash-blond wood. At its center was the black leather dentist's-style chair Feodorov had seen earlier on the colonel doctor's slide in the conference room.

"This chamber is as totally screened off from outside magnetic fields as it's possible to make it. We have to be sure they have no metal on them when they come in. But then, all they have to do is sit in the chair with their head in the helmet and relax," the colonel doctor explained. "Technology does the rest."

"Easier than visiting a dentist."

"Much. On the screen"—she indicated a TV monitor—"we'll show them thirty photographs at ten-second intervals. Twenty-eight of those photographs will be of our employees out at Novosibirsk. Neither of these men could ever have seen any of them. Mixed in will be two photographs of his victims for our psychotic killer from Kiev and photos of two of his fellow black marketeers for our Georgian. Their instructions are very simple. They must not reveal to our questioners which of the two people in the thirty they know."

Xenia Petrovna escorted Feodorov out to the control room, and the Kiev killer was brought in. Feodorov watched on a TV monitor as the man settled into the leather chair. The inmate sighed and relaxed. "He's done this before," the colonel doctor noted. "He knows there's nothing in this experiment that's going to cause him pain."

"As distinct from other experiments he's been involved in?"

"Scientific progress always has its price, Ivan Sergeivich."

"Ah yes, so it does."

Before Feodorov was a bank of computer screens. The computer installation, he noted, was American, Hewlett-Packard. He could not remember whether it had been purchased legally or brought in by his own services.

"We're ready. Start the computers," Xenia Petrovna ordered. The screens came alive in cobwebs of dancing green lights. "Focus down to his audiovisual recognition center." The device, she explained to Feodorov, could be trained in one area of the brain as small as a square millimeter. As she talked, he noticed the light patterns of the screen changing. "Now start passing the photographs."

She turned to Feodorov. "The photo of his two victims will be the ninth and seventeenth photos we'll show him."

Feodorov watched in fascination as the man followed the photos passing before him on the TV screen. Nothing in his sullen features gave any indication of an emotion, any faint flicker of recognition, despite the questions hammered at him by the operator of the machine as each photo passed.

"When his eyes see the photographs of his victims, he's going to have what we call a P300, a brain wave that will flash three hundred milliseconds after the photo appears on the screen. It is the sign that his brain's memory bank has recognized the visual image the eyes have sent to it. He can lie, say nothing, swear he's never seen that face in his life. It doesn't matter. The fact he's recognized the face will have been registered here on our computer by that brain wave. There's not a thing he can do to prevent that from happening."

"Unless, of course, he closes his eyes."

"Obviously."

"And if his eyes are held open by force?"

"Then the telltale brain wave we're looking for will be there."

The last of the thirty photos passed on the prisoner's TV monitor and the screen went black.

"Show me the reaction pattern we recorded after he saw his first victim," Xenia Petrovna ordered. "Here," she said, pointing to a wiggling line. "There's the P300 that shows he recognized him. Now give me another photo. Watch," she commanded. "That brain wave you just saw will not be there, because he didn't recognize the person in the photo."

Feodorov studied the computer screen. Sure enough, the wiggling line that had appeared as the killer's brain had recognized his first victim was absent. Xenia Petrovna screened the killer's reactions to six more photos, all of them of strangers. None contained the brain wave characteristic of his recognizing a familiar face.

"Now," she said, "here's his reaction to his second victim."

And there it was again, the same wiggling line, in exactly the same place it had been when he'd recognized his first victim.

Xenia Petrovna ordered the killer out of the chair and sent the Georgian in to take his place. The same pattern repeated itself.

"Your machine is a miracle worker as far as the eyes are concerned," Feodorov acknowledged. "But how about the act of telling a lie itself—are there any characteristics this machine will pick up to reveal that a lie is being told?"

"I'm certain there are. For every mechanical gesture the body is going to make, there is always a distinctive pattern of brain waves called 'preparation sets' which can be picked up and identified with this technology. If those characteristic waves are there for each of our mechanical gestures, I'm convinced they are also there for every one of our emotional reactions. All we have to do is find them. When we do, you'll have your infallible lie detector. And one day with this machine, we will find them."

"You and your staff are to be congratulated, Colonel Doctor. And rewarded as well."

"Our greatest reward"—a smile more playful, perhaps, than was appropriate tugged at the doctor's sensual lips—"is serving the cause of our great socialist state."

"I'm sure."

Feodorov picked up his attaché case. "Xenia Petrovna, might I have a few moments of your time in private before I return to Moscow? I'd like to discuss your recent communication about that psychic in New York and some of its implications."

Admiral Peter White, the personal physician to the President of the United States, walked up to the Executive Protection Service guard at the White House West Gate. He was dressed in civilian clothes so as to be as inconspicuous as possible. The guard carefully scrutinized his ID card and photo, found his name on the appointments list, and called the presidential appointments secretary to inform the Oval Office that White had arrived. A young man appeared a few minutes later to escort White to his meeting with the President.

Instead of taking him into the ground-floor executive offices, however, the young man took White up a back staircase to the presidential living quarters on the second floor. He led him to the end of the corridor and opened the door to the President's private study. "The President," he announced, "will be with you in just a few moments."

White settled nervously into one of the room's Chippendale chairs. This was only his second meeting with his prestigious patient. The first, a few days after the President's inauguration, had been occasioned by the most banal of complaints, an acute case of indigestion. White had used his visit to urge the President to avail himself of the extraordinary medical facilities available to him at Bethesda Naval Hospital and have a complete physical examination. That, he had stressed, would provide the President's medical advisers with the sort of complete information bank they should have ready in case any medical problems or emergency arose during his term of office.

The President had dismissed the idea before White had finished presenting it. There was no way he was going to throw away a precious workday padding around Bethesda in a white smock getting poked and scanned by a team of Navy doctors. They'd just have to make do with whatever records were available from his family GP. It wasn't likely, White thought, that the President had summoned him because he had changed his mind. There had been an edge of concern in the President's voice, a brittleness which had indicated to White that here was a man suddenly very concerned about his health.

The President's arrival interrupted his thoughts. White leaped to his feet.

"Please, Doctor," the President said, "sit down." He settled into the chair opposite White's, crossed his legs, and formed a little steeple out of his fingertips, its summit lightly brushing the point of his chin. It was a pose that had become familiar to millions of his countrymen. "Doctor, I'd like to talk to you in strictest confidence."

"Mr. President," Admiral White replied, "despite the importance of your office, I'm your personal physician. The same rules of confidentiality that bind any physician to his patient bind me to you. It's a pledge of secrecy as secure as the seal of the confessional."

"Okay, Doctor, thanks. I really don't want what I'm about to tell you to leak to the press. Not until it has to come out." The President then described in detail his attacks of dizziness, his sudden losses of balance. "I've been reading up on this," he concluded, "and I must say I'm very worried. I've got all the signs of a brain tumor."

"Mr. President." Reassurance flowed gently from the admiral's voice. "The first thing they teach you in medical school is never to indulge in self-diagnosis. The symptoms you're describing might indicate a brain tumor. But there are an awful lot of other things they could indicate as well."

The President gave a worried nod. He was not so easily reassured.

"I'd like to bring you into Bethesda for a scan, sir. We have the best in modern neurological technology over there, a thing called a magnetoencephalograph. If you've got a tumor in your brain, this will find it."

"Is this a major procedure?"

"Not at all. It's a question of forty-five minutes."

The President reflected on White's words for a moment. "Is it a fairly common thing?"

"Common, no sir. We're talking a three-million-dollar piece of equipment here. Right now it's only one of three in the country. Obviously, it's reserved for special cases."

"Yeah, that's the hitch. Some nurse or some corpsman over there is bound to blab. It'll leak to the press. It'll be all over *The Washington Post*. 'The President had to go to Bethesda for some super-secret brain study.' Can you imagine the consequences of that?"

"I can," White agreed, "but I think I know how we can avoid that, sir."

"How?"

The admiral was smiling now. "Let's do what I've been after you to do for months. Let me bring you in for a full medical. We'll do a magnetoencephalogram as a part of your regular annual checkup. That way we can pass the whole thing off to the press as just your annual physical."

The offices of senior Soviet officials all seem to have been patterned on a standard design. They are invariably somber, underfurnished, and underlit, their corners obscured by pools of shadow that convey both a suggestion of menace and the melancholia that is so much a part of the Russian character. Xenia Petrovna's was no exception. It was paneled from floor to ceiling in a dark, highly polished wainscoting. The ceiling, too, was of dark wood fixed in the rigid geometric design of a chessboard. The floor was covered by a series of Turkestan carpets in deep crimson, blue, and purple. Her desk was an immense black gilded table copied from a design by Bartolomeo Rastrelli, the court architect of the Empress Elizabeth Petrovna. Behind it was the obligatory portrait of Lenin. A set of recessed lights softened the old man's features, giving him the air of a slightly befuddled grandfather instead of that of an emaciated zealot as was conveyed by most of his official likenesses.

How strange it was, Feodorov thought, that the office of so attractive a woman should be so rigorously masculine in design. Only one feminine touch softened its severity, a faint hint of perfume someone had sprayed into the atmosphere. Perhaps, Feodorov reasoned, it was the colonel doctor's way of asserting her authority over the masculine world she commanded. She had opened her closet and was hanging up her white smock. Beneath it she was wearing a pale blue silk blouse cut to emphasize the thrusting challenge of her breasts. It was no more Russian than her black leather shoes. She pressed a button. An elderly woman opened a door leading to a private kitchen.

"Tea, Ivan Sergeivich?" Xenia Petrovna asked. "Or coffee? Or something stronger?"

"Tea would be fine." The chairman of the KGB settled into the chair by her desk and offered Xenia Petrovna a Chesterfield from a gold Dunhill cigarette case. The West's preoccupation with the hazards of cigarettes had yet to make an inroad on Soviet habits; like most of his countrymen, Feodorov remained as addicted to tobacco as Americans in the thirties and forties had been.

"The problem of the psychic in New York has been resolved," he informed the doctor. "The CIA will no longer be employing her to further their work."

His barely nuanced revelation, that the woman had been murdered, produced no indication of emotion that he could detect on the colonel doctor's lovely features. He opened his attaché case, took out her memo, read it aloud, then looked up at the colonel doctor.

"Xenia Petrovna, there is a particular and urgent reason of state why this work of yours might be of enormous consequence in the very near future."

"May I ask what that reason of state might be?"

"No."

"Very well."

As she was talking, her hands had been plucking at the pins in the bun of her hair. She tossed her head like a frisky young mare, and it fell in long rolls to her shoulders, its golden sheen glistening in the recessed light that illuminated the portrait of Lenin. "I have always maintained, as you know, that an intimate knowledge of how electromagnetic currents interact with human cells will provide the key to understanding behavior."

Feodorov was struck again watching her by what a handsome creature she was. How incongruous to sit here, he thought, admiring her physical beauty while she discusses a subject as complex and arcane as any he could imagine.

"You remember the work I was doing in Kiev a decade ago on the electric stimulation of the brain?"

"Of course." It was that work that had first brought Xenia Petrovna to Feodorov's attention. She had studied human brain functions employing a technology similar to the one Delgado used on animals. She implanted gold electrodes into certain carefully determined spots in the brain. Then she had been able to induce specific emotions in her subject—anger, euphoria, lethargy—by passing an electric current to the brain through those electrodes. Later she had wired her electrodes to a computer. Then she exposed her subjects to certain sensory stimuli: a splash of hot water on the hand, a pornographic image on a television screen, a menacing gesture. The electrodes passed back to the computer the very precise electric signal that characterized the brain's reaction to each stimulus. She had discovered she could then reproduce those reactions without the presence of the stimuli simply by sending that precise electric signal back into the subject's brain with her electrodes.

"There was and is every reason to believe," Xenia Petrovna continued, "that if you can produce these emotions in the brain with an electric current, you can also produce them from outside the body with an electromagnetic field—provided you know the very precise field to employ. And, in this case, it will almost certainly be in the extremely low frequency range, because there is no living organism on this planet that does not lie within the biological domain of those frequencies."

Her discourse was interrupted by the appearance of her elderly servant bearing a silver tray and tea service. She set them on Xenia Petrovna's table. How fascinating, Feodorov thought, watching her organize their little tea ceremony. There are certain things no political dogma can eradicate, and heredity is prime among them. Xenia Petrovna dispensed the tea with all the condescending graciousness of a grand duchess welcoming to her table a distinguished visitor but one unfortunately not favored by the benediction of royal blood.

After she'd passed Feodorov his cup, she took hers, swirling her first sip on her tongue with the studied air of a professional taster. "Now," she said, apparently satisfied, "how might those fields be used to modify behavior? The question we couldn't answer was, how do the cells of our body interact with those extremely low frequency fields?

"An Australian named Adey in California gave us the answer. The cell's membranes are covered with strands of protein tipped with calcium ions. Each strand has a negative electrical charge. Think of them as like ears of corn waving in a field in a summer breeze."

"That's a pleasant enough image."

Xenia Petrovna bestowed yet another of her condescending smiles on her superior. "Indeed. Now suppose that summer breeze is in fact one of these very weak fields. Adey and his associates discovered those strands of protein serve as exquisitely sensitive antennas that detect that electromagnetic breeze rippling overhead. The calcium ions cause a message to be sent to the interior of the cell, which orders it to respond by doing whatever it is that that cell is supposed to do. It's a phenomenon called resonance. If you have water in a crystal goblet and bombard it with one very, very precise frequency, it begins to vibrate, doesn't it?"

"Yes, I've seen that happen."

"Eventually the goblet will break. Another way of saying it is that the effect is frequency-specific. That's what happens here. Those very, very weak electromagnetic fields can't use energy to communicate their information because they don't have any. It's passed because they are operating at the one very, very precise frequency that can set those waving ears of corn on a cell's membrane vibrating."

Xenia Petrovna leaned back in her high-backed swivel chair and turned a bemused regard on Feodorov. "Let me give you another example of resonance at work which you may appreciate even more. Suppose we sit you down five feet from a television screen."

"I wouldn't appreciate that at all," Feodorov replied. "I regard watching most of our television as a form of torture."

"If we wanted that television set to generate a signal that could produce a physiological change in your body, to, for example"—Xenia Petrovna laughed with malicious delight—"give you an erection, the amount of energy that the set would have to emit to give you an erection is infinite. But suppose we turned the set on and instead passed an image on the screen of a particularly attractive woman, a young beauty from the Bolshoi, in a sensual pose? The amount of light energy coming off that screen would be negligible, barely measurable. But with a little luck, we'd get the reaction we were looking for."

"I should certainly hope so, my dear Colonel Doctor."

"Why? Because your eyes registered the visual stimuli of the ballerina's beautiful body and passed it on to your brain. There it activated your brain's command and control system. The memory bank in your cervical cortex recognized the image and ordered other glands to release a series of chemicals into your bloodstream. *Voilà*, an erection. The resonance phenomenon performing at its best."

Feodorov made a mock half-bow toward Xenia Petrovna. He was wondering if he might not invite her to one of his select Sunday lunches at his hunting lodge. "One is always grateful to science for its help and explanations, my dear."

"From what one hears in Moscow," she replied, "the explanations of science may benefit you, but its assistance is hardly necessary. Now, to continue. This man, Adey in California, demonstrated that white blood cells, skin cells, bone cells, all have this ability to receive information from these fields by resonance. What we have demonstrated here in this lab in the last month is that a similar mechanism exists in the cells of the brain."

"Please explain that."

"What your brain reacted to was a sensory stimulus, the image of that beautiful ballerina's body transmitted to it in the form of photons, electromagnetic light energy passed by the eye. Your brain recognized the image because it had been taught to by your genetic heritage and your experience. It reacted by sending out a stream of electromagnetic signals which launched a series of chemical processes. They gave you your erection."

"So obviously," Feodorov mused, "it is the signals that are the keys to the process."

"Exactly. Ultimately, each signal will have a precise electromagnetic definition. And it will almost certainly be unique to each function and to each human being, because the cells of every human are unique to that individual and the function the cells perform. But if we could discover one of these signals, could we then send it back into the brain from outside the nervous system? Could we fool a brain like yours into thinking that there was a beautiful ballerina out there, when, in fact, there was nothing, only an electromagnetic signal? Would you still get an erection?"

The sly sensuality Feodorov had so often observed in the colonel doctor was gone now. She was intense and gathered, all scientist and researcher. "The answer to that question is almost certainly yes."

"How could you hope to discover the signal?"

"The machine you saw in action today, our magnetoencephalograph, may, I believe, hold the answer to that."

"Why?"

"It can peer into the depths of the mind, and that is where these signals are being generated."

The KGB chairman could barely stifle his reaction listening to her words. My idea, he thought, my scheme just might work. "I need an accurate indication of where your work stands right now."

Xenia Petrovna sipped slowly, almost teasingly at her tea. She was not a woman to be rushed into her pronouncements.

"If by influencing behavior at a distance you mean finding a way to make you get up out of your chair, walk over to my bookcase, pick up that porcelain statue of mine"—she gestured to a modernistic sculpture serving as a bookend to a row of her medical textbooks—"and then getting you to try to bash my brains out with it, the answer is that we are light-years away. I, in fact, do not believe such a thing will ever be possible."

"No," Feodorov said. "My requirements are more

basic and simple—how to manipulate basic emotions in a general way. What I want you to do for me, Colonel Doctor," Feodorov continued, his eyes glistening with an intensity Xenia Petrovna associated with Hindu saddhus or Tibetan monks, "is find out how you can stimulate someone's aggressive impulses without his being aware of it."

"That may not be quite as easy as I made it sound."

"Don't explain the difficulties. Do it."

Xenia Petrovna started to say something, but the warning flag of Feodorov's upraised hand stopped her. "That is why you are here, Colonel Doctor. That is why this institute is here. That is why you have never been denied a ruble or a piece of equipment. You can have anything you need, any permission you request, but do it."

"And how soon do you need this?"

"Yesterday."

PART 3

"CELEBRATE,
XENIA PETROVNA.
YOU HAVE CHANGED
THE WORLD."

The three-year-old Honda Custom Cruiser represented your state-of-the-art American suburban transport. A frayed "Bush for President" sticker, surely the only one in Moscow, peeled from the front bumper. How that had survived the rigors of Russian winter was a mystery Bill Witter had yet to comprehend. Above it, both fenders displayed a standard variety of dents and scrapes, tributes, Witter liked to claim, to his wife's determination to demonstrate on the streets of the Soviet capital that American drivers were not easily intimidated. A blue-and-white Colby decal in the lower-right-hand corner of the rear window provided Witter with a daily reminder both of his absent elder daughter and the most important single drain on his annual income as a U.S. government SES2.

The militiaman at the gate gave Witter a familiar wave as he eased the car out from under the yellow facade of the U.S. embassy and into the traffic flowing along Chaykovskii Street. Like almost every aspect of Witter's life, these lunchtime jogging expeditions formed part of a rigidly patterned existence. He glanced into his rearview mirror for a sign of one of the dark green Moskvitch sedans that often trailed along behind diplomats, and particularly American diplomats, in Moscow. Today there was none. The minders were either out to lunch or not interested in yet another of the third political officer's daily jogs.

Witter moved quickly and easily down Smolenskii Avenue toward the Moskva River. Traffic jams, he'd discovered to his immense pleasure on arriving in Moscow, were not among the blessings socialism conferred on its adherents. His destination was one of his favorite jogging sites, the imposing stone facade marking the entry to Gorky Park. Its huge parking lot was almost empty, another reason, Witter thought, to sing the praises of Marx and Lenin. He did his warm-up exercises, then clipped a cassette of Pavarotti singing Verdi arias into his Walkman, fixed it onto the sweatband of his tracksuit, put on his earphones, and headed into the park.

He jogged along the familiar pathways with a measured, loping gait, breathing deeply of the moist spring air as he did. A tentative, almost shy southern breeze played at the branches of the birch trees as though questioning whether the Soviet capital was ready to receive the blessings of spring. Unassailed by the clamorous distractions of Western life, Muscovites, Witter had noticed, retained an engaging ability to savor life's simpler joys, like wandering their parks to inventory the progress of the seasons. They strode along wrapped in that mantle of silence so characteristic of the Russian masses, the outward manifestation of their ability to endure hardship. It was the symbol, to Witter, of the stoic courage that had enabled these people to turn back the legions of Napoleon and the panzers of Hitler and to suffer the endless privations that went with building the socialist nirvana.

His course took him past the Pl'zenskii Restaurant with its odor of sausages crackling on a grill, down one of the paths the park authorities flooded in winter for skaters. A few hundred yards along the path, he saw what he was looking for, an empty Pepsi-Cola can perched on a green waste receptacle. It was the signal they'd agreed on. The message was there. He swung up the pathway to the left of the trash can. As he did, he reached down to adjust the volume on his Walkman. Then he heard the familiar *click*. For all his training, Witter could not suppress a flicker of excitement at the sound.

What he was doing was performing that most mundane of spyhandlers' tasks—emptying a dead-letter box. Except to do it, he was employing the CIA's latest, top-of-the-line electronic technology. Somewhere in the two or three hundred yards ahead of him—Witter had no idea where—a tiny, battery-powered transmitter no larger than a microcassette lay concealed. The flick of the knob on his Walkman had sent a signal to the transmitter that activated its power supply. His agent's message, encoded in the usual five-letter blocks, was now flowing into Witter's Walkman at two thousand characters every thirty seconds while he listened to Pavarotti singing "Che gelida manina." The message was repeated three times before Witter heard the second *click,* indicating the transmission was finished.

The beauty of the system was its anonymity. Witter did not have to fish the message out of some tree trunk as CIA agents once did, looking over their shoulders for a KGB man ready to pounce. His agent never returned to the site where he'd left the little sender. They were expendable and once used were melted down to what might seem a cat turd by their power supply. The agent had a master encoder/recorder that fit inside a box of Belomorkanal cigarettes concealed in his house together with a supply of the transmitters. He plugged a transmitter into the device, programmed it with his message, and it was ready for use. At the moment, as Witter jogged off down the path, the transmitter was automatically erasing the message prior to activating the device's self-destruct program.

Sweating a little more than usual, Witter jogged back to his car and drove to the embassy. He went immediately to what was called "the vault," a windowless cell on the seventh floor. It was opened by a computerized lock to which only three CIA employees—the station chief, his deputy, and Witter—had the code. Once locked in the vault, he took out the CIA's copy of the colonel's one-time pad code and a little black playback machine which resembled his Walkman.

This plaything was another invention of the CIA's technological geniuses. He snapped the Pavarotti cassette into the machine and set to work. A special head in his Walkman had laid the incoming message onto his tape in the infinitesimally small space between its first and second tracks. Any KGB officer playing back the tape without the Agency's special playback machine would have heard nothing except the engaging tones of Luciano Pavarotti.

Conscious of the heavy responsibility that was his, Witter worked with slow, methodical precision. Not since the arrest and execution of Colonel Oleg Penkovsky twenty years before had the CIA had a penetration agent in the Soviet Union even remotely as valuable as Colonel Viktor Sbirunov. Defectors were the operating coin of the CIA, valuable and precious currency, but an agent in place was a blue-white diamond, an asset that was, quite literally, priceless.

Sbirunov had been recruited fifteen years earlier when he was the Soviet military attaché in Paris. Since then, he had maneuvered himself into the Military Secretariat of the Central Committee, the repository of the USSR's most secret military information. He was a man of remarkable poise and courage, and, as far as the CIA could determine, motivated, as Penkovsky had been, by the dream of an opulent post-espionage existence in the West. That dream would shortly be his; a numbered bank account at the Discount Bank on Geneva's Quai de l'Ile now contained well over three million dollars, ready for the day Sbirunov decided to come in from the Moscow cold and enjoy the rewards to which fifteen years of perilous service had entitled him.

It was an irony of the service that Witter had never exchanged a single word with the colonel, although he had, of course, seen him for a fleeting instant during brush passes and had his features stamped on his mind from hours studying his photograph. The colonel's control was the officer who had originally recruited him in Paris. To maintain that essential element of trust between agent and controller, the officer was flown from Langley to meet the colonel whenever he came West. Yet Witter felt for the man, who was several years his senior, the worried concern of a mother with a son in a particularly dangerous occupation, such as race car driver or under-cover drug agent.

That was why Witter had a sudden tremor of apprehension coupled with excitement as he reached the end of the colonel's message. He was asking for a brush pass. Clearly, he had drawings or documents he wanted to pass the Agency which he couldn't send with his transmitter. The responsibility for handling the exchange would be Witter's. A brush pass was a standard technique of the intelligence craft, an operation in which men like Witter were trained with as much rigor as marines were taught the manual of arms. Properly executed, a brush pass was almost undetectable. Nonetheless, it did bring, for however brief an instant, agent and controller into public contact. That fact made the pass one of the most challenging acts a CIA officer was called on to perform. No officer, no matter how experienced, contemplated such a pass on the streets of Moscow without the flickering finger of fear picking at his bowels.

Meetings. Art Bennington, standing in a knot of pedestrians waiting for the WALK light at F and 17th streets, almost growled the word out loud. Reach a certain level at the CIA and you spent more time taking meetings than those producers out in Hollywood sitting around the Polo Lounge did. The one which had prompted his cheerful chain of thought this morning was being held in what was referred to as the Agency's "outpatient department," a run-down office building on F Street a few minutes' walk from the Old Executive Office Building adjacent to the White House. The CIA's senior bureaucracy employed it as a supposedly discreet shelter for gatherings in downtown Washington and interagency meetings. In fact, the building was one of the places people were always pointing to with a knowing smile, which, Bennington always felt, made it about as secure a meeting place as the parking lot of the Soviet embassy.

The subject of this morning's gathering was the follow-up investigation to Ann Robbins's murder. That had led just where Bennington had suspected it would—nowhere. He went through the usual blue-blazer security procedures at the building's front entrance, then checked in with the den mother, a female officer sitting at the reception desk. She gave him the number of the room assigned to their meeting.

Most of the others were waiting. Pozner, S&T's internal security officer, was there, of course. There was an NSA officer and a lieutenant colonel from the Defense Intelligence Agency Bennington didn't know and Mike Pettee of the FBI's liaison office with the CIA. Pettee was a bulky guy who'd once been an Olympic-class backstroker. As usual, he was wearing a yellow paisley bow tie, a sartorial artifact that struck Bennington as being as out of place in the capital these days as a stovepipe hat or muttonchop whiskers would have been. Pettee had gone to Notre Dame, and Bennington figured he probably imagined those ties of his went down well with the tweedy Ivy League types he had to deal with out at Langley.

The three of them were discussing just the kind of international crisis you'd expect to preoccupy such a group of bureaucratic movers and shakers—the Redskins' picks in the NFL's latest college draft. Bennington poured himself a coffee and took his seat at the table. They were missing one man, Paul Mott of the CIA's Counterintelligence Division. The director had insisted Counterintelligence play the lead in the investigation, which made Mott the *de facto* chairman of their little committee.

Counterintelligence guys had never been wildly popular with their Agency counterparts, which was probably why the director had assigned them the lead role. The division's founder, James Jesus Angleton, "the Orchid Man," had been widely regarded by his peers as a bit of a weirdo, and his division had been tarnished by the weirdo image ever since. The problem was that they were like the credit department of a big organization devoted to sales. The clandestine guys in the overseas stations were always on the lookout for marketing opportunities.

They'd come rushing back to Langley all excited about this great potential client they'd just lined up, and Counterintelligence would come downstairs and say, "Uh-uh. This guy doesn't look so good at the bank. We get cash before we ship."

Mott entered and took his place at the head of the table. He was a gaunt man with a dyspeptic pallor who was forever sucking on a Tums. The poor guy, it seemed to Bennington, spent most of his working day worrying about his chronic ulcers, not the best therapy imaginable for that particular complaint. He was wearing an old-fashioned seersucker suit, the kind with rumpled gray-and-white stripes. It looked as if it had been cut from a mattress cover. Brooks Brothers had sold them for $29.95 when Bennington was a Princeton undergraduate. This one, he guessed, could well date back to those days.

Mott shuffled a few papers from his attaché case, then looked at the NSA man. His regard was not full of warmth and tenderness. "You have something for us, I believe."

The NSA man indulged himself in a few nervous coughs as he pulled a little black leather card holder on which he'd scrawled some notes from his coat pocket. "Yes," he said, "uh, perhaps we might have passed this on earlier, but there's no reason why this information is related to the matter we're investigating. We registered two Spetosk burst transmissions here in the Washington area, the first twenty-two days before the lady's murder, the second ten days before."

Mott cut in, "The Spetosk is the KGB's top-of-the-line burst transmitter. They're reserved for grade one, top-drawer KGB agents. We've spotted three of them in use in Europe in the last six months."

"How do they work?" Pettee, the FBI man, asked.

Mott glanced down the table, looking for a cigarette box. Nobody was smoking. "They're a little smaller than a pack of cigarettes. You can conceal one in the palm of your hand. The agent charges it up with an encoder at home. Then he takes it out into the open air somewhere. All he needs is the angle that's going to make his satellite from a particular geographic location. He points it up to the sky, pushes a button, and pop, off goes his message in a couple of seconds. Those things have data rates of a hundred kilobits a second. When the satellite passes over Moscow, the Center pulls the message down."

The NSA man seconded Mott's words with a wave of his hand. "Detecting someone using one is almost impossible. The guy will look like the Statue of Liberty for about five seconds and that's all there is to it. However, the signals these things put out are very characteristic and very particular, so it's not hard to pick them up. I mean, you can't mistake them for a fishing boat down in the Chesapeake Bay calling in for the weather.

"Now, in the first case, we triangulated the sending site to an Exxon station on the Dolley Madison Highway. The second was sent from a lay-by on Route 270 just northwest of Rockville in Maryland. We sent teams out to search both places, but of course by the time they got there the sender was long gone. The lay-by gave us nothing. At the Exxon station we figured the guy probably went out back by the restrooms to send. He wouldn't have attracted much attention back there. The guy working the gas pumps remembered three people asking for the key to the toilets that morning: a trucker with a diesel rig, a good-ole-boy type; a suburban housewife with red hair; and a businessman, suit, tie, glasses, the works."

"Did he have anything on the cars?" asked Pettee, the FBI man.

"The lady was in a gray car. A Toyota."

"Number plate?"

"Nothing."

"Great. There are probably about ten thousand gray Toyotas in the area."

"Any chance of cracking the code?" Bennington asked.

"None. They use a pad with those things."

"Do you know if the same transmitter was used in both cases?"

The way the NSA man started coughing and fidgeting, you'd think he'd been asked a question about his indulgence in some bizarre sexual perversion, mounting male donkeys or making love to schoolgirls dressed as a Roman emperor. These NSA guys are so secretive, Bennington thought, if you ask them what time it is, they'll give you an evasive answer.

"Well," he said, stifling his last cough, "I think I can say our technology does allow us to establish both bursts were from the same transmitter, yes. Each message was also repeated four times."

"And have we picked up other transmissions from this kind of radio in the area?"

Once again, the NSA man went through his agony of coughing and squirming. "Just over a year ago. Also from a lay-by, this one down near the Chesapeake shore."

"The same transmitter?"

"No."

"Must have been an illegal," Mott concluded.

"You're sure this couldn't have been someone from the embassy KGB staff?" asked Bennington.

"No way. The embassy *rezidentura* agents all use embassy transmitters. They know we haven't got a clue on their codes anymore. Illegals always use communications circuits like this one that are entirely independent of the embassy. The Center's whole idea is to keep the two operations completely separate. Absolute, watertight compartmentalization."

Mott clicked his ever-present Tums against the back of his front teeth. His conclusion seemed to give him a pallor that about matched the gray stripes of his seersucker suit.

"I'll tell you one thing—whatever motivated this was important. Only a first-class illegal would have access to state-of-the-art music boxes of theirs like the Spetosk. Second- and third-class guys don't get near the stuff. And they're not going to expose a first-class illegal unless they have one hell of a good reason for it."

The illegal program represented the proudest achievement of the KGB. It was feared and envied by every other intelligence organization in the world. None, with the exception of Israel's Mossad, had come even re-motely close to imitating it, and the Mossad had done it on only a very limited basis. In concept, it went all the way back to the days of the Cheka, the state security service whose descendants spawned the modern KGB. Stalin's paranoid police chiefs set up a second overseas service to parallel their own organization and provide a way of monitoring the allegiance of the Cheka's overseas operatives. They frequently performed the Chekists' bloodier tasks, like murdering the leaders of the White Russian opposition to the Bolsheviks in the Europe of the thirties and forties.

In the 1950s the program was targeted on the United States and set up on a more sophisticated basis. A train-ing academy was established in Bykovo, an industrial city an hour's drive from Moscow. There the KGB set out to create a replica of an American town on Soviet soil. Recruits spent years learning to become perfect little American men and women, and later, Frenchmen or En-glishmen or Latins. They learned how many times the Celtics and the Lakers had won NBA finals and when; they watched videocassettes of endless hours of profes-sional football until they knew the intricacies of the game as well as a graduate of Woody Hayes's Ohio State teams. They could recite the winners of every Super-bowl, the number of home runs Babe Ruth had hit in his career, when Hank Aaron had broken his record. They stared at tapes of American TV programs until they knew how many lovers Alexis Carrington had gone through on *Dynasty,* who wanted to kill J. R. Ewing and why. They learned how to collect green stamps, shop, cook, drive, attend church like Americans.

"Excuse me," said the lieutenant colonel from DIA, "but I'm not up to speed on this illegal program. How many of them are they supposed to have operating in this area?"

"I wish to Christ we knew," Mott answered. "It's one of the things they've managed to keep very, very secret. They have so many ways of communicating with them—a postcard, a whole series of innocuous techniques that don't get them involved in any way with the regular KGB circuits the FBI is watching."

"Yeah," said Pettee, "the in-house KGB types almost never get involved with them. We got two of them a couple of years ago by a lucky break because they broke that rule. Balch, their names were. Lived over on Connecticut Avenue in the same apartment block Alger Hiss used to live in. She was a beautician, he was some sort of vague academic. We were tailing a legal and he pitched a can of Miller Lite out the window, then accelerated like maybe he'd been counting telephone poles and got to seven or something. So the tail car checked out the can. Sure enough it had a little communication device in it. We put it under surveillance and introduced ourselves to Mr. Balch when he came by to pick it up."

"Anyway," Mott continued, "to answer your question, we guess they graduate between twelve and fifteen people a year from Bykovo. Two thirds of them are destined for the States. Some stay two years, some five, a very, very few maybe seven. The Agency's best guess is that there are a minimum of fifty Soviet illegals in the United States at any given time. And a lot of them you can be sure are here in the Washington area."

"Fifty!" snarled the DIA officer. "Fifty Soviet spies sitting here in this country and you guys have no idea who they are and where they are? That's appalling! What the hell are they doing?"

"Fundamentally, not much. That's one of the reasons it's so hard to catch them. Their purpose, as far as we can make out, is to provide an emergency standby intelligence service in case U.S.–USSR diplomatic relations ever blow up and the regular KGB group at the embassy all get thrown out. About all they do otherwise is the odd errand: 'Go see this guy up in Ottawa and tell him so and so.' Or they keep an eye on other illegals to make sure they're behaving. Or once in a while they're used for a tickle."

"A tickle?" the lieutenant colonel said. "What in the hell is that?"

Mott smiled. "About a decade ago we had a Red Army

colonel serving with the Warsaw Pact in East Germany who came walking in off the street. We debriefed him for about three years, then gave him a new suit of clothes— got him a face-lift and a new identity, put him out to pasture working for a furniture company down in South Carolina. One day he gets a call from a guy who supplies fabrics. The guy comes in, chats awhile, and leaves him a box. 'Sample of our work,' he says. 'Let's see if we can't do business together.'

"Our Red Army colonel opens the box after the guy leaves. Inside is the meerschaum pipe he'd left behind on his desk in East Germany the day he walked out to go west. 'Peekaboo. We know where you're hiding.' That's a tickle."

How the Soviet illegals functioned in the United States was, of course, no concern of Bennington's. He had, however, been frequently called on to study the behavioral aspects of the program: how the Soviets selected illegal agents, how they trained them, what psychological vulnerabilities they might have that the CIA and the FBI could attempt to exploit.

"The amazing thing about these illegals," he told the group, "is that they don't defect. Never. Here they are, all alone, living in this fine, free capitalist world we're so proud of. They're on their own. They're subjected to no day-to-day KGB discipline, only intermittent surveillance. They're free to do what they want, think what they want, see what they want. No propaganda restraints on them. They can watch Dan Rather and the CBS Evening News every night. You'd think they'd be lining up in front of the FBI building waiting to defect, wouldn't you? And how many of them have come over?" he asked Mott.

"Two."

"Two," echoed Bennington, "and one of those doesn't even count because he wasn't a Bykovo graduate. He was Abel's radio operator. Got into the high-velocity vodka. They gave him five thousand dollars to put in a tin can in some park up in New York and he figured he knew a better way to use the money. The Center invited him home to talk about it, so he decided to come in and see us on his way to Siberia."

"So what do they do, brainwash them?" the DIA lieutenant colonel asked Bennington. Brainwashing was a subject that hung over Bennington's head in Washington intelligence circles like a halo or an albatross, depending on the viewer's philosophy.

"Every time we run up against some guys from the other side whose behavior doesn't conform to what we would like it to be, we decide they're brainwashed," Bennington replied. "Brainwashing doesn't exist and it never has. The fact is, these illegals are solid Soviet citizens, good bourgeois types. And you know what motivates them? Material reward. Ever hear of that?"

"Not in the U.S. Army." The colonel laughed.

"These guys know they're an elite. When they get back to Moscow, they'll have a big apartment, big cars, a promotion, enough medals to stoop their shoulders when they put them on for May Day."

"I'll bet they're holding a father, a brother, a wife over there hostage to their doing the right thing."

"Don't put money on it. That's another thing we want to believe because it makes it easier to explain why they don't defect. I've never turned up a scrap of evidence to support it."

"What I'd like to know," Pozner asked, "is what is the likelihood that this illegal was involved in the woman's murder?"

"Who the hell knows?" the FBI man said. "All we have is the coincidence of the timing, which isn't very much."

"I don't suppose we have much chance of finding him?"

"On what we have here?" Pettee replied querulously. "None at all. This guy may never come on the air again. And if he does, he will never, never come up on anything like a regular schedule that would let us set a trap for him. Too little"—the FBI man glanced at his NSA colleague—"too late."

Mott turned to Pozner. "Where do you stand on your internal investigation out at Langley?"

"It's finished. Everyone's been polygraphed and come out clean. No documents are missing. All the computer accesses are clean. No red flags anywhere that we could find. Not even any pink ones."

Mott thought that over with a few twists of his Tums, then shifted his gaze to Mike Pettee. "How about your FBI investigation of the woman and her circle up in New York?"

Pettee rested his elbows on the table and leaned into the group like a dinner-table guest getting ready to deliver a morsel of choice gossip. "We've uncovered one possible lead. The New York office went over her client list as carefully as they could. Also friends, associates. We've flagged one of them. A woman she shared an apartment with down in the Village for eighteen months five years ago. The lady's an editor in a small left-wing publishing house."

Pettee paused, obviously savoring the tidbit he was about to deliver to the gathering. "We have a dossier on her twenty pages thick. She was one of those Berkeley Free Speech radicals in the sixties. Those nice girls that used to dump piss out the windows onto the cops and thought it was the cops who were the pigs. She's maintained her radical ties. She's big into the Save the Sandinistas stuff in New York. We've got her under surveillance, and we've asked for a court order to put a wire on her."

"Why not bring her in for questioning?" the DIA lieutenant colonel asked.

"On what grounds? That she thinks Daniel Ortega's a nice guy?"

"Is there any suggestion," Bennington asked, "that Ann Robbins was involved in any of that stuff?"

"No. She checked out clean. But they stayed very good friends. Saw each other all the time. In fact, they had dinner together in the Village two weeks before your lady was murdered. Who's to know? Maybe your lady let slip something about what she was doing for you."

Since he'd arrived in Moscow, Bill Witter had turned his Saturday afternoons into a kind of special preserve set aside for his wife and eleven-year-old son, Joey. It was an arrangement that enjoyed the blessing of his boss, the CIA's Moscow station chief. Nothing except one of Langley's nerve-jangling summonses to action stations, a flash cable, was supposed to disturb the young officer's Saturday-afternoon routine.

Invariably, the family's activities on these weekend holidays revolved around Joey. Like most American kids his age, Joey measured the progress of the seasons not by changes in foliage, flowers, or the weather, but in the shifting dimensions and shapes of the objects which excited his passions: a football, a hockey puck, and a baseball. This spring afternoon marked a signal event, the official opening of the baseball season of the American school in the Lenin Hills which Joey, along with the offspring of most of the Western diplomats and businessmen in the Soviet capital, attended. The first baseman of the sixth-grade Red Sox sat slouched in a living-room chair twisted into a position guaranteed to enhance the curvature of his spine, impatiently waiting for his parents to finish their preparations. A brooding intensity that would have done honor to one of his idols in the Fenway Park locker room on opening day marked his eleven-year-old features.

Bill and his wife, Ginny, had selected their wardrobes for their afternoon outing with particular care. They were wearing what were known in CIA jargon as "tracksuits," in Bill's case a gabardine jacket and in Ginny's a beige overcoat from Washington's Woodward & Lothrop. Both were reversible. Each had been slightly modified so that when they were carefully buttoned up, no hint could be seen of the starkly different color and pattern of the garment's interior.

Like Witter's lunchtime jogs, their outing this afternoon was not entirely innocent. The first concern of a new officer in the Moscow Station was to build up a well-defined and clearly observable routine. The purpose, of course, was to lull the minders of the KGB assigned to monitor his movements into a false sense of security about his daily routine so as to make it easier to slip their surveillance on those few occasions that mattered. Every CIA recruit had drummed into him the story of the KGB agent under diplomatic cover in London who marched out of the embassy at the same time every day for sixty-seven days to buy his London *Times* at the same news agent, returning by the same route to the embassy. Nothing, his MI5 shadows reported, ever varied in his routine until the sixty-eighth day, when he escaped his watcher's routine-dulled eyes for just seven minutes, the seven-minute interlude for which he'd been preparing for two months. Upon such patient maneuverings was the practice of intelligence built.

No place in Moscow provided a better vantage point from which to view the city than the Lenin Hills, where the American School was situated. Indeed, old Bolsheviks liked to point out that it was from these heights, then known by the more pastoral name Sparrow Hill, that their artillery had sent the first shells whistling toward the distant onion bulbs of Kremlin Square in 1917.

The school and its playing fields were sprawled over a dozen acres just below the crest of the hills, surrounded by a wooded park laced with pleasant walks and byways. Well over a hundred parents and their children were already wandering around the campus, talking, picnicking, socializing, encouraging their sons and daughters as they warmed up for the day's activities. The Witters mingled in with the crowd, then split up, moving from group to group, chatting as they went. Just before three, each went separately to the main building to use the toilet. They emerged with their "tracksuits" reversed.

Behind the main building, adjacent to one of the playing fields, a storage shed screened from a viewer on the heights above the school the entrance to a path disappearing into a nearby wood. At five minutes past three, Witter slid behind the shed and down the path. Two minutes later his wife followed. The path brought the Witters out of the woods onto a street paralleling Leninskiy Prospekt. They circled along the flank of the Lenin Hills up to the Druzhba—"Friendship"—Hotel, then, mingling with the Saturday crowds, they entered the Moscow subway at the Vernadskoyoii station.

Their destination was Arbat Street, back in the heart of the city. Of the six sites Witter employed for his brush passes with the colonel, this was the one in which he felt the most comfortable and secure. Arbat Street, he liked to joke, was the world's first socialist pedestrian shopping mall. Before the Revolution, it had been one of the favorite residential areas of the city's aristocracy. Their Empire-style mansions in pastel shades of lavender, lime green, and pale blue still lined the street, miraculous survivors of Stalin's determination to bulldoze away the remnants of Moscow's bourgeois past.

On weekends, the throngs offered Witter and the colonel the welcome mantle of a city crowd in which to lose themselves. With its shops and colorful facades, Arbat Street was also a major tourist attraction, so one more middle-aged American couple drifting hand in hand through the crowds hardly stood out. Indeed, it was on the Arbat that Ronald Reagan had chosen to mingle with the citizenry of Moscow during the 1988 summit.

The Witters entered the street at exactly three-fifty. For ten minutes they strolled along from shop to shop, talking animatedly, nudging each other with the happy complicity of a couple on a Saturday-afternoon shopping expedition deciding how to spend their ration of mad money. They were, in fact, under observation all the way down the Arbat, not by the KGB but by another CIA agent. His job was to scour the street behind the Witters trying to pick up any hint that they were under KGB surveillance: a stretched neck peering over the crowd to a figure several yards ahead, a furtive hand signal from one watcher to another. At the corner of Starokonyushennyy Per Eulok, "Old Stable Lane," the agent, who had leapfrogged ahead of the Witters, paused to glance at a state-run furrier's shop, then went inside.

Seeing him enter the shop, Witter's stomach tightened

with nervous anticipation. That was the signal he was clean. His minders were still out in the Lenin Hills pacing the heights above the American School. Had the other agent drifted up the street instead of entering the store, it would have indicated to Witter that he was being followed and he would have to abort his brush pass with the colonel.

It was now up to Witter to set into motion the carefully choreographed series of movements leading to the pass. Their purpose was to provide maximum security for the two men during that one dangerous second when they would actually be in physical contact. The first thing Witter and his wife did was to enter a shop that sold hand-embroidered napkins, tablecloths, and doilies at the corner of Silver Lane. With her discerning eye, Ginny picked out half a dozen linen napkins trimmed with a garland of hand-stitched roses.

Never move without your cover story firmly in hand was an agent's first operating principle. Now the Witters had in their brown paper bag, ready for inspection, a concrete physical explanation of what they were doing on the Arbat at this particular time on this spring afternoon.

As they left the store to continue down the Arbat, Witter saw the colonel some twenty yards ahead and to his left. He was in uniform, usual for officers of the Moscow Military Headquarters staff. Indeed, to be out of uniform would be grounds for suspicion, and uniformed men in any event made up a substantial segment of any Moscow street crowd.

Witter did not, of course, even glance at the colonel. His first function was to provide the Russian with the same service his fellow agent had just provided him: to scrub his tail, to be sure the colonel was not under surveillance. Once Witter felt sure the colonel was not being followed, he and his wife directed their steps toward a pushcart where a babushka, an elderly woman with a shawl framing a face that looked as if it had been carved out of an ancient oak tree, sold *morozhenoye,* the ice cream which Muscovites swore was unrivaled anywhere in the world. Their purchase of two cups of vanilla told the colonel the pass was on.

The agent most likely to be under surveillance—in this case Witter—initiated the pass by turning a street corner. The second agent had to be moving toward the corner, no more than a dozen feet from the intersection, at the moment the first agent made his turn. And he had to be caught up in a crowd.

This way, if the first agent really was being followed, his tail could not possibly get around the corner fast enough to see the pass. The tail would have had to have been following his quarry so closely he would have given his presence away. Witter had indicated to the colonel the street corner on which he would make his turn by shifting the bag with his newly purchased napkins from his right to his left hand while he walked past the corner on his way to the ice cream cart. It was Kalashnyi Per Eulok, "Biscuit Lane," which was always thronged on Saturdays.

As he made his turn, Ginny hugged the wall. He was right beside her, holding her hand, talking with particular animation, his gaze ostensibly fixed on her. In fact, in a quick glance he saw two things: the street was blessedly full of people and the colonel was ten feet away, peering into a shop window. He moved up toward the intersection as Witter walked toward him. As they advanced on each other, Witter kept his eyes focused on his wife, chatting with all the energy he could muster. Two feet from the colonel, he let his left hand trail by his side, its open palm resting just behind and inside his trouser seam. The two men's eyes never met. At the instant they passed, Witter felt the cold metal outline of a tube being pressed into his palm. Microfilm. For that gesture, the colonel had just risked his life.

Every CIA agent's nightmare was filled with images of little cans like this one, somewhat similar to those in which 35mm film is fitted, bouncing noisily along the sidewalk at an agent's feet after a bungled pass. Witter clutched his can as tightly as he had once clutched the first silver dollar the tooth fairy had slipped under his pillow.

After a leisurely stroll back up the Arbat, Witter and his wife returned to the embassy. He went immediately to the vault to lock away the colonel's precious roll of film. The immense relief he felt on returning to his flat was coupled with the soaring sense of elation the successful accomplishment of a brush pass in Moscow always brought him. He had just poured double scotches for his wife and himself when he heard someone pounding on the front door of his apartment. He froze. Ginny rushed to open it.

"Jeez!" shouted the angry first baseman of the sixth-grade Red Sox. "What happened to you guys? You missed everything. We won thirty-two to twenty-seven."

The black Zil limousine of the chairman of the KGB flashed through the darkened midnight streets of Moscow toward Dzerzhinsky Square. Even on a Saturday night, the Soviet capital was a strangely somber and lifeless place. No blinking signs, no gaudy pinwheels of neon light urged Muscovites into a bar, a nightclub, a restaurant, a disco. The capital's major nightspots were in hotels, most of them the domain of foreign tourists or those few Russians privileged enough to pay for an evening out in foreign currency. The rare private restaurants opened as a part of Mikhail Gorbachev's *perestroika* were inevitably packed, but they were so few in number their presence had had little impact on the capital's nightlife. Bars were masculine domains, depressing, dark, and devoted to a joylessly intense consumption of alcohol.

As they had for generations, Russians still chose to spend their evenings at home surrounded by a select and trusted circle of friends. They would gather around a table filling a tiny living room, its fully extended leaves covered with bottles of vodka, tomatoes, cucumbers, bits of sturgeon, pickled cabbage, black bread, all the snacks Russians love. In such an environment, Feodorov's countrymen came alive. All the warmth and gregariousness for which they were so famous would spill out, enriching their gatherings with a humanity made all the more meaningful by the drabness of their surroundings.

From just such a joyous evening at his lodge in Zavidovo, the forest preserve of the Soviet ruling elite, had Feodorov been summoned by a call from the colonel who presided over the Moscow Regional Security Directorate. The reason for this urgent summons had better be a good one, Feodorov reflected, as his Zil glided into the underground parking area at KGB headquarters.

A KGB guard in a khaki uniform emerged from the shadows as the limousine came to a stop in front of a square of light marking the door to the elevator linking Feodorov's office to the garage.

The Moscow security director was waiting for Feodorov in his anteroom. Standing beside him was a younger man in work clothes the KGB chairman did not recognize. "Follow me," Feodorov ordered as he swept past the two men into his inner office. He threw his overcoat into an armchair, then sat down at his desk. He left his two subordinates standing. It was his way of reminding them one did not lightly disturb the chairman's Saturday evenings.

"Ivan Sergeivich," the colonel said, "this young man is from our U.S. embassy surveillance section. He and two of his colleagues are assigned to an officer of the CIA at the embassy under diplomatic cover. Here is the man's file."

The colonel placed a folder on Feodorov's desk. Its pale blue-gray cover embossed with the seal of the KGB and the words *Tsentralnaya Registovka—Sovershenno Sekretno* ("Central Registry—Completely Secret") indicated it came from the treasure trove of Feodorov's organization, a huge central registry in which were kept the files of over fifteen million people. To begin with, every man or woman who had joined a Communist Party anywhere in the world since 1925 had a file there. So, too, did anyone who had ever applied for a visa to the Soviet Union, people who had belonged to Communist front organizations, businessmen, intellectuals, technicians, scientists who had for one reason or another caught the KGB's eye. Its core was a section devoted to each of the world's intelligence agencies in which a file was kept on all identified members of the agency in question and on anyone suspected of belonging to it.

Feodorov opened it. "Witter" was the name inside. "William W." There was a photo of Witter taken ten years earlier talking to a Syrian air force officer at a reception at the Algerian embassy in Damascus, a photo of Witter walking down Spring Meadow Road in Germantown, Maryland, en route to a game of tennis, a three-month-old photograph of the young CIA officer jogging in Gorky Park. The KGB chairman moved quickly through the file to its last notation: "Potential for Recruitment—None" was the entry written there. He looked at the colonel. "So?" he said.

The colonel turned to his young subordinate. "Tell him your story," he ordered.

The young officer flushed, clutched his hands behind his back, and began. "Sir, our target goes every Saturday with his child to the American School in the Lenin Hills. Since it's very difficult to watch him there, we have wondered if he might not use his visits as a way to escape our surveillance."

He paused to slow the nervous torrent of his words. "This afternoon we decided to break up our team to give us a wider coverage of the area. I took the street adjacent to Leninskiy Prospekt. At three-fifteen, I saw the target and his wife coming out of a clump of woods. They had both reversed their coats."

"Ah." Feodorov smiled. "Clearly an effort to avoid your careful surveillance."

"Sir." The young officer stiffened. "I followed him back downtown to the Arbat."

"Did you call for help?" Feodorov cut in.

The question clearly upset the officer. He reddened and began to stammer. "Yes—no, sir. My transmitter failed to work."

"Didn't you verify it before you left the garage?"

"Yes, sir."

What else would he say, Feodorov wondered. He stared at the colonel. "Investigate that. Continue," he ordered the young officer.

"He began a series of procedures which convinced me he was preparing to meet an agent."

"Surely," Feodorov replied, "you didn't think he'd gone to all that trouble to buy a copy of *Izvestia?*"

"No, sir. He turned into Biscuit Lane quite abruptly, next to the wall, as the CIA teaches its agents to do in a brush pass."

"How far were you behind him?"

"About twenty-five feet, so that if the CIA had a second agent in the street he would have had trouble spotting me."

"Therefore you obviously saw no sign of a pass?"

"No, sir. But I did notice passing in the crowd coming out of Biscuit Lane an officer carrying a briefcase in his right hand."

"Did you get a look at him?"

"No, sir. But I saw he was a colonel and he had the scarlet shoulder braid of a member of the Moscow Military Headquarters staff."

"You didn't go after him?"

"Sir, my assignment was to stay with my CIA officer. He returned to the embassy very quickly after that."

Feodorov got up and walked to his window overlooking Dzerzhinsky Square. Clearly, if the CIA man had gone to the trouble he had, it was to cover a pass. His target could have been anyone in the crowd. The presence of the officer could have been purest coincidence. Still, a CIA penetration of Moscow Military Headquarters would be a matter of gravest consequence.

"How many colonels do you suppose they have attached to that headquarters staff?" he asked his Moscow security director.

"I've checked, Ivan Sergeivich. Thirty-seven."

Feodorov glanced back into the empty square. If he was wrong, the Americans, of course, would expel one of his men in Washington in retaliation for his action. Nonetheless, it was a price that would have to be paid.

"I want a recent and good photograph of every one of those colonels on my desk by eight Monday morning," he ordered.

The brain conceals its infinitely complex nature under a cloak of drabness. Set on a dissecting table, it is a dull, lifeless-looking object, as uninspiring to the eye as a slab of lard. Nothing in the brain's appearance even hints at the wondrous capacities that organ possesses, at its abilities to marshal the processes of thought, of speech, of sight, of movement, of feeling, of life itself. It is three and a half pounds of compact matter, pinkish white when living, grayish yellow when dead.

Colonel Dr. Xenia Petrovna examined a row of human brains preserved in aminol in transparent plastic cubes stacked like boxes of laundry detergent on her laboratory shelf. They were dispatched regularly to her institute from mortuaries all across central Russia. All had been the brains of healthy men and women who'd died in their twenties and thirties. Her well-trained eye selected the brain whose color indicated it had spent the least amount of time on her shelf. She set the box on her examining table. Then she turned to the group of four male scientists she'd selected from her institute's staff to join her select work team. There was a neurophysiologist who specialized in aggressive behavior, a chemist, a computer engineer, and an electrical engineer.

"Gentlemen," she said as she stood gazing down on the brain before her like the high priestess of some ancient sect contemplating the entrails of a freshly sacrificed victim, "our task is urgent. It has been assigned to us by the highest authority. It is a matter of grave national concern. We must find a way to induce a pattern of aggressive behavior in an individual from a distance without his being aware of what is happening."

"Colonel Doctor," asked the neurophysiologist, "will we be authorized to experiment on our *zeki*"—*zek* was the term used for a prisoner-inmate of the institute—"as part of our work?"

"Yes. With the usual Ministry of Interior approval, of course, but yes."

Xenia Petrovna stretched a pair of elbow-length rubber gloves over her long fingers, took the brain from its plastic container, and set it on the examining table before her. She picked up a long thin knife, the kind employed to slice lettuce, from the table and placed its blade along the line demarcating the brain's two hemispheres. With a strong, swift thrust she sliced into the corpus callosum, splitting the brain in half as though she was splitting apart a ball of mozzarella cheese.

"Now," she began, "we know extremely low frequency electromagnetic fields affect the neurons, the cells of the brain. Since they do, it would seem highly likely that they can be employed to affect human behavior."

The cold, challenging way her green eyes swept the men seated before her around the laboratory table was not designed to encourage questions.

"For those of you who aren't neurophysiologists," she continued, looking at her two engineers, "let me review what we know of the aggressive reaction. First, it is the result of a series of chemicals—noradrenaline and peptides among others—being flushed into your bloodstream on the order of a group of neurons in your brain. And others, like serotonin, being simultaneously suppressed. This doesn't mean you can equate an emotion such as aggression to a chemical formula. But it does mean you can't have the sensation of anger, of rage, without an electrochemical event having first taken place in your brain."

She laid down her knife and took up a wooden stick that looked like the tongue depressor a doctor employs to check a pair of sore tonsils. It was the neurologist's standard working tool.

"We know from our work with electrodes implanted in the brain that this critical order to send those chemicals into your bloodstream comes in the form of a synchronized electrical discharge given off by a group of neurons in an organ called the amygdala. We know that because we have produced the rage reaction in patients here by implanting electrodes in a well-defined area of the amygdala and then inducing a small electric shock.''

"What exactly happens?" the computer engineer asked.

Xenia Petrovna laughed. "They try to leap out of their chair and rip you to pieces. It's a sham rage in the sense that that little electric spark replaced the visual or the auditory stimuli that usually set their rages off. But the result is real enough, believe me.''

She turned back to her neatly severed brain. "This is the amygdala right here." Her wooden instrument indicated a rust-colored organ at the base of the brain. "Every human has two, one for each brain hemisphere. They're shaped roughly like almonds. 'Amygdala,' in fact, means 'almond' in Greek. The whiter area around it"—her wooden stick swept over the clear surface enfolding the amygdala—"is the temporal lobe, the seat of most of our emotions and behavior. The grayish area on top of it is the cerebral cortex. It is, in a sense, the bank where memories are stored. Also the learning patterns, the behavioral responses an individual has developed as a result of the experience those memories represent. How do we know this? Thanks to a Canadian named Penfield. He placed electrodes into these areas during surgery and produced in his patients remarkably detailed memories of events the patients had forgotten completely.

"These track systems"—her stick traced its way along a spiderweb series of lines that resembled dried-out riverbeds in a desert seen from a high-flying plane—"carry information back and forth between the organs of the temporal lobe and the memory storage bank of the cortex. Memory, information, the responses we've been patterned to make to specific stimuli such as a bar of music, a threatening figure, a sexually arousing sight—all these things are stored in the cortex and can only be accessed by a code.

"It seems clear that these codes, which are specific to each human being on earth and are exceedingly complex, are relayed into and out of the cerebral cortices by another organ in the temporal lobe, the hippocampus, right here.'' Her stick paused at a light surface barely visible adjacent to the amygdala. Some early neurologist had decided it looked like a horse's foreleg joined to a dolphin's tail; hence its name. "In a sense, the hippocampus acts like the card index in a huge library; the information stored here in the cerebral cortices are the books themselves. With the index, you can find the book you're looking for almost instantly. Without it, you're hopelessly lost."

Xenia Petrovna offered her four subordinates a chilly smile. "A rage response begins with an outside stimulus which is interpreted as threatening by your brain. A signal flashes to the amygdala here''—her wooden stick jabbed at the organ she'd pointed out earlier—"and a massive neuronal discharge takes place in a group of neurons in the amygdala that are associated with the rage response. And our friend here''—she glanced laughing at the severed brain on her examination table—"flies into a rage."

Xenia Petrovna laid down her wooden stick and straightened up. For a second or two she was silent, fixing her green eyes on the four men before her. "The key to our hopes lies in that signal."

She paused again, crossing her arms on her chest, adding with that gesture to her already commanding presence. The timbre of her voice dropped to underline the importance of her words. "The signal is the trigger on which any individual's anger, his rage response, depends. If we can find that signal for a man, if we can unlock the combination of its electromagnetic code, then we can send him into a rage at our command. A part of his being, an essential part of it, will belong to us."

She leaned forward, her arms resting now on the examining table, and stared a second at the four men seated before her.

"We must unlock the secret of that signal, gentlemen. How do we do it?"

The course was Bill Witter's favorite jog in Moscow. It led along a bulblike bump of the embankment of the Moscow River, from the Krasnoluzhskiy Bridge past the Sports Palace and Lenin Stadium to the Andreyevskiy Bridge and back, just over six kilometers in all. It was a glorious day, unseasonably warm for Moscow, with tufts of high-flying clouds racing each other across the sky's blue canopy. Listening to a tape of Maria Callas on his Walkman, Witter felt marvelously at ease with the world. In fact, so pleased was he with himself, the day, the run, that for a moment he contemplated doing the course a second time.

Finally, he eased to a stop by the crenellated brick wall of the New Convent of the Virgin, where Boris Godunov had been proclaimed Czar of All Russia in 1598, and walked with a tapering stride back to his car in the visitors' parking lot. He opened the door of his Honda and had just tossed his Walkman onto the front seat when he felt a tap on his shoulder.

"Excuse me," said a soft voice in accented English.

Witter turned and found himself facing two men, one of whom was training the dark snout of a 9mm Makarov, the standard-issue service pistol of the KGB, at his stomach.

The second man flipped open a black plastic folder revealing an official identity card. "KGB. I don't think I need to explain who we are to an officer of the CIA, do I?"

The man smiled in evident satisfaction at his witticism, which, Witter suspected, he'd been rehearsing as he waited for Witter to return from his jog. He had a gold front tooth and a breath so vile Witter wondered if he knew what a toothbrush was. "You are under arrest."

He had hardly needed to add that phrase. Witter had understood what was happening the instant he saw the Makarov. Strangely, his first reaction had been one of almost overwhelming relief. The KGB had arrested him after the wrong jog. This morning's run had been completely innocent. He had nothing, thank God, to conceal or destroy.

"I am an officer of the United States embassy accredited to the Soviet government and protected by the 1961 Vienna Convention on Diplomatic Privileges and Immunities," Witter declared.

"You say that nicely," Gold Tooth answered approvingly. "We are, of course, aware of that. Come with us, please."

"I demand the presence of a counsel of the United States embassy."

"Please." The man with the gun moved behind Witter and pressed its snout into his kidney with a firmness that was not to be misunderstood. Resistance, Witter knew, was both futile and stupid at a moment such as this. He was caught and that was that. There were rules to this silent ballet danced out between the CIA and the KGB, unwritten rules but rules respected nonetheless by each side. They shadowboxed, danced, and sparred around their global ring, but they did not set out to kill or maim each other. When that happened to a KGB or a CIA agent, it was almost invariably the work of a renegade, a Georgian dissident, Shiite Moslem rebels, a handful of Uruguayan urban terrorists.

A difficult period was ahead of him, Witter knew, hours of intense interrogation, privation, sleeplessness. Ultimately, he would be publicly denounced and expelled. But he would not be physically abused or tortured. That was against the rules. Unfortunately, he realized, his career as a CIA operative overseas was over for all practical purposes. He would now be condemned to twenty years riding a desk at Langley. It was not to do that that he had joined the CIA.

The two KGB men guided him to a black Volga. Another pair of KGB officers were in the front seat smoking. Witter was put in the backseat between the two men who'd arrested him. As soon as the car door slammed shut, Gold Tooth cuffed him. "Go," he ordered the driver.

Witter leaned back against the seat as far as he could

and tried to relax. Name, rank, and serial number, he told himself, that's all the bastards will get from me.

The car set off down Pirogovskaya Ulitza, moving along the green lane at a leisurely pace. Wherever they were going, they were in no hurry to get there. Are they taking me to a cell at the Lubyanka? Witter wondered. Or out to the new KGB headquarters? Or Lefortovo?

Just before they reached Zubovskaya Square, the officer beside the driver turned around and tossed something on Gold Tooth's lap. It was a blindfold.

"Please," Gold Tooth remarked as he stretched its black padded folds bound to two tight elastic bands over Witter's head, then checked its placement with his fingers. As he finished, Witter felt the car lurch to the right and begin to accelerate. Oh my god, he thought, something's gone very, very wrong. This isn't the way these things are supposed to go at all.

The first of the four men to react to the imperious challenge handed down by Xenia Petrovna was the neurophysiologist, Dr. Aleksandr Borisovich Chuyev. "My dear Xenia Petrovna," he said, his age permitting him a familiarity his colleagues did not enjoy, "we have *zeki* here in the institute, I presume, who are compulsively aggressive personalities, the kind who will fly into a rage at the slightest provocation."

"More," the colonel doctor replied, "than we need. I would say we have at least fifty people, mostly men here, who suffer from that disorder."

"And you know what stimuli will trigger their rage?"

"Very often." The colonel doctor tossed up one of her icy laughs. "We have one who'll fly off the handle if we show him a photo of his mother-in-law."

"Very good. Very good." Aleksandr Borisovich nodded his head with the enthusiasm of a youngster contemplating a second helping of dessert. He was a cherubic, round little fellow with wisps of white hair that looked like puffs of smoke protruding from both sides of his otherwise bald skull. "I, of course, adored my late mother-in-law. It was her daughter who troubled me. However—'' He waved a chubby paw. ''Your magnificent new magnetoencephalograph, the one with the two hundred and sixty-five sensor points you demonstrated recently for the chairman . . .'' He offered Xenia Petrovna the pleased little smirk of a child who's just discovered one of his mother's most closely held secrets.

''What about it?''

''Can you focus into the amygdala of one of these *zeki* of ours with it and follow the electromagnetic signals it's giving off while he's going into a rage response? While he's working himself into a state contemplating a photo of that lovely mother-in-law of his?''

''Certainly.'' Xenia Petrovna erupted with another of her icy laughs. ''Of course, we'd have to bolt him into the chair to keep him there once he saw the photo.''

''But the result would give you a profile of every electromagnetic signal in the area of his amygdala from the time he was resting peacefully until the moment he was in a full-blown state of rage, would it not?''

''Of course.'' Her tolerant schoolteacher's look now glazed Xenia Petrovna's features. ''But what you don't understand, dear Aleksandr Borisovich, is that we will have thousands of signals recorded on his magnetoencephalogram during that period. How would we know which is the one we're after?''

''Still, one of them would be this magic triggering signal we are looking for, would it not?''

''Certainly.''

''Let me suggest a possible way to pick that signal out. You are one of our outstanding brain surgeons, are you not?''

Xenia Petrovna gave a puzzled nod.

''And like all of us, this gentleman is gifted with two, not one, of those little almond-shaped amygdalas.''

''Of course.''

''Could you remove one of them surgically?''

''Yes. We do that very occasionally. As a last resort for someone suffering from epilepsy that drugs can't treat. Usually we remove both the hippocampus and the amygdala from the temporal lobe.''

"Ah well." The doctor sighed. "In this case our *zek* will have to sacrifice only one of his amygdalas, and for reasons of state rather than reasons of health." The little neurophysiologist now turned his cheerful smile to their colleague the chemist. "How long would our friend's organ remain vital, reactive, outside the brain, do you suppose?''

"Twelve hours at least. More, probably, if it was handled properly.''

"A long time. A very long time indeed. Now." This time the doctor directed his attention to the electrical engineer. "Suppose we have the amygdala Xenia Petrovna has removed from our *zek* to work with? We bombard it with a series of signals. One of them happens to be this magic trigger we're after. Those neurons in our *zek*'s amygdala produce their discharge to indicate a rage response should be under way. Do you have instruments that could detect it?''

"Yes. Certainly. I would first focus a laser, a very sensitive laser, on the organ. I would also cover it with highly sensitive electromagnetic sensors," the electrical engineer said.

"And they could tell you exactly when those cells, those neurons in there, were producing the discharge we associate with the rage reaction?''

"Without a doubt.''

"How fortunate, how fortunate." Aleksandr Borisovich was positively alight with self-satisfaction. "And you, my friend." His regard was now trained on the computer engineer. "You, of course, could do a Fast Fourier Transform on those thousands of electromagnetic signals our magnetoencephalograph recorded when our friend gazed on his beloved mother-in-law? Break them down into specific frequencies, amplitudes, and so forth. That would reduce the number of signals we'd have to work with, would it not?''

"Yes.''

"With that information, you could then program one

of your computers to order an electromagnetic generator to aim, one by one, each of those frequencies at this amygdala the colonel doctor has removed from our *zek*. Say one every second."

"Yes. Perhaps not quite that fast."

"Still, in twelve hours we could subject the amygdala to close to twenty thousand different frequency combinations, could we not?"

"Yes."

Aleksandr Borisovich's attention returned to the electrical engineer. "And if one of them was this magical signal we were looking for, your laser beam and your sensors would tell us instantly that we had found it, would they not?"

"It's a brilliant idea," Xenia Petrovna cried out before the electrical engineer had even answered. "And it may well work."

Aleksandr Borisovich beamed with the delight of a child who's just been singled out for special praise by his teacher. "And once we think we have our signal, we can train it on our *zek* while he's in his hospital bed reading *Pravda* recovering from your surgery. If he goes into a rage we will know we stimulated his remaining amygdala. That will confirm the fact we have the right signal."

Xenia Petrovna walked around her examining table to Aleksandr Borisovich's seat. Like Snow White bestowing an award on one of her dwarfs, she bent down and kissed the doctor's bald head. "Brilliant, dear friend, brilliant."

Aleksandr Borisovich leaned back in his chair, basking in the warmth of her gesture. "What, by the way, will be the consequences to our *zek* of the loss of his amygdala?"

"Ah." Xenia Petrovna was already marching back to her place at the head of the table. "That will not be a problem. Assuming the surgery is done properly and we don't touch the language areas of the cortex, he will survive quite nicely."

She hesitated a moment, thinking. "We will certainly flatten out his personality. He won't have quite so much trouble containing his rages in the future. Occasionally, in the procedure, we see a need for oral stimulation, a need to suck on things, chew pencils. A lot of lip smacking.''

Her hand went down to her wooden stick, and she poked at the amygdala in the brain before her as though she were already refreshing herself on the surgical techniques its removal required. ''Sometimes these people become hypersexual. They tend to do a lot of masturbating.'' A faintly sadistic smile played on the edge of her sensual lips. ''That should have a suitably calming effect on our *zek,* should it not?''

She was interrupted by a knock on the laboratory door. ''Colonel Doctor,'' one of her aides said, ''the Center just called. They're on the way.''

A black KGB Volga, the same vehicle that had swept him from the New Convent of the Virgin at midday, delivered Bill Witter to the main gate of the U.S. embassy on Chaykovskii Street shortly after ten in the evening. At almost the same moment, the U.S. ambassador was being received by the foreign minister at the Ministry of Foreign Affairs, a massive Stalin-era tower around the corner from the Arbat where Witter had made his brush pass with the colonel.

The minister handed the ambassador a one-paragraph memorandum. It ordered Witter expelled from the USSR on the following morning's Pan Am flight to New York on the grounds that he had engaged in activities inimical to the national security interests of the USSR and was an agent of the CIA. The ambassador made a ritual protest, as the protocol of the situation required, and withdrew. He was a career foreign service officer who had little regard for the CIA and consequently viewed the affair with considerable distaste.

Colonel Viktor Sbirunov had been arrested shortly after four that afternoon as he prepared to leave the Military Secretariat of the Central Committee inside the walls of the Kremlin. At the sight of the four plainclothes officers of the KGB entering his office, Sbirunov went pale. He said nothing to the arresting officers, merely nodding to express his acceptance of their announcement that he was under arrest.

Sbirunov was taken to the old Chekist basement cells in the cellar of the Dzerzhinsky Square KGB headquarters, the famous Lubyanka, whose accommodations were now reserved for prisoners of rank and distinction. He was stripped and handed over to a team of KGB interrogators.

Some six hours later, as Witter was finishing packing for his early-morning departure, Sbirunov broke down and confessed his guilt. For the next several hours he provided his captors a full account of his recruitment by the CIA, of how he carried out his activities as a spy, and the details—insofar as he could remember them—of all the information he had passed to his American controllers. When he had finished, he was allowed to dress and given a meal. Around noon the next day, three officers of the Military Justice Division of the Red Army arrived in his cell. In view of his confession, the ensuing court-martial was simply a formality.

An hour later, a fourth officer, a colonel, appeared in Sbirunov's cell. "Citizen Sbirunov, Viktor Petrovich," he said, "I am authorized to declare to you by order of the Presidium of the Supreme Soviet of the USSR that as a consequence of your conviction of the crime of espionage by a military tribunal of the Red Army, you have been stripped of your rank and decorations and ordered to forfeit all pending pay and allowances." The colonel paused to catch his breath. "I am further to declare to you that you have been sentenced to death as a traitor to the USSR by the military tribunal. Your death sentence has been reviewed and confirmed by the Presidium."

The sentence was carried out shortly after six o'clock in the cellars of the Lubyanka. On the personal order of Ivan Sergeivich Feodorov, Sbirunov was executed in the old Chekist fashion. He was made to kneel with his back to his captors. His hands were then tied behind his back and he was killed with one round of a 9mm Makarov fired into the base of his skull.

A one-sentence bulletin released by TASS announced his conviction on the charge of "espionage for a foreign power."

At his midday briefing, the State Department spokesman vigorously protested Witter's expulsion and labeled the charges against him "baseless." A spokeswoman for the CIA informed callers that in keeping with long-standing Agency policy, the CIA would make no comment whatsoever on Moscow's charges.

Witter was met in the customs clearing area of John F. Kennedy Airport by two officers of the CIA's New York station when Pan Am's Flight 65 arrived at half past three that afternoon. In order to avoid the press, they took him out through a special customs channel to a waiting Agency car for the brief ride to the Marine Air Terminal, where a CIA plane was waiting to fly him to Dulles Airport in Washington. As they got into the car, one of his escort officers passed him a copy of the *New York Post*. The story of Sbirunov's execution was on page three.

Witter dropped the paper on the floor. For an instant, he felt a terrible need to retch. His face, suddenly pale, focused first on one, then the other escort.

"But I didn't tell them a thing," he protested. "I swear to Christ. I told them nothing, absolutely nothing."

The first escort shrugged. "Sure," he said.

The second said nothing.

Shortly after noon the following day, a middle-aged man appeared at the offices of the Discount Bank on Geneva's Quai de l'Ile. He bore a document signed by the holder of account C97164 instructing the bank to transfer to the bearer of the note the full amount in the account in the form of a certified banker's check.

As is always the case with numbered Swiss bank accounts, the name of the holder of the account appeared nowhere on the document. Instead, he had written out the letter and numbers of his account by hand on his transfer order.

An officer of the bank carefully checked the handwriting of the numbers on the transfer order against the handwriting of the same numbers by the account holder on file in the bank's archives. The match proved perfect, and a check was drawn up for the full amount in account C97164 that spring month. It came to $3,727,104.62. A few hours later, that sum was on deposit in the Voslov Bank, the official overseas bank of the treasury of the USSR, in Zurich.

The operating theater of Xenia Petrovna's Institute for the Study of Human Neurophysiology was one of the most modern in the USSR, a temple devoted to brain surgery in its most sophisticated forms. Recessed halogen lighting bathed the theater in cool but intense light. The narrow operating table could be inclined or tilted to any angle the surgeon desired with the touch of a pedal. Behind the head of the table was a bank of a dozen TV monitors. Those screens would provide an ongoing monitoring of a whole series of vital signs of the patient during the forthcoming operation, his electrocardiogram, his respiration rate, cardiac output, temperature. Three key screens at the center of the display would provide a constant computer-enhanced portrait of the interior of the brain seen from three angles, top, bottom, and side.

On them, Xenia Petrovna would be able to follow in stunning full-color detail each forward movement of her scalpel. The scalpel she would employ bore about as much resemblance to the traditional surgeon's scalpel as a hay wain does to a jet fighter. Entirely machine-run, it was a scaler diminished automated scalpel which reduced the surgeon's human gesture to the millimeter or less the delicate art of brain surgery demanded.

The colonel doctor, already dressed in her sterile greens, studied the operating theater and her assistants with the intensity of a ship's captain inspecting his radar room, her eyes alert to any deviation from the high standards she demanded in her subordinates.

"All right," she announced, satisfied with the results of her study, "wheel in the patient."

The patient was the man from Kiev who'd killed four people in a drunken rampage. He was the *zek* Xenia Petrovna had employed to demonstrate the magnetoencephalograph. A pair of male nurses transferred him from his stretcher onto the table. His arms and legs were strapped firmly to its supports so that no convulsive movement could jar the delicate procedure.

His eyelids blinked open and he stared up at Xenia Petrovna, his eyes wide with terror and pleading. How strange, she thought, this man who could murder four people in cold blood, without so much as a thought for them, and now on her operating table he'd been turned into a frightened little animal.

"What are you going to do to me?" he whispered.

She offered a faint and fleeting smile. "Improve your disposition," she said. "Make you a little easier to live with."

She motioned to her assistants to remove the green sterile towel covering his head and leaned down to inspect the surface of his skull. Marked on it in red dye were the entry points at which she would make her initial incisions.

"Attach the monitoring leads," she ordered. Her assistants began to fix the leads of the wires that would monitor his signs to different parts of his body, strapping each of them into place with a suction device dipped in electrolyte paste that facilitated the transmission of the body's electric currents to the reading devices.

While her assistants finished their work, Xenia Petrovna strode into a laboratory adjacent to the theater where another team waited to receive the Kiev killer's amygdala. Again, she surveyed the lab and her aides with a rigorous eye for the slightest error. Aleksandr Borisovich, her chief neurophysiologist, was there together with the chemist, the electrical engineer, the computer expert, and three lab assistants.

"Everything in order?"

"Yes, Colonel Doctor," the electrical engineer replied. He indicated a clear plastic vessel on the laboratory's table.

"Once the amygdala has been set into this receptacle, we'll train a high-density, high-focus laser onto the area where the neurons associated with the rage discharge are located. At the same time, we will be covering the area with an etched silicon multichannel array to detect the slightest variation in its electromagnetic field."

"You're certain this instrumentation is sensitive enough to make the readings we need?"

"Colonel Doctor, there are a billion neurons in a cubic centimeter of the brain, thousands in a millimeter. One neuron firing may not produce much of an electromagnetic signal, but be assured several hundred million of them going off together will register on our sensors."

"And you?" Xenia Petrovna said to their computer expert.

The Kiev killer had responded like a Pavlov dog to the rage stimuli presented to him while he was undergoing a magnetoencephalogram study.

"We're ready."

"How many signals are we involved with?"

"I've got to warn you, Colonel Doctor, it's a huge number."

"How huge?"

"Tens of thousands."

"That many!" The words exploded out of Xenia Petrovna's mouth. "We'll never be able to expose that organ of his to all of them in the time we'll have."

"No, we won't. But we will be able to run perhaps the first ten to twenty percent of the signals we recorded. And it's only logical that the trigger we're looking for is in the earliest phases of his reaction."

The computer expert pointed her toward his Hewlett-Packard. "We've programmed this to feed our signal generator each of those signals one by one. It will duplicate each signal exactly, its intensity, amplitude, and frequency with a resolution of a hundredth of a cycle per second."

The colonel doctor spun around and without another word strode back to her operating theater. "Are we ready?" she asked.

Her chief assistant indicated they were. Xenia Petrovna took her position at the head of the table. Her eyes swept each of her TV monitors displaying the patient's vital signs. She paused to study the computer-enhanced display of his brain, contemplating the faint outline of the organ that was her objective, his left amygdala. The patient was immobile, his breathing steady and deep. Because the brain, the organ designed to read pain's slightest warning signs, was incapable of feeling pain itself, the anesthetic required for the procedure would not be excessive. It was perhaps the only aspect of the operation not heavy with risk.

Xenia Petrovna looked at the anesthetist. "Let us begin. Needle please."

Overhead a digital clock began to click, registering the procedure's elapsed time. A closed-circuit TV system went into action filming each gesture the operating team made. The anesthetist inserted his needle into one of the intervertebrae spaces below the patient's neck.

"Penetration," he said. "How much fluid?"

"Twenty-five cc's."

One of the computer monitors flashed the words "Operation Initiated."

"Local into the incision points," Xenia Petrovna ordered.

Her anesthetist carefully injected anesthetic into the four points on the head where she would make her initial incisions. She paused thirty seconds to allow the local to take effect. "Draw back the skin," she ordered.

An assistant surgeon peeled the skin back from the area on which she would operate, revealing the pale white bone of the skull.

"Saw."

An assistant placed an electric saw, its blade a small wheel, into her hand. It came to life with a faint whir. Xenia Petrovna laid it gently against the exposed bone. Conscious of the fact that with each tiny nip of her saw she might be making medical history, Xenia Petrovna began her quest to conquer one of man's most basic emotions.

Like any good intelligence agency, the CIA operates on
a rigid application of the "need to know" principle, the
strict isolation of knowledge into pigeonholes and compartments sealed off from their surroundings as tightly as
contaminated specimens in a medical laboratory. It is
also, however, a human institution, and when a disaster
of the magnitude of the loss of Colonel Viktor Sbirunov
occurs, the "need to know" principle inevitably conflicts
with a "want to know" on the part of the Agency's officers. Art Bennington was among those with an eager ear
for gossip, and it didn't take him long to fasten onto the
few tidbits of information filtering down from the seventh
floor. The colonel, it was rumored, had been the best spy
the United States had had for years, a man who, among
other things, was supposed to have been the real reason
for the Reagan-Gorbachev arms accords. He was said to
have provided the CIA with a detailed résumé of the
Soviets' negotiating tactics, positions, and vulnerabilities.

For all his fascination, however, Bennington knew this
was not a crisis likely to impact on either him or his
Behavioral Sciences Division. He did not, therefore, assume the colonel's arrest was involved when Ann Stoddard, his assistant, marched into his office two days after
Witter's return from the USSR and announced, "The
director wants you—immediately."

This time there was no waltzing around with the blue
blazers. He was shown into the director's office without
delay. The Judge was sitting in the same seat at his little
conference table at which he'd been seated at their last
meeting. Paul Mott, the deputy director of Counterintelligence, who was overseeing the Ann Robbins murder
investigation, was there along with Bob Arnold, the head
of SR, the Soviet Russian Division of the Directorate of
Operations. SR was the holy of holies of clandestine operations. Perhaps, Bennington thought, there's been a
breakthrough in the Robbins murder.

"Sit down, Dr. Bennington," the Judge ordered.

"We've got a problem on our hands, and we hope you can shed some light on it for us." He paused, then added with an expression Bennington hopefully took for a sly grin, "And please spare us the psychic bullshit on this trip."

"Sure thing, boss," Bennington replied, etching his Christian forbearance smile onto his features as he did. "Whatever you say."

"This agent of ours who got thrown out of Moscow, Witter, is telling us a very strange story, and quite frankly we don't know what to make of it."

"Have you polygraphed him?" Bennington asked.

"Three times, and he came up clean every time."

"That means nothing," Mott interjected. "Any good agent who can get himself into a noncaring mode can beat the polygraph. We all know that."

"Fair enough," Bennington agreed. "So what's his story?"

"When the KGB grabbed him," Arnold of SR said, "they took him somewhere, apparently outside of Moscow. Drove about forty minutes with very few turns. He was blindfolded, so he has no idea where they went. Okay?"

Bennington nodded.

"He says they took him into a place like a sauna, strapped him into a seat that looked as if it could have been a dentist's chair with a helmet on it. They said to him, 'Okay, we know you're running an agent in Moscow, a colonel, and you made a brush pass with him on the Arbat Saturday afternoon.' "

"Which, I assume, he had?"

"Right. Now he swears to us he told them fuck all. Gave them nothing. Didn't say a word to them except 'I demand the presence of a U.S. counsel.' "

"A request I'm sure they rushed to fulfill."

"Oh, sure. So, still according to Witter, they said, 'Okay, now we're going to show you some pictures of some Soviet army officers and you're going to identify your friend for us.' "

"And he tells them nothing."

"At least that's what he tells us. So they show him about forty pictures."

"Including, I presume, one of this officer they just executed? Who, I also presume, was the guy they were after? The one he passed?"

"Correct. They run the pictures past him once, and then, he said, they reran about ten of them, including our man, a second time."

"And all the time he's saying nothing?"

"That's what he swears to us."

"He wasn't tortured, abused in any way?"

"Nothing. They behaved like perfect little gentlemen. *Glasnost* at its best."

Bennington tapped the tabletop with his fingers, digesting what Arnold had just told him.

"And," Arnold continued, "I've got to say this guy Witter's had a perfect sheet up until now. I considered him one of the best young officers in my division."

"I suppose the best face you can put on it," said Mott of Counterintelligence, "is that somehow he gave himself away to them with some expression, some kind of facial tic."

"Were they focusing anything on him that he could see, a camera of some kind trained on his eyes?" Bennington asked.

"Nothing. Just the pictures flicking by on a TV screen. And this helmet like a hair dryer over his head," Arnold answered.

"Touching his head? Using electrodes wired to his skull?"

"Negative. He says he was just sitting there half lying down, watching the pictures go by. Strapped into the chair, but otherwise no restraints."

"Did they give him anything to eat, drink?"

"Only a glass of water, which he says he asked for."

"Okay, Doctor." There was a clear note of impatience in the director's voice. "What do you think? Could they have given him something? LSD? Blacked him out and gotten him to talk? You're the expert on that stuff."

Sure I am, Bennington thought, and if one of your predecessors had had his way I'd be home in the garden trimming roses instead of sitting here trying to answer your question. "LSD," he answered, "no way. It's useless as an interrogation tool."

"How about a truth serum or something?"

"I don't know of any. These things at their best aren't very useful. I mean, if a guy says, 'No, I don't speak a word of Chinese,' we have some things, you can give the guy a squirt and he may start conjugating irregular Chinese verbs. That'll tell you something. But ask him how many carburetors they're making in Novosibirsk or which colonel has the Toni and that stuff's not going to be a lot of help."

"So what the hell's going on, then? Could they have found some way of reading an agent's mind, for God's sake?"

"Could have. They've been looking for a way to get someone to talk for the last forty years just as we have—without having to teach goons to feed a prisoner dead rats for breakfast or wiring his balls to a battery. We know they're deep into studying the effects of electromagnetic and magnetic fields on the human nervous system. This sounds to me like it could be something in that area."

"Oh God," the director sighed. "This is beginning to sound as far out to me as that psychic stuff of yours."

"It's all part of the same ball game, Judge, trying to find out how the human mind works. Trying to figure out the physiology of thought. I've been funding people for twenty-five years to find a way to measure brain waves so we could make the perfect lie detector. We've been looking into the idea you can detect the electromagnetic field or signal associated with a gesture, or maybe even a thought, before you make the gesture or have the thought. Maybe they got there first."

"And they've got some kind of a machine to read this man's mind? And we don't have it? I just can't believe that."

"Well, Judge"—the smile of Christian forbearance was stretched now to the outer limits of condescension—

"that's an article of faith you're just going to have to revise. We're always underestimating Soviet capacities in the scientific domain in this building. Remember how at the very beginning we were saying, 'No way they'll ever have the A-bomb before the late fifties'?"

"They had spies."

"They had good scientists, too. Just as they had good scientists for Sputnik, for their space program. The brain has been a special preserve of Russian science since the last century. Their technology isn't always up to speed, but let me tell you, there's nothing wrong with their thinking."

"And you believe their work could lead them to something like this?" the director pressed.

"It could have." Bennington lapsed into a reflective silence. "I'd like to talk to Witter. Maybe I could pick up some piece we're missing that might bring this together for me."

Art Bennington rifled through Bill Witter's file—or at least that part of it the Soviet Russian Division had been prepared to send him before he met Witter. An immense sadness overwhelmed Bennington as he read it. The guy was Joe Straight Arrow. He'd done everything by the book, a conscientious, hardworking officer with all his future glistening out there before him. His father had been an Air Force colonel, killed in action in Vietnam. Witter had probably joined the CIA to pick up where his father had left off. The kid had joined in 1972 right out of Hamilton College in upstate New York. It took guts to join the Agency in those days. Patriotism had fallen very much out of fashion. He'd been a CT, a career trainee, one of the elite destined from the outset for clandestine service.

Bennington glanced through some of the Inspector's Reports from the "farm," the CIA's ten-thousand-acre training site at Camp Peary down near Williamsburg. "Witter is not a particularly social creature, an individual dependent upon a frequent input from or exchange with others to maintain his emotional tranquillity and relatively stable frame of mind. He is basically somewhat withdrawn, with the psychological strength to endure and even enjoy isolation.''

Bennington laughed. He could see a portrait of himself as a young man in those appraising sentences. A touch of the loner. That was one of the key qualities the CIA sought in its agents. And, boy, he thought, is this poor guy going to be a loner now. No matter what judgment he might come to on the role Witter had—or hadn't had —in Sbirunov's capture, his career at the Agency was in pieces.

The source of Bennington's preoccupation knocked on his door. Witter was the picture of dejection as he entered Bennington's office. He had all the bounce, the resiliency, of an underinflated football. Poor guy's had a rough time over the last few days, Bennington thought. His left eye was blackened and a dark mouse rose from his left cheekbone.

"I thought our friends didn't beat you up," Bennington said.

"They didn't."

"You walked into a lamppost?"

"Sbirunov's controller tried to deck me. Accused me of giving his guy away."

"Wouldn't you know." Bennington sighed. One of the hallmarks of the espionage trade was the handler-spy syndrome, the intense emotional bond which is often developed between a spy in place and the agent who controls him. Penkovsky's handler had quit the CIA in a rage because the Agency, over his bitter protests, had sent Penkovsky back to Moscow for a final tour—in the face of the handler's conviction he had been compromised.

"Look, Dr. Bennington, I don't understand what it is you do or what you're supposed to do to me. All I can tell you is what I've been telling everybody in this building since I got back. I didn't tell the Russians a thing about Sbirunov. Not one fucking thing.''

"Sure, kid. But telling people around here something is a few removes away from getting them to believe it.''

"So what am I supposed to do? Cut my hand off and throw it on the director's desk? Like in the Spanish Inquisition—innocence by blood?"

"Hey, they told you this was a tough business when you got into it, didn't they?"

"Of course."

"They were right."

Come on, Bennington told himself, get out of this avuncular frame of mind. You want to help the kid, don't you? "Listen, I want you to go through the whole thing again for me. From the minute they grabbed you. Tiptoe along. Everything you can remember even if it doesn't strike you as important."

Bennington bent open a paperclip and began cleaning his fingernails as he listened to Witter's story. Nothing the young man said struck him until he was describing the moments before he was introduced into the saunalike room.

"They stripped me."

"Stripped you? I hadn't heard that."

"It was only for a minute or two. They took off my wristwatch and emptied my pockets. Then they gave me back my sweats and told me to get dressed."

"What did you have in your pockets?"

"Nothing. Just my car keys and my diplomatic ID."

"They gave them back to you?"

"Later. When they took me to the embassy."

"Anything else?"

"They asked me if I had a pacemaker. Idiots. I'm going to be out jogging with a pacemaker?"

Witter resumed his story. It varied in only minor detail from the one Bennington had already heard in the director's office. "That's all there is to it," he said, concluding. His tone was defiant, his look sullen, but Bennington sensed in Witter's eyes a desperate plea for belief. Bennington was silent for a moment.

"What do you think?" Witter asked.

"I think you told them what they were looking for, all right. You just didn't know you were doing it."

"What the hell does that mean?"

"Taking your watch, your keys. Their question about the pacemaker. That sauna you described was obviously a demagnetized chamber. We know there are signals in the brain that relate to cognition, to recognizing something like the face of your colonel."

Bennington scratched the inside of the nail of one of his index fingers with his bent paperclip as though he might be trying to uncover some secret code hidden there. "There are some people who think you might be able to read them with a thing called a magnetoencephalograph. It measures the magnetic fields the brain gives off when it's in action."

Witter's face took on the elastic cast of a drowning man who's just seen a life buoy come bobbing toward him down the flank of a retreating wave. "And you think that's happened to me?"

"Could be." Bennington heaved his shoulders. "But that doesn't mean I'm going to be able to convince your pals over in SR. My words don't generally strike the folk up on the seventh floor with the same force Saint Paul's epistles used to strike the Corinthians."

It was a sight with which millions of American television viewers had become familiar during the years of the Ronald Reagan presidency. Marine Corps One, the presidential helicopter, fluttered past the nineteen-story tower that was the landmark of the Bethesda Naval Medical Center onto the helicopter pad set on a hillock across from the hospital's main entrance. Up on the Rockville Pike, half a dozen police cars, red overhead lights flashing, shut down the avenue to traffic for the landing. A score of drivers had stepped out of their cars to gawk at the sight of the President arriving at the hospital for his first annual physical checkup.

The President scrambled down the helicopter steps and shook hands with Admiral Peter White, his personal physician. "Welcome to the National Naval Medical Center, Mr. President," White intoned. This time he was, of course, in uniform.

The presidential limousine was waiting at the pad as it always had for Ronald Reagan for the two-hundred-yard trip to the main entrance. The President scorned it and set off on foot, Admiral White and his White House Chief of Staff hurrying to keep up with his jaunty stride.

Two dozen members of the White House Press Corps were waiting for him, TV cameras on, at the entrance of the hospital.

"Mr. President!" one of them shouted. "Is there any particular medical reason you've decided to come out here for a checkup today?"

"Absolutely not." The President uttered his lie with a wide grin spread over his face. Stick it in your ear, you bastards, he thought while saying it. "I'm coming out here this morning at the suggestion of Admiral White to set a precedent I intend to follow annually during my presidency and which I hope my successors will follow as well. This magnificent institution dedicated to the good health of the men and women of our armed services contains the finest medical technology our nation possesses. I'm going to avail myself of that technology today to have the most complete medical checkup possible. Preventive medicine, they say, is the best medicine. A complete annual physical should be a part of the regular routine of every man and woman in the country, and I want my presence here today to serve as an example for you all."

That, he thought, smiling broadly into the battery of cameras facing him, ought to shut them up.

"Mr. President!" It was Britt Hume of ABC.

"You're looking a little pale, Britt. Had a good physical lately?"

The press, with the notable exception of Hume, laughed at the President's joke.

"The Senate vote on the tax hike resolution is apparently coming up around midday."

The President did his best to prevent an angry scowl from replacing his carefully fabricated grin. The Senate's Democratic leadership was trying to push through a resolution calling for a raise in income taxes in the upper two brackets by fifteen percent. Purportedly, the measure was designed to cut the budget deficit. In fact, it was meant to make him eat crow, to choke on his promise not to raise taxes.

"It looks," Hume continued, "as though the opposition may have the votes to pass it. Any comment?"

The President clenched his jaw to check his rising anger. Despite his seemingly calm demeanor, he was a man who hated losing more than anything else in life. "The Democratic leadership is playing fast and loose with this country's economy for cheap political reasons." He paused and glanced over at his Chief of Staff. "My advisers will keep me posted on the evolution of the debate minute by minute if necessary while I'm here."

With that he waved at the cameras and strode into the hospital. Admiral White marched along beside him to the elevator bank and up to the Presidential Suite on the third floor of Building Ten. Bethesda was the product of Franklin Roosevelt's devotion to the U.S. Navy. He had picked out the site himself on a Sunday drive in the autumn of 1941 and, legend claimed, sketched out the form of its distinctive nineteen-story tower on an envelope riding back to the White House that fall day.

Because Kennedy, Nixon, Johnson, and Carter had all been former Navy officers, Bethesda had gradually evolved to the status it now proudly claimed, that of being the hospital of Presidents. Its Presidential Suite in Building Ten was kept ready for an emergency twenty-four hours a day. It contained a supply of the President's blood type, emergency-room equipment, and a closet in which pajamas and a dressing gown with the presidential seal and a pair of slippers constantly waited.

White guided the President into the suite's bedroom, which, except for its hospital bed, resembled an elegant hotel room. Surrounding it were a room for the First Lady, a Secret Service anteroom, and a staff room in which three direct lines to the White House had been installed at dawn. He glanced at the Chief of Staff. "If you'd excuse us," he said, "I'd like a few words in private with my patient."

White pulled a notepad from his pocket. "Mr. President," he said, "what I've prepared for you today is the best examination modern medical science can offer. When the results of all these exams are in, I'm certain we'll be able to pinpoint just exactly what it is that's bothering you."

"I suppose," the President answered, his jocular facade now vanished, "I'd better figure on that being good news."

"Let's hope all our news will be good news. Now we'll begin by doing a complete blood chemistry series on you, so we'll start by drawing half a dozen blood samples. Then a chest X-ray, an electrocardiogram, a treadmill stress test—you're familiar with that, aren't you?"

"Intimately," the President replied. "I had to give up smoking after my last one."

"Then we'll be doing a sigmoidoscopy—"

"A what?"

White coughed. "It's a very important procedure, sir, for a man your age. We employ a fiber-optic tube a little bigger than a pencil to examine your lower colon for polyps, the growths Ronald Reagan had."

The President understood and groaned at the prospect.

"Those growths are frequent in men over fifty, I'm afraid, sir."

"How about this magic machine of yours to study my brain? That's what I'm here for, for Christ's sake."

"I was coming to that, sir, but as you requested I've set this up so that no one on the hospital staff could possibly suspect that this is anything other than a good, complete physical."

"Okay."

"We'll be giving you two scans. The first is a CT, a CAT scan. It's a machine that looks like a big doughnut. We pull you through it very slowly, and it gives us a remarkable portrait of your body. It's particularly adapted to picking up tumors, which are soft tissues, and malignant tumors, which are often warmer than normal tissue. That takes about half an hour."

"Right."

"Then we will do the brain scan I told you about, the magnetoencephalogram."

"And you're sure this will find out if I have a brain tumor?"

"Mr. President, this is the ultimate cancer-diagnosing device for the brain, period. If there's a tumor in there, it'll find it."

"How long will it take?"

"About forty-five minutes. We should have you out of here between fourteen hundred and fifteen hundred hours."

"All right. Now, my Chief of Staff's here and I want him to keep me up to the minute on how that damn Senate vote's going. Wherever I am, whatever I'm doing."

"Certainly, sir."

Colonel Dr. Xenia Petrovna Sherbatov sipped at the scalding cup of tea her attendant had set before her and started to shuffle through the postoperative notes on her desk. From them she would compile a protocol describing her surgery to remove the left amygdala from the brain of her institute's inmate from Kiev. The procedure had been long and extraordinarily delicate. As usual, the tension of those difficult hours in the operating theater had now been replaced by a profound and rather pleasurable lassitude. In its curious way, the sensation was similar to that blissful weariness she always felt after a bout of frenetic lovemaking.

Her operation had been a distinct success. The *zek* was now in the postoperative recovery room. Shortly he would be on his way back to his hospital bed, a much less menacing figure to society than he had been before the operation. The amygdala which he had unwittingly donated to the advancement of Soviet science was in the hands of her assistants in their laboratory adjacent to the operating theater. There they pursued the grail she so desperately sought, that one precise electromagnetic signal that would set off a synchronous neuronal discharge in the pinkish-white lump of matter the size of a mussel she'd plucked from a man's brain.

She glanced at her watch. Their search had been under way for over two hours. It could go on for hours more. Indeed, it could end in failure and frustration. The finite amount of time that organ could survive and respond to stimuli outside its natural environment set a limit to the number of signals their computer program could flash at it in their search for the magic trigger.

It was also possible she had erred in the theory she had constructed on how emotions originate in the brain. The brain was, after all, such an infinitely complex mechanism. To presume to understand its functionings was the ultimate vanity. Xenia Petrovna had been raised, as had everyone in her generation, as an atheist. It was a philosophy with which she lived quite comfortably—most of the time. Her moments of doubt inevitably occurred here in this institute founded by the KGB to master the wonders of the mind in the service of materialistic science. Every so often as she wrestled with the infinite complexities of the brain, she sensed the presence of some inexplicable force gliding through the densities she sought to understand. Suppose, just suppose that at the end of this searcher's road on which she was embarked, she was to find a Supreme Force playing hide and seek with her in the shadows of the mind? How would Soviet science deal with that?

In her father's day, when Stalin was alive, the answer, of course, would have been simple. Those who had seen something moving about in the shadows would have been moved themselves to Siberia and shot. Today's leaders were more pragmatic men. Still, it would confront them with an appalling quandary.

The bleat of the telephone interrupted her reverie. "Xenia Petrovna, come quickly!" It was her elderly deputy, the neurophysiologist, Aleksandr Borisovich. His voice rang with the high-pitched excitement of a child calling his mother out to see the strange snake he'd found in the garden. "Come, come."

She slithered into her white smock and rushed from

her office in the administration building across the lawn burgeoning with green new life in the summer sunshine to her hospital. The lights in the lab next to the operating theater were dimmed. The three TV monitors against one wall were all on but not functioning, a straight, unwavering green light bisecting the middle of each monitor. The amygdala she'd removed from her *zek* lay in its little bath in the center of the room, glowing a cheerful rosy color under a soft, diffused overhead light. Stepping into the room, she could sense the excitement of the men waiting for her.

"Xenia Petrovna," Aleksandr Borisovich announced, "we've found it!" Her little neurophysiologist was nervously passing the palm of his hand over his bald pate as if to caress the memory of the hairs that had once covered it. "We've got the signal!"

"Wonderful!" Xenia Petrovna emitted a sigh that combined relief and triumph in almost equal parts. "Show me."

The electrical engineer stepped from the shadows. He moved to his computer keyboard and tapped out a couple of commands. "I'm going to train three different signals on the amygdala. Watch. Number one."

Xenia Petrovna kept her eyes on the three monitors before her. Nothing happened.

"Number two . . . number three."

The echo of the electrical engineer's last word still hung in the shadows when the three monitors burst into life, a spiderweb of flashing lines and patterns. Xenia Petrovna could not decipher their meanings, but she knew what they signified. They had done it. Years ago in another laboratory, she had inserted an electrode into the brain and bypassed the visual stimuli essential to the rage process with a tiny spark of electricity. Now they had bypassed both the visual stimuli and the electrode. They had fooled the amygdala; they had deceived a human brain and sent an organ into the rage reaction, not with a stimulus perceived by the senses, but with an electromagnetic signal. The implications of what she had witnessed were staggering.

"Xenia Petrovna!" Aleksandr Borisovich was beside himself with excitement. "We have made history in this room!"

The little neurophysiologist's chest was heaving with satisfaction. "This is worth the Nobel Prize."

Xenia Petrovna laughed. "A KGB laboratory has as much chance of getting a Nobel Prize as a cat does of seeing its ears. In any event, this is one scientific advance they will certainly not be hearing about." She turned to her electrical engineer. "Tell me about the signal itself."

He tapped at the computer keyboard, and a pattern of wiggling lines appeared on one of the screens. "There it is. It's made up of three frequencies. This one"—he pointed to what looked like a tightly coiled spring—"is a high frequency component of two point six five one kilohertz embedded in two extremely low frequency carriers. This one"—his finger indicated a line that rose and fell like a Napoleonic hat—"is nine point four one seven hertz with a high amplitude. And this one"—he pointed to a gently flowing line moving across the screen—"is six point six two three hertz at low amplitude."

He tapped his keyboard, and another pattern emerged on the screen. It rose and fell in a pattern of inverted U's and V's. "This is the profile of one pulse of the signal. A very minute change in its shape and the effect disappears. The signal and the neurons in the amygdala are no longer in resonance. Even if the frequencies and the amplitudes are unchanged. And if those frequencies change by even one hundredth of a hertz, the effect disappears too."

He flicked off the screen. "It's an extremely precise and complex signal."

"Why wouldn't it be?" Xenia Petrovna asked. "The brain is an exceedingly complex organ."

Xenia Petrovna crossed her arms, adopting that schoolteacher look of hers. "Before we congratulate ourselves too much, we must play this signal on our *zek* when he's sufficiently recovered to see if he reacts to it."

"Of course, do it, my dear Xenia Petrovna," chortled Aleksandr Borisovich, "it will be the final proof. But you could celebrate now, because it will work." Impulsively, he reached out and kissed her three times on the cheeks in Russian style. "Celebrate, Xenia Petrovna," he said. "You have changed the world."

"Look on this as your dessert, Mr. President," Admiral White said, indicating the white metallic barrels of Bethesda's three-million-dollar magnetoencephalograph. "After some of the other tests we've put you through today, this one's a piece of cake."

The President looked at him with barely concealed fury. How typical of the medical profession, he thought. This guy is about to discover a tumor in my brain and he equates it with a hot fudge sundae.

"These cylinders contain liquid helium at minus two hundred and seventy-three degrees centigrade." You could sense the pride in White's voice as he described the working of his precious toy. "It's exquisitely sensitive to magnetic fields. Before we had this, we relied on NMR, nuclear magnetic resonance, to find brain tumors, but that technique depends on contrasts, on a tumor's composition differentiating it from the tissue surrounding it. With small tumors that are just starting, sometimes that difference was so small you couldn't spot it. Not with this baby, though."

The President breathed heavily. He was tense and nervous, knowing his future, his life, depended on a machine toward which his physician was displaying the affection of a teenager for a souped-up 1950s Oldsmobile.

"All you have to do, sir, is just lie down comfortably here on this table. Just relax, close your eyes if you want. Stay perfectly still and medical technology will do the rest."

The President climbed up onto the thin surgical table beneath the cylindrical sensors. His nude body was wrapped in a white hospital gown with the words "The President" in dark blue stitching lining its left vest pocket.

"This is a demagnetized chamber," White said, referring to the room in which the magnetoencephalograph had been installed. "We'll be in the next room with the computer that reads out all the information we'll get from this, but we can talk to you over the intercom."

White and the technician with him made a final check of the installation. "Just remember," White cautioned, closing the door, "lie perfectly still and don't move during the examination whatever happens."

Three technicians manned the Hewlett-Packard computer recording the information that would flow into them from the magnetoencephalograph's sensors. What they would record would be in a sense an action motion picture of the brain of the President of the United States during the forty-five minutes the machine would be on. The senior technician, a Ph.D. from Cal Tech, activated the system. A profile of a human head appeared on the first of their three monitors. The technicians used it to be sure they had a proper alignment of the sensors.

"Okay," the senior technician said, "let's go."

The computer began to hum as it started to take in information. The three screens came alive with what looked like the contour lines denoting altitude on a map. They showed the technicians the magnetoencephalograph was functioning properly. Studying the results, a laborious and time-consuming task, would be the work of a neurologist later in the day.

They were twenty-five minutes into the scan when Bill Brennan, the Chief of Staff, entered the room. "I've got to talk to him," he said. "We just got the vote results."

"Damn!" said Admiral White. "Can't it wait? We've just started. If he moves, we're going to have to start the whole damn thing all over again."

"He's the President. He gave us the order to get this to him as soon as we got it."

White sighed. The President was either going to jump for joy when he got this news or get royally pissed off. He opened his intercom. "Mr. President," he said, "I have your Chief of Staff with me. He wants a word with you. Remember, whatever he tells you, you must lie perfectly still. Otherwise we'll have to start the whole procedure all over again. And you know how you hate to waste time."

The Chief of Staff leaned down to the microphone. "Sir, we lost by one vote. We got the three Southern Democrats all right, but that bastard from South Dakota went against us."

You could almost hear the President grinding his teeth at his deputy's words. "Damn," he muttered. "Damn, damn, damn. When is that son of a bitch up for reelection?"

"Next fall."

"I'll have his ass. I swear to Christ I will."

The senior technician monitoring the computer chuckled softly. "Boy, he's pissed off. He is *really* pissed off." He leaned over to White, laughing. "You ought to ring up his systolic blood pressure and see how his heart's doing."

White glanced at the Chief of Staff. "Okay?" he said, poised to cut the intercom.

The Chief of Staff nodded. For a few moments he watched the technicians at work. "Pretty impressive machine," he observed politely, understanding nothing about it.

"Best in the world," the Ph.D. from Cal Tech answered proudly. "One of these days with this thing we'll know what you're going to think before you think it."

"Wow!" Brennan was not being polite now. This time he really was impressed. "That's incredible. Have the Russians got anything like this?"

"No," the Cal Tech Ph.D. replied, "they're miles behind us."

The Spanish Inquisition: those had been Witter's words in his office the other day, and the kid, Bennington thought, wasn't that far off. This little gathering in the director's office, presumably to resolve the young officer's situation, was beginning to take on the coloration of a Star Chamber proceeding. You could almost sense Mott from Counterintelligence twirling the gallows rope he hoped to fit around Witter's neck before the meeting was over. Arnold, Witter's boss at SR, was still trying to read the tea leaves, but he had the smarts to know his ox was going to be gored if he didn't come down on the right side of this thing. The director was playing the Judge, which was appropriate enough, but Bennington had already sensed his hostility toward the young officer. That left Bennington to play the role of Witter's defense attorney.

Unfortunately, the situation was rather straightforward. Over the years, far more Soviet spies had been nailed than the spies of any other intelligence service. That was not because the Soviets were inept. It was just that they had more spies. The CIA had precious few, and the loss of one of them like Sbirunov was a disaster for which somebody—in this case Witter—was going to have to pay.

The director put down the report Bennington had prepared after his talk with Witter and some of his contacts in the field. As if on cue, Mott and Arnold lowered theirs, too. Oh, oh, Bennington thought.

"Well," the director declared, fixing Bennington with the distant gaze of the judicious bureaucrat, "at least we're not dealing with psychic ladies fingering Soviet submarines here."

Bennington was tempted to offer the gathering a deprecatory little wave of his hand, but he thought better of it. He was right.

"Not quite, anyway," the director concluded.

Arnold, who could lip-read the boss as quickly as anyone in the building, now knew where the thing was going. "Art," he chimed in, "I for one am certainly grateful to you for taking the time you did with Witter and going to the trouble you did to research this paper. But when we get down to it, what we have here is just another fur ball, isn't it?"

"No," Bennington replied, "what we have here is one of your guys who's about to be crucified for something he didn't do."

"Well, you sure as hell haven't established that."

"What I'm telling you guys in that paper is that the chances are ninety-nine out of one hundred that this guy was run through a magnetoencephalograph. He told those guys what they wanted to know, all right. But he didn't know he was doing it."

"Just because of this business of the keys and the pacemaker?" Mott asked.

"Why the hell else would they go through that drill if it wasn't because they were putting him into a demagnetized chamber?"

"Standard procedure. Picking him apart to see if he's emptied a letterbox or made a pass."

"A pacemaker, Paul? They thought he got a pacemaker in a brush pass? This was not your normal shakedown. They were cleaning him for that demagnetized chamber."

"And then they read his mind in there with this miracle machine of theirs?"

"That's the conclusion I have to come to. We know there are signals in the brain that precede any thought you're going to have or any gesture you're going to make —like recognizing a guy's picture. And there is strong evidence that this machine, this magnetoencephalograph, can detect the magnetic fields that are characteristic of those signals."

"But no one's done that, yet, right?" Arnold demanded.

"We haven't. How do we know the Russians haven't? The Pentagon is funding a black contract out at Los Alamos to study this. They're looking, for example, for people who have superfast reaction times, the kind who make good jet pilots. Or guys who have a superior ability to resist the kind of stress officers have to deal with in combat."

"Fine, Art," said Mott, "but this isn't *Top Gun*. We're concerned here with a CIA officer who in all probability revealed the identity of the agent he was running to the KGB. Under duress, perhaps. But revealed it."

"Look, if you can get the sort of information the Pentagon is after by studying the signals coming off a man's brain, why do you think you can't read the signal that indicates he's recognized someone's picture?"

"I'll tell you why I don't believe it: because we haven't done it. And if we haven't done it, I'll be goddamned if I'm going to believe the Russians have done it."

Bennington liked Mott. They were Agency contemporaries, and in his dark days during the Church Committee hearings Mott had gone out of his way to befriend him. Nonetheless, like most counterintelligence officers Mott was as relentless as a pitbull with his teeth into a rival's throat once he'd latched onto an idea.

"Paul," he said, "there's something much bigger going on here, and you guys are missing it. I keep telling you guys the Soviets are up to their eyeballs in this business of how the brain and electromagnetic fields interact. I told you this when we lost the psychic up in New York. I'm shouting it at you now, and all I'm getting out of you is a lot of jargon about the SOP for body searches."

"We hear you, all right, Dr. Bennington," the Judge noted, "but what does it mean? It's just conjecture on your part."

"It means the first shoe has dropped, and the other one is going to come falling down on us one of these days. It means that we should start looking into this stuff more closely ourselves instead of spending our time cutting up the career of some perfectly innocent officer."

"Art, like the director says, you're talking theory." Arnold had the bone now and was off and running with it. "I can't run the Moscow station of this Agency on suppositions. I have an officer who, however inadvertently, betrayed an agent's identity to the KGB. For the sake of the morale of every asset this Agency has, that action cannot go unsanctioned."

"What do you propose to do, Mr. Arnold?" the director asked.

"I'm going to pull Witter's clearances and assign him to the historical section. He can sit down there writing up old case histories until hell freezes over."

"Good thinking, Bob," Bennington growled. "Barbecue a perfectly innocent officer because you don't want to stare reality in the face. That'll do wonders for your division's morale.''

Ann Stoddard was waiting faithfully for Bennington when he returned to his office. The TV set, its volume off, was tuned to CNN. That had become standard in all the watchtowers of the government, the National Military Command Center, the National Security Council situation room, the Pit downstairs, the offices of CIA executives and State Department officials. The President, he noticed, was boarding his helicopter, waving happily to the camera.

Art turned the volume up. ''. . . earlier the President completed his annual physical at the Bethesda Naval Medical Center. His physicians described his health as 'excellent.' '' The camera cut back to the studio. ''The President,'' the anchorman declared, ''received some of the most modern medical screening techniques as a part of the routine, a CAT scan, a magneto-met . . .'' He couldn't quite dislodge the morsel the word represented from his mouth. He smiled apologetically toward his female co-anchor before glancing down at his text. ''Magnetoencephalogram,'' he concluded, triumphantly measuring out each syllable.

Bennington cut the TV. Maybe they should learn to use the thing as a lie detector for politicians. Destroy democracy overnight. ''Little treasure,'' he said to his assistant, ''I think my contribution to the nation's security is at an end for today. See you tomorrow.''

Witter happened to get into his elevator at the third floor. He gave Bennington a hopeful glance. Bennington nodded to him but said nothing. Elevators at CIA headquarters were not exactly conversation pits. Heading into the parking lot, he sidled over to the young officer and laid his hand on his shoulder. ''I did my best for you up there today, kid,'' he said, ''but I'm afraid it wasn't enough. I'm sorry.''

You didn't need to be a psychologist to sense the hurt, the sadness in the young officer's eyes.

"To hell with the CIA," Bennington growled. "Who needs it? Go up to New York and be a stockbroker. Think of the big bucks you'll make."

A glimmer of tears in the young man's eyes gave an eloquent measure of both the intensity of his disappointment and his lack of interest in Bennington's suggestion. "Thanks anyway," he whispered. "It's good to know at least one person here believed me."

He turned and walked to his car, a dejected and forlorn figure.

Bennington watched him go. An afternoon like this, he told himself, calls for a scotch at the inn.

The Potomac Inn was barely ten minutes from CIA headquarters, just beyond the massive, eye-jarring clutter of the Tysons Corner shopping mall. It was barely half a century old, yet already its colonial portico and mansion-style verandah seemed hopelessly out of place in the asphalt jungle engirding it, turning it into a kind of vestigial remnant of the area's less prosperous, rural past. A few years back the owner had rebaptized his bar a "Tap Room," started to serve his beer in pewter tankards, and gussied up his waitresses in white bonnets and colonial skirts and dirndls like the ones the girls wore down at the Williamsburg Inn. Someone had assured him that that was the way to lure the Yuppies suddenly swelling the neighborhood onto his premises. All he had succeeded in doing, however, was discouraging his regular patrons. In deference to them and in defiance of the absent Yuppies, the Tap Room had now reverted to its original status as a bar and the girls had gone back to miniskirts and chewing gum.

Bennington ordered a Johnny Walker Black on the rocks with a twist. As he did, he thought of Witter, wondering how the kid would react tomorrow morning when he got the good news his clearances had been pulled. Taking away a CIA officer's clearances was like defrocking a priest or castrating a seed bull. And once they were gone, the officer could look forward to about as much excitement in his new professional life as the nobbled bull could expect in his. Bennington's sympathy for the young officer was real. After all, he, too, had once been down that painful road.

He took a careful sip of his scotch, savoring its warmth as it slid slowly down his gullet. The inn's stereo system was playing a tape by that girl the kids were all crazy about. What the hell was her name: Vega, Suzanne Vega. There was a plaintive softness to her voice that went down well in the perpetual dusk of saloons like this one. And with moods like his.

The bitterness left over from his own betrayal by the Agency had been muted by time, but something like the Witter business could set it churning again. His mind wandered back to the mid-seventies and the agony of those days he'd spent testifying to the Church Committee. How Bennington hated the memory of the honorable senator from Idaho. And Bill Colby. The Ford people had wanted Colby to stonewall, have the director of the CIA tell Church and his committee to stuff it, it was none of their goddam business how the CIA worked. It was the affair of the executive side of the government. But no, Colby had his own ideas about how to handle it. The best way to get the Agency off the hook, he'd figured, was to throw Church and his committee a few real juicy morsels. Chunks of sirloin for a pack of hungry dogs.

Since the LSD business had never amounted to a damn thing, giving it away wasn't going to hurt the CIA. And the assassination plots. They were ice-cold by 1976, but they were just what you needed to satisfy the Congress's and media's appetites and get them off the Agency's back.

Colby was honoring one of the prime laws of the federal bureaucracy: you cover the top guy's ass by letting some middle-grade ass hang out. No one wanted to tar the memory of the hero of D-day with stuff like drugs or JFK, the fallen hero, with assassination plots. And so Bennington had woken up one morning to find himself walking down the corridors of the capital in a daze. All his professional life he'd been trained to be faceless, to be anonymous and there he was, flashbulbs popping in his face, TV cameramen stuffing their microphones at his molars, shouting questions at him he couldn't even understand in the chaos and confusion. His boss, the man who'd recruited him for the Agency, had long since retired to the golf courses and marinas of Orange County. Two of the other men who'd been in the Chemical Branch when he'd joined the Agency had also left, so that had made Bennington the senior survivor of the LSD program.

And then, not so long after the hearings ended, the summons came to Colby's office. Old Owl Eyes was waiting, eyes blinking away behind those clear plastic-framed glasses of his, all smiles and contrived congeniality. He'd called him up, he explained, for a heart-to-heart talk, a little "just between us fellas" chat.

"I've been going through your personnel file, Art," Colby continued. "You'd be surprised what you've accumulated in there, entitlements, retirement benefits. And you're still a young guy. A brilliant neurologist." He gave what Bennington supposed was meant to be a hearty laugh. "Christ, you can hang out a shingle up on Park Avenue and be making more money than the President of the United States in no time. The point is this, Art." He leaned forward, and his voice took on the intimate tone of a father trying to coax a teenage son into doing something he thinks is going to be good for him. "We're getting an unbelievable amount of flak from the media on your continuing presence here. Quite frankly, it's becoming a bit of a problem. You know how savage reporters can be. For your own good, Art, and the good of the Agency, I think you should give serious thought to turning in your resignation. I'll personally make sure none of your entitlements are interfered with."

So there it was, just what he'd been suspecting from the moment he'd walked in the director's door. Even now, all these years later, sipping his scotch in the Potomac Inn, Bennington could still chuckle at what had followed. He was mad, genuinely, pissed-off mad. Instead of dealing with the LSD business with a midnight whisper, which was the way things were supposed to be done at the CIA, Colby had offered him up for a public skewering. And now he wanted to get rid of him to ingratiate himself with the media and Congress.

Bennington remained silent for several moments trying to throttle back his rage. "Gee, Bill," he had replied finally, his tone mockingly contrite, "it sure was good of you to be thinking about my well-being like that."

Colby beamed. "I knew you'd see it my way."

"There's just one thing, though."

"What's that?"

"I ain't going."

The director's astonishment was wondrous to behold. "What the hell do you mean, you're not going? If I decide to sack you, you'll be gone fast enough."

"On what grounds, Bill?"

"Grounds? You think I'm going to need grounds after what came out at those hearings?"

"How about what didn't come out?"

"What the hell are you talking about?"

"I've got a stack of papers a foot high putting the papal blessing on everything we did. There are a lot of paw prints on those papers. Allen Dulles's. McCone's. Dick Helms's. Why, I think if I look hard enough I can even find some papers in there with your initials on them, Bill."

"Are you trying to threaten me? After I try to ease you out of the mess you're in, let you out of here quietly with your pension money intact?"

"Nope. I'm just telling you I'm not going to roll over and stick my ass in the air anymore for you or anybody else. You want my resignation? Lay a ninety-day letter on me." A ninety-day letter was a form of Agency reprimand. All sorts of bad news were associated with it. It pointed out an officer's shortcomings and told him to either justify his behavior, pull up his socks, or face termination. "I'll hire outside counsel, get those papers, and build a little bonfire with them."

"You wouldn't pull a stunt like that."

"Try me."

Contemplating the director's face brought Bennington the first pleasurable sensation he'd experienced since he'd gotten out of his car on Capitol Hill to begin his Church Committee testimony. He'd gone pale, and his fury was so manifest it constituted a third party to their conversation.

"All right, Bennington," he snapped, "I'm reassigning you. As of right now, I'm giving you a casual assignment down in Records. And you can bet your ass the moment you walk out that door"—he jerked his thumb toward the entrance to the office—"your clearances are gone. You're going to have the need-to-know of the guys who take out the garbage."

Bennington shrugged. "That's your right. But what do you intend to do with my section and its ongoing projects?"

"Bury them."

"Not while I'm in the Agency you're not."

"You? You're going to be down there in the cellar reviewing housekeeping disbursements in the Philippines for the next ten years."

"You're the one who's on a short tether here, Bill, not me. When you came up to this office, you went off the list, remember?"

Bennington, of course, referred to the fact that in accepting the directorship of the CIA, Colby had left the bureaucracy and become a political appointee.

"Ford leaves the White House and you leave with him. But I'll still be here. And so will the Agency. It may even survive what you're doing to it. You want to bury me in the archives for a while, okay, you can do that. But don't close up my shop and don't shut down its ongoing projects."

"Your section is just like you, Bennington. It's an embarrassment and a humiliation to this Agency. I'm going to gut it."

"No you're not."

"Is that another of your threats?"

Bennington had tried to keep his reply calm and measured. "It doesn't have to be. Bill, you know as well as I do that this LSD stuff Church is so excited about was just one small corner of our research. And the LSD stuff ended ten years ago, for Christ's sake. But there are things we're following downstairs now that are absolutely vital to this country's long-term interests.''

"Your behavioral stuff? The brain work? Those people out at Stanford trying to look into missile silos from a thousand miles away?"

"They're part of it."

"Well, they're exactly what I intend to stop."

By then, Art was so wound up he couldn't sit still. He sprang from his chair with the quickness of the Princeton linebacker he'd once been looking for a figure in blue to hit. "Yeah, I could go up to Park Avenue as you suggest, make a quarter of a million bucks a year," he snapped. "You know why I don't?"

You would not have thought from the expression on Colby's face that he was desperately anxious to get the answer to that question, but Art had given it to him anyway.

"Because there's a revolution going on out there, the biggest scientific revolution of our lifetimes, and I'm part of it. It involves the brain, how it works, what influences it, how it can be influenced. Neurologists today are where physicists like Fermi and Szilard and Bohr were in 1939. But what they're going to come up with is going to make nuclear fission look like some kind of pale joke. This is where tomorrow is, Bill. This is the science of the twenty-first century. What's going to come out of this is going to change the face of the earth.''

Art had had to pause a second to rein in his emotional outburst. "This section of mine you want to gut is out there at the cutting edge of the revolution. You close my section down and you'll send this country walking into the future with its eyes closed."

"Bennington." Colby's eyes were pale and cold as ice cubes. "You're a troublemaker. That stuff of yours is exactly the kind of research I'm not going to have contaminating this Agency anymore."

"Okay, Bill." Bennington leaned his heavy arms on

the director's desk and smiled down at him. "I didn't want to leave on a threatening note, but now I will. There are a couple of senior senators over on the Hill who have a deep interest in what we're doing. Follow it very closely. They happen to agree it's vital to the national interest. I'm sure you won't mind if I inform them you're thinking of shutting the whole thing down."

Well, it had ended right about there. Bennington had been sent down to do his penance in the purgatory of Records for a couple of years. Some basic reforms had been instituted—the absolute ban on assassinations, on any form of unwitting human experimentation—but Art's section's projects survived more or less intact. The word had come down from the seventh floor that he was a maverick and that his old colleagues had better keep their hats on straight and put a little distance between him and themselves. Some had, some hadn't. For a while, he and the others who'd been burned by Church had been jokingly referred to as "war criminals." Then, as he had predicted, Colby left and his rehabilitation had begun.

Bennington's meditation was interrupted by the sudden appearance of a familiar figure circling the perimeter of the inn's horseshoe-shaped bar. It had been almost a month since he'd had his final encounter with Nina Wolfe, the hypnotherapist whose sessions had brought him such solace. As she advanced toward him, her fingers fumbled their way through her handbag as though in search of a compact or lipstick tube.

The three bowling-alley alumni beside Bennington had noticed her approach, too. This evening, Nina Wolfe was not dressed in one of the severe suits she used in her office. Instead, she wore a rather tight black leather skirt with a broad cloth belt buckled by what looked to Bennington like a turquoise-studded piece of Navajo silver jewelry. Her blouse was white silk with a kind of embroidered bolero vest over it. A low approving rumble from the bowlers beside him was the proof, if any was needed, that Nina Wolfe outside her office was considerably more attractive than the businesslike hypnotherapist inside it who'd treated Bennington. He twisted his stool so he was in the path of her advance.

"Not looking for a cigarette in there, I hope," he said as she drew up to him.

She looked up. For just a second, he noted a troubled expression pass over her face. Had he interrupted some deep and important chain of thought? Was she startled to see him? Or didn't she recognize him, did she think he was some bar hound trying to make a pass at her? Then she smiled. Her smile, he noted, was a good deal more welcoming than the professional greeter's smile in her office had been.

"Oh, hi—no," she said, looking down at her open handbag. "I'm not like the doctor with the sign on his desk saying 'Do as I tell you not as I do.' I gave them up years ago." She offered him a reproachful wag of her forefinger. "I thought barhopping was one of the activities we were trying to discourage."

"Shows how good your therapy was. Now I can come in here with the confidence of a poker player raising on four kings." Art smiled down on her as he said it. Her red hair gave her face a kind of copper halo. Like most redheads, she had pale skin. No matter. Suntans were out of fashion this year anyway. Her eyes were as bewitchingly blue as a pair of newly laid robin's eggs. "Can I offer you a drink?"

Again, for just a second, that troubled air passed across her face like a shadow on the moon. She probably felt it was wrong to associate socially with her clients, past or present. Then she smiled again. "I have to make a phone call. Check my answering machine. After that, I'd love to."

Art watched the tight mold of her black leather skirt stretched over her muscular buttocks as she strode off to the telephone. Beside him, a Willie Nelson look-alike among the bowlers burped out an envious growl. "Looks like somebody just got lucky."

* * *

Bennington waved grandly at the carousel of neon lighting up Chain Bridge road like an amusement park. "Look at that," he declared. "Anita's Mexican Food, Harry's Sushi Bar, Le Canard, the House of Hsuei, Roy Roger's. The cuisine of half a dozen nations, and all within a block of each other. And the food all tastes the same." He gave a harsh, self-satisfied laugh. His somber mood had evaporated in Nina Wolfe's presence. She'd only had a Perrier at the inn, but after a little persuasion, she'd agreed to have dinner with him. Now all he had to do was remember for the next couple of hours that he was an Exxon lobbyist named Art Booth and not a senior officer of the Agency.

"Are you hungry?" he asked her.

"Ravenous."

"Me too. Screw this glorified junk food over here. Let's go across the river and have a good meal."

He accelerated, glancing at her as he did. Her arms were folded across her chest, her well-formed breasts relaxed on her forearms, their outlines subtly suggested by the silk of her blouse. Her perfume's faint yet delicious aroma formed an unseen mist between them. Her face was lost in the shadows, but occasionally the glow of a passing streetlamp sent glints of copper swirling through her hair. Funny, he thought, I've always seen her in shadows, never in decent light: her office was kept in shadows, the bar was perpetual dusk, and now this car.

"Where to?" she asked.

"Jean Pierre's—know it?"

"No."

"French. Run by a car racer."

"I hadn't thought racing drivers were known for their skills with a saucepan."

"This one is."

They drove in silence for a while as he pointed up onto the George Washington Memorial Parkway and started to slip along the Potomac toward the capital.

"How is the world's oil industry these days?" she asked.

"Stinks."

"Why is that?"

"Too much oil. Not enough customers."

"That sounds like one of those classic dilemmas of the free-enterprise system they teach you about in college."

"Well, it isn't."

"Why?"

"Because OPEC doesn't know what free enterprise means."

Beside him, Nina Wolfe giggled. "You weren't this laconic in regression."

It was his turn to laugh. "Wait. Before the evening's out you'll be desperate to shut me up. Was I easy to deal with when I was under?"

"Wonderful. Because you weren't afraid, as so many people are, at the idea of hypnosis. I was amazed at how much you knew about the subject when you first came in to see me about stopping smoking. Much more than I ever thought someone in your business would know."

"Well." Art lifted his hand from the wheel and made one of the free-ranging gestures that always characterized his good moods. "The mind has always fascinated me. Paranormal phenomena, psychics, ESP, all that sort of thing."

"Do you believe in those things?"

For a moment he was silent, concentrating his thoughts both on her question and on the traffic sliding up to the Theodore Roosevelt Bridge. Across the river the delicate ivory needle of the Washington Monument beckoned navigators of the night to the capital as once Sugar Loaf Mountain had beckoned seafarers to Rio. "Yes," he said, finally. "I believe these things exist. In fact, I know they exist. But I sure as hell don't know why."

"Then I suppose you must be a believer. In God or whatever?"

Bennington gave a harsh laugh. "Nina, I'm like most people. I don't believe in God. Except every now and then when I really need to." He looked over at her. She was wearing very red lipstick, the kind the girls at Smith and Vassar wore in the fifties, and it played well with the stark magnificence of her pale skin and red hair. "You?"

"My parents were Hungarian. They came to this country after the revolution in 1956. I was a three-month-old baby. Atheism was about the only thing they kept from the world they were running away from. They passed it on to me."

"Ahh." Bennington mused a second. "I thought you had a trace of an accent."

"I suppose so. They never learned English very well, either one of them. I hated their accents, just like all immigrants' kids do. But some of it still rubbed off on me."

They pulled into the parking station next to Jean Pierre's plum-colored awning on K Street. Art, gastric juices already churning, almost bounded up the steps to the restaurant.

"Ah, Art." Jean Michel, the owner, beamed. "What a pleasant surprise." It was Jean Michel's way of saying, "There you go again, dropping in without a reservation." Why a restaurant called Jean Pierre's should be owned by a man called Jean Michel was one of the capital's little conundrums, but he wasn't going to get tangled up in that with Nina Wolfe.

Jean Michel took them to a quiet table in the front room. The restaurant was a favorite with Agency officers and alumni. The table opposite theirs was jokingly referred to as Dick Helms's lunchtime executive dining room.

"Drinks?" Jean Michel asked.

"Now can I tempt you?" Bennington said to Nina Wolfe.

"Only if you try." She laughed and looked at Jean Michel. "A Stolichnaya on the rocks, please."

Bennington ordered another Black Label. When the waiter set their drinks before them, Nina lifted her glass. Those stunning blue eyes of hers fixed him across its rim. "To your continued good health," she said.

"Cheers," he acknowledged.

He took a long drink and set down his glass. "Anybody ever tell you you have unbelievably beautiful blue eyes?"

"Never."

"Not surprising. Men are blind."

"If you're trying to convince me you're not a male chauvinist, don't bother." She smiled. "I know better, remember?"

"You know all my secrets before I begin," he growled.

"Oh, not all. I'm sure there are a few left in there to pry out."

The waiter moved to their table and began to recite the litany of the evening's specials with the enthusiasm of an altar boy rattling out the responses of the mass. Bennington prodded the young man with a few questions and then launched into the business of composing their menus.

"Do you always pay so much attention to what you eat?" Nina Wolfe demanded as he debated the fine points of a rack of lamb versus *magret de canard*.

"Always. It's one of my most exasperating traits."

They finally settled for soft-shell crabs and cold poached salmon for her and scallops à la Provençal and red snapper in a light mustard sauce for him. Art picked up the wine list. To the waiter's evident consternation, he ordered a California Chardonnay in preference to the French whites that filled the list.

"You know," he said, returning to his scotch, "I owe you a great deal. Without you, I think I would have turned into a misogynist."

Instinctively, he offered her the shy boy's grin he reserved for such occasions. "When I came to you, I didn't ever want to have a meaningful affair with a woman again." He snorted. "Christ, I was so bitter there was no way I could start up a new relationship."

"And now it's better?"

"Much."

"Does that mean you've found a woman to your liking? Have you started a new relationship with someone?"

"No. Well, in a sense, yes, almost. I did meet a woman up in New York I found very attractive."

"What happened?"

How do I dance my way around this one? Bennington wondered. "Unfortunately, nothing, really. The people she works for transferred her out to California before we could get to know each other. But being around her did help me to realize something very important—I'm not quite the burnt-out case I thought I was."

"You never were. It was just a question of time—and a little help from your friendly neighborhood hypnotherapist."

"A lot, I would have said." Art again made a small movement of his glass to her before drinking, a gesture designed to acknowledge his admiration and gratitude for what she'd done for him. "Do you get many cases like mine?"

"To be honest, no. Psychiatrists generally handle that line of work in this country. We tend to get left with the smokers and the overeaters. Which is a shame, because I think our techniques are a lot more effective than theirs."

Art wrinkled his nose in laughter. "In any event, your technique certainly worked wonders with me. At least now I can hear the distant trumpets of passion over the ridgeline. Who knows? Maybe I'll even fall in love again."

Nina's eyebrows arched mischievously. "Ah," she chuckled, blue eyes glinting with humor. "Love. Passion. Those are beyond the hypnotherapist's gifts, I'm afraid. And it's probably better that way, anyway."

"Why?"

"Passion." There was a sensual catch to her voice as she said it as though the word had slipped inadvertently from some secret chamber of her mind. "Passion is usually just a wonderful way of getting yourself into trouble, isn't it?"

"Sure, but don't forget what those ads for that old ocean liner, the *France,* used to say—'Getting there is half the fun.' "

"Oh, I didn't mean to suggest it isn't fun. It's simply that people who overindulge their passions tend to wind up on a psychiatrist's couch about as fast as people who overindulge their appetites wind up on mine.''

"How about love, then? What do you think about that?"

"What do you think about it?"

"You should know the answer to that already. Didn't you find all that out when I was under your spell?"

"Ah." She lifted her vodka glass to her lips and gazed at Bennington again from across the rim. "What you and I were trying to deal with was a love gone bad, remember? A love that had run its course, not one in full bloom."

"Well, I'll tell you what I think." Bennington spoke in that half-growl that was his conversational staple. "I think love's an accident. A fortunate accident, okay, but an accident that is going to overtake you when you least expect it, maybe two, three, four times along whatever the course they give you to run is."

"Not much room for scientific determinism in your philosophy."

"None whatsoever. And yours?"

"Oh, I'm a little pessimistic about love's bounty. Pessimism, unfortunately, comes naturally to people who spend most of their time listening to other people's troubles."

"In other words, psychiatrists and hypnotherapists make unenthusiastic lovers."

She brightened. "Oh, I'm not sure I'd say that." Her smile was a mocking, teasing challenge. "Perhaps they make the best lovers, because they're realists. They know how the affair ends before it begins. Like people who read the last page of a novel first."

The dour humor left over after his trying day dissolved under the impact of the evening. Dinner was a delight. Jean Pierre's food, as usual, was delicious and Nina Wolfe a charming companion. Why, Bennington wondered, didn't I realize before how attractive she is? When the waiter brought them coffee, Bennington asked for a cigar. "One of Jean Michel's specials," he added.

"Sure, Mr. Bennington."

The waiter brought him a small humidor containing a dozen unlabeled cigars. Bennington selected one and lit it.

"Your cigar smells marvelous," Nina noted. "It also doesn't smell as if it comes from Jamaica."

"It doesn't." Art smiled. There might have been no labels on the cigars in the humidor, but their aroma left no doubt of their origin.

"Aren't you ashamed?" She laughed. "A good . . ." She checked herself in midsentence, clearly shifting verbal gears to accelerate away from whatever it was she had been about to say. "I mean, an American patriot like you smoking an illegal Cuban cigar?"

"I never let ideology interfere with pleasure."

As they headed back over the Potomac and up the George Washington Memorial Parkway toward Tysons Corner, where Nina had left her car, Art began to do a quick mental inventory of his bar. After all, he couldn't very well use a cup of Maxwell House instant coffee as a lure to invite her back to his flat. His cognac was almost gone. He had some port, but a lot of people didn't like that. Suddenly he remembered a bottle of twenty-year-old Calvados he'd brought back from his last trip to Paris.

"Where do you live, Nina?" he asked.

"Off the Gallows Road in Falls Church."

"Well." He tried, not altogether successfully, to keep his voice casual. "We're practically neighbors. I live in the Park Terrace Apartments just a block east of 123 in Vienna."

"Oh yes," Nina said. "I know just where they are."

"Why don't you drop in for a drink on the way home? I was in Paris on business a couple of weeks ago and I brought back a terrific bottle of Calvados. I've been waiting for the right moment to open it."

"And look at your etchings?" She laughed.

"My ex-wife got them. We can watch the world go by on CNN. I have to warn you, though. My apartment is not exactly the kind of place you'd be likely to mistake for an award-winning *Playboy* penthouse.''

Again, she laughed appreciatively. ''No, Art, I regret to tell you that's not the life-style I associate with you.''

For a moment, she lapsed into silence, pondering, obviously, her answer to his invitation. Christ, Bennington thought, I used to find it tough enough dealing with rejection when I was twenty-one. How am I going to handle it at my age?

''You know,'' she said, ''I'm not sure it would be such a wise idea to accept your invitation, as much as I'd like to. For either of us.''

''Wise ideas I leave to the Jesuits, Nina. I hope there's not an iota of wisdom in this one. Just menace, mystery, and promise.''

He could sense she was studying him as he drove, those blue eyes cool and appraising. What's the form here? he wondered. How many nos does it take to make a no? ''What's a quiet Calvados between a hypnotherapist and a client?'' he coaxed.

''Yes.'' She smiled. ''That's a bit of a concern, isn't it?''

Sure, he thought, it's the old story—don't let them build up a dangerous emotional dependence on you. ''If it's the ethics of the thing, don't worry,'' he assured her. ''I won't tell the National Society of Hypnotherapists about us.''

''There's no such thing. We're a terribly independent lot of people.'' They were entering the Tysons Corner shopping mall. ''But I think not tonight, if you don't mind. Perhaps another time, who knows?'' She touched his arm. ''It's over there on the left, the gray Toyota.''

He pulled up by her car and stopped. As he did, Nina slid sinuously across the seat toward him. Almost before he could respond, she had coiled herself around him. She gave him a cool, lingering kiss, a carefully sensual gesture of promise and inquiry. Then, as quickly as she had slipped into his arms, she was out of them, her hand poised on the door handle.

''You're sure you won't change your mind?'' he asked.

"I'm afraid not. Not tonight." He could see a teasing smile cross her face in the shadows. "You still have my tapes, don't you?"

"Sure."

"You can listen to them." She laughed. "They're the best part of me anyway."

With that she was gone. He watched as she bent to fit the keys in her car door, her skirt taut over her sensuous hips. His eyes followed the fading red glow of her tail-lights fleeing through the parking lot, a lonely hunger rising in him as he saw them disappear into the night.

Nina was distracted and melancholy as she headed south down the Leesburg Pike toward Falls Church. Washington was a city of early sleepers, and the highway was empty. Like me, Nina thought, empty and barren. Why shouldn't I have gone back with him? Who would ever know? No one, in fact, would ever know except him and me.

How long had it been since she had felt her body locked in the pleasurable vise of a man's arms? When was the last time she'd spent a wild, exhausting night of lovemaking, her spirit burdened by nothing more complex than the joy of pleasures taken and pleasures given? What was she supposed to be, after all, some kind of overripe fruit condemned to wither too long on the vine? Why shouldn't she just turn this car around and head right back toward Route 123 and Vienna?

But she didn't. Instead, she paused at the stoplight beyond the 495 overpass. She stared moodily at the shadowy white boxes of suburbia around her, all dark, all inhabited by people locked in each other's arms, comforted and comforting.

The light changed. With a sigh, she eased the car forward. What a fool I am, she told herself. No one would ever have known!

. . .

Art Bennington shuffled through the dreary routine of his bachelor nights, pacing off the distance to his confrontation with the lonely darkness of his bedroom, to his quest for sleep's elusive caress. He took his jacket off, hung it up, undid his tie, turned on CNN. He tried as hard as he could to work up an interest in another tedious development in the never-ending Middle East peace process, to find some faint enthusiasm in his heart for the recital of the night's baseball scores. He found none.

He went out and contemplated his kitchen liquor cabinet. Maybe I should open the Calvados, he thought, have a nightcap. The idea of drinking it alone, however, was too painful. He would save it. There might be another time. She had, after all, said "not tonight" rather than "never." Thinking of her, seeing again the image of her lithe figure striding across the parking lot to her car, brought back the ache of her departure, the promise in her swift embrace. Sleep was not going to come easily tonight.

He went to the fridge for a glass of milk. His hand was on its door when he heard the buzzer. Shit, he thought, it's the computer programmer from across the hall locked out by his wife again. He jabbed the downstairs entry buzzer and was starting back to the kitchen when he heard footsteps and the ring of his doorbell. He opened the door with an angry yank. Nina Wolfe was leaning against the doorjamb, her arms folded across her breasts, looking up at him with that smile he'd noticed at dinner, the one that was half quizzical, half mocking.

"Can a girl change her mind?" she asked.

Much later, after Nina had left, Art lay on his bed, watching the dawn's gray fingertips begin their inspection of his darkened bedroom. The smell of her perfume clung to his bedsheets, the odor of her femininity still lingered on his body. He was exhausted and sad. It was always that way after such nights, an intimation of sadness riding the wake of spent passions.

He smiled to the darkness and rolled up into his bedsheets as though once again he were rolling his body into the embrace of her supple figure. Strange how sometimes a thing like this could go so wrong, a couple's mutual fumbling for pleasure marred by unspoken misunderstandings and little misdeeds. And how, on other occasions like tonight, two strangers could ride a tide of passion as surely, as deftly, as a windsurfer streaking through a roiling sea. They had loved in silence, in an instinctive synchrony of their desires, two people alone for a brief hour on a wondrous plateau.

Art closed his eyes. Sleep would come easily now. When, he wondered, would he see her again? Was there someone else already in her life? There had been once or twice for a quick instant a shadow hovering over her. Well, time would tell. Love, he'd proclaimed in his usual pompous manner at dinner, was an accident along life's route. Who knows, he chuckled, maybe I got hit by a car tonight.

Naturally, he was late heading off to Langley. He dashed out the front door, opened his mailbox, and yanked out the usual fistful of junk mail and a bill. The thought struck him as the door closed behind him: how had she known which apartment in the building was his if she didn't know what his real name was? There was no Art Booth living here.

His rush slowed to a crawl as he pondered that. Then he realized what had happened. It had been the waiter at Jean Pierre's. He'd addressed him as "Mr. Bennington" when he'd brought his cigar, hadn't he? She had picked up on that. Probably half her clients, a little ashamed of going to a hypnotherapist, gave her false names. He resumed his march to his Volvo, his stride jaunty and buoyant once again.

PART 4

"A SIGNAL
AS INVISIBLE
AS THE NIGHT WIND."

For the second time in less than a month, Admiral Peter White, the President's personal physician, found himself striding along the second-floor corridor of the White House with a representative of the Secret Service. Clutched in his right hand was the reason for his visit, a black attaché case containing the laboratory reports and the detailed findings of the two scanner examinations compiled during the President's physical at Bethesda Naval Hospital.

Once again, the Secret Service agent guided White to the President's private study. This time, White had barely settled into his armchair when the door opened and the President stepped in. He made what seemed to White the curious gesture of turning to check that the corridor behind him was empty, as though he were a hotel guest trying to slip unseen into a woman's room.

"Well?" he said to White, who had just had time to rise from his chair.

"I have all the results of your physical here with me, sir," White replied.

"I know that, for Christ's sake. What about the brain tumor?"

"There is no brain tumor, Mr. President. There is no trace of a tumor, benign or malignant, anywhere in your body."

"Oh my God!" The words escaped the President's mouth in a little gasp. "Are you sure? Are you sure?"

Curious, White thought. The President was probably a man of intense emotions, emotions he'd spent a lifetime trying to control, conceal, repress. "Positive," he said.

"Thank Christ! Oh, thank Christ!" The words were as much a verbal ejaculation as a prayer. "What the hell is wrong with me, then?"

"You're suffering from something called Ménière's syndrome. Or Ménière's disease, if you wish."

"That sounds terrible."

"It's not. It's a relatively rare complaint, though. It's a disease of the middle-ear passages."

"What causes it?"

"Quite frankly, we don't know. The result is a buildup of fluid in the middle-ear passages that produces these occasional attacks of intense dizziness, nausea, a sense of instability on your feet, a headache, disrupted vision."

"Well, what can you do about it?"

"Usually, the problem takes care of itself with time. In your case, because of your position and public exposure, I propose to put you on a mild medication called Antivert which will attenuate the effects of these attacks. In fact, it should pretty much stop them altogether until time and nature do their work."

The President waved White to an armchair and settled into one opposite him. "You can't imagine how relieved I am."

"Yes, I can," his physician said, snapping open his attaché case. He began to pull out a sheaf of papers. "You're a fortunate man, Mr. President. You're in excellent physical condition." He droned his way through the thicket of test results, blood cultures and chemistries, cholesterol, triglycerides, liver sedimentation rates, urinalysis, albumen, the excellent state of his bowels, all the technical benchmarks of an individual's most fragile and precious possession, his health. They had even, in deference to the tenor of the times, given him an AIDS test. To no one's surprise it was negative. White then displayed the full-color wizardry of the President's CAT scan and the incomprehensible swirls of his magnetoencephalogram.

"Fascinating and gratifying," the President said. "I'd like to ask the press secretary, if you don't mind, to arrange for you to brief the press on everything you've just

told me about my general state of health. I'm a great
believer in full and complete disclosure, as you know."

"Certainly, Mr. President."

The President then bestowed a regard full of under-
stated warning on his physician. "But I think we can
forget about this middle-ear business and the fact I'm
going on medication, don't you?"

White tried, unsuccessfully, to control his discomfort.
"As you wish, Mr. President," he said finally. "I suppose that would fall under the heading of patient-doctor
confidentiality."

"Exactly." The President smiled.

The room was one of half a dozen in Colonel Xenia Petrovna's Institute for the Study of Human Neurophysiology equipped with one-way mirrors so the institute's
doctors could study patients without the patients being
aware they were under observation. The patient Xenia
Petrovna and her colleagues watched with fascination
was the *zek* from Kiev, from whose brain the colonel
doctor had surgically removed an amygdala.

Xenia Petrovna was crisp and commanding as always
in her white smock. Behind her, her electronics engineer
made a series of last-minute adjustments to what looked
like a tightly wound magnetic coil sitting on a table in the
middle of their observation room. The machine was an
electromagnetic signal generator programmed to radiate
the one very precise, complex signal Xenia Petrovna's
team had discovered would produce the massive neuronal discharge characteristic of rage in the amygdala she
had plucked from the unfortunate *zek*'s brain.

Now they would make a crucial experiment. When that
machine began to beam out the signal, would it be picked
up by the *zek*'s remaining amygdala still encased in its
natural habitat inside the prisoner's skull? Would his
brain then send him into a fit of rage on nothing other
than the prompting of that signal?

Quite unaware that he was under observation and was
perhaps about to make an unprecedented contribution to

medical history, the *zek* was playing chess with his hospital roommate. To all appearances, he was calm and relaxed. He was erect in his chair, apparently alert and vigorous, his color good, remarkable in view of the fact he had undergone major brain surgery just three weeks before.

Xenia Petrovna turned to the electronics engineer. "Ready?" she commanded.

"Almost."

"When you activate the machine, will we be aware of anything? Will we hear anything?"

"Absolutely nothing. The energy it's giving off will be invisible. Silent. There will be no discernible sign that it's there. If you took a transistor radio and pulled out its antenna here in this room, you'd pick a dozen radio signals out of the air, wouldn't you?"

"I assume so."

"You would. But until you turned on your radio, you wouldn't be aware they were there. That's what this will be, just another signal riding in the air."

"And comparable to them?"

"No, it's more complex. Its wave shape, its polarity, its intensity are all critical. It's what we call amplitude-modulated, which means, basically, it varies in its amplitude or strength."

"And you're sure this will penetrate these walls, everything between here and our friend?"

The electronics engineer was in his early forties, a Ph.D. from Moscow University who'd been recruited into the Organs after long service in the Ministry of Defense. He was much more at home with laser applications in the vastness of space than he was with microbiology and dimensions so small they defied comprehension. "Penetrate these walls? It's an ELF signal. It will penetrate water. It'll penetrate lead shielding. It'll penetrate almost anything."

"From such a small device?" Xenia Petrovna looked almost contemptuously at the coils of his signal generator. It wasn't much bigger than a tomato can.

"It's only going to send the signal a short distance.

From here to the far side of his room. I measured it. It's seven meters.''

Xenia Petrovna had no idea what precise use Ivan Sergeivich Feodorov had in mind for this revolutionary technology she was trying to develop. She doubted, however, that an ability to manipulate emotions at a distance of seven meters or less was going to be particularly useful to the KGB. "Suppose you wanted to send the signal farther than seven meters?"

"No problem. Just use a bigger generator. These things follow the classic laws of electromagnetics. The power fall-off is one over the distance traveled cubed. Hit our *zek* from half a mile away and we'd probably need a generator the size of an oil barrel. You could send this signal bounding around the world if your generator was big enough.''

"Is that really possible?"

"Possible? We've done it. You know our generator at Sary Shagan?''

"The one that made that signal the Americans used to call 'the Russian woodpecker'?"

"That's it. With that we could drive this signal straight through the center of the earth and out the other side. Or get the angle right and you could send it echoing inside the space between the earth and the lower ionosphere. Get it into a wave-guide mode and cover the entire planet with it.''

"Good God!" Xenia Petrovna had just understood the enormity of some of the implications of what they were doing. "If this works, you could send our friend in there into a rage with a signal sent from—from''—she stuttered a second—"Buenos Aires?"

"Provided the generator was big enough."

Xenia Petrovna glanced through the one-way viewing panel. Their *zek* was quietly contemplating the chessboard, clearly pondering his next move. His opponent regarded him with what she took to be a certain glimmer of satisfaction. "Let us proceed," she ordered.

The electronics engineer bent toward his generator. He manipulated a black toggle switch.

"Power on," he announced. "The signal is being transmitted."

Nothing happened.

There was not a sound in the observation post, not even a hum to indicate the generator was functioning. In his room, the *zek* continued to ponder his chessboard in perfect tranquillity. It didn't work, Xenia Petrovna realized. Her theory was flawed. For one fleeting instant, her sentiments swayed between relief and bitter disappointment.

Then the *zek* looked up from his chessboard. He stared at his opponent. He looked back down at the chessboard. An instant later, he brought his head up with a jerk. Xenia Petrovna could see his face was flushed now. He shouted something at his opponent. The poor man appeared stunned. The *zek* brought his massive fist crashing down on the chessboard, shattering it, sending the chessmen popping into the air like kernels of corn leaping up from a hot skillet. He jumped up. He was shouting, gesticulating wildly. Then he leaped over the ruins of the chessboard at his opponent. He grabbed him around the throat and threw him to the ground. With furious strokes, he started to batter the man's head against the cement floor of the room.

"Guards! Quick, before he kills him!" shrieked Xenia Petrovna. "Turn the damn thing off," she ordered the electronics engineer.

Xenia Petrovna was shaking as two hospital orderlies burst into the room. They pulled the *zek,* still shouting out his rage, from his opponent. The poor man lay unconscious on the floor, a red stain of blood beginning to slip out from under the base of his skull.

"My God!" gasped Xenia Petrovna. "What have I done?"

Even Aleksandr Borisovich seemed stunned by what they had witnessed. "You have become heir to the great Pavlov, to all our masters of the mind," he whispered. "Imagine! You have fooled a man's brain into ordering him to do something he had no reason to do. With a signal you sent to him. When you wanted to. A signal no one can see, no one can hear. A signal as invisible as the night wind."

For Admiral Peter White, the President's personal physician, it was a moment of unprecedented glory. There he was in full uniform, three rows of ribbons sparkling on his whites, addressing the White House press corps in the briefing room employed by the presidential press secretary for his daily confrontations with the press. At the back of the room a battery of cameras, including those of the three networks, CNN, and PBS, recorded the admiral's words on videotape. In front of him, two dozen reporters dutifully noted them down in their notepads.

What the admiral would only come to realize later in the day when he set himself in front of his TV, bourbon and branch in hand, was that there was no chance whatsoever that any of that footage would ever be aired by a TV network. The reporters so faithfully noting down each of his phrases were, in fact, bored stiff by this little exercise the press secretary had arranged for their benefit. It had been a four-color peep show with blowups of the President's CAT scan, a glimpse of some of the voluminous data recorded off his brain by the magnetoencephalograph, a stunningly candid revelation of the vital numbers which constituted the parameters of his well-being.

"So what we got here," called out the *Los Angeles Times* man from the back row, his voice weighted to the ground with boredom, "is a paragon of physical perfection. I mean, to hear you tell it, the President's a walking, talking example of good health."

White beamed. "He's in excellent physical condition for a man his age. Or indeed for any age." White had conveniently forgotten the little problem with Ménière's syndrome.

"Doesn't this guy have anything to make him like the rest of us?" complained *The New York Times* man. "I mean, doesn't he have backaches like I do? Has he had to learn how to spell 'relief'? Doesn't he get occasional heartburn or acid indigestion like the rest of the country does every other night if you believe the TV ads?"

The admiral became serious. After all, *The New York Times* was *The New York Times.* "Of course, the President's subject to the occasional complaint that besets us all. But his basic health is wonderful."

As he was saying those words, a little bell went off in his mind. Anecdotes, he thought, the press love anecdotes. That was part of the lore of the federal bureaucracy—feed the press anecdotes the way you feed elephants peanuts.

"One interesting thing did happen during his exam," White said. "You'll remember he got his exam the day the Senate passed the budget bill. Well, he'd just begun his magnetoencephalogram when the news came. He'd insisted he get it straight away. Now you've got to stay absolutely still while you're getting that exam. He was a real soldier. He didn't budge when we gave him the news. But boy oh boy, was he ever mad!"

"How did you know he was so mad if he couldn't move?" someone asked.

"His systolic blood pressure took off like a rocket. Gave us another quite unexpected example of just how good his cardiovascular system is."

That ended White's moment of glory. His briefing earned a one-sentence remark on the three network news shows. *The New York Times* and *The Washington Post* gave it four paragraphs on an inside page the next morning. No one except the AP and the UPI mentioned the incident during the magnetoencephalogram. They both carried it in a brief item on their overnight world wires.

A half-empty bottle of Georgian champagne, their second, rested on Xenia Petrovna's black Rastrelli-style desk alongside a bubbling samovar of tea and a tray of caviar and sturgeon canapés. Ranged around the colonel doctor's desk were the members of her elite work team —her neurophysiologist Dr. Aleksandr Borisovich Chuyev, her electronics engineer, and her computer wizard. They were reviewing the sight they'd all witnessed earlier in the afternoon with the exhausted sense of excitement of a coaching staff analyzing a close victory or a husband and wife discussing a particularly successful party after the last guest has gone.

"God!" said the electronics engineer. "I couldn't believe it. The way he shot out of his chair after we turned the signal on!"

"How's his cellmate?" the computer wizard asked.

"He'll be all right," Xenia Petrovna assured him. "The hospital told me he has a slight skull fracture, nothing more."

The electronics engineer was still shaking his head. "Listening to all your theories was one thing. But seeing it happen! Seeing someone get angry just because his brain picked up a radio signal which could have come from halfway around the world!"

"Ah, my dear Xenia Petrovna, it is at times like this one regrets the nature of our employers," said Aleksandr Borisovich, sighing. "The implications of what we saw today for modern medicine are staggering, aren't they?"

Xenia Petrovna nodded slowly and thoughtfully. It was true. The implications arising from the fact they had been able to trigger an event in the brain with a signal from outside the central nervous system were extraordinary. If you could do that, could you, for example, trigger defective brain cells to release dopamine on signal and cure Parkinson's disease? Or amino-sugar cells to release insulin and cure diabetes? How about bypassing a severed nerve in the spinal column with the signals related to movement? Would you be able to deliver a cripple from his wheelchair with that?

She shook her head. Those possibilities were stunning, but they were not the concern of her little team. The time for exhilaration was over; it was time to refocus her group on the problem Ivan Sergeivich had assigned her.

"Really," she declared for her associates, "what we succeeded in doing was proving a theory: that there is, in fact, a precise signal that can trigger an individual's rage response."

Her associates nodded their concurrence.

"But that signal we found is absolutely specific to the gentleman from Kiev, is it not? No other human being on this globe will respond to it?"

"Quite correct, my dear." Aleksandr Borisovich beamed. "What responded to our signal? The cells in the man's amygdala. Every human being's cells are unique to that human being. They are, if you will, our genetic fingerprints, stamped on us by our genes at birth."

"So what, in practical terms, can the KGB do with this great scientific advance of ours?" she asked.

"Keep getting one individual mad over and over again," chuckled the electronics engineer.

"Exactly." Xenia Petrovna leaned forward. "You all know, I assume, who assigned this task to us?"

"Presumably the chairman."

"Correct. Now, I don't think his interest in the technique is based on a desire to cure Parkinson's disease, do you?"

"Why not?" It was the electronics engineer exercising his sense of humor. "When you look at the age of some of the people who run this country?"

Xenia Petrovna laughed with the others, then continued, "In practical terms, what could the KGB do with this Kiev lout of ours? I suppose they could send him off somewhere, bring him face to face with some enemy, and have a KGB officer nearby flash our signal at him. Presumably, he might then be counted on to do away with the gentleman in question for us."

"There's no way of predetermining that. This technique can elicit an emotion but it can't give someone an order," Aleksandr Borisovich cautioned. "There is much that is unpredictable in anyone's rage response. The only thing we can be sure of is that he'll get mad. He may try to kill someone since that's the pattern with him. But maybe he won't. Or maybe he'll kill the wrong person."

"Colonel Doctor, that sounds to me like a plot from one of those bad thrillers they like to read in the West," observed the electronics engineer.

"Indeed," Xenia Petrovna agreed. "One assumes our

chairman has far more secure techniques for dealing with such problems." It occurred to her as she said the words that she had had adequate proof of that in the case of the CIA's psychic in New York. "We must assume, therefore, that what he has in mind for this technique is going to require a higher level of sophistication than the one we've reached. That is our real challenge. How do we move from the specific of our *zek* from Kiev to the general? How do we now proceed to find the signal that is going to trigger your rage response, Aleksandr Borisovich? Or yours?" she added, looking at her electronics engineer. "Or, God help you all, mine? And is it possible to find that signal without physically removing an individual's amygdala?"

"Colonel Doctor?"

It was the computer wizard. He was thirty-eight, a child of the computer revolution, a man whose life's frontiers seemed to coincide with the dimensions of a computer screen. Xenia Petrovna had recruited him from the Bekhtereva Brain Institute in Leningrad. He had specialized in programming his computers to record certain specific signals sent from the brain by electrodes. Those signals were then played back to the brain by the electrodes to see if the reaction they produced was similar to the one they'd first been associated with.

"I think I have an idea that might at least eliminate the need to perform surgery to get this signal we're after."

"Please." The computer wizard was hunchbacked, wore Coca-Cola-bottle eyeglasses for his desperately bad astigmatism, and looked fifteen years older than he was. But Xenia Petrovna had great respect for his skills.

"I went back to the *zek*'s magnetoencephalogram, the one we took when we sent him into a fury before you removed his amygdala. I located his trigger signal on it. Now, I can fix the signal's location in a very, very precise way in reference to a series of bearings in the readout, the spot in the brain it's coming from, time parameters relative to a whole series of other signals, and so forth."

"A speck of salt in a shifting sea, isn't it?" Xenia Petrovna warned.

"Maybe. But suppose we acquire a little database? Perform the procedure just as we did here on half a dozen more *zeki*. Attach them to the magnetoencephalograph, and while they're being examined, provoke them into a rage. Then remove the left amygdala of each, expose it to our instruments to locate each man's trigger signal, and study where that signal is showing up on each *zek*'s magnetoencephalogram."

"Why should we do that?"

"I have a hunch from the work we were doing in Leningrad that those signals are always going to occur in precisely the same place on the magnetoencephalogram. Suppose as a result we learn exactly where to look for them? Suppose we can develop a precise set of bearings to pin down where an individual's signal is going to occur on a readout? Then what we'll have is a way to pick that speck of salt out of our shifting sea every time.

"This way, at least," her computer expert concluded, "we would have a way to get someone's rage signal without performing surgery on him. A magnetoencephalogram taken when he goes into a rage would be enough."

Xenia Petrovna bestowed a smile on her shriveled little computer wizard. "It's worth a try."

Xenia Petrovna sent her Citroën DS21 gliding down the straight, deserted highway eighty miles northeast of Moscow at close to a hundred miles an hour. Driving her Citroën at speed along the uncluttered roadways outside the capital was, for the colonel doctor, an act of purest sensual pleasure. It was rendered all the more pleasurable by the certain knowledge that no militiaman was ever going to award her a speeding ticket—not with the KGB identification she carried.

Her car had been a gift to the late Secretary General of the Communist Party, Leonid Brezhnev, from the French government. Brezhnev had been obsessed with foreign cars. Each time he set off to make a state visit, his ambassador would discreetly inform his hosts which product of their automotive assembly lines would provide the Secretary General with a suitable memento of his visit.

The result had been an immaculately kept collection of over twenty cars sheltered in Brezhnev's private garage. Regularly, he would visit it, select a Ferrari or Mercedes, and go tooling through the Moscow countryside at a hundred miles an hour. Andropov had seized the collection when Brezhnev died and distributed the cars to particularly deserving institutions in the capital. Technically, Xenia Petrovna's Citroën belonged to her institute. For all practical purposes, however, it was her private car. That was what it meant to be a "privileged person" in Soviet society.

She glanced at her watch. Seven minutes to one. She would be right on time, a courtesy the KGB chairman expected, even in attractive women. She drew up to a gate at the edge of a forest of fir and birch. A pair of young men wearing pale green shoulder boards and the blankly arrogant stares of the KGB advanced on the car. An officer followed. Politely, he asked Xenia Petrovna for her papers.

"Ah yes," he said, studying them and referring to his clipboard, "the chairman is expecting you, Colonel Doctor."

He went back to his station and made a telephone call, alerting the guards farther down the road to her arrival. He handed back her papers with a smart salute. "The third turning on the left, Colonel Doctor. Have a pleasant afternoon."

Xenia Petrovna smiled and entered what was, after the interior of the Kremlin, the most exclusive swath of land in the USSR. Zavidovo was the 130-square-mile private hunting preserve of the Politburo. Developed in the Brezhnev era, it was, in a sense, the ultimate fulfillment of the Marxist-Leninist canon that privilege is the reward of power. Only members of the Politburo, and their personal guests—and, of course, the small army of foresters, gamekeepers, beaters, and guards required to maintain the preserve—were allowed inside its confines. Each member of the Politburo had his own hunting lodge tucked into a grove of ash and birch lining a large lake at one edge of the preserve. Zavidovo reflected two characteristics of the Soviet power elite: it was an exclusively masculine world, and its members all shared a passion for hunting. There were probably more matched pairs of Purdey shotguns per head among the members of the Politburo than there were among the members of the British Royal Family.

Alerted by the sound of her tires crunching along his gravel drive, Feodorov himself opened the door of his lodge and came out to greet her. He was wearing stone-washed blue jeans, designer jeans she was sure. His had undoubtedly come not from a foreigner's suitcase, the usual source of jeans in the USSR, but direct from New York or LA. Over them he had on a traditional muzhik's peasant tunic, except his was cut from heavy silk, a fabric not generally associated with the Czar's peasantry.

"My dear, how nice to see you here today."

He helped her from the car and started her toward his lodge. It resembled a two-story Swiss chalet. Indeed, Feodorov had given the architects a set of photographs of chalets in Gstaad, Switzerland, to fuel their inspiration. They had succeeded right down to the rows of flowerboxes red with geraniums lining its second-floor balcony and the blowtorch-darkened planking of its frame.

"I invited Pavel Orlov and his wife, Tania, to join us for lunch. I thought you'd enjoy meeting them."

"The playwright?"

"Yes. A fascinating man."

"I'm sure."

This man does amaze me, Xenia Petrovna thought. Orlov was a well-known intellectual dissident who'd spent at least three years in a KGB prison camp. His latest work, *The Dark Hours,* a scathing denunciation of Stalin's terror, was a Moscow sensation. What was a man like that doing having Sunday lunch at the hunting lodge of the chairman of the KGB?

"We'll let our business wait until after they've left, if you don't mind," Feodorov continued.

"Of course."

The main room of Feodorov's lodge was paneled in oak, with heavy antique beams set against the white plaster of the roof. At its far end was an enormous walk-in fireplace edged in rough-hewn stone. The walls above and to each side of the mantelpiece were adorned with Feodorov's hunting trophies: moose, elk, bear, wild boar, even a rare white snow leopard. Xenia Petrovna knew that Western millionaires paid the Soviet government thousands of rubles every year to hunt the exotic and rare animal. In the corner of the room was a Sony large-screen TV with a matching videotape player. Beside it was a cabinet full of tapes. Xenia Petrovna felt a pang of jealousy looking at that assembly. She'd been scheming for some time to find someone who could bring one back from the West for her.

Feodorov introduced her to the dissident playwright and his wife. The dissident looked the role. A mass of curly graying hair exploded from his head in every imaginable direction. He had thick horn-rim glasses that seemed condemned by the pull of gravity to rest well below the ridge of his nose. He was wearing a T-shirt from a 1988 Prince concert in Copenhagen, which, Xenia Petrovna hoped, was designed to make a statement rather than denote his musical tastes. A surprisingly well-nourished stomach drew its cloth taut; evidently he'd made up for the privations of KGB camp since his return to Moscow. His wife was a quiet, mousy little woman, clearly intimidated by her surroundings. Xenia Petrovna guessed she was the kind of woman who had spent three years handing in hopeless petitions pleading for her husband's release from camp—and probably now endured with equal patience her husband's numerous infidelities.

Feodorov guided them all to a long low table at one end of the room. It was covered with trays of Russian delicacies, bottles of iced vodka, Georgian champagne, and, Xenia Petrovna noted with delight, two bottles of Château Talbot. Clearly the assembly was the work of Feodorov's domestics, but none of them were in sight now. Instead, the KGB chairman played the role of a charming and attentive host.

He offered them each a drink—she took the Bordeaux —then raised his glass. "To good friends, beautiful women, and the good health to enjoy them both," he said.

Xenia Petrovna blushed slightly and sipped her wine. Her green eyes coolly appraised Feodorov. He was an attractive man. He possessed great power, and like most women, she found power very sexually stimulating indeed. And there was his reputation in Moscow. Xenia Petrovna liked that. Men with such reputations represented a challenge, and she enjoyed challenges.

Opposite her, the playwright raised a silver thimble full of vodka. "*Mir y druzhba*—peace and friendship." He laughed mockingly as he uttered the Brezhnev-era toast, then gulped down his vodka in a single swallow.

An oil painting on the wall behind Feodorov caught Xenia Petrovna's eye. It was Feliks Dzerzhinsky. Curious, Xenia Petrovna thought. Was it the obligatory icon in a residence of the chairman of the KGB? Or did Feodorov feel some affinity for that strange and cruel man?

He caught her eyes on the painting and turned to it as well. "Bizarre personality," he said. "Did you know he often wept signing the death warrants of his victims?"

"I didn't," Xenia Petrovna replied. She wanted to say, "And you? Do you weep for yours?" But instead she noted, "His tears don't seem to have slowed down the motion of his pen much, do they?"

Feodorov laughed. "Perhaps speeded it up. He was a tangle of contradictions." He looked at the playwright. "You know, he and Stalin shared the same youthful ambition. They both wanted to become priests."

"What do you suppose drew them to that?" Xenia Petrovna asked.

"Probably the same thing that drew them to Marxism —a love of authority, order, a rigid hierarchy."

The playwright grimaced. "There is nothing more satisfying than a rigid hierarchy—provided you're at the top of it."

Once again, Feodorov laughed. He gestured to another portrait on the wall behind him, this one of Lenin. "Now, he would never have darkened the door of a seminary—unless, of course, he wanted to blow it up."

This time they all laughed with him.

"Thank God he was a lawyer," Feodorov sighed. "Do you know why?"

"Because lawyers are pragmatists, not dogmatists like priests?" asked the playwright.

"No," Feodorov said, "because like most lawyers he left a paper trail a mile wide behind him. His writings are like the Bible—rummage around in them long enough and you can find a quote to justify anything, even, I suppose, incest if you're so inclined."

Feodorov lapsed into silence for a minute, smiling at his guests over the rim of his glass. People instinctively try to cover a silence, and the policeman's golden rule is, if you want to inform, talk; if you want to learn, listen. Finally, he made a gesture with his glass. "What would our poor Secretary General do without Vladimir Ilyich's writings? They're his security blanket. Every time he wants to throw one of Lenin's ideas into the trash can, he has to go poking around in his writings for the quote to justify it, doesn't he?"

Is that what he really thinks? wondered Xenia Petrovna. Or is he trolling the waters to find out what we think? She didn't answer. No reticence, however, fettered the playwright. "Maybe he can find something in there about the inner harmony produced by standing in a line. After all, that's what good socialists spend most of their lives doing, isn't it?"

Feodorov shrugged. "Alas, talk seems to be the only commodity *perestroika* has produced, doesn't it?"

"And cynicism," added the playwright. "Communism and idealism were linked once, remember?" He barked out a laugh, hardened, Xenia Petrovna imagined, by memories of the gulag. "Trying to convince someone today that his grandparents became Communists because they were idealists is about as easy as convincing a Palestinian in Gaza that the Israeli soldier who's beating him

on the head with a rifle butt is there because his grandparents were Zionist idealists.''

"Ah, yes." Feodorov smiled. "Power corrupts. Let's
for the moment corrupt ourselves." His dark Georgian
eyes flashed out their mischievous challenge to Xenia Petrovna. "Now, my dear," he said, "with what can we
nourish that superb figure of yours this afternoon? Sturgeon? A touch of caviar?"

He remained the charming, attentive host all through
their lunch, open and witty in his conversation, covering
Xenia with numerous small attentions. They concluded
with tea and wild cherries, an Armenian brandy, and a
Cohiba cigar, Fidel Castro's old favorite, for the playwright. When the playwright had finished his cigar, Feodorov stood up.

"Would you excuse us, my dear?" he said and escorted the playwright and his wife outside to a waiting
KGB car.

His farewells took some time. Xenia Petrovna strolled
to the mirror to check her appearance. She, too, was
wearing blue jeans, a pair of tapered Calvin Klein jeans
that fit inside her knee-high suede Italian boots. She still
filled them remarkably well—not quite as well as the girls
she saw advertising them in the Western magazines, but
well enough for a woman of her age. She had on a pale
blue blouse, and the mirror echoed a suggestion of a
white Christian Dior bra beneath it. How she enjoyed the
bra's silken caress on her breasts! Western lingerie was a
luxury for which a good socialist lady might kill, she
thought with a smile.

As she turned from the mirror, she glimpsed Feodorov
walking in the woods outside with the playwright. The
mousy wife was evidently waiting in the car. With that
one vision, it all became clear. It had not been his harsh
memories of the gulag ringing through the playwright's
laughter at lunchtime. It was the sound of self-loathing.
The man was a KGB informer. He was Feodorov's eyes
and ears into the Moscow intellectual community. Its
members were Mikhail Sergeivich's most enthusiastic
supporters. If ever the time came to roll back the advance

of *glasnost*, Feodorov, thanks to the playwright, would know exactly where to strike.

She was looking at his collection of videotapes when he returned. "We can watch one later if you like," he said, gliding up behind her. He glanced at their luncheon leftovers. "Let's walk down to the lake while they clean up."

The path to the water's edge led through a thick stand of towering fir trees. Sunlight fell through their tops to the path at their feet in an uneven cascade, dappling the ground with the coloration of a fawn's skin. The lodge was beginning to fade behind them when Feodorov turned to her, an eager smile enlivening his face. "At last you and I can talk. How is your work advancing? Tell me everything. You can't imagine how important it is to me."

Oh yes I can, she thought. That look on your face just told me that. She folded her arms across her chest and walked a stride or two before answering. This was the instant she'd been dreading all day.

"Not as well as we had hoped, I'm afraid, Ivan Sergeivich."

"What?" There was no smile now. She could see the muscles of his jaw constricting in anger. "I don't understand it. Your initial report was so encouraging. What's happened?"

Xenia Petrovna had sent him a detailed account of her first operation, their success in finding the *zek*'s aggressive reaction trigger and finally in playing it back to him from an adjoining room. Now, as she advanced along the carpet of pine needles under their feet, she was intensely aware of his disappointment. And disappointment was not a sentiment one aroused lightly in the chairman of the KGB.

"I've got to have that technique, Xenia Petrovna."

She sighed. "There's another way. You could put a strand of stannous oxide in a tube of flesh-colored plastic the size of a human hair and implant it in the brain. No one would know it's there, not even the person you planted it in. No X-ray would find it. You could use it as a radio antenna. Send him a microwave signal and you could make him angry or gigglingly stupid or sexually aroused, depending on where you'd planted the device."

"How would you ever plant a device like that?"

"Surgery. It could be quick, easy. While he's in a dentist's chair having a root canal drilled. All he'd feel would be a thump on his head for a second."

Feodorov strode ahead, pine needles carpeting the path crackling under the angry jabs of his heels. "It's no good. It would never work. That implies we would have to have the man under our control." He smashed his right fist into the palm of his left hand. "We have to be able to do it without direct physical contact. That's essential. It's got to be done the way you originally suggested it could be."

The fury enveloping Feodorov surprised Xenia Petrovna. He was, after all, a man known in the KGB hierarchy for the cool, almost detached way in which he exercised his authority. What did he want this for? What could be important enough to get him into such an agitated state? What else could she suggest to calm him down, or at least direct his anger away from her and her institute?

"Ivan Sergeivich," she declared, "there is one thing we've learned since our last report. Not a great advance, but still progress."

"What?"

"We performed five more amygdalectomies on inmates at the institute. The procedures we followed were exactly the same as those we used in the first procedure. We have compared the six magnetoencephalograms we made of each man when we got them angry before their surgery."

"What possible interest would that have?"

"We discovered that there was a very, very precise point in each readout where the aggression signal always occurs. A spot we were always able to locate and identify correctly."

"I'm sorry, but I don't seize the significance of that."

"It means that if we had a magnetoencephalogram of a man taken when he suddenly got very angry, we could determine what his aggressive trigger was—without surgery."

Feodorov stopped. He was trying to remember . . . of course! That two-paragraph item from the Western news agencies that passed across his desk: it had been an addition to the President's psychological profile, the one about his annual physical exam.

"You're sure of that? Absolutely sure?"

"Of course, Ivan Sergeivich."

"You mean that if I could deliver you the—the whatever it would be, the computer readout of a man's brain made by one of those machines when he suddenly got angry, you could find in there the precise signal that was triggering his rage?"

"On the basis of the work we've done, certainly."

"And you could then find out how to duplicate that signal? Send it to him and get him angry on demand?"

"I believe we could."

"Believing's not enough."

"It's worked on all six people we've tried it on so far."

Feodorov resumed his walk in silence. Xenia Petrovna followed half a step behind him. His brooding air did not invite conversation. It was only several moments later when they'd reached the edge of the lake that he turned to her.

"This is the device you demonstrated to me, isn't it? The one we used to force the CIA agent to identify the spy he was running?"

"That's the one."

"As I remember, you were using a Hewlett-Packard computer to store the information you were reading off the brain with your device, weren't you?"

"One you got for us through Sweden. The very newest, a Precision Spectrum."

"In the West, when they use that device to give someone a brain scan, how do you suppose they store the information they're recording off his brain?"

"I imagine the same way we keep ours. Right there on the hard disk of the computer."

"How long would that disk remain in there?"

She tossed up her hands. "Months. Years. It's a nine-hundred-megabyte disk. It can hold thousands of scans."

"And each patient would be identified on there? By name?"

"Oh no, not in the West. I'm told it's different there. Each patient would have a code number. Only his neurologist would know what it was. He'd be given a print-out of his patient's scan, and perhaps a copy of the data on a floppy disk, and no more. You could never identify a patient from the master disk because of the code. All you'd have would be the date, the code, and the time the scan began and ended."

The date and the time, Feodorov thought. That would be easy enough to establish. Of course, there was always the chance they had recorded the President's scan on a separate disk. Or erased it. But it was just as likely they hadn't. The Americans were lax in their security on things like this. There was every chance they'd feel sure their code gave them the protection they needed.

They had reached the edge of the lake. Feodorov bent down, picked up a flat stone, and sent it skimming into the blue waters. He counted, three, four, five skips of the stone. His record was seven. Maybe that was a good omen. He turned back to Xenia Petrovna. The mischievous smile of the lunch table once again enlivened his Georgian features.

"You underestimate your achievements," he said.

The new Soviet embassy in Washington, D.C., stretches along Tunlaw Road in the Cathedral Heights section of the capital. It is situated, certainly not coincidentally, on the highest ground in the District of Columbia, across Wisconsin Avenue from the U.S. Naval Observatory. That the location would be the ideal spot from which to monitor microwave communications in the U.S. capital was a thought which unfortunately had occurred to the solons of the State Department only after the Soviets had bought the land and broken ground for their embassy.

Technically, the white marble chancery was not supposed to be occupied by the embassy's diplomats until after the controversy over the bugs planted in the new U.S. embassy in Moscow had been resolved. For Colonel Viktor Andrevich Gorokhov, the KGB *rezident* in Washington, however, that was only a technicality. Officially listed as a third secretary in the Economics Section of the embassy, he had a pro forma office in the old embassy downtown, but his real headquarters was here.

As he did every morning, he arrived in that office at seven o'clock sharp. His overnight duty officer had a cup of coffee and the morning press review waiting for him on his desk. The review contained nothing of interest, and Gorokhov rang for the overnight cable log, the list of all the communications the forest of aerials on the roof of one of the embassy's eight-story apartment complexes had pulled in during the night. The KGB maintained its own strategic communications network, complete with its own satellites, land lines, and radio networks. It functioned independently of the military and the foreign ministry's communication nets and was supposed to provide the party leadership with a communication channel "secure" from the military and the technocrats—which it did, at least to the extent the KGB's senior leadership wished it to.

At the top of the list a red designation number indicated that a *V Ruki Lichno Rezident*—"Personally to the hands of the Resident"—message from the Center had come in during the night. Gorokhov unlocked his safe, took out his personal one-time pad, and walked down the hall to the registry. He entered a code in the keyboard by the room's heavy steel door, and a peephole snapped open. An armed KGB guard scrutinized him, then activated the door's mechanism. Once Gorokhov was inside, the guard entered his arrival in his log and Gorokhov stepped to what could have been a bank teller's window, complete with bulletproof glass, and asked the communications officer for his message. Again he was signed into a log before receiving it. Then he settled at a desk and chair to decode it.

His first efforts revealed that it came from the KGB

chairman. Like all of Feodorov's messages, it was succinct and precise. But what, Gorokhov wondered, could possibly interest the chairman at the Bethesda Naval Hospital?

As soon as he got back to his office, he summoned his deputy and briefed him on the chairman's request.

"Put three men on this," he ordered. "Have one go through all our computer banks. Run it through *The New York Times* databank. Send someone down to the periodicals section at the Library of Congress. Check the registry to see if we've ever had an asset out there. I want the answers tonight."

"Tonight?" his deputy asked, as though hoping for a stay of that deadline.

"Tonight," snapped Gorokhov. "It's for the chairman."

His staff did as they were ordered. By dusk, the information was on Gorokhov's desk. The KGB had never had an asset at the hospital, only a couple of garrulous physicians, now retired. He was bemused, however, preparing to encrypt his reply for transmission to Moscow. Like so many American institutions in the eighties, the Bethesda Naval Hospital had been struck by the virus of venality. Four sailors had been court-martialed in 1980 for stealing goods from the hospital's PX and warehouse. Three civilians had been arrested in 1984 for belonging to a ring stealing personal computers from the desks of the hospital's doctors and administrators. They'd been tried in federal court for stealing government property, fined, fired, and given six-months suspended jail sentences. One was still in the area, working as a sales clerk in a Radio Shack in Silver Spring, Maryland. Gorokhov shook his head in disbelief. Pull a stunt like that in the USSR, he thought, and you'd have gray hair before you saw the last of the Siberian snows.

Nothing sets the drabness of the city of Bykovo, an hour's drive from Moscow, apart from the equally depressing drabness of any of the hundreds of industrial cities just like it in the USSR. There are the same ranks of smokestacks belching their daily ration of pollution into the skies, the same blocks of workers' flats marching in dreary conformity along the horizons, the same billboards of square-jawed workers and heavy-breasted women exhorting their fellow citizens to the fulfillment of their production norms. There is a weed-filled People's Park and the obligatory bronze statue of Mother Russia grieving her sons lost in the Great Patriotic War on the lawn in front of the local party secretariat. And, of course, there are the lines, always the lines, of a patient citizenry twisting down the city's streets in their eternal quest for a day's nourishment.

Outside the city's northwest corner, however, sheltered by the protected screen of a birch-and-fir forest—and, more suitably, by a triple barrier of electric fences and minefields—was the institution which rendered Bykovo unique. Indeed, the Central Intelligence Agency would gladly have handed over a king's ransom to get just one asset past the barrier through which the dark limousine of the KGB chairman now slowly made its way. Inside was the proudest possession of Ivan Sergeivich Feodorov's organization, the Illegal Operations Directorate.

His rivals in the intelligence agencies in the West tended to refer to the Bykovo training complex as a "campus." It was anything but that. As Feodorov himself had once remarked, an institution designed to form men and women for the most demanding of roles bore nothing in common "with a school or a sausage factory." So rigorous were the institution's security procedures that the three dozen agents being prepared at Bykovo at any given time were never allowed to meet each other. That way, they could never give away the identities of one of their fellow agents should a Western security service catch them once they'd been inserted into a foreign country. And they would never know which of the people crossing their path once they'd gone underground was, in fact, another illegal checking up on them for the Center's benefit.

Feodorov's limousine drew up to the administration building, a three-story cement structure with no redeemingly original features unless the bronze profile of Iron Feliks above its main entrance could somehow be deemed original. The deputy in charge of the directorate, alerted by the security guards when Feodorov entered the compound, was waiting for him with a handful of his staff.

"We are honored by your presence, Ivan Sergeivich," he intoned as Feodorov descended from the car. In fact, he was more concerned than honored. Visits of the chairman of the KGB to Bykovo were rare. Rarer still were those such as this one, the purpose of which had not yet been revealed to the deputy or his staff. Inevitably, apprehension that something was wrong was the first thought the announcement of Feodorov's arrival aroused at Bykovo.

The deputy ushered Feodorov to the sitting room adjoining his office. The table at its center was set with a tea service, with careful pyramids of oranges and little silver trays of sweets and biscuits. Czarists or socialists, Russians set great store in the ritual manifestations of civility. From the bread and salt offered to an arriving stranger to the ritual toasts that accompanied a meal or a drink of vodka, these hallmarks of courtesy, of hospitality, of respect were embedded in Russian social mores.

Following the polite ebb and flow of conversations around him, Feodorov reflected on how much those values permeated even the KGB. They underscored the importance of respect and patience, he thought, and patience, after all, was the hallmark of the KGB. His CIA rivals were always evaluating their operations in good capitalist terms such as cost-benefit analysis. An asset didn't produce, jar him and risk exposing him or cut him off.

Not the KGB. The Organs knew how to wait, to let an asset sleep for years until an opportunity came to use him, and nothing proved that better, Feodorov thought, than this remarkable illegal operation. With a barely perceptible flicker of his eyes, he indicated to his first deputy that the time for business had come. Following the man's lead, he rose, bid his staff goodbye, and went with him into his office.

"The reason for my visit is twofold, dear friend," he told his deputy as they settled into chairs. "First, we may shortly be undertaking an operation in Washington. It is of the utmost importance that the embassy, our organization, indeed, the *Rodina* should not be associated with it in any way whatsoever should anything go wrong."

"I understand," his deputy replied. What he understood, of course, was that the nature of the operation to which Feodorov had just alluded was too secret to be any concern of his.

"To put it into effect, we will therefore have to activate one or perhaps two of our illegals in Washington. I'd like to review the dossiers of our people there to get some idea of who the most promising candidates might be."

"We have twenty-nine assigned in the District of Columbia area," his deputy replied. "Every indication is that they are all functioning satisfactorily." There was no mistaking the pride in the man's voice as he proffered those figures to the chairman. It was, after all, an extraordinary achievement; more than two dozen Soviet agents sitting patiently in Washington, D.C., undetected by the Americans, untempted to defect by the glamour of capitalist society.

Feodorov nodded. "I also wish to speak with the young officer who led the recent Department V operation in New York."

"Captain Tobulko. He's an instructor with us here, as you know. I'll summon him immediately."

"Please. But before he comes in, I'd like to study his dossier."

"Of course." The deputy barked a quick order to his secretary to get Tobulko's personnel file. The operation of his Illegals Directorate was, in fact, divided into two parts. The first involved the implantation of long-term illegals in the West. The second, much less well known, handled *zondstarki*—probes. The men and women assigned to it were an elite, members of perhaps the most exclusive society in the world. All had successfully completed a tour as illegals in the West. They were employed for short-term, "in and out" operations in the countries they knew well and in which they moved with ease. Check out the new immigration procedures at the U.S.–Mexican border; get hold of copies of all the documents required to get a job at a plutonium-reprocessing plant in France—work permits, social security papers, the forms which had to be completed for a security clearance; deliver a package or make a pickup of something the KGB didn't want to pass through the diplomatic pouch. And, on occasion, an elite among them was employed by Department V, the "wet" section, to carry out KGB-sanctioned assassinations.

A young officer laid Tobulko's file in front of Feodorov. He studied it methodically, page by page. Valentin Tobulko reflected the qualities the KGB looked for in its recruits for the illegal program. He was not a zealous Marxist ideologue. The leaders of the Komsomol, the eager beavers who never missed a Young Communist cell meeting during their university days, were rarely recruited for Bykovo. Zealots of one ideology all too frequently made easy recruits for a rival ideology.

Tobulko's grandfather had been a muzhik, a small landowning peasant shrewd enough to read the handwriting on the wall and join the collectivization program at its outset. His father had been a much-decorated Red Army colonel who died in 1962 from the wounds he'd received in Sevastopol during the war. Through the intervention of one of his father's old comrades and his gift for languages, Tobulko had received an appointment to Moscow University. He'd come to the attention of the GRU —the KGB's rival, the Red Army intelligence service— during his military service, but rejected its overtures because he did not want a military career. He, in fact, dreamed of becoming an actor.

It was at the Academy of Dramatic Arts that the KGB's eyes first fell on him. A facility with languages, a gift for acting out a role—those were, in fact, excellent recommendations for a recruit for the illegal program.

The prestige and the immense, by Soviet standards, material rewards of the program were enough to overcome Tobulko's attraction to the theater. Besides, a year's study at the academy had been enough to make the young Tobulko realize how limited his acting gifts were. He spent three years at Bykovo, then five as an illegal, serving, Feodorov noted approvingly, in Bethesda, Maryland, where he operated a small photo equipment store. So he knew Washington well. His record there had been impeccable, although, like most illegals, he had had to perform only a few minor tasks. On his return he'd been sent to the KGB counterespionage station in Kabul. That assignment had exposed him in swift and gory abundance to the less savory side of life in the Organs.

He hadn't flinched. He'd supervised "heavy" interrogations, the Organs' euphemism for torture sessions, helped the Afghan loyalists arrange a trap in which three mujahedeen chieftains were murdered in cold blood, knowingly sent his share of agents off to die as Soviet spies behind the Afghan Moslem guerrilla lines. That record, and his illegal experience in the West, had recommended him for special training in what might be described as Department V's school for assassins and his subsequent assignment to murder the CIA's lady psychic in New York.

Feodorov indicated with a gesture that he was ready to see the young officer. His deputy brought Tobulko in, then discreetly withdrew to leave the chairman and the young man alone together. Feodorov waved Tobulko to the armchair beside his with an offhand gesture meant to put him at ease and introduce a touch of informality to their meeting. Tobulko was in his late thirties. He had a medium-sized frame with pale blue-gray eyes, blond hair he wore in a neat, American-style crew cut, high cheekbones, and a jaw that thrust slightly forward. Still, Feodorov noted approvingly, there was nothing distinctive about his appearance. His was a face one could easily forget.

His deltoid muscles sloped away from his neck at a sharp angle, and the chairman could sense the knot of his shoulder muscles, the bulge of his biceps beneath his tan suit jacket. His dossier had noted that he ran six kilometers every day, lifted weights in the gym, and practiced regularly tai chi chuan and the more deadly martial arts taught at Bykovo.

"Permit me to congratulate you, Major, on your recent success," Feodorov began.

"Captain, Comrade Chairman," Tobulko corrected.

"Major," Feodorov insisted with a smile. "It has been decided."

The young man did not appear flustered by the news of Feodorov, but his pleasure was manifest nonetheless. "You obviously carried out your duty with great professionalism. There's been no indication the New York police suspect anything other than what they were supposed to suspect."

"I'm pleased to hear that, Comrade Chairman."

There was no taint of boastfulness in the words, Feodorov observed with satisfaction, but rather the assured air of a man who had never doubted the quality of his work. Good.

"What did you use to fire the capsule?"

"Technical Services provided me a ballpoint-pen gun which fired by pushing its pocket clip sideways with the thumb."

"Ah. And how did you inject it into her without her realizing what was happening?"

"I was standing right behind her in a checkout line in a little grocery store around the corner from her apartment. To conceal my action I pretended I had to bend down to pick something up."

"She didn't notice anything?"

"Oh yes. She turned around right away, but I had my arms full of groceries with the pen concealed beneath them. She swatted the back of her knee and said something about how many insects there were in New York."

"Difficult, I suppose, to have to go into her apartment later and do the cutting."

"Not pleasant," Tobulko admitted, "but she was already dead, of course. That made it easier."

Feodorov studied Tobulko's face as he said the words, scrutinizing the young officer for any hint of regret, of revulsion, for what he had done. People who could perform the deadly work of Department V and come away psychologically unscathed were rare. The first major KGB officer to flee to the West had been an illegal who had defected because he could not bring himself to murder a White Russian exile leader in West Germany.

"Still, to kill someone, whatever the reason, is a harsh assignment."

"I'm sure the reasons were sound," Tobulko answered, "and that the proper procedures were followed in ordering the task to be done."

Yes, Feodorov thought, studying him, I really believe you do. "I have another assignment I'd like to ask you to undertake for me," he said. "Fortunately one that does not involve any wet proceedings. I think there's a way it can be done without any direct involvement on your part."

"I would be honored, Comrade Chairman."

Feodorov glanced at his watch. "Could you come back to the Center with me at three? I'll explain the mission to you in the car. We'll have to prepare your documents with some care, and I'd like to get you on the way as soon as we can."

Three separate steel doors, each electronically operated, each preceded by its own security check, led to the underground holy of holies of the Illegal Operations Directorate. It contained a dozen office suites, one for each of the countries in which illegals were stationed, and communications and coding rooms. Communications with illegals were rigorously restricted to minimize the chances of exposing them, but they all originated here. The few that were sent by radio were encrypted in these vaults, then relayed by land line to the Center in Moscow, where they were beamed to the satellite that would subsequently downleg them to North America or Western Europe. Similarly, return messages from illegals were pulled

off the passing satellites and sent, still in code, to Bykovo. Most communications, however, went by much
more innocuous channels: a postcard, a letter from a relative, a phone call containing a banal phrase which would
alert the illegal to a specific task: go to a preselected spot
where a message or another illegal bearing instructions
from Bykovo would be waiting. It was all part of a complex exercise to keep the Illegals Directorate wholly isolated from and independent of the other branches of the
KGB.

Feodorov's deputy guided him to the North American
Control Center. It was, in fact, nothing more than a large
office manned by a duty officer twenty-four hours a day.
One wall was covered by a map of Canada, the United
States, and Mexico. In a curious way, it might have been
the KGB's equivalent of the ''homes of stars'' maps tourist agents hawk in Beverly Hills. The location of every
illegal agent in the United States was marked and identified by a code number on its surface. There was a tight
circle of marks around Washington and other marks
around the country at those sites where activity in a crisis
would be of major interest to the USSR: Hingham, Massachusetts, on Cape Cod, for the Phased Array Early
Warning Radar System, the FPS85; outside Cheyenne
Mountain in Colorado to cover NORAD, the North
American Aerospace Defense Command; near the
United States' most important ICBM and Minuteman
fields.

Around the room were filing cabinets which contained
the complete dossier of each of the illegals: his real personal background, recruitment and training reports, his
relatives in the USSR, fitness reports. All the details of
his legend, or cover, and how it had been compiled, the
evaluations made of him since he'd been in the United
States, some made with his knowledge, some without,
and, of course, copies of all communications Bykovo had
exchanged with the illegal plus his one-time pad codes
and the predesignated indicators they'd been given for
specific actions.

One by one, the duty officer brought the dossiers of the

twenty-nine Washington-area illegals to Feodorov. As he
went through them in his usual meticulous manner, his
deputy hovered nervously nearby. Feodorov laughed at
the man. "You look as anxious as a bordello madam
while a client's looking over her girls," he said.

Certain patterns, of course, characterized the illegals,
and Feodorov was familiar with them. Most ran independent one-man—or one-woman—enterprises, a radio repair shop, a wine store, a videotape rental service. The
KGB wanted them in occupations in which their hours
and routine could be flexible and there would be a regular
flow of people in and out of their stores or offices, and
which did not require a detailed educational or professional background. Bykovo would not, for example, set
up an illegal as a doctor or dentist. The fabrication of
eight years of complex schooling at precise locations with
detailed records of each was too difficult and too apt to
fall apart under the first close scrutiny.

Finally, he selected three possible candidates. The
first, 3792, offered a great advantage. He'd trained as an
electrical engineer in the USSR before being recruited by
the KGB. He had been in the United States for only three
months, however. Would he be familiar enough with the
country, sufficiently confident of his cover, to operate
effectively? The second, 4106, worked as an oysterman
on the Maryland shore. His credentials were first-rate,
but one problem concerned Feodorov. He'd been in
place six years, and it had been two years since he'd been
thoroughly vetted. Was he still as reliable in person as he
appeared to be on paper?

The third, 2641, was a woman. She'd been brought
back to the USSR for a routine vetting just six months
earlier by a technique the KGB liked to use with illegals.
They took a European vacation, visited Denmark or Sweden. There they were slipped onto a Soviet cruise ship
for a three- or four-day visit to the *Rodina*. There was
never any problem slipping them unnoticed past the
Danes or the Swedes. She was the asset who'd furnished
the information concerning the CIA's psychic in New
York. Her most recent communication concerning the

New York psychic was proof of both her alertness and her reliability. And, Feodorov thought, there was something else in her favor, her sex. Women tended to attract less attention than men in operations.

Seventy-two hours after his meeting with the chairman of the KGB, Major Valentin Tobulko was in East Berlin. He was wearing a dark blue suit from the Brooks Brothers store in Washington, D.C., a white button-down oxford-cloth shirt, and a blue-and-red-striped rep tie. He'd gotten them all off the rack of the KGB's "warehouse" in Moscow, an emporium supplied with clothing from over two dozen countries for Soviet agents who needed walking-out suits for a visit abroad. Tobulko could feel the surreptitious glances of envy and curiosity cast at him by the knot of spectators gathered in front of the German Democratic Republic's War Memorial between the foot of Unter den Linden and Alexanderplatz. Clearly they were mistaking him for a visiting American businessman, which was just what they were supposed to do.

Tobulko was fifteen minutes early for his *treff*. This monument to "the triumph over fascism and militarism" seemed as good a place as any to spend the extra time. The exterior of the building looked to Tobulko like something a nineteenth-century Prussian architect inspired by a temple in the Foro Romano might have designed. The interior was suitably austere. A perpetual flame flickered beneath a crystal block which refracted its light through a series of triangular prisms. Behind it were the tombs of an Unknown Resistant and an Unknown Soldier.

Tobulko could not suppress a faint smile. Just what uniform was it, he wondered, that that Unknown Soldier had been wearing when he'd been killed? As he strolled back outside, a new set of guards of the elite East German regiment assigned to the monument marched out of their barracks. They wore knee-length olive-green greatcoats and gleaming black boots, and their white-gloved hands held AK-47s at trail arms as they advanced. Fifty feet from the monument, they stopped and shouldered arms. On an order they started forward again, this time those black boots slamming into the pavement in a goose step, each set of feet flailing the ground with the enthusiasm of a squad of SS storm troopers marching into a Nazi rally in Nuremberg. To Tobulko's left were half a dozen of his compatriots, older men of his father's generation, with their heavy chests and puffed faces, and a little line of medals pinned to the lapels of their suits. He studied their impassive Slavic regards, searching for some sign of emotion, some hint of the feelings this little demonstration really stirred in them. He saw none.

It was time to go. Tobulko started back up Unter den Linden to his *treff*. The shop windows, he noted, were full of goods: Algerian wines, Bulgarian olives, Hungarian sausages, Polish hams. There was no doubt about it, this center of East Berlin was the showplace of socialism. Its new steel-and-glass buildings matched anything he had seen in his years as an illegal in the West. Mixed with them were the old, solid Prussian structures that had survived the war: dignified brown-gray edifices built to mirror the stolid rectitude of the German burghers they'd once housed.

He paused at the display window of the German Textile Industry. It was almost opposite the Soviet embassy. Tobulko gazed with satisfaction across the street at the two-story-high marble bust of Lenin planted on the embassy's front lawn, its cold gaze peering down Unter den Linden to remind these modern German burghers who was the reigning prophet here now.

As he turned to stare into the display window, he saw a young man, a blue Malev Hungarian airlines carry-on bag over his shoulder, glide up beside him.

"The brown suit would go well at the opera in Budapest," he said.

"Yes," Tobulko agreed, "particularly if you had a nice green tie to go with it."

The young man nodded, and whispered, "Follow me. I have a car." They walked a few blocks to a gray East German Wartburg sedan, then drove in silence to Friedrichstrasse Station. With a curt nod to an armed guard, the young man drove unchallenged into an underground garage and up to a door.

"Wait," he ordered, and disappeared through the door. He was back in a few minutes.

"Come," he said.

They certainly teach our cousins of the East German State Security Service to husband their words, Tobulko thought, following him.

His escort took him up a long flight of stairs to another door. There he pressed a button on a panel. It sent a message to the major of the *Grenztruppen*, the border guards, in his control booth overlooking the station border post fifty yards distant. There long lines of West Germans and foreigners filtered through ten checkpoints, each a tunnellike corridor controlled by a *Grenztruppen* guard in a screened-off booth. After a meticulous study of each crosser's documents, the guard activated a switch which opened a swinging door that allowed the crosser to leave East Berlin and enter the passageway leading to the Friedrichstrasse platform of the U-Bahn that ran to West Berlin.

Now, on the major's command, the doors all stayed shut. The passageway drained of people. When it was empty, Tobulko's escort opened the door and waved him into the passageway. No one, except his escort, Tobulko noted with satisfaction, knew he had surreptitiously entered that passageway. Even the commander of the East German border guards had no idea of what he looked like, although he certainly knew an agent was being infiltrated into West Berlin. In fact, since he'd slipped out of the KGB compound near Schönefeld, the East Berlin airport, there was no one except his SSD escort who had any notion of his real function and identity.

From Friedrichstrasse, two S-Bahn lines headed into West Berlin. One went north to Wedding and Tegel in the French sector or south toward Mariendorf in the U.S. sector. The other went west to Zoo Station and the Kurfürstendamm. Tobulko sauntered up the steps to the Zoo Station platform and mingled with the crowd waiting for the train already hissing slowly into the station. He stepped into the train, and five minutes later he saw the enormous pylon topped by a Mercedes-Benz symbol that was a kind of capitalist beacon marking the frontier between the two Berlins.

There was no control of any kind as he got off the train at Zoo Station and wandered out into the streets of West Berlin. The reason was simple. The Western Allies refused to recognize the division of Berlin. To set up border control points would be to give *de facto* recognition to the Communists' action in dividing it. For forty-five minutes, Tobulko wandered the Ku-damm area applying the techniques of tradecraft he'd learned at Bykovo to be sure he wasn't being followed. When he felt certain he was clean, he got into a taxi for Tegel Airport.

At Tegel, he bought a ticket for the next flight to Frankfurt. Again, there was no control either leaving Berlin or arriving in Frankfurt. In Frankfurt, he took a taxi to the Bahnhof and got on the first train to Basel and Zurich.

A few minutes before the train reached Basel, West German and Swiss customs officials strolled through Tobulko's car checking travel papers. He offered them an American passport. The document was genuine. It had been issued to Roy Banwell, of Minneapolis, Minnesota, an executive with Cargill, the grain merchants. Six months earlier, Banwell had been spending a quiet weekend with a lady other than his wife at the Ledra Palace Hotel in Nicosia in Cyprus. While the couple were sunning themselves by the pool Saturday afternoon, a thief, with the complicity of a friend in room service, had entered their suite and stolen Banwell's wallet and passport and a handful of his girlfriend's jewelry. He'd kept the cash and made a few quick purchases with Banwell's credit cards before destroying them. That night, he'd offered the jewels to his own girlfriend, a stripteaser in a nightclub in Limassol. He'd also taken the occasion to sell the passport to the club's Lebanese barman for a hundred dollars.

Later that night, the barman had sold it in turn to a Palestinian contact for two hundred dollars. The Palestinian belonged to the Arab Organization of May 15, Abu

Ibrahim Faction, a Syrian-supported group. He forwarded the passport to Damascus. There his superior had no immediate use for it, but he knew the KGB was always in the market for American passports. He sold it to his KGB contact for four hundred dollars, and the passport wound up in the Center's Documentation Division.

Banwell's age, as registered in the passport, was thirty-seven, identical to Tobulko's. When Feodorov ordered the major west, he was assigned the passport. Banwell's photograph was lifted and replaced with Tobulko's. The Center had an ample supply of recent State Department seals to stamp the photo to the page. A few immigration stamps from Western Europe were pressed into it for currency's sake and Tobulko had become Roy Banwell.

The passport would never, of course, have gotten Tobulko past a customs officer at a major U.S. airport. A series of lines, invisible to the eye, cross the photo of the holder of a U.S. passport and the page to which it is affixed. Tamper with the photo and the fact will be immediately evident to a customs officer when he slips the passport under a special ultraviolet light because the lines will no longer match.

Tobulko, however, had no intention of entering the United States on this passport. It was perfect, on the other hand, for what he needed it for, moving about in Europe. The German and Swiss customs inspectors scrutinized the passport in turn, then handed it back to him. Tobulko returned to reading the copy of *Time* magazine he'd bought in Frankfurt. He smiled. How easy it had been to cross two Western borders in less than twelve hours.

These little Thursday dinners were as much a weekly ritual for the KGB *rezident* in Damascus as Friday prayers in the Umayyad Mosque were for his guest, Major Abdul Hamid Hatem, the head of the Havarat, the Syrian intelligence service. In the cold months, they met in downtown Damascus in the Sheraton Hotel, surrounded by belly dancers, Syrian businessmen, and Palestinian plotters of every imaginable political coloration. In the warmer months, on a nice night like this one, they came out here to dine in one of the garden restaurants by the River Surati, running fresh and cool off the flanks of what the Syrians call Djebel Sheikh and the Russians, like most Westerners, Mount Hermon.

The *rezident* feigned both admiration and friendship for Hatem. In fact, he despised him. Hatem was a toady who held his post, the *rezident* was convinced, because he belonged to the Alawite religious sect and consequently was unwavering in his loyalty to Syria's dictator, Hafez al-Assad. Like his service, Hatem was a creature of the KGB, and like the spoiled son of a wealthy businessman, he had now become somewhat patronizing to the wise old tutor his father had chosen to form him.

Smoking after-dinner Havana cigars, the two men set off on a leisurely stroll along the riverbank. As they walked, Hatem attempted to explain the intricacies of Middle Eastern politics to a man who had mastered them before the Syrian was born. The *rezident* listened respectfully, however. The KGB knew Hatem was one of Assad's intimates, the perfect backstairs channel to the Syrian dictator. Whisper Hatem a secret and Assad would have it within an hour. Furthermore, Moscow was convinced Assad was a closet Westerner despite his loud, public proclamations of undying Soviet-Syrian friendship. The *rezident*'s job, therefore, was to scrutinize men like Hatem who were mirrors of Assad's thoughts for the first warnings of the treachery Moscow was certain was endemic to the Arab character.

Finally, they reached Hatem's car and the pair of Land Rovers bearing his bodyguards. The two men exchanged back-thumping Arabic embraces, Hatem's rough beard scraping up and down the *rezident*'s cheek like a brace of little thistles, to the Russian's intense displeasure. He stood by the roadside waving a mock respectful farewell as Hatem's departing cavalcade drove off.

Then he got down to his main business of the evening.

The *rezident* was perfectly aware that the Havarat kept him under surveillance. Detecting signs of their surveillance had been simple. The KGB, after all, had taught the Syrians everything they knew about the art. The *rezident* had also noticed that the one time they never bothered to tail him was on evenings like this one when he was dining with Hatem. That made every one of Hatem's pompous little lectures worth listening to. He was using Hatem as the perfect vehicle to cover his truly secret meetings, his *treffs* with a handful of people he never wanted the Syrians to know he was seeing.

This evening's contact was waiting for him along with his driver bodyguard in the shadows by his car at the back of the restaurant's parking lot. They shook hands warmly and got into the backseat of the car. The driver headed north along the Aleppo road, an area the Russian knew would not be subjected to any Syrian police roadblocks this evening.

"I bring you warm greetings from Ivan Sergeivich," the *rezident* informed his guest.

"Please give him my best regards in return," his interlocutor replied.

"Indeed," continued the *rezident*, "it was he who asked me to meet with you tonight."

The man beside him said nothing, but his attention was now riveted on the *rezident*. Like the *rezident*, he was an officer of the KGB, a man with close to a decade of devoted and effective service to the Organs. He was also a Palestinian Arab born in a refugee camp of parents who had fled Jaffa in 1948 at the beginning of the Arab-Israeli conflict. In that he was a rarity indeed. While the KGB was active in training Palestinian terrorists, supplying them, manipulating them, and using them as agents, only three men had so earned the Soviet's trust that they had been enlisted into the ranks of the KGB. Abou Said Dajani was the senior member of the trio.

"He is planning—or rather contemplating—an operation in which he needs your help."

"He shall have it, *inch'Allah*."

"For now, we need you to select four men for the operation."

Dajani nodded.

"At least two of them must speak German, and all of them will have to be comfortable working in Europe. Preferably they will have already performed tasks there."

"Will they require special training, qualifications?"

"They will all have to be thoroughly familiar with explosives. The rest will be taken care of." The *resident* took a Camel cigarette from his jacket and offered one to Dajani. The Palestinian lit his with a match, instinctively cupping his light in the pocket of his hands like a man long accustomed to lighting his cigarettes in the open, in the face of the wind.

"And this is most important—I want them all to be Hez'bollah."

Dajani shrugged. He was a *hamullah,* a kinsman of Abu Nidal. That relation had earned him his first introduction into the PLO as a Young Tiger in his refugee camp at age twelve. It had also helped his steady ascension in the ranks of Arab terrorism to the position he now held as Abu Nidal's third-in-command and liaison with the Iranian-sponsored Hez'bollah in Lebanon's Bekaa Valley. His kinsman completely ignored, of course, as did all his associates, his ties to the KGB.

"That is not a problem."

"Compensation?"

"The Qaddafi scale."

The Qaddafi scale was a graded list of payments for terrorist actions, established by the Libyan in 1984 and frequently used by Middle Eastern terrorists since. Its payoffs, in British pounds, ran from five thousand pounds for delivering explosives to a hundred and fifteen thousand for the family of a martyr lost in a suicide bombing.

"Do I say anything about the target?"

The *resident* reflected a moment. "Only that it will be American and in West Germany. I assume," he continued, "the Artist remains in business in Beirut."

"Of course."

"When you've selected your team, take him their photos and have him make them four 798s. These are the identities he must put on them." The *resident* passed

Dajani a piece of paper, which the Palestinian slipped unopened into his pocket.

"Do you know the Artist personally?"

"No."

"Good. When you order the passports, indicate somehow you're Hez'bollah."

"Are these people going to need visas?"

"No. We'll send them out of Nicosia or Tehran to Berlin on Interflug when the time comes."

"And do I offer any reason for the operation?"

Again, the *rezident* reflected for a moment, pondering his own terse and limited instructions from the Center. "Suggest to them it's vengeance for the Airbus the Americans shot down. Believe me, if this goes through there'll be enough bloodshed to avenge a whole squadron of Airbuses."

Twenty-four hours after his surreptitious passage into the West, Major Valentin Tobulko was strolling along Zurich's Bahnhofstrasse with all the relaxed assurance of an American businessman long accustomed to working and traveling in Western Europe. Swinging from his right hand was an expensive Vuitton leather attaché case, exactly the sort one would have expected a man of his stature to be carrying. He'd picked it up a few minutes earlier at the left-luggage counter of the railroad station.

Whistling softly, he stopped at 249, a solid brownstone structure whose occupants were identified by a series of discreet bronze plaques beside the door. He checked to be sure the firm he was looking for was indeed there and then walked up to the third floor. The reception room could well have been a doctor's waiting room: half a dozen armchairs, a highly polished circular table, three discreet oils of alpine scenes. The papers and magazines on the table, however, the *Financial Times*, the *Wall Street Journal*, the *Economist, Business Week*, made it clear that medicine was not the concern of visitors to the office. It was the headquarters of the Privat Kredit Bank, as its name implied a private, small, and uniquely Swiss institution.

Tobulko smiled a warm good morning at the receptionist. "I'd like to purchase a banker's draft, if you'd be so kind," he said.

"Of course," replied the young woman. "In what amount?"

"A hundred thousand dollars."

"Please have a seat. One of our officers will be with you in just a moment."

A few moments later a pale young man in horn-rim glasses, enrobed in that antiseptic look Swiss bankers cultivate, greeted Tobulko and led him to another room, this one rigorously empty of furniture except for a heavy table with two chairs. He motioned Tobulko to one and took the chair opposite. "How may I help you?" he asked.

Tobulko repeated his request for a one-hundred-thousand-dollar banker's draft.

"Certainly. Would you like it made out to bearer or to a designee?"

Tobulko reached into his pocket and handed the banker the Banwell passport. "I should like it in my own name, if you would."

"Fine," the banker agreed. "Our commission for the transaction is one half of one percent."

Tobulko laid his attaché case on the table and opened its combination lock. Inside were neat stacks of hundred-dollar bills, one hundred bills or ten thousand dollars in each stack. An employee of the Voslov Bank, the Soviet's Swiss banking house, had fitted them into the case twenty-four hours earlier, then checked it at the Zurich railroad station. A second bank employee had later delivered the claim stub in a sealed envelope addressed to Banwell at the Baur au Lac Hotel. Time might be the art of the Swiss, but security was the art of the KGB. Tobulko counted out ten stacks of bills and an additional five hundred dollars and passed them to the banker. With a fine Swiss display of meticulousness, the banker counted them out in turn, bill by bill. Then he took the passport and the bills.

He was back in minutes with an obsequious smile, the passport, and a banker's draft for a hundred thousand dollars.

Tobulko's next stop was yet another bank, this one the massive Zurich headquarters of the Crédit Suisse, where he asked to meet a bank officer for the purpose of opening an account. The young man to whom he was introduced, every bit as antiseptic as the first banker had been, looked with respect at the line of zeros on the banker's draft that Tobulko laid before him. Nothing, the KGB officer thought, commands a banker's attention as those little zeros do. He was going to be traveling in Europe for the next few weeks, he explained, and while he had every confidence in the Privat Kredit Bank, his normal Swiss bankers, they did not have the European-wide facilities of a bank like the Crédit Suisse.

The young man beamed a warm endorsement of his visitor's wisdom, took the Banwell passport, and helped Tobulko fill out the forms needed to open an account.

"Shall I order you some Eurocheques and a Eurocheque card?" he asked.

"Yes," Tobulko replied. "It would also be helpful, perhaps, to have a VISA card. You can direct-debit the charges to the account."

"Certainly. What would you like to establish as the card's credit limit? Ten thousand dollars?"

"That should be plenty." Tobulko smiled. The young man fussed his way through a few more papers, then offered Tobulko an earnest handshake to welcome him officially into the worldwide family of Crédit Suisse clients. His checks and cards would be ready in forty-eight hours.

As Tobulko strode back out of the bank's double door, just the suggestion of a smile played across his face. Latin American drug dealers were not the only people skilled in laundering money. He would now have access to the one indispensable accouterment of travel in the United

States, a credit card. And no one would ever be able to trace it to its rightful owners, the KGB.

Feisal's Café. Just walking by the dingy café across the Rue Bliss from the gates of the American University of Beirut stirred all the nostalgia of which Abou Said Dajani's soul was capable. As they had been in his days as a poor Palestinian student, his tuition funded by the PLO, the café's windows were a pastiche of posters, notices, ads, cartoons. They summoned the university's undergraduates to every imaginable distraction from karate classes to a dozen different demonstrations to protest all the ills, real and imagined, to which the Arab world was subject. For a second, he was tempted to duck inside, order a cup of *masbout*—sweetened Arabic coffee—and a foul sandwich, and let the impassioned ravings of the students engulf him.

That exercise in nostalgia would have to wait, however. He had more important things on his mind. He continued his march up the Rue Bliss to the Rue Sadat. There he turned left, silently cursing the Lebanese as he did for their failure to expunge the Egyptian traitor's name from their street directory. Halfway up the street, he found what he was looking for, a camera shop so shabby, so run-down, Dajani wondered if its proprietor had sold a camera since the Lebanese troubles had begun a decade earlier. Given the man's real occupation, it was probably immaterial whether he had or not.

A little bell tinkled as Dajani thrust open the shop's front door. When he stepped into the shadows of its interior an overwhelming odor of cat's urine assailed his nostrils. It seemed to hang in the air, moist and revolting, like a fog drifting slowly earthward. One of its authors scampered off the shop's empty shelves; another growled at him from out of a darkened corner of the room. Finally, Dajani heard a rustle of wooden beads, and a woman, her head wrapped in a scarf, her bulk swaddled in a loose black wrapper, came toward him. On her left cheek he recognized the blue tattoo of the Howeitat Bedouin tribe.

She did not utter a word of greeting. Instead, she glared at him in sullen, unwelcoming silence.

"I've come to see Abou Daoud," Dajani said.

"Who is this Abou Daoud? Who are you?"

"A friend."

"We have no friends."

"I come from Baalbek."

"I don't care if you come from the moon."

"From the Imam Fadallah. He is my friend. He sends his respectful greetings to Abou Daoud."

The mention of the imam's name clearly registered on the woman's hostile features. He was a Shiite imam, schooled in the terrorist camp of the Ayatollah Hussein Ali Montazeri in Qom in Iran, then sent to Lebanon's Bekaa Valley to organize and run the Hez'bollah, the fanatical Shiite organization which had left its bloody imprint on scores of terrorist actions and hostage seizures.

Dajani took a small card, the imam's personal calling card, from his pocket. Dajani served as his liaison to Abu Nidal, and the Iranian cleric had given him the card as a kind of safe-conduct pass to the violence-prone communities around Baalbek in the Bekaa Valley. He handed it to the woman.

"I can't read."

"Abou Daoud can."

The woman thought that over a moment. She glared up at Dajani. "Wait," she commanded. She padded out of the room, her departure signaled by another rustling of the beaded wooden curtain at the rear of the shop.

It was at least five minutes before Dajani heard a sound except for the hostile meowing of the half-dozen cats infesting the shop. Finally, he heard the labored slip-slap of a pair of felt slippers advancing across the floor behind the beaded curtain. A hand shot through the curtain and flicked on a light. Then a man emerged, a shriveled old man well into his seventies. It was one o'clock in the afternoon, but he was still wearing his pajamas and a bathrobe knotted around his waist with a rope. On his head was a symbol of an Arab world long dead, a red tarboosh. He peered at Dajani through horn-rimmed glasses, the kind with flat, perfectly round lenses you saw diplomats wearing in the old newsreels from the 1930s.

Dajani smiled in greeting. The shrunken little figure before him was a living legend, Abou Daoud Sinho, the Artist. There was virtually no document in the world he had not reproduced. Hong Kong driver's licenses, Swiss passports, U.S. green cards, Kenyan hunting permits, French resident's permits, German *Gastarbeiter* passbooks—if the document was rare and valued, it was virtually a certainty that at one time or another the Artist had forged it.

Dajani made a half-salaam before the Artist's frail figure. "I bring you warmest greetings from the imam," he intoned with the solemnity of a muezzin reciting the morning prayer call.

The Artist clutched the imam's card in his fingers. They were long, bony, and colored like old parchment by the thousands of cigarettes he'd smoked in his lifetime. "Please extend all courtesies to our friend Abou Said Dajani," the imam had written on it. The Artist studied those words suspiciously. Suspicion was, after all, the trait that kept him commercially prosperous and physically healthy. Finally, his mind made up, he passed the card back to Dajani.

"Coffee?" he asked.

Dajani nodded.

The Artist clapped his hands. *"Et nain masbout*—two coffees," he barked to the woman in black. He nodded Dajani to a taboret and took another beside it himself.

After they'd sipped at their coffee and worked their way through a few dispirited bits of conversation, the Artist looked up at the Palestinian.

"Shou—so?" he asked.

"I . . . we need four 798s," Dajani said. He drew an envelope from his pocket and slid four passport photos across the mother-of-pearl-inlaid table between them. "For these men." Then he placed the paper the KGB *rezident* in Damascus had given him on the table. "Here are the identities."

"798s are difficult."

"I understand."

798s were Moroccan passports. They belonged to a packet of blank passports stolen from the Moroccan Foreign Office in Rabat and were called 798s because the serial number of the first passport used had begun with 798. No one knew exactly how many passports had been in the stolen packet or quite how they had wound up in the Artist's custody. He doled them out with the parsimony of a miser handing out his last gold coins. Because they were genuine passports already bearing the Moroccan royal seal, detecting them at a border crossing was virtually impossible. That made them immensely valuable to the myriad terrorist organizations the Artist served with fine impartiality.

"They will be thirty thousand Lebanese apiece."

"Agreed."

"Half now. Half on delivery."

"Agreed."

Dajani reached inside his black leather jacket and drew out a brown manila envelope the size of a book. Slowly, he began to count the money onto the little mother-of-pearl table. When he'd finished, the Artist picked up the notes, stuffed them back into their envelope, then thrust it inside his bathrobe like a hot-water bottle.

"In ten days, *inch'Allah*," he said.

"Ladies and gentlemen, Captain Graham has just switched on the 'No Smoking' sign indicating we're beginning our final descent into Toronto International Airport. Please fasten your . . ."

Valentin Tobulko did his best to shut out the Air Canada hostess's weary recital and concentrate his thoughts on the moments ahead. The young KGB officer had complete confidence in his documents, his training, and how easy it was to enter Canada on a stolen U.S. passport.

After all, he'd done it barely three months earlier on his way to New York.

Still, it was the first critical moment in his mission, and despite his efforts to calm himself, he felt a knot of nervous tension tightening his bowels. A few moments later he was standing in front of a Canadian immigration inspector in his glassed-in booth. He laid Banwell's passport on the counter. The officer scrutinized it, checked Tobulko's face against the photo in the passport. Then he flattened it out on the ledge of his cubicle and picked up a thick binder. Panic swept Tobulko. Was this some new Canadian procedure the KGB did not know? Had the State Department started to communicate stolen passports' serial numbers to the Canadians?

Tobulko could have spared himself the worry. The binder contained a list of U.S. citizens wanted by various Canadian authorities, and Roy Banwell's name was not on it. The inspector passed him back the passport with an indifferent gesture.

The Russian collected the suitcase he'd bought in Zurich to give himself the air of a tourist returning home on this trip and left it in the baggage check room. An attaché case alone would be the right cover for the next stage of his journey. Then he took a taxi to downtown Toronto and found a stationery store, where he bought a padded manila envelope. He slipped the Banwell passport inside, addressed it to Roy Banwell, General Delivery, Florida Avenue Post Office, Washington, D.C., and set off in search of a post office to mail it from. He was not going to be caught entering the United States with a stolen passport on his person.

An hour later, he was in a train for Windsor, Ontario, just across the Detroit River from Detroit, Michigan. He found the local Hertz car rental agency and rented a car. His own car, he explained to the attendant on duty, had been banged up in a minor accident. He was going to have it fixed in a garage on the Canadian side and come back to pick it up in a few days.

For identification, he used the VISA card issued by the Crédit Suisse in Zurich and a Michigan driver's license made out in Banwell's name. It was a forgery prepared by the Center's Documentation Division, but it was so good there was only one way an immigration official could discover it had been counterfeited. That would be to run the operator's license number through the Michigan Motor Vehicles Department computer in Lansing. The results of that check would have revealed that license number 0915161821 had, in fact, been issued to a sixty-two-year-old widow named Schulte in Grand Rapids.

Tobulko spread copies of the *Wall Street Journal* and *The New York Times* on the seat of the car. Neither journal, he reasoned, was the sort of reading matter a U.S. immigration inspector would associate with an officer of the KGB. Then he headed for the Ambassador Bridge and his passage into the United States.

As he'd been warned it would, the rented car raised a little flag at the border-crossing post. He showed the inspector his Michigan license, then, when the inspector asked him why he was driving a Canadian rental car, Tobulko gave him the story of his own car's breakdown. He garnished it with a remark about the idiot woman who'd hit him. It was the kind of scene he'd played out dozens of times with the instructors at Bykovo. Be natural, be relaxed, were the watchwords.

The inspector glanced at his reading matter, then passed him back his license.

"I'd like to have a look in the trunk, sir."

Tobulko got out and opened it for him. He'd been expecting the request. Drug smuggling, he knew, was the chief concern of these inspectors.

A few minutes later, he was on his way to Metropolitan Airport. He dropped off the Hertz car and found a Northwest Airlines flight for New York's La Guardia Airport. From there he caught the eight-o'clock shuttle to Washington. He rented a car at National Airport and drove across the Potomac into the capital.

By shortly after ten o'clock that evening he was sitting in the bar of the Washington Hilton savoring the first sip of an ice-cold vodka martini. Despite the jet lag under which his system was beginning to crumple, he was exhilarated. He was in the capital of the United States, his presence and his purpose there unknown to anyone, not even the KGB *rezident* at the Soviet embassy. For a moment perched on his bar stool he felt as though he were reliving a childish fantasy. He was invisible, drifting through these people around him, listening in on their conversations, contemplating their moves and actions, an unseen shade in their little world.

No job the Central Intelligence Agency offered was more dangerous or more difficult than that exercised by the Agency's Beirut station chief, Ray Reid. On his office wall was a photograph of his predecessor, William Buckley, kidnapped by Shiite extremists, brutally tortured, then murdered. Reid kept it there as a reminder, should ever he be tempted to ease up on the security procedures that governed his life, of just how perilous this assignment of his really was. His cover was the role of the embassy's second political officer. It was as transparent as the cellophane wrapping on a box of strawberries at the corner supermarket. There were only half a dozen diplomats still assigned to the once enormous U.S. embassy in Beirut, and determining which one of them was the CIA man required no more skill than reading the morning paper.

Trying to carry out his job without exposing himself or his assets to unacceptable risks was about as easy, Reid liked to joke, as making love in a shop window on Fifth Avenue during the Christmas rush without anyone noticing you. His telephone was tapped, his mail opened by "friendly" Christian forces. Venturing into Moslem West Beirut with its gangs of Shiite fanatics was out of the question. Whenever he moved around Christian East Beirut, Reid estimated he was under surveillance by three different organizations, the Lebanese Deuxième Bureau and two rival Christian militia. And, in any event, he couldn't step out of the embassy compound without an armed escort, a pair of Christian Lebanese. Who knew who they reported to?

Yet the irony of the situation was that the Agency retained a solid network of reliable assets and informers in the Lebanese capital. Beirut had always been a Third World spy center, a place where intelligence agents flourished as they once had in wartime Lisbon and Istanbul. The problem was communicating with them. To do it, Reid had been forced to go back to tactics developed by the anti-Nazi resistance during the war, when the book on clandestine operations was written.

That was, in fact, what he was doing now, riding down the main shopping street of Ashrafiyeh in Christian East Beirut, his bodyguards in the front seat, the economics officer beside him discussing baseball. As the car inched through the heavy noon-hour traffic, Reid's eyes glanced from time to time at the shops and crowds along the street. They found what they were looking for a hundred yards from the Greek Catholic Church of the Holy Martyrs, the stall of a sidewalk flower vendor. What a tribute to the resiliency of the human spirit, Reid thought, that after the horrors the last decade had visited on them, the Lebanese could still buy and sell flowers. At the base of the stand, set just a bit apart from the rest of the vendor's display, was a green vase containing three stalks of bright red gladiolas. It was his sign. There was a message waiting for him in the letter box used by one of the Agency's most precious and secret assets in the city.

Later that afternoon, on his way back to the embassy from a meeting at the ambassador's residence in Yarze, he decided to stop at a little shop he occasionally visited in Furn-el-Shebak. Once, in Beirut's glory days, its proprietor had owned a souvenir gallery on the curve of the corniche above the Saint-Georges Hotel. Now he eked out a living selling hand-hammered brass and copper trays, coffeepots, vases, and urns, and boxes of cedarwood inlaid with mother-of-pearl. They came in all forms —backgammon, checker, and chess boards; boxes for playing cards, jewelry, buttons, and bric-a-brac. At Christmas and Easter, an occasional Beiruti would send one to a relative in some distant corner of the globe, a souvenir of the tortured homeland they'd been forced to abandon. And a few people like Reid collected them.

He left one bodyguard to protect his car and the other posted at the entrance to the shop. For a few moments, he chatted with the proprietor about Beirut's golden days, then began a fascinated survey of his merchandise.

It took him twenty minutes to find what he was looking for. It was a cigarette box with a Cedar of Lebanon wrapped in a kind of halo of triangular wedges of mother-of-pearl on its cover. One of the thirty-odd triangles was inverted. He picked up the box, selected a second box at random, and took them to the proprietor. They went through the expected ritual of bargaining over their price, then Reid paid the man, pocketed his boxes, and walked back to his car.

"Harry," shouted the manager of the Silver Spring Radio Shack from his post at the front of the store, "guy here wants to talk to you."

Harry glanced up angrily from the Tandy II he was playing with in the PC section. It was three minutes to his lunch hour. The last thing he needed was some bullshit conversation with a jerk who probably wasn't even going to wind up buying an extra set of pencil batteries for his pocket calculator. He looked at the man walking over to him, a blond guy with a crew cut in a State Department suit. Never saw him before in my life, he thought. How come he wants to talk to me?

"Banwell," said the man, offering Harry a warm smile and a friendly handshake. "Roy Banwell. I understand you're a real computer whiz."

Harry gave a shrug that defined just how indifferent a salesman he was. Banwell didn't seem to notice. He launched enthusiastically into a complex question on modeling computer graphics. Finally, hungry, Harry stopped him. "Look, mister," he said, "can this wait a little bit? My lunch hour's just starting."

"Oh!" Banwell's tone was both surprised and apologetic. He glanced at his watch. "I'll make a deal with you. There's a Chinese restaurant down the street, Empress of China, terrific place, know it? Come talk computers and I'll buy us lunch down there."

It took Harry just over a millisecond to decide to accept the offer. He knew the Empress of China all right, but mostly from being outside looking in. Lunch there was certainly going to beat the shit out of the Big Mac that was his usual lunchtime staple.

Somewhat to his surprise, their conversation during lunch didn't really get focused in on computers. It was only after their cute Chinese waitress brought them some jasmine tea that Harry sensed Banwell beginning to move toward the point of their lunch.

"You know," he remarked, "I'm an avid reader of the press."

"So are a lot of people."

"I was going through the *Post* the other day." Banwell paused a second. "For May eleventh, 1985."

Harry felt a chill in his stomach. That was the day he'd been given a six-month suspended sentence in Federal District Court for stealing government property. How did the son of a bitch know that? What was this? Some kind of a shakedown?

He gave Banwell a stare which was not exactly suffused with gratitude for the good lunch he'd just eaten.

"Boy," Banwell went on, "I gotta say the Navy really fucked you over, didn't they? I mean, the way they treated you, firing you, slapping that suspended sentence on your head after you offered to give them back their crummy computers. They acted like a bunch of first-class bastards."

Harry made a noise that was as much a growl as it was a gesture of assent to Banwell's words. Banwell reached out and for just a moment rested his hand gently on Harry's wrist.

"Harry, I want to be absolutely up front with you. Get the cards all down on the table, so to speak." Tobulko had been working on his idiomatic English at Bykovo, and he was delighted to see how easily it was rolling off his tongue. "I work for a medical-equipment company out in St. Louis. American Medical. Ever hear of us?"

Harry shook his head.

"Never mind. We're into the forefront of medical technology. Right out there on the cutting edge where it's all happening. I need your help."

"Mine?" said Harry. He couldn't have been more stunned if Banwell had suggested they drop into the White House for a cup of coffee with the President.

"Right. One of the things we're working on is a new device to study how the brain works. Real state-of-the-art stuff. We've got one major competitor, and right now they've got their machine installed over at Bethesda in the Radiological and Diagnostical Facility."

"Hey, wait a minute, mister. If you want me to go poking around Bethesda, forget it. I walk in the front door out there and bells'll start ringing."

"I don't want that, Harry. Hear me out. This machine they got over there is a magnetoencephalograph. Made by some good folks out in San Diego. They got it wired up to a Hewlett-Packard Precision Spectrum computer. What I need is a copy of, say, the last four months of data on the master disk in there. So we can be sure these guys' machine isn't doing something our machine can't do. Product development research, you know what I mean?"

"Sure I do, mister. But like I told you, there's no fucking way in hell I can get through the front door out there at Bethesda. If they brought me in dying on a stretcher, they wouldn't let me into the emergency room."

"Bastards. How many years did you work out there, Harry?"

"Seven."

"Seven, okay. You had friends, right?"

"What do you mean?"

"Here's my deal, Harry. I need somebody who can go in there, copy some of the data on that disk for me. Take a few minutes at the most—it should all fit easily on one high-density floppy. No sweat. No danger. No big deal. You think about the guys you knew out there. Maybe a guy who was boosting the computers with you, didn't get caught. You put him on to me and he agrees to do it, you got five thousand bucks, cash, in your hand, under the table. Nobody sees, nobody knows."

"And the guy?"

"He gets another five the same way when he gives me the floppy disk. Nobody knows anything. Out in St. Louis, it goes down as medical research."

Harry digested his words for a few minutes. Five thousand bucks was a lot of dough. What was he doing illegal in this? Nothing he could figure. He began to work through his mental Rolodex of his friends out at Bethesda.

"Let me think about it," he said as the waitress laid the check and a pair of fortune cookies at Banwell's elbow.

"No problem."

Banwell paid the waitress and cracked open a fortune cookie. He pulled out the little white ribbon in its core. He read it, laughed, then passed it to Harry.

"Hey," he said, "I think this one's yours."

Harry stretched it out.

"Listen to the words of the wise man," it said, "and good fortune will smile on you."

On the pine-covered hills of Awkah climbing out of the Mediterranean north of Beirut, it was already night. Only the marine guards downstairs were still in the building that served as the provisional U.S. embassy in strife-torn Lebanon. Ray Reid opened his safe and took out the cedarwood box inlaid with mother-of-pearl which he'd purchased earlier in the day.

He snapped off the cover, then took a knife from his desk. Carefully, he cut away the piece of wood around the triangle of mother-of-pearl that had been inverted in the halo of wedges around the cedar tree on the box's cover. Next, he took a razor and slowly, very cautiously, picked at the mother-of-pearl triangle until he'd pried it from its resting place.

He turned the piece of wood upside down over his desk and tapped it. What he was looking for fell out onto his desk, two black specks of microfilm no larger than a small child's fingernail.

Reid fitted the film into a photo magnifier and focused its light onto a piece of white paper on his desk. A triumphant smile crossed his face as the images of the film took form before his eyes. The old bugger had earned his money again. Below him were four 798 photographs, the serial numbers of four Royal Moroccan passports, four sets of identities, certainly all false, and one word: "Hez'bollah."

It was a few minutes before midnight. The Bethesda Naval Medical Center was muffled in the special silence of hospital nights, in the knowledge that somewhere in its dim corridors, a life was ebbing away, another thrusting toward existence. The naval medical corpsman on duty at the main reception desk didn't even look up from his paperback when Pharmacist's Mate First Class Eddie Ruggiero pushed through the revolving doors. As the color-coded ID badge pinned to his uniform breast indicated, Ruggiero was one of the senior enlisted men in the hospital's lab facility.

He walked across the empty reception room toward the gangway leading over to Building Nine, which housed the center's diagnostic facilities. The sailor manning the command duty desk, perched above a sign reading "Safe sex—do you know your partner?" glanced at him as he walked by.

"Hey, man," he said, "I didn't know you were on watch tonight."

"Naw," answered Ruggiero. "Just gotta check out a couple of cultures."

He strolled over the gangway into Building Nine, then skirted along the purple doors of the Radiological Facility in the main deck. Just as he expected, there was a plastic card like a hotel "Do Not Disturb" sign hanging from the doorknob of the main entrance to the facility. "Duty Attendant in the Cave," it said.

Ruggiero ambled along the corridor toward the Cave, a twenty-four-hour cafeteria for the center's personnel in the middle of Building Nine. There were barely a dozen people sitting around pulling coffee, smoking. He spotted the Radiological Facility duty attendant in the midst of an animated conversation with a pretty black nurse from the emergency room. Twists of steam were rising from their coffee mugs. They were going to be there for a while.

Reassured, he ambled back up the corridor, trying to slow the nervous gait of his footsteps as he advanced on the purple door of the Radiological Facility. Twenty-five yards from the door, his nerves began to crumble.

Damn, what the fuck am I doing this for? I'm putting sixteen years in the Navy on the line. What will they do if I get caught? Maybe I'll wind up in the brig at Portsmouth with those fucking jarhead guards who beat the shit out of you if you look at them cross-eyed.

He was abreast of the door now. He glanced back over his shoulder. The corridor behind him was empty and silent. So, too, was the area ahead of him. There was no one to notice him slip through the purple door. Five thousand dollars. Five thousand dollars cash for one little disk, that was what Harry's guy, the guy from St. Louis, had promised. Almost automatically, his hand slid to the doorknob and turned it. The door was unlocked, just as he'd figured it would be. He slid inside.

He leaned against the door. He was panting nervously. What the hell was he going to tell them if somebody caught him in here? O'Rourke—he was looking for Charley O'Rourke, see if he had the watch, see if he wanted to go down to the Cave, get some coffee. It took an effort of will to shove himself away from the door and start down the long passageway giving access to the facility's treatment stations.

"Are you pregnant?" two signs screamed at him in Spanish and English. "If you are, please tell the X-ray technician."

Holy shit, he thought, am I pregnant? At least I got a

lump in my belly right now big enough to make me think I'm pregnant.

The magnetoencephalography installation was at the end of the corridor past the other scanner facilities. There was a little sitting room in case a patient had to wait. Behind it was the installation itself, the device in its sauna-like demagnetized chamber, and the control room in front of it. At its center was the gleaming white Hewlett-Packard computer he'd come to violate. Looking at it, the nervousness surged over him again.

He was going to have to turn that damn thing on. Have it light up like a Christmas tree. Look at the directories on the master disk and find the scan data files. Then copy the last four months of scan data to a floppy disk. Christ, the whole thing was going to take more than a few minutes. What the fuck was he going to say he was doing with this damn thing whirring away like a sewing machine if somebody walked in? Looking up Charley O'Rourke's address, for Christ's sake?

Five thousand dollars, he whispered to steady his nerves. His shaking fingers pulled the blank floppy disk he'd brought with him from his jacket. As he looked for the computer's power switch, his eyes fell on the rack beside the control panel. It contained two series of floppy disks. The first was marked "Blank Disks." The second section beside it was labeled "Scan Data." He looked at the disks it contained. Obviously they were copies of all the scans done, with a disk for each quarter. The guy had said he wanted the last four months. Fuck starting the machine, Ruggiero thought. He reached out, grabbed the disks for the last two quarters, and slipped them into his jacket. He spun around and in a second was on his way back to the purple door and safety.

The traffic, bumper to bumper, crept along L Street toward 14th. Valentin Tobulko smiled in amazement at the spectacle on the sidewalk. They were barely five blocks from the White House, and who did the pavements belong to at two o'clock in the morning? Not politicians, but whores. He watched the spectacle hungrily. The girls were mostly black, flaunting satin miniskirts clinging like elastic stretch pants to their high muscular buttocks, their long brown legs tapering sensually to the outrageously high heels on which they pranced along the sidewalks and darted out to the passing cars. He savored the stiffening between his legs. Did he dare spend some of the KGB's money on one or two of these girls, get a hotel room near here, have a wild debauched night before he went back to Moscow? No one would ever know. But there was AIDS. All American whores had AIDS, they said. Particularly the black ones. Like so many of his countrymen, Tobulko was fundamentally a racist. Yet these proud defiant black girls exuded some mysterious, challengingly strong sexuality that aroused him as no one in Moscow did.

He nosed the car into the curb at Vermont. Two of the girls swayed out to the car, laughing and shaking their breasts as they advanced on him. One poked her head into the open car window. Golden curls cascaded from her wig, and a cloud of her cheap perfume seemed to roll into the car like a fog bank drifting in from the sea. "Hey, honey, how about a date?" she challenged.

At that moment, he saw the sailor, in civilian clothes, moving out of the shadows to the car. "Here's my date," Tobulko laughed. The whores turned to Ruggiero. "Yech!" screeched the one with the blond wig. "AIDS bait!"

Ruggiero slipped onto the seat beside Tobulko. The KGB officer pointed the car back into the stream of passing traffic.

"Get it?"

Ruggiero tapped his jacket. "Right here. Better than what you wanted, Banwell old boy. I got disks for the last six months."

Tobulko whistled softly. "Let's have a look."

Ruggiero pulled the disks from his pocket and held them up. In the gleam of a streetlight, Tobulko could see the seal of the U.S. Navy and the words "Bethesda

Naval Medical Center" printed on the label pasted onto the disk.

"You got mine?" the sailor asked.

Tobulko drew an envelope from his pocket and passed it to Ruggiero. "Count it."

The sailor's greedy fingers picked a slow, deliberate path through the hundred-dollar bills in the envelope. He was exhilarated. He'd pulled it off without a hitch. His mind was already planning how to spend the money. First a quick visit to the corridor up on Harvard Street, get a little marching powder from one of the sidewalk salesmen up there. Then back to the Whirlwind Bar to meet Regine the exotic dancer, with the tits the size of an elephant's balls. He'd look a little better to her, he knew, once he'd stuffed some Colombian sugar up her nose.

Tobulko watched scornfully as Ruggiero completed his count. His mind was on his future plans, too. Gone now was the temptation to spend the night with a couple of L Street whores. Tomorrow he'd pick up the Banwell passport at the General Delivery window of the post office by the hotel, head up to New York, and fly out to London. Leaving the United States on a stolen passport was no problem. Then he'd fly to Stockholm and get onto the Leningrad ferry.

"Count's right," Ruggiero said. "Pleasure to do business with you, Mr. Banwell."

Tobulko moved the car back to the curb. He extended his hand to the sailor. "Thanks for the help," he declared. "You may not realize it, but you made a real contribution to medical science tonight."

Art Bennington slammed down his telephone. She was on her answering machine. She was always on her goddam answering machine. He picked up a paperclip, twisted it into a pretzel, and hurled it into his wastebasket. Maybe she was away. Didn't pick up her messages. He closed the center drawer of his desk with an angry slam. This was all so stupid. He was a grown man, for Christ's sake. Why was he working himself up like a high school kid with a hard-on? He locked the drawer and stood up. He really did want to see her again. There was also that nagging suspicion: had she in fact learned his name when the waiter used it at Jean Pierre's? A minor point, but one he still had to lay to rest.

He sighed. Now he had a different sort of treat waiting for him. He had to go upstairs and have lunch with the director. Just a private lunch, the director's secretary had said when she called to make the appointment, the Judge wanted to have a chat with him. Those words had sent a cold chill down his spine. Was this little chat going to turn out to be as friendly as his last chat with Colby had been?

A blue blazer showed him into the director's private dining room adjoining his office suite. Lunch would be private, all right. The table was set for two. The director, the blue blazer explained, was on his way back from across the river. He'd be a few minutes late. It was ten minutes past one when he finally burst into the room. "Christ, Art, I'm sorry," he said. "I was up on the Hill. Oversight Committee. Those guys simply can't stop talking." He glanced at the mess steward. "I'll have a Bloody Mary. Join me, Art?"

That was sufficient invitation for Bennington. He ordered one as well. The director waved to the table. "Let's eat. I'm starved."

Resting on each plate was a handwritten menu card. They made their selections while Fernando, the mess steward, handed them their drinks.

"Cheers, Art," the director said. "I was a little brusque with you at our last meeting. I apologize. I was furious about losing that asset. Still am."

What am I seeing here? Bennington wondered. The first contrite director in the history of the CIA? Or is he spreading anesthetic on my back so I won't feel the knife as it goes in? "No apologies necessary, Mr. Director. Brusqueness is a prerogative that goes with your office."

"You know," the director continued, "I was thinking back on our last meeting. When we talked about your psychic woman who was murdered up in New York, remember?''

"I sure do. Unfortunately we haven't been able to turn up any leads on who fingered her to the KGB. Except for one old left-wing pal the FBI's investigating.''

"You probably gathered at the time I was completely, totally skeptical about this paranormal business you're overseeing.''

"Yeah, you could say that. But then you're in good company.''

"Am I?" asked the director. He nodded his head three or four times as though trying to find the answer to some momentarily puzzling riddle. "I'm not so sure.''

Bennington stiffened. That was certainly not a phrase he'd expected to hear this man utter.

"I had an experience about a week ago, to be quite frank, a rather jarring one. That's why I asked you up for lunch today. I want to describe it to you—strictly in confidence, of course. With your medical and scientific background, you know more about these things than anybody else in this building does.''

The director took a long swallow of his Bloody Mary, holding the liquid on his tongue as he ordered his thoughts.

"It happened last Thursday. My wife woke up screaming in the middle of the night. A nightmare. She said she'd dreamed her sister was drowning and calling out to her for help. She'd dreamed they were both children swimming in a lake they used to go to in the Ozarks. Now, we have an alarm clock with a luminous dial, so I saw what time it was. It was four thirty-two in the morning. I calmed her down. After all, Kelly and Eldon, her sister and brother-in-law, were driving through France. One of those eating trips where you use the Michelin Guide for a road map.''

"I know the kind." Bennington laughed. "Forget the museums and cathedrals, just take me to your three-star restaurants.''

"Right. So that was that. Or so I thought. Tuesday when I got in here, I had a call from our ambassador in

Paris. Kelly and Eldon's car had been swept away by a flash flood during a torrential downpour in the gorges of the Tarn. They were both drowned.''

The director took another sip of his drink. He was a shaken man. ''Now this is what I have a hard time dealing with, Art. When that flood hit their car, its generator went out. All the electrical circuitry stopped.''

Bennington felt the same fleeting tap on his shoulder, the same swift brush on his cheek that he'd sometimes known working with Pat Price or when Ann Robbins's uncanny results came in—the hint of a fleeting visitation from across the frontiers of the spirit.

''The dashboard clock read ten thirty-two when they found the car. The French are six hours ahead of us. That's four thirty-two A.M. here in Washington.

''My wife and I haven't been able to think of much else since,'' the director went on. ''I haven't mentioned this to anybody, because, quite frankly, I'm afraid of making a fool out of myself. But the experience has sure as hell shaken up my belief system.''

''Don't feel like an odd man out, Mr. Director. People have been having experiences like yours for four thousand years. Tell it to a bunch of hard-nosed scientists, though, and they'll say, 'Yes, that's very interesting. Thank you very much.' And forget it as soon as you walk out the door. As they like to point out, there are thousands of predictive dreams like that every night when nothing happens. The car doesn't crash.''

''But it happened to me, Art. Or rather to my wife. I know it happened for a fact. I saw that alarm clock with my own eyes.''

''Mr. Director, I don't doubt that. Any more than I doubt some of the things I've seen in the thirty years I've worked on this stuff for the CIA. But until we find a way to fit them into some solid scientific framework, it's all just folklore.''

''But how do you explain it? How could it possibly happen?''

''I can't explain it. Nobody can. All we can do is toss up theories.''

"Such as?"

"Well, it's assumed in Western culture that our consciousness, yours, mine, is particulate." Art tapped his Bloody Mary glass and then fingered the director's. "Distinct objects, as these glasses are. Each localized in time and space. Suppose that assumption is wrong? Suppose consciousness has a duality to it? Suppose it has a wave-like nature as well as its particulate nature?"

"That sounds physically impossible."

Art shrugged. "Light has that dual character. When physicists get down to the microlimits of reality, they find subatomic particles like the rho prime that apparently have it, too. So why not our consciousness? That would give consciousness access to regimes of time and space that otherwise wouldn't be accessible."

The mess steward glided up with their lunch plates and set them on the table. "Coffee? Tea?"

"Ice water," Art said.

"My usual tea," ordered the director. "Well, I find all this fascinating, puzzling, and, I've got to say, very unsettling."

"Dangerous, too," Art cautioned. "There are big risks associated with this. Political risks. Public-opinion risks. And some people get a bit loopy when they get overinvolved with it. Christ, we had a guy here once who wanted to use a medium to talk to our great spy Penkovsky after the Russians shot him. See if there was anything he'd forgotten to tell us."

The director laughed. "Maybe we'd better get that guy back to arrange a chat with the asset we just lost."

Art took a mouthful of his grilled sole and smiled at the director. Forgotten now was the foreboding with which he'd entered this room. "You see some funny things in this area. Old man McDonnell of McDonnell Douglas was big into it. Thought it was wonderful the Russians were so intrigued by the paranormal, because he was convinced they'd find God at the end of the line and blow Marxism right out of the water."

"With a little luck we won't need God for that." The director chuckled. "We've got Gorbachev." He finished off the last of his Bloody Mary. "That damn dream has changed my whole perspective on your work."

"It's been around for a long time, Mr. Director. After all, the Bible is in some ways a catalogue of psychic phenomena. Aristotle, the great rationalist, was fascinated by prophetic dreams like your wife's. Sir Francis Bacon, who after all founded the scientific method, wanted to investigate psychic healing."

"Quite a roll call."

"And how about dowsing? People have been going around looking for water with little forked sticks for four thousand years. They're still doing it despite all the gains science has made in this century."

The director tilted back in his chair, cocked his head, and smiled at Art. "Well, after all these years, Art, you must have come up with some personal explanation for this, some rational stuff a pragmatic old Missouri mule like me can sink his teeth into. How do you deal with it when you can't get to sleep at night?"

"By worrying about other things, like stretching out the paycheck."

"Seriously, Art. How do you look at it as a medical man?"

Art shrugged. "My pet theory involves something called Schumann resonances. They reverberate back and forth between the Van Allen belts in the ionosphere and the earth's magnetic field on the surface of the earth. Been doing it for eons."

"How do you get from them to my wife's dream?"

"With a couple of leaps of the imagination, mostly." Bennington laughed. "An awful lot of the frequencies in those Schumann resonances are down around ten hertz. Among other things, that's the frequency of the earth's own electromagnetic field. So as life, animal, plant, human, emerged on the earth, it was being constantly exposed to an electromagnetic sea in that ten-hertz range. You might suppose that the life forms that evolved would retain some special sensitivity to those ten-hertz frequencies, right?"

"Yes," the director agreed. He'd left his salad half eaten. "I suppose you would."

"And they do. When you feel good, the alpha waves in your brain are pulsing at ten hertz. Same thing if you flex your biceps. It's a frequency spectrum we are constantly finding insects and animals use in their sensing mechanisms."

There was more interest written on the director's face now than Bennington had seen at either of their earlier encounters. "So," the director noted, "those frequencies could account for my wife's nightmares?"

"It's a theory. About as good as any of the others you're likely to come across. It's pretty well established that human cells can detect those signals, interpret them. But we have no explanation for how a cell could send a message. None. Where's the power source? There isn't any."

"In other words, you can explain how my wife got that message but not how her sister sent it?"

"In theory, yes. Which brings me back to the point I raised in that meeting about our murdered psychic. For the moment, the traffic on this ELF street seems to be all one-way—it's all going into cells. There's nothing coming back out we can see. But that's dangerous enough. It could open the way to using these things to influence behavior." Bennington sensed the director would soon have to cut this off. He drained his ice water. "You remember that story of the guy at State who said, 'Gentlemen don't read each other's mail'?"

"The idiot who almost lost the Second World War for us by trying to put us out of the cryptanalysis business?"

"That one. Well, gentlemen aren't supposed to try to pry open each other's minds, either. But I'm afraid they may be able to do it before long."

The procedure was SOP, the bookend that closed a week's routine, the last gesture Arlene Doxie had to accomplish before embarking on a weekend's freedom. The floppy disk for the current quarter was updated only once a week, because each time the Bethesda magnetoencephalograph was employed, other copies of the computer data were made immediately, one for the main backup files, locked up in the hospital's record center, one for the researcher from the National Institutes of Health, Brain Sciences Division, who employed it in his work, and sometimes one for the patient's neurologist.

When she reached for her backup disk file this Friday afternoon, she was puzzled to discover that the backup disks for the current and preceding quarters were missing. Strange, Arlene thought. Maybe she'd mixed them in with the blanks. She checked the blanks. They weren't there. Yet she was meticulous in her work habits, which in view of her master's degree in computer science from USC was hardly surprising. Recreating the disks, of course, was no big deal. All the files were still on the hard disk, and copying them onto fresh floppies wouldn't take long. Probably the originals had been mailed in error with a patient's exam record to a capital-area neurologist. She would check that on Monday. I wonder, she thought, should I tell the administrator? Or just forget it?

In any event, all that could wait. She gave herself a blast of Arpège and headed for the door. She had better things on her mind this evening.

Night had already fallen by the time Xenia Petrovna reached the security gate. Autumn in Moscow was such a brief interlude, a nostalgic sigh for a lost summer before the interminable winter began. An allegory, perhaps, for her affair with Ivan Sergeivich? By now the KGB guards at the entrance recognized her Citroën. It was, after all, her fourth visit to the chairman's hunting lodge since their affair had begun that Sunday afternoon. Still, the young captain on duty was going through his security routine with maddening slowness, as though he derived some perverse pleasure from slowing her journey to his boss's bed.

Feodorov heard the sound of her arriving car and came to the door of the lodge. He would have a fire roaring in his huge fireplace by now. The fur rug, its hairs so silken they could have been sable, would be spread before the flames. They'd made love on that rug in front of the dying embers on her last visit. Remembering those luxurious instants electrified her body's nerve ends. Despite her rising desire, however, she slid from her car with calculated slowness and advanced on Feodorov at a measured glide. By both instinct and desire, Xenia Petrovna was a temptress.

He must have arrived only moments earlier from Dzerzhinsky Square. As she reached him, she gave a toss to her cascading blond hair and eased a smile that was both mocking and inviting onto her lips. Wordlessly, she slithered into his arms. Their embrace was long and sensual. As they kissed, she pressed her hips and thighs against his groin and held them there, delighting to sense him stiffening in response to her pressure.

She drew away slowly and looked up at his dark, almost saturnine regard. "So, how is my Georgian despot tonight? You seem worried."

"Not anymore. Not now that I have you to hold."

"Vaniusha, Vaniusha, do you really expect your women to believe such charming lies?"

"Believe them? No. Accepting them is enough."

He took her arm and they walked toward the lodge, hips pressed together in a kind of promissory communion. For the first time this fall, she saw her breath's silver filigree drifting through the air. Another harbinger of winter.

"I want to get out of this suit," Ivan Sergeivich announced, entering the lodge. He ran his strong fingers slowly down her spine, playfully letting them pause at the knob of each vertebra along their route.

As she always did on such occasions, Xenia Petrovna had selected her clothes with considerable care. From her French silk lingerie to her form-hugging leather pants from Frankfurt to her white cashmere sweater from Harrods, they were all, of course, from the West. The effect they had produced was precisely the one she'd intended.

When he came back in jeans and a heavy wool sweater,

he had an expression on his face she'd often seen there, a regard she'd always found curious in a man whose power was as complete as his was. It was the look of a little boy who wanted—but didn't quite dare—to suggest a forbidden game to a friend.

"Let's do something different tonight," he proposed.

"Not too different, my angel," she said. "Your earlier programs have been just fine."

"Come," he ordered. He flicked a number of switches on a control panel by the lodge door, then led her outside. Recessed lanterns marked out the path down to the water's edge.

"A swim would be different, all right, *dorogoy*—darling," she informed her lover, "but I think I'd also find it about as sexually arousing as eating a bowl of boiled lentils."

"For a brilliant neurologist," Feodorov remarked, "you have a disturbing tendency to leap to the wrong conclusions."

At the lake's edge, he turned her left along the shore. About a hundred yards ahead, she saw a splash of light flowing out of the shadows onto the lake's waters. It came from a low-lying, one-story log hut, an updated replica of the traditional peasant *izba*—cottage. He opened the door. Inside was the KGB chairman's luxury version of an institution that had been a constant of Russian life for eight centuries, a *banya*, a bathhouse. There was a small room to leave their clothes, a washing room, the *parilnya*, the steam room with its wide wooden benches, and a cold pool. Finally, there was the resting room, a mecca waiting to reward the bathers at the end of their ritual progress. An ice chest rested in one of its corners. Bottles of vodka, beer, mineral water, and champagne poked through a blanket of ice cubes. Their visit to the *banya* was not entirely spontaneous.

Feodorov locked the door behind them. "I love a bath after a hard day." Indeed, a long, relaxed evening in a bathhouse was very much a tradition among the Soviet elite. Not the sort of bath the chairman of the KGB had in mind, however. He slipped Xenia Petrovna's jacket off and placed it on a hook. As she started to pull her cashmere sweater over her head, she felt his palms caress her rib cage. His fingers moved hungrily forward, their tips playing over the taut surface of her stomach. Then they thrust their way imperiously under the belt of her slacks, over the silk sheen of her panties. He pulled her body against his, and again she felt him stiffening, this time pressing against her buttocks. For a moment, he held her like that, their bodies locked together, swaying slightly. Then she squirmed free.

"First things first, Vaniusha," she chuckled. They finished undressing and went into the washing room next door. She took a bar of soap the size of a small brick and thrust it into a bucket of hot water. Then she started to slide it over his body in long, teasing strokes. Gradually, he took on the air of a statue glistening in the rain, a slick of water and soapy film mixed with garlands of bubbles sluicing down his chest, back, and legs. Next, she took a scrubbing mitten, a fingerless glove covered with rough, uneven horsehairs. "The fun's over for a while," she announced, applying its scratchy surface to his skin. With a firm hand, she scoured him from his neck to his ankles, each gesture of the mitten applied with the uncompromising determination of a mother offering a weekly scrubdown to a recalcitrant child.

"You scraped away an inch of skin," he murmured when she'd finished. "I don't think there's a single pore you missed."

"I hope not, *moy sladkiy*—my sweetheart. Now it's your turn to lather me." She gave him a lighthearted kiss. "Gently, please."

When he'd finished, they were both covered with a slippery slick of soap film like ancient Greek wrestlers, their bodies oiled for combat. Laughing, they fell into each other's arms, their bodies slithering together, in uncertain sensuality.

Feodorov led her to the showers and then into the ceremonial heart of the *banya*, the *parilnya*, the steam room. Its huge open furnace was full of scalding stones, some glowing in the heat of the bellows below them.

The chairman grabbed a bucket of water and tossed it onto the furnace. A hissing cloud of steam churned up to the bath's wooden ceiling. He did it again and again and again until the bath was wrapped in a silvery fog of moist steam and beads of perspiration mixed with condensed steam bathed their naked bodies.

In one corner of the room were a dozen *veniki,* bundles of birch twigs, an indispensable part of the almost mystic Russian rite of self-purification the bath represented.

"Lie down, Vaniusha," Xenia Petrovna ordered.

The chairman stretched out on his stomach on one of the wooden benches lining the bath. Xenia Petrovna took a bundle of birch twigs from the pile and, with a swishing sound, drove them through the moist air onto Feodorov's wet skin. It reddened under the twigs' slap. She raised her bundle. Again she whipped it onto his back, harder this time. He squirmed silently. Birching with these twigs was supposed to promote circulation, and good Russians were meant to endure it in stoic silence. We'll see just how good a Russian you are, Xenia Petrovna chuckled to herself, lifting the bundle high again.

When they could no longer bear the suffocating heat, they stumbled next door to the cold plunge. That provided a brief, sobering interlude on their way to the bath's ultimate reward, the resting room. Feodorov had designed it as a kind of room-sized bed. They toweled themselves dry and tumbled onto the enormous double mattress covering most of the room. Feodorov scrambled to a cassette player and slipped into it a cassette of Mussorgsky's *Pictures at an Exhibition.* Then he filled two small tumblers with ice-cold vodka. He clinked his glass to Xenia Petrovna. "What shall we toast?"

She thought a moment. "Do you know the Jewish toast?"

"No."

"They say *L'chayim*—to life. I like that. How marvelous life seems at moments like this." She clinked her glass back at his. *"L'chayim."*

He swallowed his vodka in a gulp, she in a series of sips. Momentarily spent by the bath's enervating heat, they lay back on the mattress, bodies intertwined, letting the music and vodka sweep over them. The steam and shock of the ice-cold bath had dampened Feodorov's ardor. Not for long, however. Xenia Petrovna's fingers saw to that. When her work was done, he rolled on top of her with a delighted growl. She was more than ready for him. He entered her swiftly and so fully he could feel the bones at the base of his groin pressing against her. They moved together like that very slowly, barely accelerating the rhythm of their gestures until Feodorov felt his climax beginning to move up from some dark well deep inside his being. Sensing the first warning rush of pleasure, his breath began to come in tightening circles.

At that moment, Xenia Petrovna stopped. She placed the heels of her hands against his hipbones and, laughing, pushed him from her.

"Oh no, no, no. It's much too soon for that, *mi sladki*," she whispered.

He groaned. She rolled him over until he was flat on his back. Then she knelt astride him, sitting erect, and slipped him back inside her. She tilted slightly backward, her palms resting flat on the mattress for support, and resumed her circular movements. Pinned between her knees, he started to follow her gestures.

"Don't move," she commanded.

Slowly, very, very slowly, refusing to accelerate her movements to accommodate his groans or his quickening breathing, her magic pestle did its work, setting their rhythm to the progress of her own delight.

Beneath her, his body began to quiver slightly. He rolled his eyes skyward. *"Da, da, da,"* he groaned. "Now."

She laughed. "I'm not going to let you ejaculate, Vaniusha. I'm going to make you explode."

With that, she resumed her movements, even slower now, bending slightly backward, holding his oncoming pleasure a prisoner of her own. He was sweating and panting, begging for release, but still she refused to accelerate those tantalizingly calculated movements of hers, savoring the tightening inside her.

"Now, Vaniusha," she called out as her own delight started coursing through her. "Now! All for me!" With a final imperious thrust, she forced him to orgasm.

"*Gospodi! Gospodi!*—God! God!" he cried out. "*Ya umirayu*—I'm dying."

His hips rose quivering to her as he indeed exploded, then fell back spent to the mattress. She remained astride him a moment or two, delighting in the diminishing spasms of his pleasure. How extraordinary, she thought. This man exercises such remarkable power, yet for these few moments he's completely under my domination.

Laughing softly, she slid away and lay down beside him, her face looking onto his. She gave his upper lip a playful tweak with a scarlet fingernail.

"Darling Vaniusha," she whispered in a throaty giggle, "don't you think someone in your position should invoke a different sort of deity when he's making love? Perhaps you should try crying 'Vladimir! Vladimir!' or maybe 'Karl! Karl!' to see if it has the same effect."

She was starving by the time they got back to the lodge. The fire was roaring, the side table covered as always with trays of delicacies. They satisfied their hunger in the lazy silence of the sexually spent, then, when they'd finished, he slipped the tape of a James Bond film into his video deck. The chairman of the KGB, Xenia Petrovna knew, found Bond films immensely amusing. The film had just begun when she heard the sound of a telephone ringing somewhere in the lodge. Seconds later, a buzzer sounded.

"That's a call I've got to take." He walked to a nearby phone. "*Da*," he barked. There was a pause.

"Wonderful!" he shouted.

Another pause followed.

"Wonderful!" he exclaimed again. "Put him in a car and get him out here as fast as you can."

"Good news?" she asked as he settled back onto the rug before the TV screen.

"Excellent," he answered and snapped off the pause switch on his remote control.

A few minutes before Bond's final spurt of cinematic gymnastics, Xenia Petrovna heard the sound of tires rolling over the drive's loose stone.

"I've seen the end of this," he said. "You look at it and I'll be back in a few minutes."

"Vaniusha," she replied, "I'll go. You have work to do."

"No, no. Stay. I want you here."

He was back shortly after the film ended, a manila envelope dangling in his hand. "I'm afraid we must now return to our worldly concerns." He indicated the envelope. "This contains computer disks of one of those magic machines of yours in action."

"A magnetoencephalograph?"

"Exactly. You must find on them the record of the exams that were run August seventeenth."

She nodded.

"We are interested in an exam that was made that day. It could not have begun before twelve-fifteen in the afternoon and it had to have been finished by two-thirty."

"It shouldn't be difficult to find. A complete examination takes forty-five minutes."

"We have good reason to believe the patient went into a rage crisis while he was being examined."

He drew a pair of disks from the envelope and tapped them thoughtfully against his fingertips. He handed her the disks. "You told me that if you had a magnetoencephalogram taken of a man when he flew into a rage, you could find the electromagnetic signal that provoked his rage."

Xenia Petrovna felt her temples grow taut. Of course I told you that, she thought. I can find that signal on a disk I've made on my magnetoencephalograph in an exam I've conducted in my lab on my conditions. Not on a disk made by God knows who, God knows when, God knows where. She said nothing, however, and took the disks.

"Find me that man's signal, Xenia. I've got to have it."

She glanced at the disks, then looked at him, startled. "The Bethesda Naval Medical Center? In America? Who would you be interested in there?"

He focused his regard on her, the same dark stare that had terrorized a generation of dissidents. He did not have to tell her never to mention to anyone what he was about to say. The glisten in those Georgian eyes of his told her that.

"The President of the United States."

Admiral Peter White glanced at his watch with ill-concealed impatience. As the head of Bethesda's Medical Department, the President's personal physician had to attend these weekly staff meetings. One by one, each of his fellow department heads would tick off his little triumphs of the past week, a statistical litany of inconsequential achievements down to and including his department's contribution to the United Way. That was occasionally followed by the admission of a minor failing or two, sins of such calculated venality their confession could not possibly stir the composure of the center's director. Important achievements were jealously trumpeted elsewhere; major failings were, whenever possible, swept under the table. The result was meetings worth, White thought, a zero on the Richter scale.

He had a different concern to worry about at the moment, a golf game at Chevy Chase Country Club. He was due on the first tee in forty-five minutes, and if the administrative officer of the Radiological and Diagnostical Facility didn't get on with it, he was going to be late for his foursome.

The gentleman was talking about computers, reminding the gathering of the trouble the center had had a few years back with computer thefts. Well, they had noticed last week that the two most recent backup disks of magnetoencephalographic data had gone missing, presumably stolen. Someone had probably stolen them to erase and use on a home computer. They were instituting a review of their security procedures governing the safekeeping of valuable property, and the center's other departments might wish to follow their example.

It was only half an hour later as he was driving into the Chevy Chase Country Club parking lot that it occurred to White that the data for the President's magnetoencephalogram would have been on one of those disks. The thought was father to a momentary spasm of apprehension. Being only ten minutes away from his assigned tee-off time helped quell it. The President's ID, White assured himself, was coded. And besides, who the hell would want that useless mass of information anyway?

"It's all there!"

Gennadi "Four Fingers" Glebov, the head of the KGB's Fifth Directorate, responsible for the repression of ethnic unrest in the USSR's fifteen republics, waved the stump of his missing forefinger at the report he'd just set before the chairman of the KGB. "Everything we got out of them during their interrogation, plus a complete inventory of everything we found in that cave, right down to the last bullet."

Feodorov glanced at the report, then at his deputy. Four Fingers had the look of a man who'd just sniffed some singularly unpleasant odor, a dog's turd perhaps, and was about to order someone to find it and clean it up for him. The analogy, Feodorov reflected, was not altogether inaccurate. This report was a pile of dog turds, all right, and Four Fingers was certainly going to expect him to take drastic action to clean it up. Feodorov was already aware of its general outline. A pair of children playing by a riverbed in Tadzhikistan had stumbled on a cave full of weapons. The KGB had put the cave under surveillance and caught two young men delivering a load of arms to the cache. One was a former Afghan guerrilla, the other a Tadzhik, a Pamiri from the mountains of Tadzhikistan who spoke Farsi and had spent three years studying illegally in Tehran.

"Did they indicate what they intended to use all this for?" he asked Four Fingers.

"Use it for? They had enough arms in that damn cave to equip a battalion of infantry, Ivan Sergeivich—AK-47s, American M-11s, three kinds of mortars, machine pistols, even two TOW missiles. What the hell do you think they were going to use it for? Do you know anybody who hunts wild boar with TOW missiles? They're going to start a goddam revolution, that's what they're going to do."

The rich color of Four Fingers' face was a measure of his fury and exasperation. He was such a perfect example of the older generation of KGB officers, all bluster and brutality, capable of no gesture more subtle than a slap in the face. Feodorov sighed. "I hadn't expected they'd be giving them out as elocution prizes on May Day, comrade. I meant, did you learn when they intended to start using them, how they intended to use them? Do they have a concerted attack plan to go with all this?"

"They said they had orders to keep them hidden for something they called the Rising of the Martyrs. They had no idea when that was going to be. Presumably when they've stockpiled enough arms."

"Did they know about other arms caches?"

"Specifically, no. They claimed this was the only hideout they'd smuggled arms to. But one of them, the Afghani, did admit he'd heard they had a whole network of arms depots in Tadzhikistan and even up into Kazakhstan."

Feodorov pursed his lips as if to whistle, but he didn't. "Could he have been bragging?"

"Not the way they were questioning him."

The logic of that, the chairman of the KGB knew, was irrefutable. There was no way to escape the implications of this. There was a network of hidden arms depots out there, all right. How many? Where? If these Moslem bastards had been able to smuggle what they'd found in this cave across the border without getting caught, how much more had they been able to bring into the country? This meant there was the hand of an organization behind this; an organization that knew exactly how and when it was going to use these arms. "I suppose they were Sufis?"

"Naturally, the bastards."

"Did they give anybody else up?"

"No one. Their only contact was their *murshid,* and he always made contact with them. They were getting their arms down in Afghanistan, though, from old mujahedeen stockpiles, then smuggling them up here."

"They're both still alive?"

"Barely. But we won't be getting anything else out of them. We squeezed them dry."

Feodorov got up. He had never bothered to tell Four Fingers to sit down, a gesture of his contempt for the old Chekist. Now, however, he threw a comradely arm around his shoulders. "Good work, comrade. Good fast work."

He began to pace his carpet, hands clasped behind his back. It had gone farther and faster than even he had thought it would.

"We're going to have a colonial war on our hands down there, Gennadi Petrovich. Like the one the French had in Algeria or the English in Kenya. Like Somoza and the Sandinistas, or Castro against Batista. Except this time, we're the ones who are going to be the colonialists. Can you image that? We, the heirs to Marx and Lenin? We, who always gave our support to wars of liberation? We're the ones the world's going to be screaming at! We're going to be the goddam imperialist oppressors!"

The irony, the bitter irony of it all, enraged Feodorov. "Those bastards will turn every trick we ever taught them against us. Every single tactic we ever showed them, the PLO, the IRA, the Red Brigades, the whole damnable lot of rascals. They are going to turn us into a bunch of pariahs before the world. Fifty years of our work is going to be destroyed."

He stopped and jabbed an accusing finger at Four Fingers as though it were his deputy, not a horde of faceless Moslem mystics, that was about to foment an insurrection. "I'll tell you *exactly* what they're going to do. One of these nights on the Prophet's birthday or the anniversary of one of those Islamic battles they're always going on about, they'll break out those arms. They'll attack anything Red: our offices, police headquarters, party headquarters, maybe even army barracks. In a hundred different places.

"And we'll react like a herd of stampeding elephants. Which is exactly what they'll want us to do. Overreact. We'll send in the KGB. We'll send in those half-baked troops of the minister of the interior who'll shoot if someone laughs at them. We'll send in the tanks, the Red Army. And by the time we've finished overreacting, there won't be a Marxist-Leninist left in any of our Moslem republics. We'll organize the biggest goddam mass conversion the world has ever seen!"

The uncharacteristic outburst stilled Four Fingers' rage. "So what are you going to do about it, Ivan Sergeivich?"

"I'll present your report to the Secretary General at the next meeting of the Politburo."

"You'll what?" Four Fingers exploded. "What the hell good will that do? He's the one who's got us into this mess in the first place. With his *glasnost*, letting every idiot in the country complain if he doesn't like the way the sun comes up in the morning. Sucking up to those damn Balts. Letting the Armenians get away with murder."

"He's the Secretary General of the party, comrade," Feodorov murmured in reproach.

"Not my party. Not the party of Marx and Lenin and Stalin I was brought up to believe in. His party is the party of five hundred Moscow intellectuals." The old Chekist spat out the word "intellectual" like a man spitting out a bitter fruit.

"And a majority of the Central Committee." Feodorov laughed as he said the words, but his voice contained about as much mirth as would be found in a funeral oration.

"Showing him that report is going to be as useful as putting a mosquito's dick on an elephant," Four Fingers rasped.

A laugh, a real one this time, burst from the chairman. As it did, a buzzer warned him he had an urgent call.

"Da!" he barked, grabbing the phone.

"Colonel Dr. Sherbatova is on the line," his male deputy said.

"Yes." His tone softened as he heard her.

"Ivan Sergeivich. I'm with three of my associates. We've found the examination on the disk you gave us. It began at twelve-ten that day, five minutes before the time you cited. It concluded at one o'clock."

"And?"

"At twelve twenty-seven the patient had a rage crisis."

"You're sure?"

"The image area concerned lit up like a beacon. We ran a spectral analysis on it to get the signal you want. It's as clear as the chimes of midnight."

Feodorov had been standing. Now he sank back down into his desk chair with the air of a man collapsing under the weight of some shocking bit of news. "There's no question it's the right signal?"

"None whatsoever. It's locked in precisely the same place on the computer readout relative to his rage response as all the others we've studied have been. And its three frequency components are right in the spectrum we expected."

"I'll call you back."

Feodorov hung up. For a moment he sat in silence staring at his desk. So that was it. It could be done. All that was required was the courage to do it. Succeed, and he would spare the *Rodina,* the motherland, the ordeal this report under his eyes promised as sure as the winter promises snow. Fail, and there was no question what the price would be. An earlier generation of Bolsheviks had stood ready to die for their beliefs. Did he? He looked up at his deputy.

"Our meeting is over, comrade," he said. "Return to your directorate. I will deal with this."

Forty-eight hours after his telephone conversation with Xenia Petrovna, the chairman of the KGB was standing at the edge of a pine forest, a double-barreled Purdy shotgun resting in the crook of his elbow. To his left twenty-five yards away, he could just see the figure of his Polit-buro colleague Yigor Ligachev, profiled against a stand of trees. Somewhere to his right, out of sight in a neigh-boring grove, was the third member of their shooting party, Feodorov's predecessor at the KGB, Viktor Che-brikov. An expanse of open ground, its rolling surface blemished with thick tufts of underbrush, stretched away from their forest grove toward a second tree line a quarter mile distant. There the beaters had just begun to advance, moving forward in a loose semicircle, their long staves whacking at the underbrush, a guttural chant rising like some Zulu war cry from their oncoming line.

The three guns watched them, sensing the birds scur-rying through the copses along their route, moving inex-orably toward open ground and death. Just under one hundred yards from Feodorov's point, the first pheasants broke cover, clawing frantically toward the illusory sal-vation of the sky. He swept his Purdy to his shoulders, tracing a male bird's ascending arc, offering the cock a brief chance of escape. Sensing him reach the peak of his rise, he fired.

His shot was perfect. For one poignant instant the pheasant hung suspended in the sky, his wings struggling to wrench him free of gravity's embrace. Then, lifeless as a stone, he dropped to earth. Watching, Feodorov was reminded of one of his researcher's discoveries, a "death light," a flash of radiation emitted by a cell in the instant life leaves it. Was it that he'd just witnessed in the instant his pheasant had poised at the peak of his rise, his "death light"? Could it be, he wondered, a metaphor for me as well?

When the last pheasants had been flushed, the beaters gathered up the dead birds while the three Politburo col-leagues wandered back to Feodorov's lodge. A fire, of course, was roaring in the fireplace, and the table was covered with food and drink. For a quarter of an hour they ate and drank before the fire, laughing, telling dirty jokes, swapping bits of Kremlin gossip. The two men represented the leadership of an older, harder core of

Marxists in the Politburo, the embittered foes of *glasnost* and *perestroika*, of everything those reforms symbolized and stood for. Finally they fell silent. They knew the chairman of the KGB had not invited them to his lodge just to shoot pheasant. Feodorov read their silence as an invitation to begin. He took a pair of reports from his attaché case, Four Fingers' paper and a résumé of the deteriorating situation in the Moslem republics. "Read these, comrades," he asked.

Chebrikov finished first. "It had to come to this, didn't it? What else did he expect with all this *glasnost* business? Sooner or later, we were bound to have an uprising on our hands, the Georgians, the Ukrainians, the Armenians. But the Moslems! Nothing could be worse than that!"

Ligachev, the hardened socialist realist, tossed the paper back to Feodorov with an angry snap of his wrist. "So what do we do?"

Feodorov was waiting for the question. "We can do three things. We can move in there massively right now. Seal the border with the deployment of the Red Army. Order preventive arrests of the people we suspect are involved in this, get them out of there to Siberia. Impose martial law, dusk-to-dawn curfews, scour the countryside for their arms depots. We'll break a few eggs doing it, but we'll find their damn arms before we're through. Execute anyone we find with a weapon or in one of those hideouts."

"Right!" Chebrikov exulted. "That's exactly how problems like this should be handled."

Ligachev pondered his enthused expression with an air of bemused contempt. "Viktor Aleksandrovich, you are right, of course. That's exactly what any sane leader would do. However, there's a problem here."

"What problem?"

"We haven't got a sane leader. This Secretary General of ours would give Siberia to the Americans before he'd do that. What's your second option?" he asked Feodorov.

"Do nothing except alert our people. Wait for the Moslems to make the first move, to come out in the open. Then crush them with one swift counterblow when they do."

"That's not a solution," Ligachev rejoined. "It's a recipe for suicide. People who let their enemies strike the first blow lead short lives."

"There is a third way."

The way in which Feodorov said those words made it clear to his two interlocutors that this was why they'd been invited to shoot pheasants on this autumn afternoon. Slowly, with painstaking attention to detail, he took them through his plan. At each step along the way, he assessed the benefits and dangers it represented. They were stunned when he'd finished, mesmerized by the idea as much as they were frightened by its dangers. Ligachev, a veteran of three decades of Kremlin intrigue, was struck by something else as well. What a clever bastard Feodorov is, he thought. No wonder he runs the Organs. By telling us the details of his plan, he's trying to compromise us.

Chebrikov worked his way through the scheme with a policeman's mind, looking for the flaw its architects had failed to take into account in constructing it. "Why won't the White House pick up those electromagnetic signals you're sending? After what we did to their embassy here with our microwave bombardments, they're obsessed with electromagnetic signals."

"The White House has the most sensitive electromagnetic screening system in the world." There was no way Feodorov could keep the edges of a triumphant smile from accompanying his next words. "But it has one major flaw. It begins screening for signals at one hundred hertz. Our signal is going to be down around fifteen. It will slide right underneath that protective electromagnetic fence of theirs."

"How can they be so stupid?"

"They're not stupid. Our security systems don't pick up those signals, either."

"Why the hell not?"

"Because they have no ability to activate anything, any hidden devices, or transmit any messages. So why screen for them?"

Chebrikov, it seemed to his former deputy, was marking a cross on some mental checklist he'd drawn up. "How about the President? How can you be sure he's going to react the way you want him to?"

"I can't be." Chebrikov was about to erupt, but Feodorov held him in check with a warning gesture of his hand. "I can only be sure of one thing—that periodically during this crisis, he's going to become violently angry. When people get violently angry, when they lose control of their temper, they tend to do irrational things. Particularly people with a psychological framework like his."

Ligachev had gotten up as they were talking and walked to the fire. He stood there, one arm leaning on the heavy stone mantelpiece, staring down at the flames. What the hell's going through his mind? Feodorov wondered. He was the key. Without his support, Feodorov wouldn't dare go ahead with this. It would leave him totally exposed if it went wrong.

"There's something else," he said. He addressed his words to Chebrikov, but they were destined for Ligachev brooding by his fire.

"The President of the United States is a much more powerful individual in a crisis than our Secretary General is. He's the commander in chief of their armed forces. He even has the sole authority to use the so-called red button. No individual has that power under our system."

Ligachev turned away from the fire. "It's a dangerous plan, Ivan Sergeivich. Very, very dangerous."

"I realize that."

"If it ever got out to the West that we were behind this, Ivan Sergeivich, God help you, because I won't."

"So be it, comrade. I am prepared to accept the responsibility of failure."

"In fact, I may even have to call for your execution in the Central Committee myself."

Feodorov inclined his head in what was meant to seem a meek acknowledgment of that very prospect. Yes, he was thinking, right after I've played the Central Committee my recording of this conversation, you can make your suggestion.

"If we were ever, in any way, associated with this it would be a disaster." A scowl as immutable as the outline of a seal pressed into the surface of a signet ring was affixed to Ligachev's face. A permanent scowl, Feodorov often thought, must be issued to each new member of the Politburo along with his Kremlin security pass.

"There's no reason for that to happen. The American's eyes will go right where they're supposed to."

"Ivan Sergeivich." Ligachev pronounced the KGB chairman's name like a judge uttering a prisoner's name before handing down his sentence. "I see nothing in your plan but risks, terrible risks."

Tensions were warring inside the man, Feodorov sensed, tensions Ligachev had yet to reconcile fully.

"And we do not like risk playing a role in our decision-making." Ligachev hesitated a moment. "But there is one risk greater than all your risks combined—the risk of a Moslem uprising against our rule. Let one nationalist uprising break out, and we'll have ten nationalities screaming for independence." The Soviet leader gave a heavy sigh, a kind of nostalgic gasp for a USSR that was fast receding and of which he remained the last great advocate and spokesman. "These Westerners! They think our empire is Hungary and Poland and Czechoslovakia. The fools! They don't understand our empire is right here, at home."

He walked slowly back to the side table and poured himself a tumbler of vodka. This was no time to jar his thoughts, Feodorov realized. Ligachev looked angrily into his glass before swallowing its contents in a gulp.

"Let one of these ethnic movements succeed and the Soviet Union will fly apart. We'll have five, six nations in our homeland, not one. A superpower!" He laughed harshly. "We'll become a third-class power, an India or an Argentina begging for a few crumbs from the West's table.''

"I gather you feel we should try my plan," Feodorov prodded.

Ligachev hurled his glass into the fireplace. It exploded against the stones in an angry tinkle. "We may all hang for it. But what the hell else is the KGB for?"

PART 5

"A SEARING BURST OF WHITE LIGHT."

". . . the only thing the President will notice, besides his rage, of course, is a slight tightening at the temples—the kind of sensation he'd associate with a severe headache."

Beside Major Valentin Tobulko, the chairman of the KGB tilted his head back as he looked at the colonel doctor who ran the KGB's Institute for the Study of Human Neurophysiology.

"How long is the President's anger state going to last?"

"Ten minutes or so. Once our signal causes his brain to release the chemicals associated with rage into his bloodstream, he'll go on feeling anger until those chemicals work their way through his system."

"Exactly as he normally would?"

"No, his anger is apt to be a little more intense. It may last a little longer, too."

"Once the effects of his rage crisis wear off, how is he going to feel about any decisions he made while he was angry? Is he likely to go back on them?"

Tobulko was struck by the evident affection in the look the director of the institute gave the chairman.

"The answer to that, my dear Ivan Sergeivich," she said, "lies more in psychology than neurology."

"You did study our psychological profile on the man?"

"I did. Clearly, the President is someone who hates to appear inconsistent. He was very sensitive to the accusation of being weak and indecisive during the presidential campaign. The last thing the man is going to want to do is demean his position, his presidential authority, by making a strong decision and then going back on it. If he's made a decision while he's angry, he'll use every rationalization he can think of afterward to justify it. People like that don't say 'I'm sorry. It was a mistake. I overreacted.' "

There was a fourth person present in their meeting room, a balding forty-year-old Feodorov had introduced to Tobulko as the colonel doctor's electronic wizard. Now the chairman pointed a commanding finger at him. "We're ready for you." His dark eyes shifted their focus to Tobulko. "Major, what we're going to review now concerns your role in the operation." Another, less confident, superior would have ordered Tobulko to pay close attention to the engineer's words. Not Feodorov. He let his eyes do that for him.

The engineer lifted what looked to Tobulko like a medium-sized metallic trash can onto a table. His grunts made it clear that the can was heavy. "This is the device that's going to generate and send out our signal. As you suggested, Comrade Chairman, it's designed to be functional within a circle two miles in diameter centered on the White House. In fact, we've built a safety margin into it. It generates fifteen kilowatts of output power. Since its power fall-off conforms to classical electromagnetic law, one over the distance cubed, you'll have some extra distance to play with if you need it."

The engineer stooped down behind the table on which he'd set his generator and pulled up an enlargement of a map of downtown Washington, D.C. It was in the form of a circle two miles in diameter with the White House at its center. The arc of the circle swept all the way to the Kennedy Center, Watergate, and the Potomac in the west, past Dupont Circle up to New Hampshire and R Street in the north, beyond Massachusetts and 6th, almost to the Capitol in the east. To the south, it encompassed largely open ground, parts of the areas around the Reflecting Pool, the Tidal Basin, and the Mall.

"After studying the problem," the engineer said, "we've come to the conclusion that the best course is to employ two generators, one in a fixed location—an apartment, a hotel room, or a garage—and the second mobile in a truck or a van. The idea is to intersect their fields on the White House. If you consider your fixed generator, wherever it is, as being at high noon on the circumference of a circle, your mobile generator in the van can transmit from anywhere between three o'clock and nine o'clock. That gives the mobile generator plenty of room to circulate in and will make it very difficult for the Americans to locate it.''

"How long," Tobulko asked, "are the signal generators going to be emitting each time we decide to turn them on?"

"Forty-five seconds."

"That's all?"

"Yes."

"Can we emit while the van is moving?"

"No. You'll have to stop to adjust the mechanisms that will angle the signal at the White House. But the whole process will only take a minute and a half. Then you can drive away and stay out of the area until you have to come back into it to make another transmission.''

"And when we're not sending out the signal there's nothing to lead the Americans to the van?''

"Absolutely nothing.''

"That will make it impossible for their signal detection apparatus to locate us, won't it?'' Tobulko's confidence in the operation's prospects had increased measurably in the last five minutes.

"Impossible, no. But very, very difficult. Assuming they even notice the signals are there, which we have every reason to believe they won't.''

"And how about the NSA and all their listening devices? Won't they pick it up?''

Feodorov looked at his young major with growing esteem.

"Five miles from the White House," the electronics engineer replied, "this signal will have died without a trace. The NSA's interception stations are farther away than that, outside the District of Columbia.'' The engineer turned away from his map. "There is a further sophistication we're going to employ here. We want to guarantee that our two output signals are identical, that they hit the White House at exactly the same time. So we're going to phase-lock them. That means you're either going to have to rent a van that's already equipped with a cellular telephone or install one. The chairman assures us that's easy to do in the United States."

"Very." Tobulko's knowledge of the country he'd now entered illegally half a dozen times left him no doubt of that.

"You'll then purchase a telephone modem at a computer store and link the phone in the van to the phone in your fixed location. That will allow you to synchronize the transmissions of the signals perfectly."

"And there's going to be enough electrical power in the van, and in the electrical circuits of, say, a hotel room, to work this?"

Once again, Feodorov felt he had good reason to congratulate himself on his choice of Tobulko. They had, of course, studied the problem he'd just raised, but the young major's insight in asking the question spoke well of his abilities.

"Plenty. You'll have a three-hundred-horsepower engine in the van. All the power you'll need, especially when you're standing still. In an apartment, it's the power you'd need to run a couple of air conditioners."

"Will this have to be hooked up to an antenna of some sort in the apartment or the hotel room in order to get the signal out?"

"No. The only thing you will have to do with the equipment we're going to provide you is set the proper sending angle for your bearing on the White House. The signal will go through anything—bricks, mortar, cement, concrete, wood, steel. Only one thing will stop it, a barrier of liquid helium—and I can assure you that that is not a part of the White House's electromagnetic protection systems."

Tobulko laughed. "How do we get these two things into the United States? By diplomatic pouch?"

"No." Feodorov took over the query. He and his planners had already given the matter considerable study. "I want to limit your contacts with the *rezidentura* to a minimum. Essentially, these two devices are really nothing more than a few thousand turns of number-fifteen copper wire around an iron core. There are a dozen places you can buy them in the United States when you arrive."

"This is the key." The electronics engineer was waving a plaque covered with a silver cobweb of microchip circuits. "The electronic circuitry we've constructed here defines the signal, its precise frequency lines, the amplitude of each, to give us exactly the signal, the shape, the pulse we have to have. It has to be very precise, because even the most minute change in the shape of the signal will affect its ability to impact on the President's brain cells. You'll wire one of these plaques to each of the two generators and they will order out the signal."

"You'll have to take those plaques back with you," Feodorov declared. "Our friend here is going to teach you how to hook them up to these generators. You'll be doing it in your sleep when he's finished with you."

Abou Said Dajani squatted by the side of the road, a hooded shepherd's burnoose enveloping the stillness of his body. In the darkness, from a few yards away, h took on the profile of a small rock pyramid, like sou. primitive stele marking out the course of a medieval caravan route. Behind him, a chill wind blew off the peaks of the Jebel Lubnan, the Anti-Lebanon mountain range. In front of him, a road ran southwest straight down the valley to the village of Saidnaya, six kilometers away. His jeep was nearby, hidden in a defile. Dajani had crossed the mountain range in it earlier, twisting the vehicle down tracks worn into the steep hillside by the tread of ten centuries of smugglers.

He was finishing his third Camel when he finally saw the headlights cresting over the horizon. They dipped three times. He rose and walked to the roadside. From there he guided the Damascus *rezident*'s car up a rough path so that in the unlikely event another vehicle should come by during their *treff*, the KGB chief's car would not be seen.

He got in and wordlessly shook hands with his superior. Neither Dajani nor the *rezident* was inclined to excess speech.

"*Shou*—so?" Dajani asked.

"It has been decided."

"I am ready."

"Good. Send your people to East Berlin on Interflug." Interflug was the East German airline. "Send one from Beirut, two from Damascus, and one from Baghdad so no one sees them together and their names aren't linked. Not that Interflug is likely to show anybody its passenger lists."

"When?"

"Start them Monday."

"It shall be done."

"Ivan Sergeivich wants you to go to Berlin to coordinate their work. If you leave before them, can you be sure they'll get to East Berlin as you've instructed?"

"For sure, my friend."

"Good. Then go via Interflug from Beirut. You remember the location of the compound?"

The East Berlin headquarters of the KGB were in a walled compound of half a dozen bungalows in the Treptow neighborhood a hundred yards from the Spee River, well away from the city center.

"No problem."

"Someone from the Center will be waiting for you there. He will have all your instructions for you."

A moment of silence, its frontiers defined by a suggestion of menace, passed between them. It was clear to Dajani that the *rezident* knew at least some of the details of the operation. It was equally clear he had no intention of telling Dajani what they were. The Palestinian, for his part, knew better than to ask.

"Is that all?"

"Not quite. There is one last matter. A rather unpleasant one, I'm afraid. Ivan Sergeivich would like you to supervise it personally."

"Oh?"

"The Artist."

"The Artist?"

"Yes. His usefulness is over."

Abou Said Dajani leaned back against the Lada's stiff cushions. The taking of another man's life was not a matter to raise undue moral scruples in a close associate of Abu Nidal. As always, however, it posed problems and risks that had to be carefully studied.

There was not another soul within ten miles, yet the *rezident* leaned over to whisper the words to Dajani as though someone might overhear him. "Ivan Sergeivich asks that you make certain that the Lebanese authorities lay the matter firmly at the doorstep of the Hez'bollah."

"My dear Major, I'd like to ask you to read this file and give me your opinion." Feodorov liked to ask his subordinates for their advice on matters of little consequence. It gave them a sense of importance and the illusion of being a party to his inner thoughts, which, of course, they never were. "In the circumstances, it wouldn't have been appropriate for you to review the list of our illegal postings to Washington. I had to perform the task for you and select a candidate we can activate to be your deputy." He passed Valentin Tobulko the personal file of KGB Captain Dulia Vaninya. "If there is anything in her file that bothers you, any failings I've overlooked that you think would make her difficult to work with, let me know and I'll find someone else."

Tobulko grasped the file from the chairman's extended hand. One thing is certain, he thought, the chairman is holding this very, very close indeed. With the exception of the colonel doctor and her electronics expert at Zhukovskii, he had gotten all his instructions directly from Feodorov. No one, not even the chairman's top aides, had been present at any of their conversations. "I'm sure, Comrade Chairman, you've made an excellent choice."

Feodorov studied Tobulko as he was speaking. The major's face was remarkably expressionless, a blank sheet of paper on which life had yet to leave the mark of its joys and pains. And that despite the fact he had murdered in the name of the state. Clearly, emotions did not trouble this man. That was good. Emotions bred doubt, and operations such as this one were no place for doubters.

"She possesses one of our new Spetosk burst transmitters, which only a few of the illegals in Washington have. Another reason for choosing her." Feodorov stood up and began to pace his office floor. "Which brings us to the last two points we have to review before you leave, control and communications." Intelligence agencies, like the military, respond to the same basic imperatives the world over, and while the terminology that describes them differs from service to service, their substance never does. Command, control, cover, communications, intelligence: every espionage operation undertaken in the world is informed by those five considerations. Feodorov's was no exception.

"For your basic communications with the Center, you will employ her Spetosk and her one-time pad. She has the schedule of the satellite overflights and the transmission angle each requires. Our technical people will fit a one-time pad for your use in an emergency and a copy of the necessary satellite data inside the framework of your attaché case."

Feodorov's was the tone of voice officers of the Organs had been trained to employ with departing agents since the days of Iron Feliks: patient, precise, reassuring. It reflected the golden promise extended to every Soviet agent sent overseas: the Center cares. If something happens, it will raise heaven and earth to get you back.

"Now," he continued, "emergency communications. I must stress that you should contact the Washington *rezidentura* only in the direst of emergencies. No one there, including the *rezident*, will know anything whatsoever about you or your operation. We will provide you with a code phrase to identify yourself personally to the *rezident*. When he hears that phrase, he will know he has to relay any message you give him to me in his personal cipher immediately.''

"And the return message?"

"It will come on your satellite transmissions. We'll use her pad for the cipher, with the one we'll place in your attaché case as a fallback.'' Feodorov circled back to his desk chair and settled into it with a slow and considered gesture. "Which brings us to the most delicate and difficult part of your mission—determining exactly when to employ the equipment you'll have. In this we are going to have to rely to a large degree on you.''

"There is no direct communications link we could employ?"

"One I'll explain in a moment. Now, we know how the U.S. government will respond to this crisis we're arranging. What they'll do is set up a special committee to deal with it which will take over the National Security Council situation room in the White House. All their incoming information will be funneled into that room. Sometimes the President will join in their work, sometimes he'll carry on with his normal schedule. You must monitor CNN, the news TV network. It will tell you a great deal about what is going on and what the President's schedule is. You can be sure that within fifteen minutes after every important announcement is made, the President will have the news and he will be reacting to it.''

"And presumably that would be when you would wish us to activate the device?"

"Yes. With one critical exception, of course. Not if the President is at a public function, a state dinner, a reception in the Rose Garden, making a speech to some big group.''

Feodorov picked up what looked like an old-fashioned fountain pen from his desk. "We will also be able to control the flow of some of the information coming in on the crisis, and we must have a fast way of instructing you to use your equipment. This is the indirect communication tool I mentioned. It's a very directional, very penetrating, but very short-range transmitter. All one of our people has to do is drive by the hotel, the apartment, or the house you're using, point this at it, and press the cap. It will beam a message to a special listening device with which we'll equip you. Since it's such a short-range device, no scanner is going to be able to detect it."

"But that's going to involve the local *rezidentura*."

Feodorov sighed. "To an extent that is, alas, inevitable. The agent we will employ will know he's sending a message to someone. But he will not know who or why, and the message will be in code, of course."

"And if the FBI is following him?"

"Let them follow him. They'll have no way of detecting the fact he's made a transmission. He doesn't stop. He doesn't slow down. He just drives by, points the transmitter, and the message has gone."

"And how do we get the listening device?"

"I've given that a great deal of thought. I don't want you to take it in your attaché case. You can explain away those microcircuits as computer or TV parts if your case is opened. But the listening device might excite a customs officer's curiosity. Suppose we have one of our officers in Washington lease your van for you, then leave it somewhere where you can pick it up? With the device inside? That will give you one further margin of security. You'll be able to monitor the van's delivery to be sure the operation is clean."

"What would he use to lease the van? For a license? For a credit card? That couldn't be traced to the embassy?"

"The Documentation Division can handle that."

"But suppose the police stop me for missing a red light? My driver's license won't match the name on the van's rental papers."

"Yes it will." Feodorov couldn't resist a triumphant grin. That was just the question he'd wanted to hear. "The Documentation Division already produced one Mr. Banwell for us. We'll ask them to produce another."

MAZE
• • •

Nina Wolfe opened the mailbox in the entrance gallery of her Tysons Corner professional building. It was filled with the usual clutter of junk mail: handbills for the weekend sale at the local Stop and Shop, from Sears Roebuck and K mart, Don's Electronics and Al's TV offering yet another series of unbeatable bargains with no down payments for six months and easy terms thereafter. How she loathed this wretched flotsam of a society gone mad over material well-being.

As she reached the bottom of the pile, she stopped. Her fingers trembled ever so slightly at what they found there. It was a postcard. She looked at it. The picture was of the public market at Aix-en-Provence in the South of France. The postmark was five days old. She turned it over.

"Dearest Nina," it read. "Having a wonderful trip. Don picked up our rented van at the Nice airport, then we drove along the seacoast to Saint-Tropez and on to here. Had dinner last night in a Chinese restaurant just like the China Paradise you like so much. We fly out of Marseille for London at 1830 on the 23rd, then back to the good old USA."

The signature was illegible. She waved the card for a moment like a fan, then tucked it into her pocketbook. The junk mail she threw into a wastebasket. Walking slowly up the stairs to her office, she tried to hold back the sense of excitement rising through her being like a mist. All her years of training, the months of patient waiting, would come to something at last.

Violent death in the capital of Lebanon is an affliction as banal as the common cold. For the two Lebanese policemen and the officer of the Sûreté, the corpse lying on the floor of the camera appliance shop on the Rue Sadat two blocks east of the campus of the American University of Beirut presented a professional interest about as great as a double-parked car would offer a traffic cop in Manhattan or Paris. The scene's only reminder of the human cost each life lost in Lebanon represented was a Bedouin woman in black keening out her ritual grief in the piercing ululations of the Arabian Desert.

"Tell her to shut up," snapped the officer of the Sûreté as he bent down to peer at the corpse.

"Shut up, old woman!" ordered one of the cops.

The woman looked at the policeman, her mouth agape in outrage at his insensitivity to her well-practiced lamentation. For a second, she was silent. Then she drew a full breath and bleated out a new lament in a tone so shrill it might have shattered glass. From somewhere in the shop, a pair of cats joined in. The cop shrugged and turned to the corpse.

In the shadows on the ground behind it, he saw a maroon tarboosh. He picked it up. He had an uncle up in Zahlé who liked to wear them. As he did, he noticed an object that looked a bit like a fat earthworm on the floor beside it. He peered curiously at it.

"*Sayed*—sir," he said, pointing it out for the officer of the Sûreté. The officer picked it up, then dropped it in disgust. It was a human tongue.

He pried open the dead man's jaw and confirmed what was self-evident: this was the orifice in which that tongue had functioned before the victim's throat had been cut. Clearly, it had functioned a bit too well and a bit too often. The officer glanced around looking for an additional sign. He found it marked in green grease pencil next to a calendar photo of the Mosque of al-Aksa in Jerusalem, a crescent of Islam. He closed his notebook and stood up. Murder investigations had long gone out of fashion in Beirut. And the thought of trying to investigate the bloodshed caused by the city's Shiite fanatics excited an absolute minimum of enthusiasm among the city's few remaining police officers.

"Fill out the papers," he ordered the two policemen, "and tell her to get him ready for the graveyard. Maybe that will shut her up."

•   •   •

From under the wings of his Interflug TU-5 jetliner, Abou Said Dajani glanced down at the serpentine twistings of the Berlin Wall, a white welt of scar tissue stretching along the city's heart. Then, as the pilot of Interflug Flight 104 positioned his aircraft for his final approach into East Berlin's Schönefeld Airport, the Mariendorf sector of West Berlin swept through Dajani's line of vision.

How different East and West were. Socialism, he thought, comes in precise geometric patterns, with everything set out in straight lines and rows, in well-planned, tidy units with all their rough edges rounded off. There was no place down there in East Berlin for the ideologically divergent loop or impure design. As nature abhors a vacuum, socialism, it seemed, abhorred the unplanned form.

By nature and preference, Dajani's taste ran to the less rigid formulations of the West. He was, after all, an Arab. His conversion to Marxism-Leninism had come not from a burning zeal to reorder the lot of mankind, but because in the slaughter of the Chatilla refugee camp in 1982 he had understood that power orders the world. There was only one power unequivocally committed to aiding his people, and he, in turn, had made his personal and unequivocal commitment to that power.

Dajani endured the slow, sullen East German immigration and customs process along with everyone else. His status as a KGB major offered no help; he was here under cover. He picked up his suitcase and walked out to the airport taxi rank. Through some minor miracle, there was actually a taxi waiting. He gave the driver an address three blocks from his real destination and settled back into his seat. As he did, an odor he always associated with East Berlin struck his nostrils. It was that faintly sulfuric smell of coal smoke, still the basic fuel of the DDR's industries.

The Palestinian knew East Germany well, although he knew West Germany better and much preferred it to the East. He'd gone to West Germany in the late 1960s as a recruiter/talent spotter for Abu Nidal among the many

Palestinians studying there. His harvest had been prodigious—almost fifty handpicked candidates for the PLO's secret training camps in Algeria. How many, Dajani wondered, were still alive? Ten? Fewer?

He let the taxi disappear before setting off on foot for the KGB's Treptow compound. The compound was strictly Russian territory; there were no East Germans, not even cleaning women, inside its walls. The KGB guard in civilian clothes at the gate gave Dajani a look of instant, withering hostility as he approached. Racism, Dajani wondered, or just the natural surliness the KGB attempted to breed into its watchdogs?

Whatever its motivation, the look disappeared the instant Dajani identified himself. "We've been expecting you, sir," he said, activating the compound gate and at the same time alerting the headquarters to his arrival. A KGB officer, a colonel, bounded out to meet him. The colonel allowed Dajani forty-five minutes to rest and clean up after his trip, then returned to the room they'd assigned him. "Ivan Sergeivich asked me to give you his warmest personal regards," he declared. "He would like to have you return to your duties via the Center so he can extend those greetings to you personally."

"I shall, of course, be honored," Dajani intoned.

The colonel drew an envelope from his pocket and extended it to Dajani. "This is the mission directive."

After a quick glance at its outline, Dajani looked up at the colonel. "This would mean the end of Soviet-American détente if . . ."

The colonel interrupted, then continued Dajani's sentence for him: ". . . if ever the faintest evidence of our involvement should get out. That is why Ivan Sergeivich attaches the utmost importance to security. The Americans must never, under any circumstances, have any reason to suspect our involvement in this. Besides, of course," and the colonel smiled engagingly, "the CIA's usual paranoia that sees our hand behind every firecracker that goes off anywhere in the world."

Well, Dajani mused, returning to his mission directive, this is going to be quite a firecracker.

"The intelligence is excellent," he observed.

"RAF—Red Army Faction," the colonel explained.

"I didn't realize they worked with us."

"They don't. They think they're doing it for their Third World brothers."

"And you're sure we can count on their information?"

"Absolutely. They're very Teutonic. They have a file on every American military base in West Germany—the entries, the exits, the security procedures, how many sentries are on duty at each post, when they change them. Which ones tend to be sloppy. Everything. They have copies of the ID the Americans use, the GIs, civilians, dependents. Maps of all the bases."

"How the hell do they get all that?"

"They cultivate the menials, the Turks, the Pakistanis, that collect the rubbish, do their housekeeping. And they have a whole network of bargirls who work the bars around the bases." The colonel moved his head from side to side very slowly. Those naive American GIs. A few beers, some dope, a Fräulein's fingers at their crotch, and out came the information that could be used to blow them and their bases into unrecognizable fragments. Fortunately, that was not a problem confronting the Red Army in Eastern Europe. Red Army recruits rarely got past their barracks gates.

"We've got a Red Army Faction contact in West Berlin for your commando. They will give them a last-minute briefing before they strike."

"And this event, whatever it is, we're going to strike?" Dajani knew little of American ways and customs beyond what he'd retained from an occasional viewing of *Dallas* and *Dynasty*.

"It's one of their three major social events of the year."

"Then won't their security people be on alert?"

"The RAF has been watching this place for a year. It's wide open. Anybody can drive in and out without the slightest security check."

"That sounds incredible."

"It is. But it's true. We checked on that ourselves.

They only set up their security checkpoints when they have some sort of intelligence that a terrorist commando is in the area. Since your commando isn't going to leave Berlin until the morning of the attack, they should have no warning. Obviously, the members of your commando have got to go in there looking like GIs.''

"Should we put them in American Army uniforms?"

"Perhaps. We've thought about that. Although the Americans don't wear their uniforms on Saturday night unless they're on duty. Obviously, where your commando's going, people aren't going to be on duty.''

Dajani started to glance back down at his mission directive, but the colonel continued. "Let me emphasize how important the timing is. It's designed to give your commando the time to substitute the charged car for the getaway car, drive back to the Frankfurt airport, catch the last plane back to Berlin, clear Tegel Airport, and be on their way back here before the Americans can react.''

"If they miss the plane?"

"They drive to France. They've got to get out of Germany fast. But they must not miss it.'' The colonel hammered each word to underline the point. "That's the guarantee we have them back here where we're sure they can never talk.''

"What are we going to use for explosives?"

"Semtex.'' Semtex was an extremely effective and efficient plastic explosive manufactured in Czechoslovakia and furnished by the USSR in vast quantities to Libya, Syria, and the terrorist groups in Lebanon. It was the explosive of choice of Arab and Iranian terrorists in Western Europe, the explosive that had blown apart Pan Am 103 over Scotland.

"Is there a stockpile available in West Berlin?"

"No. You'll have to be the conduit to get it to them.''

"Me!'' Dajani's voice, usually so soft it was almost plaintive, soared an octave or two. "You think I'm going to walk into West Berlin with a suitcase of plastic under each arm?"

There was an edge of scorn in the colonel's answering laugh. "Of course not. Although I can promise you no one would stop you over there if you did. We have an absolutely safe, reliable way for you to pass it to the commando. What's vital is that one of your commando be fully qualified to handle plastic. He'll have to pack the car and set the timers himself. Without blowing up the neighborhood. Have you got someone who can do that?"

"I was instructed to have someone, Colonel, and I do."

"Well, he'd better be good. The Syrians made an awful mess here a while ago on two separate occasions. In one, they couldn't even assemble a simple suitcase bomb and had to send back over here for help from West Berlin twice. Then they wired up six of our M82 mortar shells in the trunk of a car they meant to set off at Tempelhof, the American airport. They were wired to such a primitive remote-control electronics device their bomb was activated by someone using a beeper to open his garage door as they were driving past his house on their way to the airport."

There was no warmth and a minimum of respect in Dajani's reply. He did not like to be patronized and did not like this man's indirect allusion to what was known in intelligence circles as the "Abdul Factor," the conviction that at some point in any operation, the Arabs could be counted on to bungle it.

"My man could rig up a Tinkertoy so it would wipe out half this compound," he answered. "He wired the van that did the American embassy in Beirut. He's done sixteen car bombs. There is no one, no Russian, no Israeli, no German, no one, as skilled as he is. Believe me, he will give you a sound-and-light show neither you nor the Americans are ever going to forget."

Forty-eight hours after the corpse of Abou Daoud Sinho, "the Artist," had been found in his camera shop on Beirut's Rue Sadat, a copy of the terse police report on the circumstances of his death was on the desk of CIA station chief Ray Reid in the temporary U.S. embassy in East Beirut. The nature of the Artist's activities as a forger of documents for the various terrorist groups operating out of the Lebanese capital had, of course, long been known to the Lebanese Sûreté. Given the nature of his friends and supporters in the city, however, it had been deemed impolitic by the Sûreté's senior officers to interrupt his work. One of them passed the report of his demise to Reid as a routine matter. It was just the sort of action which justified the monthly retainer the Agency paid him.

Reid was genuinely upset by Sinho's murder. He had never met the old man or even laid his eyes on him. The Artist was an asset he had inherited from his predecessor, and their contacts had always been arranged through cutouts like the owner of the souvenir shop. Nonetheless, he had been an immensely valuable source of information. At least five terrorist operations against American or Israeli targets in Western Europe had been thwarted thanks to intelligence the Artist had furnished the CIA. Replacing him was going to be a difficult if not impossible job.

Reid immediately cabled the news to the DDO, the deputy director of operations in charge of the Agency's overseas stations and covert activities. The DDO contemplated informing Mossad's Branch 40, the unit of Israeli intelligence that dealt with terrorism, about the loss, but decided against it. He preferred wherever possible to keep the Agency's setbacks in-house. In view of the Artist's loss, however, he sent a communication to the Counterterrorism Standing Group which joined representatives of the CIA, Britain's MI5, the West German BND, the Israeli Branch 40, and France's DGES. It stressed the importance of the last information the Artist had supplied the Agency—the identities and passport numbers of the four Hez'bollah members to whom he had furnished his Moroccan 798s.

Said Dajani's rendezvous with the colonel was at the head of Unter den Linden just south of the Brandenburg Gate. The site was convenient because it was only a couple of minutes by foot from the Soviet embassy, where the colonel had to pick up the Royal Moroccan passports of Dajani's four-man commando. The Palestinian made a point of being ten minutes early. He had no intention of giving the colonel any pretext for another allusion, however disguised, to the Abdul Factor.

Dajani was not a student of history, but it was impossible to be insensitive to the special significance of this ground he was pacing waiting for the colonel. Ahead of him were the heroic arches of the Brandenburg Gate, their approaches barred by barbed wire as though East Germany's new rulers feared some emanation, some radiation evocative of Germany's militaristic past, might somehow still flow from those dead stones. Just to his left was a block-long stretch of empty ground—nothing more than stubbly grass, a few odd chunks of stone and mortar cast up from some abandoned excavation. Yet it was on that ground that Hitler's Reichschancellery had once stood, and under it his Führer's Bunker had been planted. Nothing, no sign, no bombed-out ruin, no faded inscription remained to remind passersby like Dajani of the bloody tyranny once exercised from those few hundred square meters of land.

He paced along Wilhelmstrasse above the Soviet embassy looking for the colonel. There were only a handful of cars running across the T where Wilhelmstrasse crossed the head of Unter den Linden. Imagine, Dajani thought, there was more traffic flowing here in September 1939 than there is today, half a century later. How many places are there in the world about which you can say that?

He saw the colonel turn the corner into Wilhelmstrasse, his head down, a cigarette between his lips, concentrating on the pavement at his feet with the intensity of a mathematician pondering an intractable formula. He looked up, saw Dajani, and fell into step beside him. The Lebanese felt him press a bundle into his hand.

"They've all got East Berlin student visas on page four," he said. "If they're stopped over there, all they have to do is show them. Just say they came over to look around for the day."

This divided city was a bundle of anomalies, Dajani knew, anomalies such as this one which allowed an Arab or, in fact, anyone studying in East Berlin to wander into West Germany without any verification of his documents or identity whatsoever. In their determined refusal to acknowledge the city's division, the Allies and the West Germans had made it an earthly paradise for clandestine operators like Dajani.

"When are you sending them over?" the colonel asked.

"As soon as I give them back their passports. I've split them into two teams. I've told one to hole up in Kreuzberg, the other in Wedding. We'll have one of them buy the getaway car—the other car we'll use for the bomb."

"Good," the colonel said.

"I've told them to drive one of the cars down to Frankfurt to reconnoiter the site and familiarize themselves with the area."

"Excellent. We'll pass them their plastic on the way back. Do they speak German, by the way?"

"One in each team does. Enough to get by, anyway."

"Don't go over there yourself until you have to," the colonel cautioned. "Stay at arm's length. Remember, nothing that could come back to us."

"I understand." There were some KGB officers like the *resident* in Damascus who could get across half an hour's worth of information in three cryptic phrases. And then there were some like his friend the colonel here who felt they had to repeat any thought worth thinking at least three times. Or, Dajani wondered, is he doing this for the benefit of my poor, dim Palestinian soul?

The colonel nodded and turned away back up Wilhelmstrasse. Dajani walked down Unter den Linden to Alexanderplatz and got on an S-Bahn for Rosa-Luxemburg-Platz.

As each member of his four-man commando had arrived, Dajani had ferried them from the airport to a safe flat furnished by the KGB just off the square named after the famous female revolutionary. Now they were waiting for him in a café on the ground floor. It was almost as bleak and depressing a place as the safe flat was. The lighting came in shades of gray, the furniture consisted of primitive wooden chairs and tables. The air was so thick with cigarette smoke you could almost pull it apart with your fingers like puffs of cotton. The waiter came over for his order. Another Berlin anomaly. In this shabby Communist café whose clients were all in sweaters and shirt sleeves, the waiter was wearing a dinner jacket and a black bow tie.

Dajani tasted his beer, then slipped his men their passports under the table. He had gone over every aspect of their mission in mind-numbing detail with them. They were all fairly reliable, although perhaps not the paragons of disciplined behavior he'd suggested to the colonel. The explosives expert, Ali Nasreddin, was a true fanatic, a cold, soulless individual who lived to blow people apart with the efficiency of an assembly-line robot. Two members of the commando, Ali Kazemi and Sayed Hakim, had been in and out of Western Europe as petty drug smugglers before becoming Hez'bollah gunmen. Drug dealers, like terrorists, had to learn to live outside the legal margins of society. They knew how to move without papers, without leaving footprints behind them. The fourth member of the commando, Hussain Ansari, was Dajani's youngest and least-experienced recruit. He was here because he'd studied at West Berlin's Free University and spoke excellent German. He'd paired him with one of the drug dealers and the bomber with the other. Better, he'd figured, to keep the drug smugglers apart.

He nodded to Kazemi. "You two go first," he said. "The others will follow in half an hour." He raised his glass. "Vengeance," he said. "Vengeance" was the name he'd given their commando. Everything had to have a name in the Bekaa Valley.

His four commandos raised their glasses. Two, in deference to the tenets of Islam, were drinking lemonade. "Vengeance," they said.

● ● ●

Some guys get to spend their Saturday mornings washing the family car or following the wife around the supermarket carrying her groceries or taking the kid to Little League. Lucky bastards, Chick O'Neill thought. For the last four years, Saturday had been a work day for O'Neill and his partner, Denny Strong; boring, routine work days on the heels of KGB agents in Washington for the FBI's Washington field office countersurveillance unit. Right now, they were engaged in an activity that consumed most of their Saturdays, waiting, doing nothing.

Their government-issue Plymouth was poised on the left-hand side of the White Haven Parkway where it angles into Wisconsin, so that the car's outline was screened from the line of vision of a vehicle driving down Wisconsin by the bulky structure of the Divine Science Church. They could monitor traffic flowing down to Georgetown, while it was almost impossible for a driver going down Wisconsin to make them.

Their assigned target was Dimitri "Antsy" Yashvili, a KGB officer who used the embassy's Cultural Affairs Section as his cover. They knew Antsy all too well. He'd been one of their regular weekend assignments for eighteen months. Most Saturdays, Yashvili liked to spend his midday wandering the neighborhood around Q and Connecticut. O'Neill had given him the nickname "Antsy" because he was always popping in and out of the stores in the area, the Melody Record Shop, Kramer Books, the Foreign Press Center, fingering the merchandise, occasionally buying a record or a book or a French newspaper. They'd even caught him popping into the Lambda Rising Homosexual Bookstore a couple of times, which prompted the suspicion he was gay, a crime both FBI agents rated at least as serious as that of being an agent of the international Communist conspiracy. For the moment, however, the permanent surveillance post across from the embassy's main entrance at 2645 Tunlaw Road had picked up no sign of Antsy's sky-blue Honda. O'Neill and Strong slumped against the front seat of their car, trying not to smoke, relieving their boredom with the traditional pastime of cops on a stakeout, storytelling.

"I ever tell you about this Czech we made going out to Bowie every Sunday, playing the ponies and not having all that much luck?" O'Neill asked his partner.

"Naw."

"Number two in Czech intelligence, he was. And as a horseplayer, I gotta tell you, he stank. Then we found out something real cute about him. He was fucking his boss's wife." O'Neill rasped out a low chuckle at the memories that inspired. "So we wrote him a letter. Sent it to him right there in the embassy. How did he figure his boss was going to feel when we told him he was shtuping his old lady? Did he figure that would be a career-enhancing move in Czech intelligence? Of course, we pointed out there was a way to handle the problem." O'Neill began to giggle, recollecting the Czech's dilemma.

"Sure glad you like your own stories," grunted Strong.

"Not only does the guy come over, the night he comes he goes into their coderoom, takes a sack, stuffs it with codebooks, messages, Christ knows what else, and jumps out of a window like Santa Claus coming down the chimney."

"Never fuck the boss's wife, Chickie, that's the moral of your story. At least our guys never had to worry about that with old J. Edgar, did they?"

Their radio rasped before O'Neill could answer. From his vantage point at a seventh-floor window of the Tunlaw Apartments opposite the embassy's big, black electrically operated sliding gate, the duty agent in the Bureau's twenty-four-hour surveillance post had just spotted Yashvili's blue Honda approaching the gate. He peered at it with high-resolution binoculars from behind a window ledge lined with potted plants and teddy bears. Somehow, those homely items were supposed to convince the Russians the FBI really wasn't up there.

"Blue Bonnet three thirty-nine," the duty agent whispered to his radio as Yashvili's car cleared the KGB control at the gate and pointed along Tunlaw heading for 39th Street. A block away from the embassy, a first FBI tail car started to slide up Davis Place toward Tunlaw. As the KGB officer's Honda flashed past the T ahead of them, the two agents accelerated toward the corner to take the initial surveillance. Yashvili turned on to 39th, then right on Wisconsin heading down toward Georgetown.

"Ameche," the first car's driver announced to his radio. That told O'Neill and Strong Yashvili was coming their way. They spotted his car gliding down Wisconsin and dropped into traffic two cars behind the tail car in a move only a very alert KGB officer could have detected. At P, Yashvili turned right. The first tail car dropped off, leaving the surveillance to O'Neill and Strong. The Russian headed across the upper fringes of Georgetown, going toward Connecticut.

"Off to see the Yuppies again, Antsy is," O'Neill remarked. They followed their KGB agent until he found a metered parking spot on 19th. "Take him," O'Neill ordered. "I'll park."

Antsy was wearing jeans and a bulky white knit sweater covered with brown-and-black zigzags and carrying a green-and-white Benetton shopping bag. In a sweater like that you could make a guy in a crowd from half a mile away, Strong thought, drifting along behind him on sidewalks thronged with weekend shoppers.

For an hour, Antsy went through his Saturday routine, peering in here, poking around there, picking through the foreign press in the shop at Connecticut and Q. The two agents alternated coverage, communicating through the button mikes in their coat collars. Finally, Antsy strolled into one of his favorite haunts, Kramer Books. The bookstore had entrances on two streets—one off Connecticut onto its stacks, and the second onto 19th from a little restaurant, Afterwords, that was a part of the bookstore. Those dual entrances made the place an automatic security concern to Antsy's FBI tails.

O'Neill took up a spot across Connecticut just down from the Janus Theater. Antsy's white-brown-and-black sweater was clearly visible through the bookstore windows as he browsed with maddening slowness along

Kramer's display counters. Finally, after half an hour, he picked up several books and headed for the cashier.

"He's coming out your side, Denny," O'Neill announced.

Five minutes passed. Antsy did not show up at either exit. "Where the fuck is he?" O'Neill whispered into his mike.

"Maybe he went to the can," Strong said.

"I'm going in there," O'Neill announced.

"Wait, for Christ's sake. He'll make you sure as hell." Strong had barely finished his sentence when he saw their target picking his way through the tables packed with the Saturday lunch crowd toward the 19th Street exit. "Here he comes," he whispered with considerable relief. "We got him back."

Antsy stepped out the door and peered at the terrace of Afterwords. All its little tables were full. He appeared to hesitate a moment, debating, perhaps, whether to go up the street to the Mexican Cafe Reale. He frequently ate Saturday lunch at one of the two restaurants.

"What'll it be, Antsy?" Strong growled. "Tex Mex or good old American?"

A client gesturing to a waiter with his check and a twenty-dollar bill made up Antsy's mind for him. He moved over to take the seat at the curbside table under a bright red parasol, settling into the chair as soon as the previous client got up. He placed his Kramer Books shopping bag at his feet, picked out one of his purchases, and began to read in the warm Indian-summer sunlight.

"I hope you're not hungry, Chickie," Strong whispered. "He's there for a good hour."

Forty-five minutes later, engrossed in his book, Antsy finally finished the last of his avocado salad and signaled for the waiter.

"Get ready, Chickie," Strong reported. "I think he's asking for the check."

Two minutes later, Strong saw the waiter reemerge.

"Holy shit!" groaned Strong, spotting what the waiter was carrying in his hand. "Would you believe it? The guy's gone for the chocolate pecan pie."

"He's got no shame," replied O'Neill from his post on Connecticut Avenue. His own stomach had been sending out impatient signals for an hour now. "Doesn't he know how many calories they got in there?"

It took Antsy a good ten minutes to go through the pie. When he'd finished, he called the waiter again. This time the waiter returned with a cappuccino. Antsy said a few words to him, then pressed his book flat on the table and stood up.

Strong was able to follow Antsy's progress through the café window as he returned to the inside of the café, then moved through the cluster of tables toward the men's room, just out of his line of sight adjacent to the kitchen.

"He's going to the can again," he whispered.

Alerted, O'Neill turned his attention to the Connecticut Avenue entrance. Five minutes went by and there was no sign of Antsy.

"Where the fuck is he?" Strong said. "Nothing on your side?"

"Two girls and a guy in a raincoat and felt hat. Maybe he's got a bad prostate," O'Neill joked from Connecticut.

Five minutes later when there was still no sign of Antsy, the bantering tone had disappeared from the voices of the two agents.

"I'm going in and have a look, Denny," O'Neill said.

"Roger," his partner replied. "I'll meet you at the 19th Street entrance."

Less than a minute later, the two agents came face to face by Antsy's table. His cappuccino rested untouched beside his copy of Tom Clancy's latest novel. "The bastard's flown!" O'Neill hissed in a whisper venomous with hate.

"You sure?"

O'Neill whipped a green-and-white Benetton shopping bag from behind his back. "Had this all morning, didn't he? But not when he came out here for lunch. It was in the trash can in the toilet. The fucker stashed it in the can when he went in there the first time. He had his walking-out clothes in it. He was the guy in the raincoat and the fedora!''

Kazemi and Ansari, the ex-student from Berlin's Free University, were the first members of Said Dajani's commando to cross into West Berlin. Ansari led the way through the East German controls up to the Friedrichstrasse railroad platform. A white strip was painted down the platform three feet from its edge. As the train eased into the station from the East Berlin marshaling yards, uniformed East German border guards toting machine pistols were posted every one hundred yards along the line to hold back the fifty-odd passengers, all West Berliners, who'd come over to get a good seat on the train. While the Westerners looked on scornfully, the East German border guards scoured the train for defectors. Search teams with ladders opened all the toilets to peer inside while others with mirrors scrutinized the train's undercarriage for anyone crazy enough to want to flee the workers' paradise of East Germany. A guard's whistle pronounced the train sanitized, and the two Lebanese piled on.

Trains out of Friedrichstrasse Station run through West Berlin, across East Germany to West Germany, and then on to Paris, Zurich, Amsterdam, and Brussels. They stopped twice in West Berlin, Ansari told his companion, at Zoo Station and Wannersee to take on passengers. No West German officials bothered to check anything or anybody, however, until the train left Wannersee and was sealed for its run through East Germany.

Minutes after they boarded, the train was in Zoo Station. The two terrorists walked downstairs and onto the U-Bahn for their final destination, Kreuzberg, a prewar working-class neighborhood that had become home to most of West Berlin's migrant workers: Turks, Iranians, Arabs.

By the time they reached Kreuzberg, their two confederates were passing through the East German border controls at Friedrichstrasse. Like the two who had preceded them, they had no problems with the East German guards. It was only their fellow East Germans that interested the *Grenztruppen*. They went deep down into the station's bowels to the subway platform that the KGB's Valentin Tobulko employed on his crossings into the West. They, however, took the northern leg of the subway up toward Wedding and the French sector of West Berlin. Under East Berlin, the old subway stops were all closed, gray, lifeless caverns, covered in dust and grime, their dark passages patrolled by armed *Grenztruppen* in case a defector should try to leap onto a passing train. Coming into the first animated, brightly lit station in West Berlin was like walking out of a darkened movie theater into the sunlight of midafternoon.

Dajani had ordered them up to Wedding, "Wedding the Red" of Berlin of the 1920s, then a stronghold of National Socialism. Largely untouched by the Allied bombing in the war, it remained a lower-middle-class working area. Sayed, the former drug runner, had a better idea, however. He had an address on Residenzstrasse in a more prosperous area just south of Wedding.

The place he was looking for was at number 50, the Pizzeria Capri. The two Lebanese walked in and ordered espressos at the bar. The pizzeria was small and neat, a couple of lobsters' carcasses crawling up the wall, a fishnet dangling from the ceiling, and its principal decorations, postcards sent back to the proprietor from sunnier climes, tacked up anywhere there was room.

"You Giuseppe?" Sayed asked.

The barman nodded.

"My brother, Abou Khalifa, said to say hello."

The news did not appear to excite Giuseppe unduly. He grunted and continued to polish his already gleaming espresso machine.

"We're looking for a pad to stay in for a while," Sayed continued. "Know anything in the neighborhood?"

Giuseppe continued to stroke his espresso machine with the affection of an elderly woman petting a favorite cat. Finally, he pointed a finger toward the café window, indicating a four-story brick-and-gray-stucco structure across Residenzstrasse's divided highway. "Ask the caretaker over there," he said. "Tell him I sent you."

The two men finished their espresso and paid. *"Ciao,"* Sayed said.

"Maaq'salaam—goodbye. Say hello to Abou Khalifa," Giuseppe answered with a perfect Arabic accent.

They crossed the divided highway. On the corner opposite, Sayed noticed with considerable interest, was the Moonlight Sauna. Next door was an open-air used-car lot. His instincts had been right. This was obviously what you'd call a full-service neighborhood.

He led the way through the archway at 97/98, an entry big enough to let a coach and four pass, and found the caretaker's lodge. The caretaker led them up a back stairwell to a third-floor apartment containing a sitting room, two bedrooms, and a clean if rudimentary kitchen and bath.

"Five hundred marks a month," the caretaker announced. "Two months' rent and a month's rent as a deposit in advance."

Sayed looked at his partner and exchanged a few words in Arabic. "It will be fine," he announced and counted out fifteen hundred-mark notes for the caretaker.

A few minutes later, the caretaker was back bearing an official form. "You must fill these out and take them to the Landes Einwohner Amt at the police," he explained. "It is the law."

Sayed nodded gravely. They would, he assured the caretaker, give the matter their urgent attention. When he'd left, Sayed suggested a visit next door to the used-car lot. The cars were lined up in the open air. They inspected them one by one, their attention finally settling on a 1987 Opel with 47,000 kilometers for 9,500 marks. Its red TUV automobile inspection sticker was good, Sayed noted, for another three months.

Sayed got the price down to 9,250 marks and closed the deal. The dealer took Sayed's passport and filled out a purchase order. Then he collected the 9,250 marks cash and an additional 180 marks which would give them a sixty-day license and insurance permit until they got around to registering the car themselves.

Their day's work was a source of considerable satisfaction to Sayed. Dajani had given each team fifteen thousand marks for their car and five thousand marks for an apartment. Their transaction left them with close to ten thousand marks profit. Why give it back to Dajani? Or why share it with his colleague, the car bomber? His only interest was blowing people up. Sayed, however, knew how to start putting such a windfall to good use. He said goodnight to the bomber and headed down to the Moonlight Sauna to enjoy the rewards of a good day's work.

Across Berlin in Kreuzberg, the day had been equally satisfying for the other two members of the commando. Kreuzberg meant "Hill of the Cross," an irony few of the neighborhood's Moslem inhabitants understood or appreciated. The graffiti spray-painted on the walls of the nineteenth-century Bismarck-style dwellings, "PLO" and *"Yankees aus raus,"* made the two terrorists feel right at home. They too turned to a café for help finding lodging, the Samsun Donner Kebab House on Oranienstrasse. The owner, as it turned out, had a cousin who owned the building nearby at 82 Adalbertstrasse, and within two hours, Karemi and Ansari had settled into a ground-floor flat. No one mentioned filling out any official forms to register their presence in the building. Bureaucratic procedures were not held in high regard in Kreuzberg, which, among other distinctions, had the highest crime rate in Berlin.

To get a car, Ansari took his accomplice to a drive-in theater in Mariendorf which he'd discovered in his student days. During daylight hours it functioned as a kind of automotive flea market. Half a dozen prospective sellers were lined up with vehicles for sale, cardboard signs with their asking price in their windshields. They studied the offerings and, after some ritual rubber-kicking, settled on a 1986 Ford Granada for 8,700 marks. Its TUV still had three months to run. The owner counted out their money on the hood of the car, signed the title over to Karemi, and gave them the keys. That was all the protocol required. The car was theirs.

Later, back in their flat, Karemi decided to furnish them both with some relaxation. He went out and with his flair for such things, found what he was looking for in less than twenty minutes, a plug of high-grade Nepalese hashish.

Never go to a meeting you haven't organized yourself without first carefully studying the meeting site for surveillance or a trap. The graveyards of the world's intelligence agencies were, after all, filled with agents who'd forgotten that principle. For this, the first *treff* of her career, Captain Dulia Vaninya intended to follow KGB procedure rigorously. She got to the parking area in front of the China Paradise Restaurant in Tysons Corner an hour before the six-thirty rendezvous assigned to her in her postcard from Aix-en-Provence.

She parked her gray Toyota in front of a laundromat about fifty yards from the restaurant's blue-and-white awning and at right angles to it. Carrying a sack of laundry, she walked inside, found a free machine for her wash, then, as the machine thumped into action, picked up a copy of *Cosmopolitan* and sat down in a kind of lounge area before the laundromat's plate glass window. She pretended to be absorbed in an article addressing the burning question "Condom Courtesy—Yours or His?" —an issue which, to her regret, she had never had much cause to study in her three and a half years as an illegal in the United States. In fact, of course, her eyes and attention were on the area in front of the China Paradise. Her vantage point afforded her as good a place as any to scrutinize the parking lot for any hint it was under surveillance without making her interest obvious.

For fifty minutes she watched, recharging her washing machine as the occasion required. Three and a half years, she thought. For three and a half years she'd been living in what had become for her a warm, secure womb, the personality of this woman she had created, Nina Wolfe.

The first six months, there had been moments of panic and anxiety, but for the last three years, she had felt safe, comfortable, unmenaced. Now in a few moments she was going to have to open the door of a van, get in, and drive off. With that act, she would have broken cover. She would have left her sheltering womb; no longer could she hide in safety in the personality of Nina Wolfe.

Stop it, she ordered herself. Watch. Study. Check. Shortly after six-fifteen, she saw a beige van enter the small parking lot. She could sense the driver's hesitation as he searched for a parking place. He drove slowly past the China Paradise, past an empty spot. Her eyes were on the lot behind him, looking for any sign he was being followed.

He circled once, came back, and eased the van into the empty spot just beyond the restaurant's blue-and-white awning. Making no apparent effort to study his surroundings, he got out, took off his raincoat and hat, tossed them into the backseat of the car, and strolled away. Captain Vaninya followed his white-brown-and-black knit sweater disappearing from view, alert for any indication he was being followed—she saw none.

She waited ten more minutes, until her last load of laundry tumbled from the dryer, then headed back to her Toyota. She went around the block and parked. Now, she thought. A slow, controlled breath to ease her tensions. Open the door. Walk back around the corner without a care in the world. Was there an FBI agent watching the van from a window in the mall? If there was, don't think about him.

She was in front of the van. She reached out, opened the door, and got inside. Panic hit her like a blow in the stomach. There were no keys. Where were the keys? It was a trap. Wait, she told herself, be calm. Under the driver's seat? Her finger patted the rubber mat below her. They were there.

She glanced into the backseat, to where the courier had tossed his coat. She saw the outline of a suitcase under it. Very carefully, aware that this was not the moment to scrape someone's fender or run a stop sign, she started off.

Since their KGB quarry's flight, Chick O'Neill and Denny Strong had done the only thing they could do: stake out his car and wait for his return. Strong had "tagged" it by placing a button-sized transmitter that emitted a continuous radio signal under one of its fenders. That would make following Antsy even easier when he returned from wherever it was he'd gone—except, as O'Neill had pointed out, he was going to head straight back to the embassy, and following him back there wasn't going to be all that much of a problem.

"Here he comes!" Strong whispered from his post on 19th shortly after six-thirty. "He's just turned off the circle. He's back in the sweater. Must have dumped his walking-out clothes." He paused for a moment. "Yeah, he's walking straight to his car. I swear to Christ, Chickie, the bastard's got a smile the size of an elephant's asshole all over that dumb face of his."

"Why wouldn't he? He made us weeks ago. He's been setting this up for months."

Nina Wolfe gave the fat teenage girl a reassuring pat on the shoulder as they walked to her office door. "Now be sure to listen to your tapes just before you go to sleep at night and as soon as you wake up in the morning. That's going to help that posthypnotic suggestion I tried to implant in your unconscious to work the next time you want to go out for a milkshake or a hot fudge sundae."

The girl looked at Nina with the grateful eyes of a cocker spaniel contemplating a bone. "Gee, thanks, Doctor. I sure hope it works. My boyfriend, he really don't like fat girls."

"Not Doctor," Nina said firmly, opening the door to the landing outside. "I'm just a friendly counselor."

The girl disappeared, and as she did a man stepped out of the shadows by the stairwell. He was tall, with a blond crewcut, washed-out blue eyes, and the vacuous smile of a male model advertising aftershave lotion. An FBI agent, she thought. They'd been watching. They followed me back here when I picked up the van.

"Miss Wolfe?"

"Yes." Be calm, she told herself. Don't give yourself away by appearing frightened.

"May I come in a moment?"

"Could you come back tomorrow? I was about to close up."

"It's urgent. I've got to stop smoking. My doctor's orders. My heart."

I'd better talk to him, she thought. If he is an agent, refusing is only going to make things worse. She showed the man into her office, seated him in a wing chair, took her place at her desk, and drew out the questionnaire she always filled out with clients anxious to stop smoking.

"So," she asked, "how many cigarettes do you smoke a day?"

"I don't smoke."

Her head jerked, and she looked at him, frightened and puzzled.

"Three times the new apples ripened."

Her mind went blank. She sat there for a second or two staring back at the man, her lips half open as though her sinuses were blocked out and she had to breathe through her mouth. The words had been in and out of her consciousness for days, since she'd gotten the postcard. Now, when she needed them, they'd dropped through a black hole in her mind, as the name of a close friend come upon unexpectedly at a street corner sometimes will.

"Three harvests from fields were gathered." She blurted out the line from Vadim Strelchenko's "Native Land" with a relief so evident the visitor smiled.

"Major Valentin Tobulko," he said. "My congratulations, Captain, on how efficiently you scrutinized your rendezvous site with the van. You haven't forgotten what they taught you at Bykovo."

"Thank you, Major. May I offer you something?"

"Are you expecting anyone else?"

"No. That really was my last client."

"Good. We're going to be working together for the next ten days on an assignment of great importance."

Captain Dulia Vaninya sat back in her chair. "I am at your orders, sir."

The man took a map of Washington from his pocket and spread it on her table. "First," he said, "I'd like you to rent a small furnished apartment for the two of us to use here, in this neighborhood." His index finger traced a small arc running from Connecticut Avenue through New Hampshire to 13th Street. "It must have a telephone. Pay cash. Take it for two or three months. Say we're a married couple working with IBM. Down here for a training seminar of some sort. I presume you have sufficient currency?"

"Yes, sir."

"Move in as soon as you find it. Take a minimum of things with you so if anyone's watching you, it won't occur to him you're changing locations. For your clients, make it appear as though you've just gone away for a few days."

"My car?"

"Leave it. The police could trace you through it. When you get the apartment, leave a letter for me, Roy Banwell, at General Delivery at the post office at Florida and T. Spend as little time outside the apartment as possible until I arrive. Take your Spetosk and your codes with you when you leave, of course. Is there anything here or in your flat that would indicate your ties to the Organs?"

"Nothing."

"Double-check anyway before you leave. If you find anything, destroy it."

"Fallback?"

"The laundromat by the Chinese restaurant, Wednesday at fourteen-thirty and each succeeding day one hour later." The major stretched out his hand. "I'll need the keys to the van."

She dipped into her handbag for them.

"And the suitcase that was on the backseat." He rose. "Try at all costs to be installed by Monday at the latest."

"That doesn't give me much time."

He shrugged and started for the office door. "Tell me," he said, opening it, "can you really make people stop smoking?"

On the night of Monday, October 25, Said Dajani ordered his four-man commando to drive to Wiesbaden in one of their newly acquired cars. The purpose of his order was threefold: he wanted them to reconnoiter their target and familiarize themselves with the roads they would take to it five days hence; he wanted them to get the reassurance of seeing for themselves how easy the border-crossing procedures along their route were going to be; and finally and most important, he had to hand over to them the sixty kilograms of Semtex high explosive they would employ in their car bomb when they drove back to Berlin through East Germany.

The four left just after dawn the next day. As they had been told, there was no check leaving West Berlin. Entering East Germany, they were stopped by the East German border police, who took their passports, then returned them with transit passes which gave the time and place of their entry into East Germany. The regulations covering their trip were simple. They had to stay on the autobahn that was designated as a transit corridor at all times. They could stop for gas, to eat, to use the toilet facilities, but that was all. The reason for the regulations was simple. The same autobahn was used for ordinary East German civilian traffic. The East German traffic flowed on and off the autobahn at normal exits. Those exits were only occasionally monitored by the East German police. They didn't want Westerners employing them to go poking around East Germany, and one of the key checks at the East German exit post was the amount of time a Western driver had used for his journey. If it exceeded the normal time span, he had better have a good explanation.

The trip through East Germany was slow and boring. Despite the light traffic, they rolled at a steady sixty miles an hour. Dajani had warned them there was nothing the East German police enjoyed more than handing out speeding tickets, which were payable in hard currency on the spot. They crossed back into West Germany just beyond Eisenach. At the frontier the East German guard carefully examined their transit passes and passports to be sure they were who they were supposed to be. He did not, however, make any attempt to search their car. A couple of hundred yards on as they entered West Germany, the border guard didn't even look up at their passing car.

They reached the city of Wiesbaden spread across the hills that constituted the northern banks of the Rhine just before noon. As they'd been instructed, they got off the autobahn at the Wiesbaden-Erbenheim exit and pointed their way along Route 455 toward Königstein. There, across from a potato farm, where the plateau crested and began its descent to the Rhine, was their target. In German, it was called the Siedlung Hainerberg, in English the Hainerberg Military Housing Area. Its triangular shape embraced a commissary, a PX, a church, three schools, and eighty-one three-story, prewar Luftwaffe barracks converted by the U.S. Armed Forces into family dwelling units for enlisted men and their wives and children. Over five thousand of them lived inside that compound. Adjacent to it a couple of hundred yards from its western edge were two more housing areas for officers and senior NCOs and their families.

A silence inspired by both fear and awe struck the four terrorists as they sighted their target. They started along the northern face of the triangle, the potato field to their right, the compound to their left. The barracks were built in the style inspired by Kaiser Wilhelm's architects, squat, solid, with sharply sloping roofs. They were painted tan, lime green, faded yellow, and each had four numbers stenciled in black paint at its base. A green metal fence eight feet high topped with a single strand of barbed wire enclosed the compound. Two minutes through their journey they passed the main entrance to the compound at Washingtonstrasse. The car ahead of them turned off Route 455 and entered its precincts.

"I don't believe it!" whispered Ansari.

"It's incredible," echoed one of his confederates.

There was absolutely no security at the gate to protect the area: no guardpost, no checkpoint, no MP controlling traffic, nothing.

"It's easier than the Marine barracks or the American embassy," declared the man who had wired up the bombs that had shattered the embassy.

Slowly, they circled the area three times, along 455 to New York Avenue, down to the tip of the triangle, then back up Abraham Lincoln Avenue to 455. With each voyage around the target, their confidence and their amazement grew.

"It looks so easy, you'd think it was a trap," Karemi declared.

"Except it's not," Ansari answered. "They're crazy, these Americans are. Crazy. Crazy."

For a minute they debated whether to enter the compound, to scout out the precise location at which they intended to place their car bomb Saturday night. The risk appeared unnecessary. They decided not to take it. They headed instead back to the number 66 autobahn and the Frankfurt airport. Driving slowly, the trip took exactly thirty-three minutes. Ansari, who was the least Arab-appearing of the four, went into the airport and bought four tickets on Pan Am Flight 660 back to Berlin at five minutes to ten Saturday night. He gave the counter clerk four false names he'd selected from the sports page of the *International Herald Tribune*. By three o'clock, they were on their way back to Berlin.

Captain Dulia Vaninya tossed the keys of her car into the center drawer of her desk. She studied her office, methodically going through the mental checklist she'd prepared for herself. She had $7,600 in cash in her pocketbook, most of what she'd accumulated in her checking account at the Riggs National Bank. Her clients for the next ten days had all had their appointments rescheduled. She'd left messages on both her answering machines and told the Mexican who cleaned her flat she was leaving for Europe. There was nothing, she assured herself, she'd overlooked. She walked out, locked her office door, and hung the little sign she'd prepared on her doorknob.

With nothing more than the handbag under her arm, she walked up to Tysons Corner to catch the bus to the District across the river. Nina Wolfe, hypnotherapist, had, for the time being at least, disappeared from the face of the earth.

"Are you sure they're not going to miss the lay-by?"

"Yes, Colonel, I'm sure." Abou Said Dajani did his best to conceal his exasperation at his KGB superior's question. They were pacing the gravel of an autobahn lay-by two kilometers north of the junction of Route 246, not quite twenty miles from the East German border with West Berlin.

"I wish I shared your confidence. With these people . . ." The colonel squashed his cigarette underfoot, leaving the rest of his phrase unspoken.

"I understand why the West Germans never search the traffic coming off the autobahn," Dajani said, preferring to change the subject, "but I don't understand why the East Germans never search cars."

"Because our idiot diplomats made a mistake in 1971. We signed an agreement that said the three access autobahns to West Berlin were a facility for West Berlin civilian traffic and the traffic wouldn't be interfered with. So, the East Germans don't search cars."

"Come on, Colonel!"

"We respect our agreements." In the darkness, Dajani sensed the colonel was looking at him. "You should know that."

"It must cost you, that respectful attitude."

The colonel lit a cigarette, thought for a moment or two

before answering. "It does. Do you remember that agent the English had inside the KGB? In the Center?"

"The one that had been working for MI6 all those years? In Scandinavia?"

"Yes. That's how they saved him. Got him to East Berlin, put him into the trunk of a British soldier's car, and drove him straight through Checkpoint Charlie. They know we never search cars that belong to Allied soldiers."

Dajani whistled softly.

"We know there's an organization in West Berlin that smuggles people into West Germany. The smuggler drives down from West Berlin and stops in a lay-by just like this. The East German is waiting. He gets into the trunk and out he goes. Fifty thousand Swiss francs they charge."

"Who in hell can afford that in East Germany?"

"No one. It's paid by friends, relatives in the West."

The sound of a car's tires on the gravel interrupted their conversation. The colonel drifted into the shadows. Dajani recognized his commando. *"Salaam,"* he said. "How did it go?"

"It will be easy," Karemi said. "For sure, it will be easy."

Dajani walked to his car and took out two suitcases.

"Open the trunk," he ordered. He laid the suitcases inside, then leaned into the car. "Everything you asked for is there," he told Nasreddin, the bomb expert. "Call me if you need anything else and I'll bring it over." He whacked the car door as a wrangler might slap a horse. The commando drove off.

"So, Colonel," he said getting into his own car. "Arabs can understand directions after all."

Half an hour later, the commando and their deadly charge drove unmolested back into West Berlin.

In a strange way, this neighborhood the captain had chosen for their hideout reminded Valentin Tobulko of the area he'd lived in off Gorky Street in Moscow when he was studying to be an actor. Like that neighborhood, Church Street was lined with trees, maples, which in spring and summer would shelter the narrow street under an awning of shade. The buildings certainly predated World War I. They had cupolas and cornices edging the roofs, bulblike lumps for bay windows swelling from their facades, and like so many of Moscow's old buildings, their masonry was painted in pastel shades: lime greens, pink, violet, beige, pale blue. Above all, it was quiet. Just as his neighborhood had been a kind of time capsule preserving a prerevolutionary Moscow, this one seemed to preserve the memory of another Washington, the sleepy Southern capital of an adolescent nation.

As he strode down the street toward the number she'd given him, he passed a sign wired to a lamppost. "This neighborhood reports all suspicious activities to the Metropolitan Police," it warned. Well, not all of them, I hope, he thought, suppressing a laugh.

The house he was looking for, 1750, was beige, its wooden trim painted dark brown. He paused, saw the half-flight of stairs descending to the basement apartment, walked down, and rang the bell. She answered immediately.

"You made an excellent choice," he assured her. "Congratulations."

"*Spasibo*—thank you, Major," she said.

"And you will now forget my name. I'm your lover, Roy Banwell, Nina Wolfe. And we will not speak another word of Russian to each other until our feet are back on the soil of the *Rodina*. I'll be back in a few minutes."

Ten minutes later, he returned with the van. He brought in a pair of heavy crates the size of rubbish cans and unwrapped them. When he'd finished, he took two panels of microchip circuitry from his attaché case and began to connect them to the devices he'd removed from their crates.

"May I ask what those are?" she said.

"Generators designed to emit one very precise, complex signal. I've got to assemble them, test them, then inform Moscow they're ready for use. When, and if, they send us back the mission-proceed order, I'll tell you what we're going to do with them.''

An hour later, he'd finished.

"These work very simply," he said. He picked up the electrical cord attached to one of the signal generators. "All you have to do is plug this into the wall socket, then turn this switch on"—he indicated a toggle switch on the top of the generator—"and it will start emitting its signal." For his test, he had positioned the generators so they would beam their signals due north, away from the White House.

"You won't see or hear or feel anything. You will, in fact, have only this red light"—he indicated a red bulb on the top of the generator—"to let you know the signal is actually going out. Is that clear?"

She nodded.

"We're going to test them now. I'm going to get in the van and drive off to another location. I'll call you when I get there. I want you to turn on first one generator, then the other."

"That sounds simple enough."

Tobulko was putting on his suit coat as she spoke, and for an instant he froze, one arm halfway into his jacket. She sensed there was something he wanted to tell her, a warning, perhaps, that what they were doing was not quite as simple as he'd suggested. Whatever his thought, it remained unspoken, however, silenced by the precepts of their service.

Tobulko had selected his test site with considerable care. He'd chosen the intersection of Lanier Place and Ontario, a block from Columbia Avenue. The corner was just about half a mile from the basement flat at 1750 Church Street, approximately the distance separating Church Street from the White House. More important, if their basement flat represented the junction at the base of a V, the intersection was only a few degrees off a center line bisecting the V. The signal the generators would emit was narrowly focused. By the time it got here, half a mile from its source, it would span a narrow arc. He could be sure that at this location, he would be inside that arc. If the signal hit his van, then there would be no doubt that, turned 180 degrees around, it would hit the White House.

He found a place adjacent to the intersection, parked, and drew what looked like a radar speed trap detector from the van's glove compartment. Indeed, his device worked on the same principles as detectors designed to pick up police radar signals, except for one thing—it picked up signals lower on the electromagnetic spectrum, at frequencies ranging from one to thirty hertz.

He switched it on. A miniature digital display counter like four postage stamps aligned in a row lit up. A series of numbers outlined in red moved on and off the counter. Sometimes a precise four-digit number would be frozen on the display for a second or two; at other times the numbers would flick on and off like numbers on a car's radio rapidly spanning the AM band. What the device was picking up was the ambient ELF "noise" around the van, extremely low-frequency electromagnetic radiation, most of it probably being thrown off rotating electrical machinery around Columbia Avenue.

He called the flat on his cellular phone. "Switch number one on," he said. He could hear her high heels clicking over the tiles as she walked to the generators.

Suddenly, four numbers, the four numbers he sought, glowered in a bright red outline from his digital counter. They did not move. They did not flicker. They stayed there frozen onto the counter's face like a bead of rubies set against a jeweler's black velvet display board. It was just as they had told him in Moscow it would be. The signal coming from the generator half a mile away was invading the van with a force so overwhelming it drowned out any trace of the electromagnetic noise in the area.

"Turn it off," he ordered, "and turn on the second one."

Exactly the same thing happened. The signal fixed its four characteristic numerals to the digital counter as though it were a digital clock that had stopped at a precise instant in time. The signal was there with him in the van. It was in the air he breathed, in the space his fingers stroked, behind him, above him, beside him, an invisible shroud whose presence only the black box in his hands could detect. In a few days, in response to his command, the electromagnetic ghosts swirling around him in his van would be unleashed on the White House. No corridor, no closet, no cubicle, no conference room would be impervious to their unseen and unfelt presence. Even that unassailable citadel, the mind of a man, of the President of the United States, would fall within their domain.

Valentin Tobulko had set out for his test beset by doubt and worry. He returned to Church Street wrapped in a serenity akin to that of a Tibetan monk in the throes of meditation. Above all, he stood in awe of the achievement of Soviet science he'd just witnessed, of the socialist system of which he was, at this moment, a particularly proud Praetorian guard.

Three hours later, he was on a barren hillock off the Indian Head Highway in Maryland behind Fort Foote Village. To anyone who might have seen him—and no one did—he would have looked like a bird watcher tracing with his outstretched arm the path of some exotic creature along the horizon. It was, in fact, the flight of a bird he followed, a Soviet communications satellite to which, with Captain Vaninya's Spetosk transmitter, he burst out the news of his successful test.

Preceded by the click-clicking of a Tums tablet against his teeth, Paul Mott of Counterintelligence entered Art Bennington's office. His J. Press sports jacket and gray flannel slacks were so rumpled you would be forgiven for thinking, Bennington told himself, that Mott had been using them for pajamas for the past couple of weeks. Mott's investigation into the Ann Robbins murder had, alas, remained mired where it had always been, on square one. It was, he'd informed Bennington, the reason for his visit.

"How's the stomach, Paul?" Bennington asked, waving him to a chair.

"I don't have a stomach, Art," he sighed. "After

twenty years in this building, I've got a vat of acid below my rib cage."

That launched them into a few moments of chatter about the trials of Agency life. Then Mott said, "Something's just come in I thought you ought to know. Quite frankly, it isn't much. In fact, it isn't anything when you get right to it, but that Spetosk transmitter came on the air again yesterday over in Maryland."

"The one the NSA picked up before our psychic was murdered?"

"That's what the NSA says."

Art mulled that one over for a moment.

"There's one other thing," Mott continued. "One of our friends from the embassy ditched his baby-sitters Saturday. The whole thing was so constructed that there's no question it was deliberate. He had a meet somewhere. Could it have been with the owner of the Spetosk?"

"Yeah," Art agreed. "That's a possibility you'd want to at least consider, isn't it?"

"The likelihood is the guy was either emptying a letter box or taking a meet with some agent he's running. Still, it's something to think about."

That was just what Bennington did after Mott left, think about it, immobile in his chair, staring at his office wall on which Nina Wolfe's face seemed to flash at him from time to time like a subliminal perception taking on form. He picked up the phone. He had to set the nagging doubts still swimming through his mind to rest. It was something he couldn't let ride another day. Furious, he slammed the receiver down. The answering machine, always that goddam answering machine. She was sitting there in that half-darkened room of hers trying to get some overweight teenager to stop breakfasting on Hershey bars. She didn't return his calls—at least not at night. He hadn't been able to leave her his office number, for Christ's sake.

Well, he'd have to go over there. She took her last appointment at six, he knew. Take her up to the inn and lay it on her as gently as he could. Which was not something he did all that well. "Oh, by the way, dear, just how is it you knew my name?'' And hope to hell she gave him the right answer.

"Little sugar," he called out to his assistant, Ann Stoddard, "another day's heroic work in the service of the nation is over as far as I'm concerned."

Ali Nasreddin was given the choice of which of the two cars to booby-trap. He selected the Ford, because it was more spacious, and the following day took it to a secluded wood on the shores of Lake Wannsee where he could work undisturbed and unobserved.

His Semtex plastic explosive was packed in twelve "loaves" of plastic, each weighing five kilograms. Properly detonated, they would represent an explosive force almost as deadly as that he had employed against the American embassy in Beirut, a bombing that had killed sixty-three people.

The problem was making sure that each of his loaves exploded with maximum effectiveness. To do that each loaf had to be individually detonated, and yet the detonations had to be triggered simultaneously. The method Nasreddin used was to detonate his charge in a series of parallel chains. First he laid four loaves of plastic along the floor of the Ford's trunk. They could later be concealed under a blanket. Next he took out the backseat of the car, cut out its springs to make more room, and packed four more loaves into the space he'd given himself. The last and most difficult job was fitting two loaves under each of the car's front seats. Semtex, like most plastic explosives, was a malleable material, and Nasreddin had to knead the loaves into flatter shapes which would fit beneath the seats.

Once he'd packed the loaves into the car, he inserted individual detonators into each loaf. He then wired the detonators into four chains of three loaves each, one in the trunk, one under the rear seat, and one under the front seat. The four wires he connected in turn into a central socket which plugged into his firing device. Normally, Nasreddin was an enthusiast of the button bomb, a bomb detonated by remote action employing a radio-control device operating somewhere in the two-to-six-meter VHF bands. You could make these devices yourself, using, for example, the radios kids employed to maneuver model airplanes. In this case, however, they would be hundreds of miles from the site when the bomb exploded, so he'd had to use a timer set for eleven o'clock. It looked very much like an ordinary clock, and, indeed, it was, except that when the hour hand reached eleven it would close an electrical circuit which would release a charge of electric current simultaneously into his four explosive chains.

All that was the easy part. The dangerous part Nasreddin would have to perform once the car had been delivered to the bomb site. He was going to use the car battery as his power source. That meant he would have to hot-wire the ignition leads into his timer so that when the hour hand closed on eleven the battery's twelve-volt charge would storm into his chains.

Hot-wiring cars, however, was something Nasreddin could do in his sleep. For the moment, immensely pleased, he stood back and surveyed his handiwork. His wiring had all been concealed under the car's rubber floor matting. The timer was taped to the base of the steering column, well out of sight. Glance into his Ford Granada and you would never imagine that it was as deadly an instrument as his skilled hands could assemble.

"It's very simple," declared Wolfgang, the Red Army Faction terrorist giving Sayed Hakim a final briefing. "You drive on Washingtonstrasse, follow its bend to the right, and take your second right on the left, Florida-strasse. Yours is the last big building on the left. You can't miss it. Its number, 7777, is written right across it. As you look at it, the parking lot is to its right."

"You're sure they won't have security?" Sayed asked for the second time.

Wolfgang sneered. Beside him, his girlfriend, Ulla, gave a little smirk. She was pale, with blond hair so unkempt and dirty she might have considered shampoo a toxic waste. "Not unless you call to tell them you're coming," Wolfgang said. Ulla giggled admiringly.

"The football game will be over by four o'clock. From six to seven, there won't be anybody around. You drive in and leave your getaway car as a blocking car in the parking place nearest the building. When you bring the charge car back at nine, you'll have a reserved parking place waiting there for you."

"It seems stupid to me to go in there twice." Sayed's voice had a pleading tone to it, like that of a youngster asking if he really has to run an errand in the dark.

Wolfgang's sneer had now become a permanent part of his features. These Arabs. They liked soft targets. "Listen, you don't use a blocking car like I tell you and when you get there there won't be any places left in the parking lot. You'll have to stick your car out in the back somewhere. All that nice bomb of yours will do is bounce a few cars around."

"Okay, okay." Sayed sighed.

"The uniforms are in the bag under the table," Ulla whispered.

"We go now," Wolfgang concluded. "Please. Don't leave for five minutes."

The two Germans got up and strolled out of the café, leaving a very worried Sayed to brood over his coffee.

Abou Said Dajani listened carefully as his four-man commando reviewed their plans for him.

"Change back into your own clothes on your way to the airport," he ordered. "Get rid of the uniforms. Don't leave them in the car."

Then he went out to inspect the Ford. "Sleep tonight," he said when he'd finished. "You must have clear minds tomorrow." He embraced each man in turn.

"Vengeance," he whispered, then turned and walked away.

•　•　•

MAZE

He walked up to the Kottbusser Tor U-Bahn station at the center of Kreuzberg and boarded the subway line Berliners called the Orient Express. He had one last errand to accomplish before returning to East Berlin, and the colonel's instructions had been very precise. He got off the U-Bahn at Kochstrasse and walked up to the street. Ahead of him, he could see a handful of cars exiting East Berlin through Checkpoint Charlie. As the colonel had instructed, he crossed the street to 60 Kochstrasse. There in front of a bedding store where the colonel had said they would be was the line of three yellow phone booths. He stepped into one and took out a stack of coins, inserted them into the phone, and dialed the number the colonel had given him, 00 98 34 2716.

"Bah key kaar dareed?" the man who answered said in Farsi. "Whom do you want to talk to?"

"Tell the boss the package has been prepared and will be delivered tomorrow," Dajani said in Arabic. Then he hung up.

As the crowd roared out its delight, the flames of the bonfire stretched their rosy fingers into the night. Somewhere a cannon boomed out its salute. Yipping a series of delighted squeals, half a dozen cheerleaders in white sweaters and miniskirts ran into the circle around the exploding fire. The Homecoming Weekend of General H. H. Arnold High School in Wiesbaden was officially underway.

Like most of the schools in the Department of Defense's Overseas Schools System, General Arnold High strived to be as American in tone and taste as the schools back in the homeland its students' parents were overseas to defend. To the crowd's cheers, the coach of the Arnold High School Warriors introduced his team one by one. They wore their letter sweaters and warmup jackets. Young eyes shining with pride and emotion, they thumped each other as they were introduced as though they were getting ready to play in the Super Bowl.

Over two thousand people had gathered around the

bonfire, most of the faculty and the nine hundred students, their parents, dozens of younger kids from the enlisted personnel quarters in the Hainerberg Military Housing Area, GIs and airmen enjoying a spectacle that was a perfect replica of ones they themselves had lived not so long ago.

As the rally wound to a close, a willowy black cheerleader stepped to the microphone. Joan Mallory was the vice president of the student council and captain of the cheerleaders. She also had a lovely contralto voice, a pair of 700-plus SATs, a 3.8 grade average, and an ambition that thrilled her father, a master sergeant in the maintenance section of the nearby U.S. Army helicopter base —a scholarship to Harvard. She reminded the crowd of the weekend activities—kickoff of the big game against Frankfurt American High at two-thirty, the homecoming dance, of which she was the cochairman, in the gym at eight. Then she led the crowd singing the high school's fight song.

"Let's go, Warriors!" she shrieked as it ended, leaping up before the dying flames with all the exuberance of her glowing youth.

Art Bennington walked up the three flights of stairs to Nina Wolfe's office with a tread about as gay and lighthearted as that of a condemned man advancing to the hangman's noose. There was no way that he could figure that their relation, or whatever it was you would call one night of blissful, wonderful lovemaking, was going to survive the coming confrontation. After all, what do you say? "Look, darling, there's this one little thing that's bothering me about how you might just be, well, you know, I mean, uh, a spy, a KGB agent." I should have written to Ann Landers and asked her how she'd suggest popping that query, he thought as he turned onto her landing.

As he did, he saw the white sign hanging on her door. Anxiously, he picked it up and read it. She'd gone to Santa Fe on vacation. She'd be back in a few days. At the bottom was that infuriating line which seemed as much a part of social discourse these days as "hello" and "goodbye": "Leave a message on my answering machine and I'll be back to you as soon as possible."

Bennington was so relieved, so happy, he almost galloped back down the stairs. If she was out in Santa Fe on vacation, one place she couldn't have been was over in the Maryland hills the other day popping up a burst transmission to Moscow Center. This vacation was probably something she'd been planning for some time. Maybe she'd gone out there with some guy she'd been seeing before that night. Maybe right now, at this very minute, she was starting to let the guy down easy, setting him up for the end of the affair.

He was whistling as he crossed the parking lot to his car. In the twilight he saw her car in the area reserved for the building's tenants, the gray Toyota right in front of the white wooden sign reading "N. H. Wolfe." Looking at it brought him a sense of reassuring warmth, the kind of feeling a man has when he smells a woman's scent in the air of a room in which she's just made love or stumbles on some familiar object, a cigarette lighter or a barrette, left behind after a rendezvous.

The thought hit him with the force of a fist in the stomach as he was two steps away from his own car. It was what Pettee, the FBI guy, had said during their meeting downtown on the Ann Robbins murder investigation: "a suburban housewife type with red hair . . . driving a gray Toyota." The joy he'd felt reading the sign on her door was over. Once again, the cancer of suspicion resumed its malignant advance. Was she really in Santa Fe? What the hell should he do? Should he go down and see Mott in the morning, and admit he'd subjected himself to hypnosis without informing his superiors? Could his career survive a blip like that? Maybe I'm becoming paranoid, he thought. Realistically, what are the odds she's not what she seems to be—one in a hundred? A thousand? Ten thousand? Should he jeopardize his career for that?

He got into his car and slouched in his seat. He felt an overwhelming desire for a cigarette. Funny, because it was cigarettes that had gotten him into Nina Wolfe's office in the first place. He turned the key in the ignition. I'll think about it, he decided. Stew on it overnight.

The four-man commando, traveling in two cars this time, left Berlin at eleven Saturday morning, October 30. By six they were at the rendezvous they'd selected on their first trip, a rarely used lay-by on the E5 autobahn just north of its junction with the A66. Joking to mask the nervous tension that had now crept over all of them, they got into the U.S. Army camouflaged battle dress the Red Army Faction had provided them.

Ali Kazemi and Hussain Ansari set off in the Opel they would use as a getaway vehicle. Nasreddin and Hakim followed in the bomb-carrying Ford. Kazemi and Ansari drove into the compound as they'd been instructed and found the gym, a big square building opposite the church at the end of Floridastrasse. As their RAF allies had said it would be, the parking lot adjoining the gym was empty. The game had been over for almost two hours, the crowds and players had all left. The crowd for the homecoming dance had not yet begun to arrive. They were able to take the slot closest to the gym, some twenty-five yards from the football team's locker room. They walked off, leaving the blocking car unlocked. If someone should become suspicious of it, a team of military police could inspect it and see that it was just another parked car.

Halloween: a night for hobgoblins and witches, jack-o'-lanterns and ghosts and the frivolous menace of trick or treat. That was the theme Joan Mallory and her dance committee cochairman had chosen for the General Arnold High School's homecoming dance. Orange and black streamers ringed the basketball court of the gym. Witches in peaked black caps rode their broomsticks high overhead. Ghoulish masks lit up by bulbs peeked out of corners and doorways.

To get in, the students entered through the varsity

dressing room. Its passageway into the gym had been turned into a kind of fun-house corridor. A fluorescent cardboard skeleton dropped out of the darkness at each passing couple. The kids loved it and grabbed, of course, the excuse to leap into each other's arms.

By nine o'clock the dance was going full-blast. A German disco group that specialized in running dances had set up their musical control system in the basketball court's pressbox high overhead. On Joan Mallory's instructions, the Germans ran a neat split between rap and rock, a tactic designed to conciliate the high school's two rival musical factions.

The parking lot outside was packed with cars but sat almost deserted under the light of a full moon. No one paid any attention to the GI in camouflage battle dress who strolled into the lot, got into the Opel next to the side of the gym, and drove off. Nor did the appearance of a Ford Granada a minute later heading toward the empty space stir anyone's interest. Indeed, only one person even saw the exchange. It was Walt Clemens, the nose tackle on the Arnold High School Warriors football team, and Clemens had much more important matters on his mind. His girl, sitting beside him in his father's Chevrolet, had just announced to him their six-week love affair was over. Groping for a reply to that stunning news, Clemens let his eyes follow the departing GI as he walked past his car. Asshole, he thought. He's out of uniform. Adidas sneakers instead of combat boots on his feet.

Five minutes after Nasreddin had deposited the booby-trapped car, the four exultant terrorists were on their way down the A66 to the Frankfurt airport. They stripped off their uniforms and dumped them on the car floor. By nine thirty-five they'd parked the car in the airport's huge parking lot and were on their way to Gate B41 and their Pan Am flight to Berlin.

The plane coasted up to its landing spot at Tegel at ten minutes to eleven, five minutes early. With no baggage, the four terrorists had only to walk through the airport to the taxi stand outside. Hakim got in front, the others in the back. "Zoo Station," Hakim told the driver.

"We made it!" Ansari, the youngest member of the team, exulted in Arabic. "Would you believe it? Everything worked perfectly."

"Shut up, donkey's asshole, don't speak Arabic," Hakim hissed. "Unless you just want to tell this driver we're Arab?"

They continued their drive in rigid silence.

At about the time their plane had been coming into Tegel, Walt Clemens, the jilted football player, had returned to the parking lot with his girlfriend for another backseat conference in his dad's Chevy. He happened to notice the license plates on the car parked by the side of the gym. They were not U.S. Forces plates but German plates from Berlin. Must belong to the guys doing the disco, he thought. Then he stopped. The guy getting out of the car had been a GI—and out of uniform.

"Holy shit!" he said, grabbing his girl by the arm. "We gotta go find Mr. Swensen!"

Ignoring her protests, he ran back into the gym and found Swensen, the assistant principal and track coach. The boy, thought Swensen, was unduly alarmed, but he was a conscientious man and followed Clemens back into the parking lot. He tried the car doors. They were locked.

"My dad's got a flashlight in his car," Clemens said.

"Get it."

Swensen took the light and shone its beam into the car. It was reassuringly empty. There seemed nothing unusual about it until he ran the light's beam down the steering column. There was a package of some sort taped to its base. And he couldn't be sure, but it looked like there just might be a set of wires running into it. He thought for a moment.

"Walt, get back in there and evacuate the gym—by the front entrance. I'm going to try to break into this car."

Swensen's decision saved an incalculable number of lives but cost him his own. He was still trying to pry open the window when Nasreddin's bomb went off with a searing burst of white light and a roar that shook windowpanes on the other side of the Rhine, three miles away.

PART 6

"...RELIEVE
THE PRESIDENT
OF HIS OFFICE."

Abou Said Dajani and the colonel peered through the command post's one-way glass down into the crowds surging up to the East Berlin Friedrichstrasse border control point. The flow of traffic was strictly one-way. Hundreds of people were backed up waiting to cross into West Berlin. The one-day visitor's visas for East Berlin issued by the *Grenztruppen* ran out at twelve midnight. Miss the deadline and the reward was a day in an East Berlin jail. Very few people were heading east, however, which made it easy for the two men to scrutinize each arrival individually. Behind him Dajani heard the phone ring and then noticed the *Grenztruppen* duty officer obsequiously tiptoe over to the colonel, a black telephone receiver in his hands.

"*Da*," the colonel said, grabbing it from him. He listened a few moments, added "*spasibo*—thank you," and handed the phone back to the East German. When the German had retreated into the shadows, the colonel leaned over to Dajani. "They did it," he whispered. "The American Armed Forces Radio just interrupted their programs to announce the bomb."

Dajani registered the news with a shrug. He had never doubted his commando would do it. Barely thirty seconds later, he nudged the colonel. Nasreddin had stepped up to one of the two *Grenztruppen* checking the documents of people entering East Berlin. One by one the other three followed Nasreddin past the control point. "Well done," the colonel whispered. "Well done indeed." He stood up.

"I've arranged a welcoming celebration for them back

in their safe flat. It's the least they deserve. Go do your errand and come back and join us.''

Dajani moved off down the interior stairways to the door giving direct access to the U-Bahn platforms under the station. He stepped onto the first train heading into the American sector and got off one stop later at Koch-strasse. As he had done the night before, he crossed the street to the three yellow public phone booths and stepped into one. He again dialed the number the colonel had furnished him. "Your package has been delivered," he announced as soon as a voice came on the line. "The messengers have all returned safely." He hung up the phone and headed back down to the U-Bahn station.

It was the kind of scene television dramas do well: the blinding red-and-blue lights of the police cars and fire trucks, the firemen in yellow slickers darting back and forth, blue-white pillars of light picking across the wreck-age, the wail of sirens and the occasional anguished scream of the wounded for background music. Except, in the still-smoking wreckage of the General Arnold High School gym, it was all real.

The colonel commanding Rhein-Main Air Force Base had parked his mobile command post next to the high school's main building and taken charge of the rescue operation. Yellow U.S. military and orange German ci-vilian fire trucks surrounded the ruins. An emergency medical triage and evacuation post had been installed in the corridors of the main building opposite the front en-trance of the gym.

Litters from the dozen ambulances that had reached the scene covered the floor. Crying softly or just staring at the ceiling in stunned silence, the wounded waited for treatment, lying under the photos of the Warriors Ath-letic Hall of Fame, of classmates cited for academic achievement. A dozen doctors and medics applied the medical philosophy the Army had developed to care for its wounded in Korea and Vietnam: stop the bleeding, open the breathing passages, treat for shock, and go like hell for the nearest hospital.

One doctor, a lieutenant colonel, allocated priorities and destinations, getting the most seriously wounded down to the football field and into a CH-60 Blackhawk helicopter flown in from the Darmstadt Army airfield. The half-dozen badly burned kids were helicoptered to Landstuhl near Ramstein Air Base, the military's European burn-treatment center. No first aid was going to help them. Head injuries were shipped to the Army's 97th General Hospital in Frankfurt. Crushed or punctured lungs, of which there were many, went to Wiesbaden.

The Rhein-Main crash rescue team, engineers and aircraft maintenance men, worked the wreckage, following the whimpers of the wounded and dying through the rubble. They had cranes, jacks, and heavy-duty inflatable balloons to shift and move the wreckage. The balloons, designed to lift a shattered airframe, were remarkably effective. They could be slipped under a tiny gap beneath a slab of fallen masonry. Inflated by an air compressor, they would lift tons of debris and open up a space through which a rescue worker could crawl to a wounded victim.

Military police from the Lee Barracks in nearby Mainz had been trucked in to set up a security cordon around the disaster site. Outside, German police sealed off the entire triangle of the Hainerberg Compound, leaving only the Washingtonstrasse gate open to traffic.

While Hainerberg was an American installation, the soil it rested on was German, and thus the ultimate police responsibility for investigating the bombing was German. As it happened, the Federal Crisis Investigation Office, responsible for investigating major terrorist incidents, was in Wiesbaden. The office was the home of "Big Brother," a giant Siemens computer whose treasure trove of terrorist data made it the envy of most of the world's police agencies. As soon as the importance of the gym bombing became apparent, the head of the office, Horst Wegener, was summoned to the scene.

Forty-five minutes later he arrived with a pair of deputies to take charge of the investigation. An Army lieutenant colonel from the Counterintelligence Corps was designated to assist him while the embassy's antiterrorist expert and the CIA's chief of station were driving down from Bad Godesberg.

Wegener ordered a circle fifty yards in diameter sealed off around the crumpled wreck of the booby-trapped car. No one except members of his explosives search team was allowed in the circle. They would work their way through it on their hands and knees, picking over every scrap of metal they could finger, looking for clues that would identify the explosive used and, perhaps, the make and registration of the car.

As they were setting up their lights to start work, an Air Force major rushed up to Wegener. "Sir," he gasped, "they're just pulling the kid who saw the car out of the debris."

"How is he?"

"Bad."

Wegener and his American deputy rushed to the ruins of the gym. The Rhein-Main rescue team had inserted and inflated a rubber balloon under the huge piece of the gym's roof that had collapsed on Walt Clemens's shattered body. The opening it offered was barely a foot high. A pair of medics, at the risk of their own lives, had crawled in and were easing Clemens out of the rubble.

"Is he alive?" Wegener whispered to the doctor supervising the medics.

"Barely."

"What are his chances?"

The doctor shook his head sadly.

As the medics got the upper part of Clemens's body free of the wreckage, Wegener knelt down to whisper in his ear. "Courage, son," he said. "They're going to get you out of here. They'll have you in a chopper in no time. Just hang in there."

Clemens's bruised and swollen lips opened. "Yeah," he whispered.

"Son," Wegener said, "the car with the bomb. Can you remember anything about it?"

The young football player's lips moved. For an agonizing second he tried, unsuccessfully, to frame the words floating through his dying mind. Finally, they came. "Berlin," he whispered. "A Ford from Berlin."

The colonel had arranged the dreary safe flat in which Dajani's four-man commando was quartered with the care of a mother preparing a birthday party for a six-year-old. The table had been covered with a brocade tablecloth, heavy silver, delicate Meissen porcelain. On it were heaped plates of caviar, smoked salmon, foie gras, sturgeon, roast beef, fresh fruit. At the center of the table was a pitcher of freshly squeezed orange juice. More discreetly set on the sideboy were bottles of vodka and whiskey and a box of Cuban cigars.

The colonel, like the proud mother throwing open the doors of her dining room to her child's guests, was waiting for the four when they returned to the flat.

"Welcome!" he cried. "And congratulations. The American radio just confirmed the success of your mission."

He stepped over and embraced each man, introducing himself as he did. "Our friend Abou Said Dajani will join us in a few minutes.

"Come, my friends," he urged, leading them to the table, "a celebration, a reward you've earned." He picked up the pitcher of orange juice and poured a glass for each man. Then he poured himself a tumbler of vodka from the bottle on the sideboy. "I appreciate the traditions of Islam do not allow you to drink alcohol," he laughed, "but it's one of our Russian failings."

Sayed coughed to indicate that not all of the members of the commando felt constrained by the dictates of Islam.

The colonel understood. "Of course." He smiled and topped off the glasses of the two drug dealers with generous dollops of vodka.

"I raise my glass," he announced, "to the brave members of the Vengeance Commando. You have struck an unforgettable blow at your enemies. Vengeance is yours! Success is yours!''

He lifted his tumbler full of vodka toward the ceiling. For a second he held it there like a priest consecrating the wine in his chalice. Then, drawing it to his lips, he poured the fiery liquid down his throat in a few hearty swallows. The four terrorists, awed by the sight, enthusiastically followed his example.

The new President had brought to his White House an air of informality that had not been present during his predecessor's reign. He had spent his Saturday jogging and playing tennis, a reflection of his obsession with physical fitness. In the evening, he'd invited two of his sons, their wives, and four of his grandchildren to the executive mansion.

He'd served them all barbecued ribs for dinner, then taken them downstairs for popcorn and a movie. By ten-fifteen they'd left and he was ready for an early bedtime when the NSC duty officer disturbed him in his second-floor study. He had the first, fragmentary reports of the Wiesbaden bombing in from Stuttgart, the headquarters of the U.S. armed forces in West Germany.

The President frowned as he read the paper the duty officer had handed him. His instincts told him this might turn into a very bad situation. ''Get General Trowbridge,'' he ordered. General Kent Trowbridge was his National Security Adviser. ''Tell him to stay on top of this for me. If it looks justified, have him set up an EXCOM meeting for tomorrow morning.'' His top advisers weren't going to like having their Sunday ruined, but lost Sundays, unfortunately, were the price of high government office.

By the time Abou Said Dajani had crossed back into East Berlin, the area around Friedrichstrasse Station was deserted. The itinerant peddlers selling their souvenirs and primitive handicrafts had disappeared. Only a pair of currency black marketeers were loitering under the spans of the S-Bahn. As Dajani passed one of them, he hissed, "Dollars? Deutsche marks? Good price." I wonder, Dajani thought, how pleased he would be to learn he'd just propositioned a major of the KGB.

Naturally, there were no taxis at the cab stand. The S-Bahn wasn't running, so he set off for Rosa-Luxemburg-Platz on foot. The walk took twenty minutes, and that, plus climbing the three flights of stairs to the safe flat, left him puffing. He paused a second before the door, fumbling for his keys. His commando, it occurred to him, wasn't going to keep the neighborhood up with the sound of their celebration. He flung open the door to find the dining-room table heaped up with food and the colonel sitting beside it in the flat's only armchair smoking a cigar.

"Where the hell are the others?" he asked.

The colonel pointed his cigar toward the half-open door to one of the flat's three bedrooms. Dajani had to walk through the sitting room to peer inside. Two of his commando were sprawled on the beds. One lay facedown on the floor. The fourth, Sayed, was jackknifed into a corner of the room, his head propped against the wall, his mouth hanging open.

"What the hell is wrong with them?" he demanded. "Are they drunk?"

"No," said the colonel. His face was as cold, as lifeless, as the snows of Siberia. "They're dead."

"Dead?" Dajani reeled at his words.

"Arabs talk too much. They won't talk now."

"You son of a bitch! You filthy murdering son of a bitch!" Dajani shouted.

"Orders." The colonel was still sitting there in his armchair, his Cuban cigar dangling from his left hand, as composed as a banker contemplating a loan applicant.

"You bastard, wait until Ivan Sergeivich—"

"Ivan Sergeivich gave the order," the colonel interrupted. As he spoke, he shifted slightly forward in his chair.

"That wasn't the only order he gave," he continued.

His right hand slid inside his suit jacket. The 9mm Makarov was out of its holster and trained on Dajani so quickly the Palestinian had no time to move, to hide, to duck into the bedroom, to leap at the colonel.

"You talk too much, too, Dajani," he said. The Palestinian saw the cylinder of the silencer around the snout of the pistol at the same instant he heard the three quick pops. He felt the blows hammer his stomach. He tumbled backward under the force of the bullets' impact. As he hit the floor, he tried to shriek out the name of his protector, Ivan Sergeivich Feodorov, but all his lungs could produce was a gurgle and a fine red spray of his blood.

Horst Wegener, the head of the Federal Crisis Investigation Office, paced the area outside the brightly illuminated circle in which his explosives search team looked for scraps of evidence. His hands were clasped behind his back, and he was wearing one of those knee-length black leather coats still much favored by German policemen despite their associations with an earlier, less respectable period in German police history. The dying boy's information was, unfortunately, of limited value. How many Fords, he wondered, would carry Berlin registrations? Twenty, thirty thousand?

A shout from one of his searchers interrupted his ruminations. The man walked over to Wegener with his hands cupped in front of him like a communicant awaiting the host. In his hands was a scrap of red metal. Wegener looked at it with the affection of a courtesan contemplating a ruby. Indeed, for the German policeman that piece of metal was, at the moment, about as priceless as a ruby would have been. It was a TUV, the metal German roadworthiness plaque attached to a car's license plate, and like all TUVs it bore the month in which it expired. Since there was almost certainly only one unidentified German car in the bomb area, the booby-trapped car, the number of Fords whose owners the Berlin police would have to trace had just been reduced by a factor of twelve.

MAZE

• • •

The haunting summons of a telephone ringing in the night echoed through Louis Doria's bedroom. The Frenchman stirred and, half awake, reached out to the blaring instrument. Doria represented the French security services in Berlin. He was a cop by trade and a Corsican by birth. That, he liked to assure his colleagues in France's Police Judiciaire, was a potent if somewhat unusual marriage.

"Monsieur," the duty officer at the Quartier Napoléon outside Wedding said, "there's been a bomb against the Americans down in Wiesbaden. It looks bad."

Doria groaned and struggled out of bed. Tegel Airport was in the French sector of Berlin, and Doria was responsible for its security procedures. He was in his office in ten minutes, ordering his German colleague to set up identity checks on all incoming flights until further notice. Then he walked down to the Pan Am office and asked for the passenger manifest for the last flight in from Frankfurt. The flight was light, only thirty-two passengers. It was, after all, Saturday night. None of the names on the list had a Middle Eastern ring, but as Doria well knew, that meant nothing. "Get the stewardesses on the phone for me, will you?" he asked the Pan Am duty officer.

The two girls were sound asleep at the Intercontinental Hotel. Rather angrily, they informed Doria that four of their passengers had, in fact, looked like they might be Middle Easterners, Turks or Arabs or whatever. They'd been the last passengers to board the plane in Frankfurt. No, the girls said, they hadn't spoken to them, nor had they heard them talking to each other in a foreign language. The four were young men in their late twenties or early thirties, clearly traveling together, rather subdued for a Saturday night.

It wasn't much to go on. Berlin was full of Turks. Doria, however, prided himself on being a good cop, and good cops worked with their noses as well as their heads. He returned to his German counterpart and suggested they assign a police officer to the taxi stand to ask each driver coming in over the next twenty-four hours if he'd picked up four Middle Easterners around eleven that night. It was a long shot, but in Berlin, as in many cities, a certain number of taxi drivers liked to work the airport run. You could never tell what the check might turn up.

Doria called back into the Quartier Napoléon to brief the duty officer on what he'd done. *"Merde!"* he said to his German colleague when he hung up. "They just found out the car with the bomb in it had Berlin plates. There goes Sunday."

The door to the President's bedroom eased open, and Pablo, the White House mess steward, tiptoed into the room in his blue blazer with the presidential seal, bearing the President's Sunday indulgence, two scrambled eggs, five slices of lean bacon, and an apple Danish. The President stirred as Pablo switched on his bedside reading light.

"What the hell time is it?" he growled.

"Six-thirty, sir."

"For Christ's sake, it's Sunday morning, isn't it?"

Another figure emerged from the shadows behind the steward. It was Lieutenant General Kent Trowbridge, the National Security Adviser, and he was in uniform. That could mean only one thing—major trouble.

"Shake me, wake me, was what you said, Mr. President," he said. "We've got a problem."

The President sat up, groped for his glasses on the bedside table, put them on, and blinked half a dozen times to root sleep's morphia from his mind.

"You remember the item that came in last night? About the car bomb outside the gym of the Armed Forces high school over in Wiesbaden?"

"I do."

"It's turned into the worst terrorist incident we've had since Pan Am 103."

Terrorism. The nightmare of each new presidency. The President slumped back onto his pillows. "Okay, how bad is it?"

"Awful. We may have a hundred or more dead and

injured on our hands before we're through. Most of them perfectly innocent teenage kids slaughtered at a Halloween dance.''

"Do we have any idea who's behind it?"

"We don't yet. The Agency, the NSA, the Germans are working all-out on it."

Trowbridge moved forward and dropped the Sunday editions of *The Washington Post* and *The New York Times* on the President's bed. "The papers are full of it. The networks are climbing all over it, too. Pan Am Flight 103 all over again."

"The bastards!" growled the President. "This time we're going to get them."

"I've convoked a meeting of the EXCOM for noon in the situation room."

"Good," the President said. "I'll preside. You tell everyone I want the absolute latest intelligence on who might be behind this thing when we convene. And I want the Joint Chiefs looking at options for us. Real options. I don't want to hear the word 'sanctions' mentioned. And tell the press secretary to brief the media on the meeting. I want to make sure the media and the public realize we're on top of this."

"Yes, sir," General Trowbridge said, leaving the President to his thoughts and a breakfast for which he'd lost his appetite.

Art Bennington was up early that Sunday morning. He had not slept well. His night had been troubled, as he knew it would be, by his nagging doubts about Nina Wolfe and her gray Toyota. He did his calisthenics with less than his usual angry energy, then showered and padded barefoot into his kitchen. His hand went like a robot's arm to the bran flakes on the shelf. "Screw it," he growled, before his fingers could wrap their way around that loathsome box of goodness, "it's Sunday morning." He turned to the freezer and pulled out an English muffin. That, with some butter and a few slices of bacon, was the way to start the day, he told himself, popping it into the microwave. As he did the phone rang.

"You seen the morning paper yet?" asked John Sprague, his boss, head of the Deputy Directorate for Science and Technology.

"No."

"Then turn on CNN. There's been a ghastly terrorist bombing over in Germany at one of our high schools. The director wants an interdirectorate coordinating committee set up to staff the thing for him. You know Germany. You're more or less up to speed on explosives, aren't you?"

"More or less."

"Then you're going to represent S&T on it. Get your ass into Langley as fast as you can."

As soon as he hung up, Bennington turned on his television set. The network was running a tape of its Bonn correspondent standing in a searchlight's glare in front of a smoking mass of rubble, part of the remains of the General Arnold High School gymnasium. He listened horrified for a moment to the account of the bombing, then headed to his clothes closet. Nina Wolfe was, for the moment at least, forgotten.

Across the Potomac River in a basement flat, another set of eyes was riveted to television. Major Valentin Tobulko had been up since five watching CNN. From Bonn, the news desk cut to the White House press room. The President, the press secretary was saying, had summoned the Executive Committee of the National Security Council to an emergency meeting in the White House at noon.

Tobulko snapped off the TV set and beckoned to Nina Wolfe, who'd been sitting quietly in an easy chair behind him following the broadcast.

"We'll make our first transmission then," he announced. "At twelve-thirty. By that time, they'll be right into the heart of their discussion."

· · ·

The Berlin Polizei Präsidium is a massive four-story khaki-colored building, one of a series of similar buildings enfolding the concrete pillars of Berlin's monument to the 1948 Airlift. It resembles any police headquarters in the world. The floors are linoleum, a dull, insipid gray. The walls are painted in that sickly green favored by police stations since desk sergeants were invented. It was the wall decorations, the photos of surly, disheveled German youth, survivors of the Baader Meinhof gang and the Red Army Faction, lined up under the label *"Terroristen,"* that gave the place its distinctive local flavor.

On the fourth floor of that building, in room 4415, was the office of Manfred Schmidt, the chief of Berlin's Staatsschutz, or State Security Service, the man with the unenviable job of controlling terrorism in a city almost uniquely designed to facilitate the terrorists' task. On Sunday, October 31, Schmidt had been in his office since five-thirty dealing with the possible Berlin connections of the Wiesbaden bomb. When his three Allied colleagues walked into his office, he was on his sixth cup of coffee and a package of Marlboro cigarettes already empty lay on his desk. Like everything else in Berlin, police investigations were enmeshed in the cobweb of the city's complex political structure. The city was run internally by the Berlin senate, and policemen like Schmidt were responsible to the senator for the interior, who in turn was responsible to the three Allies.

In fact, the Berlin police ran their police business on their own with a minimum of contact with the Allies. In cases such as this one in which Allied interests were involved, the Allies and Schmidt cooperated as far as possible, but there was no question who was boss. The French, American, and British officials coming into Schmidt's office could give orders for one thing: takeout Sauerbraten dinners furnished by the nearby Shultheiss Brewery. Other than that, they offered suggestions; Schmidt gave the orders.

The three men pulled up chairs in front of Schmidt's desk. The Frenchman, Louis Doria, shared the affinity of the cop's trade with Schmidt. Terry Breslaw, the American, and Alex Campbell, the Englishman, were intelligence officers on detached service. As long as the crisis lasted, the four men would meet periodically to review the investigation's progress.

"Okay," said Breslaw, "what have you got, Manny?"

Schmidt sighed. Some policemen seem to fill a room with the majestic authority of the law. Schmidt's was an almost invisible presence, a sort of gray shade flitting through the shadows. He was an intense little man who bore his worries in a frown as evident as a bishop's pectoral cross.

"Fuck-all," he said in perfect precinct-house English. "We've got the make of the car that had the bomb, the date of its TUV, and two numbers of a Berlin license plate. The KVA computers are breaking out all the cars that fall in that category now." The KVA was the West Berlin automobile registry. "We'll start a canvass of the owners as soon as we've got the computer breakdown, but if the car was done here you can bet the thing was staged here, too."

Doria then informed them what he'd learned the night before from the Pan Am stewardesses.

"Yeah," Breslaw growled. "What odds would you lay they headed straight for Zoo Station? If those four were our guys, I mean." He snapped open his attaché case. "I've got a little contribution here, too." He passed Schmidt the photos, identities, and Moroccan passport numbers the Artist had furnished the CIA before his murder. "There's reason to believe some or all of these guys may be involved."

Schmidt studied the documents. "I don't suppose you're going to tell us where these came from?"

"No." Breslaw smiled. "I don't suppose I am."

"I'll get them out to the men working on the car canvass right away, and we'll let those Pan Am girls look at them."

"Manny," Doria said, "why don't you push them at your drug people? Run them by the neighborhood pushers? Flash them at the whores and bargirls? These Arabs like the big blowout before the big blowup. Throw their money around. Maybe somebody will make them for us."

"Yeah, we're already quizzing our drug informers," the German agreed. "We're leaning on our Arab friends down in Kreuzberg, too. You never know what you'll come up with with them." Not so long ago, Schmidt's office had grabbed one of the *Achille Lauro* hijackers when he was fingered by one of his relatives. "The girls are tougher."

Doria shook his head in mock despondency. As a good French police officer he was constantly struck by the failure of the German police to penetrate the bargirl/prostitute world with informers. Deprive the Police Judiciaire in France of their snitches among the pimps and prostitutes and their arrest rate would be cut in half.

"You remember the last problem we had down there in Wiesbaden?" he asked Schmidt. "That GI who picked up a girl in one of those clipjoints? They went out for a ride in his car so she could give him a blow job. Some blow job! She gave it to him with a .357 Magnum. And the next day his car shows up on an American base wired for a sound-and-light show. I tell you, that *milieu* is always involved in these things."

"I know, I know," Schmidt groaned, "but you know how we operate. I'll send those names over to the LEA." The LEA was the Landes Einwohner Amt, the central registry in which the occupants of all Berlin's dwellings were supposed to be inscribed. "Maybe they'll come up with something."

Alex Campbell, the Englishman, laughed. "I shouldn't count on it if I were you, Manny."

"Oh, believe me, I don't." The postwar Germany Schmidt helped to police was built on a marvelously thorough, well-thought-out, and all-embracing system of checks and controls. It reposed, however, on one indispensable premise—that Germans are methodical, disciplined, law-abiding—and law-fearing—folk and will do what they're supposed to do, register where they're supposed to register. Drop a few grains of foreign sand into the system, people who, God forbid, didn't react as good

Germans did, and they became invisible, unlocatable, lost to view in an otherwise perfect machine.

"Manny," Doria said, "if the four guys on that Pan Am plane were really our guys, they had to get from Wiesbaden to the Frankfurt airport, right? Presumably in a getaway car. Which they must have ditched in the Frankfurt airport parking lot. Chances are that if they got the booby-trapped car here, they got their getaway car here, too. So why don't we have the Frankfurt police do a run-through at the airport lots looking for Berlin cars?"

Schmidt smiled at his colleague. "Now that," he said, "is a worthwhile suggestion indeed."

It was just two minutes past twelve when the telephone rang in the President's private study on the White House second floor. "Mr. President," Kent Trowbridge, the National Security Adviser, announced, "the members of your Executive Committee are assembled in the situation room."

The President walked quickly to the elevator, which took him to the basement. A Secret Service agent was waiting, holding open the dark oak door of the situation room, when he arrived. As his lean, slightly stooped frame appeared in the doorway, the half-dozen men in the room rose. All six were the President's longtime political associates. Two were close personal friends as well. Yet such was the aura of the presidency that even there, in that select group, they had come to their feet spontaneously. Theirs was a tribute to the immediacy of the burdens he carried, the responsibilities he bore, the power that was his to exercise for good or evil. And, more subtly, it reflected something else. There was a majesty to the presidency of the United States that was attached to no other office in the world. The Founding Fathers had not intended that. It was history and the onslaught of technology that had determined it. But the result was an awesome authority invested in one man, an authority that inspired both respect and reticence. One did not say no easily to a President.

The President moved silently to his seat at the head of the oval teak table that almost filled the room. To his right was General Trowbridge, the National Security Adviser, and to his left his Chief of Staff, and longtime political ally, Bill Brennan, former governor of Oklahoma. Also present were the Secretaries of State and Defense; General Harold Schumacher, the chairman of the Joint Chiefs; and the director of the CIA. Missing was the Vice President. He was on a golfing weekend in Del Ray, Florida.

The President settled into his russet-colored seat and turned to Trowbridge. He was familiar with the routine of crisis meetings. He'd sat in on them for years in his own days as a White House Chief of Staff. "Okay, Kent," he said, "I want as full a briefing as you can give me at this point in time on this outrage. And I want appropriate recommendations for whatever actions seem called for by the situation."

Trowbridge turned to the Secretary of Defense. The Secretary picked up a piece of paper from the table, flicked it with his fingertip, and said, "Casualties. Our latest report gives eighty-seven dead, seventy-two wounded, forty-six severely, with many of them not expected to survive. Three of the dead are German nationals. The rest are American."

The Secretary laid the paper back on the table with a little sigh, his personal lament for the young lives lost in the explosion. "The German federal police are the lead agency in the investigation, since it took place on German soil. CIA, the BND, and Army and Air Force Intelligence are all providing support. It's been established thus far that the car they used carried a Berlin registration. The explosive employed has been identified as Semtex."

"Any indication of where it came from?" the President asked.

"No, there's no way to pin that down."

"Mr. President." It was the director of the CIA. "What we do know is that indigenous European terrorist groups like the Red Army Faction don't seem to have access to it these days. They've been reduced to *The*

Anarchist's Cookbook—weedkillers and sugar and that sort of thing. The only exception to that is the IRA. Qaddafi supplies it to them, but they're not sharing it out with anybody. It's pretty much the trademark explosive of Middle Eastern terrorists. As you know, it was used on Pan Am 103. All those Paris bombs in the fall of '86 were Semtex.''

"Okay, Judge," Trowbridge said, "what else have your people got?''

"First, the usual anonymous caller to the Associated Press in Beirut. Claimed it was done by an outfit called the Vengeance Commando.''

"Do you have anything on them?" the President asked.

"No, but that doesn't mean anything. These people, whether they're Palestinian or Hez'bollah, will toss up an ad hoc group and assign them a name for a specific operation.''

"Have you got any penetration, any inside pipeline, into those Middle Eastern terrorist groups that can tell us who the hell was behind this?" the President demanded.

"We've pulsed our assets, Mr. President," the Judge replied. "We're on to the Israelis and the Saudis, who have good penetration, for anything their sources throw up. And we have one piece of intelligence in our possession right now which may very well bear on this." He recounted the story of the Artist, his murder, and his delivery of the information on the last Moroccan 798s he'd issued. "If these people were involved with this, we'll know one thing. It was Hez'bollah out of either West Beirut or the Bekaa Valley. We've seen these passports used before in bombings just like this. A couple of years ago, two Arabs bought a car at an open-air car market in Gravenbrück outside Frankfurt, then wired it up and planted it at the Frankfurt PX. They used these passports as ID to buy the car. The guys who hijacked the *Achille Lauro* had them.''

"Do we know anything about the four people on those passports?''

"We ran them through our computer. Two of the

names registered. A pair of Beirut Shiites who spent a year being trained at Ali Montazeri's terrorist school in Qom. The one that masquerades as a religious institution. One of them was a key player in the bombing of the Marine barracks.''

Trowbridge hesitated for a second to be sure the President had completed his line of questioning before turning to the chairman of the Joint Chiefs, General Schumacher. "Hal?"

"Until we've focused in on just who's behind this, we can't really begin to put up action options for a reprisal attack. We've got a whole range of shelf options we can dust off, but we aren't going to get very far studying them until we know who we'll be directing them against.''

"What's your defense posture?" Trowbridge asked.

"We've gone to DEFCON 4." DEFCON 4 was the Armed Forces' second-lowest readiness state. "We'll hold there. No sense getting the Soviets' teeth on edge, since they don't seem to be involved in this.''

"The Delta Force?" the President asked. "Have you put them on alert?"

"No, sir," the general answered. He was a taciturn man with a face so scrubbed and so closely shaven it seemed to glow. His black hair, or what was left of it, was pasted down on his head like strips of black adhesive tape. He was thumbing a blue cellophane folder stamped "Top Secret" as though it were some kind of Holy Grail. "Without information, it's difficult to ascertain what part they might play in a reprisal. Also, Mr. President, the Delta Force can't burp down there without the press picking it up. Alert them and they'll be on the evening news.''

The President cocked his head sideways as though he could see Schumacher better from that perspective. "Maybe it's not such a bad idea the press gets that. Let the public know we're really on top of this thing."

Schumacher was a soldier's soldier. Public-relations exercises never engaged much of his interest. He was also a man who could say no, even to Presidents. "Sir," he replied, "if those men of mine down there are going to have to get involved directly in this, I'd just as soon keep them standing down until we need them, if it's all the same to you."

It wasn't, but the President let it pass. Trowbridge turned to Jack Taylor, the Secretary of State. He had been the President's closest political ally for years. "Mr. Secretary?"

"We've had the usual expressions of concern and sympathy from the Allies. Implicit in them all, I might add, is the plea 'Please don't do anything rash, fellas. We really can't handle another bombing raid on Libya.' "

A murmur of amusement spread through the group at his words. They had surprised no one. Indeed, they echoed a refrain all were accustomed to hearing at such moments.

"Whose hand do you see behind this?" Trowbridge asked.

"Libya. Syria. Iran. A Bekaa Shiite wild card. Take your choice. The moving hand hasn't writ very large on the wall yet. Personally, I'd be inclined to rule Qaddafi out. He's been pretty much out of the terrorist business since Reagan stepped on him. He's playing with germ warfare and long-range rockets, but those figure to be military arms for use against Israel, not terrorist weapons."

"Syria?"

As the Secretary of State began his analysis of Syria's relations with international terrorism, the beige Econoline van was edging along Constitution Avenue past 15th Street between the Ellipse and the Washington Monument. The Sunday traffic was sparse. Tobulko pulled to the curb. With his compass, he made a quick adjustment to the angle at which his signal generator would pour forth its signal stream. Then he called the flat.

"Go in five seconds," he ordered Dulia Vaninya, then set the phone into the cradle of his modem. Exactly five seconds later, the ruby light on his signal generator came on. Forty-five seconds later it blinked off and Tobulko slid his van back into the Constitution Avenue traffic.

"Nawaf Hawatameh, Abou Nidal, and Abou Ibrahim's Fifteenth of May group are all capable of an action of this sort," the Secretary of State was saying when a curious sight caught the attention of the director of the CIA. It was the President's hands. He was clenching and un-clenching his fists, straining more forcefully with each tightening gesture, his knuckles glowing white. The Judge glanced up at him. His jaw muscles were working as though he were clenching down hard with his teeth as someone will trying to suppress a cry of pain. There was the faint glisten of sweat at his temples, and his eyes, behind his plastic-framed glasses, seemed to have bulged slightly outward. He's really pissed off and he's trying to hold it in, the Judge thought.

"My candidate would be Abou Ibrahim's people," the Secretary of State continued. "They're extremely so-phisticated terrorists. Twenty-two bombing attacks in Europe to their credit, plus two unsuccessful attempts on El Al. Hawatameh is—"

"Goddammit!"

It was the President, and he roared out the curse like a Marine drill instructor shouting at a bunch of left-footed recruits. "This is just a lot of diplomatic bullshit, Jack! American kids have been killed! I want to know what the hell we're going to do about it! I want to know what we're going to do to hammer those bastards! These are the kind of people that did Pan Am 103! These are the guys that did the Marine barracks. These are the sons of bitches that kept our hostages. This time, goddammit, we're going to make them pay for it. General!"

"Yes, sir."

"I want to know what we can do to hurt those people. Hurt them real bad. Hurt them so much they'll never want to lay their filthy hands on an innocent American again."

General Schumacher coughed and let his fingertips run

over the blue folder before him as though it might be a Ouija board that would guide him to an answer. The chairman of the Joint Chiefs of Staff was, after all, used to dealing with questions that were more specific in nature than the President's.

"Well, sir, the Sixth Fleet's on station out there in the Eastern Med. Its carrier attack groups have very considerable air-strike capabilities. They can be tailored—"

"Air strikes!" the President roared. "The Israelis have been running air strikes on those PLO camps out there for ten years, and what good do they do? Make more terrorists. I said I want to hurt those people." Again the President's fist crashed into the table. "We used the *Missouri*'s big guns on them in 1983. That didn't stop the bastards, either."

"You're not suggesting, are you, sir, another Marine intervention in Lebanon?"

"No. All that would mean is more American casualties. I want to hit them. Once. Hard." The President's jaw muscles constricted again. His eyes narrowed to a squint for a second, then blinked wide open. "Those new Tomahawk cruise missiles! Don't we have some of them out there?"

"Yes, sir. They're deployed on the *Ticonderoga* in the Med and the *Valley Forge* outside the Persian Gulf."

"They have those dial-a-yield warheads, right?"

The "dial-a-yield" warhead, officially the W60, was a recent sophistication of the U.S. Armed Forces. By manipulating the detonation system of certain nuclear warheads or limiting the inflow of booster material into its explosion, the magnitude of the warhead's yield could be programmed with precision from one kiloton all the way up to a megaton.

"Yes, sir." General Schumacher's voice had taken on a slightly reproving tone. "We have that type of warhead available out there, that is correct."

"Well then why the hell don't we just crank one of them down to three or four kilotons and let those bastards have it? Dump it right into the middle of that terrorist cesspool in the Bekaa Valley. That'll do it!"

A stunned silence greeted his words.

"Mr. President, we don't even know the terrorists came from the Bekaa Valley. We don't know where they came from or whose orders they were following."

The President's anger was momentarily checked by General Schumacher's words. The Judge could sense his quick, shallow breathing. "Well, find out, goddammit! Find out!"

"For a French cop, Louis, you turn out to be a pretty smart guy." Manfred Schmidt hadn't even bothered to say hello over the telephone. It was the kind of shorthand the head of the Berlin Staatsschutz had developed working with Louis Doria over the past three years. "The Frankfurt police found seven Berlin cars in the airport parking lot down there. We were able to run a check on the owners of all of them by phone. Six checked out. Guess what happened with the seventh?"

"I'm not sure I want to know," said Doria.

"The owner sold it to a used-car dealer up there on Residenzstrasse three weeks ago."

"And he in turn sold it to a Middle Eastern gentleman?"

"Correct. Two Middle Eastern gentlemen, in fact. I've got one of my men heading up there right now with those photos Breslaw gave us."

"I'll meet him there." That was not Doria's function, but Residenzstrasse was in the French zone, and his personal relations with Schmidt were so good the German welcomed his collaboration on a case, something he was not inclined to do with their Anglo-Saxon colleagues.

"There's something else you ought to know," Schmidt said. "They found a bunch of U.S. Army uniforms in the trunk."

That's it, Doria thought. The Abdul Factor at work. That had to be the getaway car. How typically careless of those guys to leave the uniforms in the trunk. Ten minutes later he was with the German inspector in the corrugated-steel hut that served as the dealer's office.

The dealer showed them his carbon of the purchase order Sayed had filled out when he bought the car. On it was the number of his Moroccan passport, 7983429.

"Bingo!" Doria whispered softly, seeing the number. The German inspector produced the four CIA photos.

"Him," the dealer said without hesitation, fingering Sayed's photo. He continued studying the other three photos. "That guy," he added. "He was the other one." It was Nasreddin, the bomb expert.

The name the dealer had taken off Sayed's passport was not, of course, his real name but one of the identities the *rezident* had furnished Dajani in Damascus. As his address, Sayed had listed the Free University of Berlin. Doria laughed seeing that.

When they'd finished, Doria stood outside watching the traffic flowing up and down Residenzstrasse, studying the neighborhood. It was growing dark. Across the street, a sign caught his eye, the Pizzeria Capri. It meant nothing to the inspector behind him, but it registered with Doria. The restaurant figured on an Interpol watch list of Berlin establishments involved in the Middle Eastern drug traffic. Drugs and terrorists went together like beer and pretzels. "Let's see if anybody in there recognizes these photos," he suggested.

Giuseppe, the barman who'd welcomed Sayed and Nasreddin, was on duty when they came in. Doria stood off a bit scrutinizing Giuseppe as the German inspector showed him the photos of Sayed and Nasreddin. The barman picked up each photo in turn, studied it with great care, then laid it down on the bar.

"Arabs," he said. "They all look alike. I never saw these guys in here. Maybe they came in late at night when I'm not on. Who's to know?"

"He was lying." Doria made the declaration with the assurance of a jury foreman delivering an evident verdict the moment they were back out on the street.

"How can you know?" the German inspector asked.

Doria stroked his nose. "This. In France, pal, we call it 'system D.' Smell your way to the shit." He pointed across the street. The neon lights of the Moonlight Sauna had just blinked on. The little French inspector firmly believed that it was as difficult for most criminals to walk past a whorehouse as it was for most Irishmen to pass up a free drink. "Let's check it out," he suggested.

Reluctantly, the German inspector followed him across the street. The four young ladies of the resident faculty greeted their arrival with courteous, commercial interest. The presentation of the German inspector's police identity worked an instant transformation in their hospitable attitude. The madam came bursting out of the back room like a bull charging into a bullring.

"This is a clean place, mister. No dope here. My girls go to the doctor every week. Twice a week. No AIDS," she shrieked. "No sex here. Never. Just a nice healthy massage. I swear on my son's head. No sex."

"Of course, Fräulein." Doria invoked the resources of his Gallic charm. "What happens behind these doors doesn't concern us. We're here to ask for your help."

With the relieved madam's blessing, they produced their photos for the girls. If those men had done anything wrong, she assured Doria, they would all be only too happy to assist the police in their duty.

One of the girls, a blonde with long stringy hair wearing a frayed pink negligee over her black silk underwear, recognized Sayed's photo with a giggle. "He was here three times, that guy. Big tipper. Big joint, too."

"When?"

"Three, four days ago."

"What did he do?" the German asked.

"Do?" The girl was aghast at the question. "Come on, mister. What do you think we do in here? Listen to the opera? I massaged his joint."

"Did he seem nervous to you, tense, under a strain?" Doria asked.

"Not after I got through with him," the girl laughed.

"Have you got any idea where he lived?"

"I think maybe around here somewhere," the blonde replied. "He left a sweater here the second time he came in. It didn't take very long for him to come back and get it."

"Maybe he saw it was missing when he got outside?"

"Maybe," the girl concurred. "But he had a black leather jacket on, too. He probably wouldn't have noticed he didn't have his sweater until he took the jacket off."

The two men looked at each other. That was enough. They dashed back to the inspector's car and called in to Schmidt. Within fifteen minutes, Schmidt and two dozen plainclothesmen had joined them to start a canvass of the neighborhood looking for any lead to the terrorists' residence.

Most of the men in the office of the director of the CIA were living on three or four hours' sleep and powering their biological motors with Washington's crisis fuel, coffee. The Judge glanced at his watch. He was due at the White House for the day's first Executive Committee meeting in forty-five minutes. He had digested all the most recent information his subordinates had to report on the Wiesbaden bombing. It was disappointingly little.

"We've got to pull out all the stops," he reminded the members of his interdirectorate committee. "I've known this President for ten years, and I've got to tell you I have never, never seen him as mad as he is over this. He was really pissed off in there yesterday, and God help the Agency that doesn't deliver on this one."

He stood up and started to arrange the papers he'd take with him to the White House. "I want one of you to come downtown with me." In crisis committee meetings it was the general practice for each of the principals at the NSC conference table to have a senior deputy backing him up. He relayed his superior's calls and processed the inflow of information to him. "Art," he said, "I think I'll take you with me. You guys"—he gestured to the representatives of Operations and Counterintelligence—"are probably going to be more productive out here."

. . .

The young ladies of the Moonlight Sauna on West Berlin's Residenzstrasse were fascinated by the police activities suddenly overwhelming their premises. Manfred Schmidt had decided to make it his headquarters for his door-to-door canvass of the area looking for any indication of the two terrorists' hideout. A huge map of the neighborhood was on the parlor floor. As each building was cleared, it was marked off the map.

The phone was constantly ringing. The Polizei Präsidium was checking the electric company's computers looking for subscribers in the area who paid their bills in cash. Terrorists always paid cash. Ordinary citizens seldom did. Whenever the computer turned up a cash payment, headquarters called the information out to the sauna.

Three hours after the canvass had started, one of the inspectors rushed into the sauna. "We've got them, " he announced.

The caretaker who'd rented Sayed and Nasreddin their flat was waiting under the arch of 97/98 Residenzstrasse, basking in the importance the moment had conferred on him.

"Are they up there?" Schmidt asked.

"I don't know. I haven't seen them for a day or so. But those are the two men, all right. I never forget a face. Never. My mother used to say—"

"Get your master keys," Schmidt ordered, quite indifferent to the opinions of the man's mother. Doria, Schmidt, and two inspectors went up the stairs to the flat, weapons drawn. No one answered their knocks.

"Open the door," Schmidt commanded. It took the concierge three tries to insert his key with his trembling fingers.

The policemen pounced into the flat. It was empty. The registration forms the caretaker had given Sayed and Nasreddin rested on the table.

"What do you think the chances are they'll come back?" Doria asked.

"Zero. But we'll stake it out anyway." Schmidt turned to one of his deputies. "Get the laboratory people up here to pick the place apart. And the dogs. Maybe they'll find some trace of the explosives.''

He put his Mauser back into his shoulder holster, then bestowed a faint smile to his French colleague. ''Got any other good ideas?''

The CNN's White House correspondent had been doing so many stand-uppers on the lawn in front of the building's familiar portico that he had begun to look like a part of the landscape. Now, at midmorning Monday, he provided an update on the aftermath of the Wiesbaden bomb crisis, reviewing the latest information released by the White House Press Office.

The Executive Committee of the NSC, he reported, would be back in session later in the morning. The President was being kept regularly informed of the progress of their work and occasionally joining in their deliberations. He was lunching privately in the White House so he could be close to the ongoing investigation into the bomb incident and at one-thirty would be meeting with the congressional leadership to discuss the budget deficit.

Half a mile from the White House, Valentin Tobulko followed the broadcast with puzzled intensity. Ivan Sergeivich had ordered him to use their devices sparingly, at what he sensed might be the critical moments of the crisis. How could he possibly determine when they would be from this sparse, uninformative news bulletin? All it told him was when not to use his equipment, when the President was having lunch and talking about the budget deficit.

After several minutes of interior debate, he told Nina Wolfe he was going to take the van and cruise the half-mile arc around the White House in which the signal generator would be operative. She was to stay in the apartment watching CNN. Each time the network broadcast some new development concerning the bomb she would call him on the cellular phone, describe what was being said and shown. They would decide when to use their equipment as a reaction to whatever was going on.

For the personal command post of the most powerful man in the world, the NSC situation room in the basement of the White House's West Wing was a singularly unprepossessing place. The looks, however, were deceiving. Three of the room's four walls were paneled in dark wooden squares which could be drawn aside by pressing a button. Concealed behind them were all the appurtenances of crisis management, the indispensable technological crutches to decision-making. There were monitors to display the data from the nation's most secure and secret computer nets, a bank of telecommunications equipment, laser disks geared to handle high-resolution large-screen displays for the big screen covered by a curtain on the fourth wall. In the adjacent room was the White House Communications Center, which ran CROWN, the President's personal, secure voice communication system. Each seat at the teak conference table had its own secure red telephone on which any of the Executive Committee members could communicate with any point on the globe.

Art Bennington sat directly behind the director of the CIA. The situation room was so small the back of his chair touched the wall. Still, it was the first time in all his years of government service that Art had sat in on a crisis at the highest level, and he was mesmerized watching this tableful of heavy hitters. The group had expanded since Sunday. Now NSA, the head of the FBI, and the Attorney General had joined in. The chairman of the Joint Chiefs had three deputies: a rear admiral and a pair of major generals from the Army and Air Force.

They had been in quasi-permanent session for some time, and what had struck Art above all else was the predominance of the confusion factor. Two or three of the red telephones beside the principals seemed to be ringing at any given minute. The Secretary of State was incapable of lowering his voice as he talked to Jerusalem or Paris or Bonn. At the far end of the room, the Secretary of Defense, the chairman of the Joint Chiefs, and their aides constituted a cell within a cell, all whispering frantically to each other, calling up displays on their computer terminals, scribbling furiously on their leather notepads. The head of the FBI and the Attorney General seemed to be in a constant conference about the legalities of getting the terrorists out of West German hands in the unlikely event that they were ever caught.

What I'm looking at, Bennington thought, is the way the U.S. government handles crises, anything from a hijacking to the arrival of nuclear Armageddon. Even a beginning behavioral scientist could see the system was full of holes. Kent Trowbridge, the National Security Adviser, was unable to impose a sense of discipline, to establish a set of priorities in addressing the crisis and making everybody stick to them. That was at least partly because he was junior to everyone else in the room, yet it was he who was supposed to keep the whole thing focused.

The cabinet members had tremendous egos. What else would you expect? They were forever going haring off after side issues that interested them. One of them, Bennington thought, was always turning to the National Security Adviser saying, "Mr. Chairman, I've just learned that . . ." Secretaries from the support groups in the offices outside the room kept darting in and out with urgent pieces of paper that were never as urgent as they seemed.

But what really struck Art was the stunning suddenness with which all that changed the instant the President stepped into the room, as he had twice already. Just the sight of his figure in the doorway focused things. People stopped whispering and talking. Even the Secretary of State shut up for once. Egos which had been scrapping for turf thirty seconds before suddenly were deferring to the President.

The U.S. cabinet, Art knew, didn't vote on issues the way the British cabinet did, or for that matter the way the Politburo in Moscow did. The President listened, if he wanted to, to what his advisers had to say. But he made up his own mind, came to his decision by himself. No one in this room, Bennington thought, had the authority to countermand a presidential order: with the exception of the military, for whom he was the commander in chief, those guys at the table were all presidential appointees, serving at the pleasure of the man they advised. He could sack any of them in a second. Only the Vice President could countermand a presidential order, because he, too, was elected to office.

Of course, they'd have to get him off the golf course first. But one thing was sure: if he or any other Vice President ever tried to do that, he'd better be ready to set off a *Caine* mutiny by saying with his next breath, ". . . because we're going to remove the President from office on the grounds that he's nuts." That was about the only justification any Vice President would ever have for doing it.

At that instant, Trowbridge interrupted his thoughts. "Gentlemen. The President's on his way."

Two minutes later, the President entered the room. His angular jaw was set, and Art could sense a composed coldness to the man. "All right," he said, sitting down, "a couple of points before we begin. I've spoken with the congressional leadership of both parties to assure them this crisis is receiving our full attention. There is a broad consensus in both houses that we cannot let this go unchallenged. Furthermore, I've been informed the switchboard has been swamped all morning by angry citizens demanding we do something about this outrage. So clearly, the heat's on. Okay, Kent, take over."

The NSC adviser reviewed the latest casualty figures, then declared, "The CIA has arranged for a direct, secure patch to the officer in the Berlin station who's monitoring the investigation, Mr. President. He'll give you an up-to-the-minute update."

"Put him on."

Terry Breslaw's voice filled the room, its tone so clear he might have been standing at the table addressing the meeting. First, he reviewed what the German police had learned and the fact that two of the terrorists had been positively identified as the holders of two of the four Moroccan passports the Artist had forged in Beirut. "The police," he went on, "have also just located the owner of the vehicle used in the attack. He sold it in an open-air market last week to two men. He identified them as the holders of the other two Moroccan passports. About two hours ago, a drug dealer in Kreuzberg also identified one of the two men as someone who made a buy from him last week. The police are doing a door-to-door canvass right now in the area the dealer works trying to locate their residence. But at least we now have positive ID on the four terrorists involved."

"What are the chances they're still somewhere in West Berlin?" The President's tone was grim but controlled.

"I'd have to say, sir, that based on our past experiences they're pretty damn slim."

"Which means they're hiding out in East Berlin."

"Could be, sir, but they could be long gone, too. Interflug has planes out of East Berlin for Beirut, Damascus, and Baghdad every day. They were probably out of there Sunday morning."

The President gestured to General Trowbridge. He'd learned enough from Berlin. "Review for me exactly what we know about these four people," he asked his National Security Adviser.

"What we've been given by the CIA. That they belonged to Hez'bollah. That two of them were trained in Ali Montazeri's Qom terrorist school. And I think we can assume they came from either West Beirut or the Bekaa Valley," Trowbridge replied.

"And we know Iran runs the Hez'bollah, don't we?"

"That's a yes, but, Mr. President—" began the Secretary of State.

"Oh Christ!" sighed the President. "When was the last time a Secretary of State gave a straight answer in a crisis?"

"When Yassir Arafat asked George Shultz for a visa," Taylor laughed. "There's no doubt the Hez'bollah people feel their allegiance is to Tehran. But in the hostage business we've had plenty of indication they don't always respond the way Tehran wants."

"How about Assad and Syria?" Bill Brennan, the President's Chief of Staff, asked the Secretary of State.

"Assad summoned the ambassador at midnight last night and spent half an hour expressing his condolences and sending us his assurances he had nothing to do with it."

"Cover-up," scoffed Brennan. "He's behind it and now he's scared shitless we're going to take a whack at him."

"I don't agree," the Secretary of State rejoined. "I've read the ambassador's report and I'm convinced Assad is sincere."

"You're ruling out Libya, Qaddafi?" the President asked.

"The four people using those passports were probably Lebanese Shiites. Qaddafi and the Lebanese Shiites hate each other, because the Lebanese are convinced Qaddafi murdered one of their religious leaders. So it's very unlikely they'd be in this together."

"Well, that leaves Iran, doesn't it? Two of these people were trained in Qom, weren't they?"

"The moving hand still hasn't written, Mr. President," the Secretary of State cautioned. "We don't have any hard evidence of that. But the finger is pointing toward Tehran, I'll agree. Or maybe to West Beirut."

"All right," the President said. He stood up. "I'm going up to have lunch and listen to the news. Then I'll be meeting with the party leadership on the budget." He looked down the table to General Schumacher. "General, when I get back, I want to look at some options for action against either Iran or West Beirut. Real options, not off-the-shelf stuff." To the general's relief, the President said nothing about cruise missiles. That was an option which, for the moment at least, he seemed to have forgotten.

Valentin Tobulko's Econoline van was in the parking lot of a Riggs National Bank not quite half a mile from the White House on 8th Street near H. It had seemed as innocuous a spot as any in the area to the KGB major. His radio was tuned to the capital's all-news station. The major himself pretended to be interested in a newspaper. At one o'clock he called the Church Street apartment.

"Tell me what CNN has from Wiesbaden," he ordered Captain Vaninya.

As she did, something leaped into his mind. It was one of the pages in the report Ivan Sergeivich had given him to read about the President—the one that discussed his sister and how close he had been to her as a teenager, how upset he would get when their father beat her in a drunken rampage.

"Nina," he ordered, "we generate right now."

The President was having lunch on a tray in his second-floor sitting room, all four of his TV monitors on but with the sound limited to CNN. He had barely finished his shrimp and avocado salad when he stopped, too sickened by the images on the screen to continue eating. CNN's Bonn correspondent was inside Wiesbaden General Hospital, moving from bed to bed talking to the victims of Saturday night's bomb. He had paused at the bedside of a pretty blond teenage girl, her hair arranged in a golden halo on her pillow. She had been blinded by glass shards. As the cameras focused in on her bandaged eyes, she was sobbing softly for the world she'd lost forever.

The CNN reporter moved to the bedside of another victim, another girl, this one slightly older, her once handsome face swollen with bruises as though she had been savagely beaten. The President felt his temples tightening and a tide of rage sweeping over him. Growling, he leaped to his feet, almost knocking over his lunch tray as he did.

The President was halfway into the NSC situation room before anybody even saw him. One thing immediately struck Art Bennington. He still had his white linen napkin clutched in his left hand. He was squeezing it with such force you might have thought he had some small animal whose neck he was trying to break concealed in there.

"Did you see those pictures on CNN?" he barked. None of the men in the room had any idea what he was talking about. "Well, I did! I saw them! Those poor kids torn apart, a pretty teenage girl blinded! It was those goddam Iranians. I'm going to get them. The ones who took our embassy! The ones who killed all our marines! Blew up Pan Am 103! The ones who took our hostages! Well, this time the bastards are going to pay!"

The President raised both his fists and sent them crashing down onto the table, his napkin trailing behind his left hand like a plume. Bennington's eyes swept the men in the room. They were stunned by the President's outburst. But they were all also completely focused on the man, following what he was saying with intense, unquestioning interest.

"General!"

The chairman of the Joint Chiefs of Staff turned respectfully to his commander in chief. "Sir."

"What contingency plans do we have for a reprisal attack on Iran?"

"Sir, we have plans for a carrier-based air strike on Kharg Island's oil terminal facilities and refinery. We drew it up during the Gulf crisis. That would cripple their oil industry and really pinch them economically."

"Oil?" the President shouted. "These people killed innocent American teenagers and you're talking about oil, for God's sake? Making a few Iranians miss their supper?"

"What did you have in mind, sir?" Schumacher's tone was respectful, Bennington noted, but far from obsequious.

"Have we got a plan to target on Qom?"

Schumacher turned to the Air Force major general behind him. He called up the National Strategic Target List, the data files on all potential U.S. targets, on his computer terminal.

"No, sir," said the major general.

"How about Tehran?"

Again the Air Force officer manipulated the keys of his console. "No, sir."

"I don't believe it!" the President raged. "You mean to tell me that after a decade of the worst possible relations with those people, those Khomeini savages, we don't have a plan to take out Tehran? Our relations with them are a hundred times worse than they've been with the Russians and you're sitting here telling me we haven't got plans targeted on those people?"

Bennington was watching the President carefully. A few seconds before, the man had discovered, almost accidentally, that he was still clutching his lunch napkin. He'd stuffed it into his pocket. There was a slick of sweat at his temples and he was constantly clenching his jaw muscles.

"How about those Tomahawk cruise missiles out there on the *Valley Forge* and the *Ticonderoga* we talked about yesterday? Why the hell don't we target one of them on Tehran? Right now?"

"Mr. President!" General Trowbridge was appalled by the question. "We can't do that. Tehran is filled with embassies. We'd have every nation in the world screaming for our blood if we committed an outrage like that."

"All right, then Qom. How about that, General?" the President barked at the chairman of the Joint Chiefs.

"That would take some time to plan, sir," Schumacher answered.

"Why, for God's sake?"

"Cruise missiles are very accurate, but they have to have a preprogrammed flight plan. To make their TUR-COM guidance systems work requires a territorial mapping program furnished by one of our satellites of the terrain on the route to the target. We need a clear picture of the target and a series of navigational reference points for the cruise along the way. We have to collect the radar signatures the missile's going to encounter going in. All that takes time. It's not a trivial matter."

"And, of course, we haven't got that data on Iran?"

"No, sir."

"Well, how long do we need to get it?"

"Twenty-four hours. The satellite's got to do its work and relay the images back. The information's got to be passed through the Joint Strategic Target Planning Staff out at Offut Air Force Base in Omaha. It's got to be digitalized and then sent out to the ship. Then the ship has got to cut a tape with all that data on it and program the cruise."

"Well, we should do it. Right now." The President, Bennington saw, was breathing in little short snorts, the sure sign of a man whose blood pressure has surged. "If we have to hit those bastards, this is the way to do it. The last time when we went after Qaddafi it cost us two men and a plane. We had to get permission from the whole damn world to fly over their airspace. This eliminates all that."

"Yeah," growled Bill Brennan, his Chief of Staff, "that's a damn good point, Mr. President."

"And we won't have any more American casualties, either. Get that program ready, General," the President ordered. "I want that option available. And something else. I want a four-kiloton dial-a-yield warhead ready to go in there." He slapped his hand on the table as he said the words, his face an angry mask again. "That will put an end to these terrorists once and for all."

"Mr. President, I know of no U.S. nuclear planning that has as its targeted objects cities or civilian populations."

"Well, you know of one now!"

The President snapped out the words like an angry curse. Bennington studied Schumacher. How often does a four-star general hear someone address him like that? he wondered. Except for maybe his wife. He looked around the room. This time at least some of those faces were beginning to register dismay at the President's words. No one, however, seemed ready yet to give voice to that dismay.

"Mr. President, what level of destruction would satisfy you?" There was just an edge of exasperation in the general's voice. "I mean, how much rubble do you want? We'll get it for you with conventional warheads."

"Exactly, sir." It was the Secretary of Defense. At last, Bennington thought. "We can do plenty of damage with conventional warheads on those missiles, but they won't have the opprobrium attached to their use that a nuclear warhead would."

"Sure you can!" the President retorted. "If you can hit the goddam target. We've never fired these things for real, have we? Who the hell knows where they'll hit? In some goddam cow pasture, and we'll be the laughing-stock of Iran. Put four kilotons in there and who the hell cares where it hits? We'll take out Montazeri's school, his terrorists, the whole damn works. That's what I want to do."

"Mr. President, we'll also kill hundreds of innocent women and children in Qom."

"Innocent women and children in Qom? What about those kids in Wiesbaden? What about the people on Pan Am 103? Weren't they innocent? What is this, some kind of double standard of innocence? Americans are less innocent than others?" As the President was talking, Bennington was watching, fascinated and horrified, at the movement of his hands. He couldn't keep them still. He kept knotting them until his knuckles were white, then loosening them. Sometimes he'd clasp them together as though in prayer, but he would squeeze them together so tightly his knuckles whitened his skin. Is there an edge of irrationality to this man's anger? he wondered.

He studied the cabinet members at the table, men who knew the President well, who saw him, in some cases, daily. He didn't read any distress signals on their faces. They were following a debate, listening to an argument, not concerned about their chief's behavior. Maybe, he thought, I'm the one who's being irrational.

"You've seen those Iranian mobs howling for blood on TV, haven't you?" the President was saying. "Cheering Khomeini and his mullahs, screaming their approval for every bloody declaration those savages make. Just the way the Germans cheered Hitler in the thirties. The Germans paid for it, didn't they? Well, the Iranians are damn well going to pay for it, too. They lost their innocence when they put those fanatics into power."

"Mr. President." It was Jack Taylor, the Secretary of State. About time, Bennington thought. "I can't seriously believe you would consider using a nuclear weapon on Qom."

"Can't you? I want every damn option I can have available," the President snarled.

"Such a reaction would be all out of proportion to the provocation. It would unite the entire Moslem world against us. There wouldn't be a Moslem from the Philippines to the Atlantic coast of Morocco who wouldn't hate us after this. We dropped two nuclear weapons on Japan after a long and bloody war, and our action is still controversial today. This would destroy us in the eyes of a third of the world. The Arabs, the Moslems, would throw themselves into the Soviets' arms."

"Listen, Jack, you know those Sunni Moslems hate the Shiites. Look what happened when Reagan zapped Qaddafi. Half the Arab leaders in the world came up to him and whispered, 'Way to go.' " The President snorted.

"Well, I'll tell you guys one thing." It was Bill Brennan, the Chief of Staff. "This presidency is going to go right down the tubes if we lie down on this one. We've been pushed and shoved around by these fanatics long enough. The people out there want action, decisive action."

"Bill, for God's sake, action, okay, but this would be a catastrophe. The Germans would go crazy. Mention the word 'nuclear' in the same room with them and they go into hysterics. It would kill NATO. Forty years of work in ruins, for what?"

"To let the damn world know the day of terrorists is over!" exploded Brennan. "To let the folk out there in the Middle East know once and for all that the day when you can kill and maim innocent Americans is over, that's what for!"

The Secretary of State cordially detested the Chief of Staff. They were rival suitors for the same lover, the

President. "You may think you've got the public on your side now—"

"The public? Are you kidding? Ninety-two percent want action in CBS's overnight poll." Like most politicians, Brennan believed God's ultimate truth was written on the impermanent stone of political polls.

"Do this and you'll have people marching against this administration in every city in the country."

The Attorney General had now decided to enter the argument. "There are some of you people who want to make nuclear weapons into something sacred, something special. Well, they're not. They're just large conventional weapons, but nobody wants to admit it. General," he said, looking down the table at Schumacher, "one of our low-yield, low-radiation warheads on Qom wouldn't produce even a tenth of the radiation Chernobyl did, isn't that a fact?"

The question appeared to distress Schumacher. "Yes, sir, that's about right," he admitted almost grudgingly.

"Set the thing for ground burst, or let it burrow into the ground a bit, and all you'll get is one hell of a roar and an end to those troublemakers," the Attorney General said. "We've let ourselves get paralyzed with fear about using those things. The military wanted to use them at Dien Bien Phu in 1954 in Vietnam. Ike didn't want to. It would have ended the whole damned Vietnam mess right there. Saved thousands of lives. Is Vietnam a better place today because Ike didn't have the guts to use the nukes?"

"Right on!" the President snapped. "I favored the use of tactical nukes in Vietnam if it was militarily prudent."

Bennington was studying the President closely. He was partially slumped in his chair, visibly paler than when he'd entered the room. His hands rested palms down on the surface of the table, trembling slightly. It struck Bennington that here was a man who'd gone through a paroxysm of rage and now, as the chemicals drained from his bloodstream, was recovering. The chief executive stirred. "I've got to get off to the budget meeting. General?'' He looked down at Schumacher. ''I want that option programmed.''

"It's available, sir,'' Schumacher said, ''but I still feel it's not a sound course of action. Just having that damn thing sitting out there programmed to go is a risky business.''

"Program it,'' the President ordered.

He was already striding toward the door. We're on a slippery slope, Bennington thought, a very slippery slope indeed.

Within fifteen minutes after the President had left the National Security Council situation room, the machinery which would program a Tomahawk cruise missile with a nuclear warhead on Qom had been set in motion. Twenty-four thousand miles above the Indian Ocean, one of the nation's most modern KH IV satellites, designed to provide real-time photoreconnaissance in instantaneous, high-resolution images of the earth's surface below, was triggered into action.

Set in geosynchronous orbit, the bird, twenty-three feet in length, was equipped with both Schmidt infrared telescopes fitted with lead sulfide heat sensors to pick up the energy generated by a Soviet rocket launch and cameras of such power they could photograph a man pacing on the earth's surface in a street below. Primarily designed to survey the southern fringes of the Soviet Union where it abuts the landmasses of Iran, Afghanistan, Pakistan, and India, the satellite now started to send back a series of thousands of images of the terrain the missile would have to follow from its platform on the *Valley Forge* two hundred kilometers off the Iranian coast in the Gulf of Oman to Qom, one hundred kilometers southwest of Tehran. The missile would make its landfall just south of Minab opposite Oman, then streak northwest twisting its way through the valleys of the Kun-i-Rud and Zagros mountains to Isfahan, where it would swing north to its target.

Not only would the images now flashing back from

space reveal in stunning detail the topography of the land along the missile's path, but its in-built sensors would allow the Air Force's cartographers to gauge the depths of pockets in the earth's surface, the height and configuration of objects like mountain peaks or rock outcroppings along its course. A cruise missile finds its way to its target by bouncing its guidance radar off such salient earth features. Selected by the men who plan the missile's flight path, they become the signposts pointing it to its target.

First terrestrial stopping-off point of that torrent of information was a secret U.S. installation code-named Casino in the Australian outback near Nurrungar northwest of Adelaide. There the stream of binary bits was processed through the station's IBM 360-755 computers and then put on an undersea cable to San Francisco. From there it would go by land line to the headquarters of NORAD, the North American Aerospace Defense Command at Cheyenne Mountain, Colorado.

The officers and men who received the information at NORAD had no idea of the purpose for which it was intended. Their task was simply to forward it to its ultimate military consumers, the Joint Strategic Target Planning Staff at Offut Air Force Base in Omaha, Nebraska.

The Judge's limousine slipped quickly through the traffic on Constitution Avenue toward the Potomac River and the George Washington Highway out to Langley. Sitting in the back beside the director, Art Bennington chuckled as he looked at the glimmering sheen of the Reflecting Pool. His first CIA office had been out there on that trim green lawn in a drafty emergency barracks thrown up by the Army Engineers during World War II. Two hundred yards of space and about five light-years of time separated him from the site right now.

Neither he nor the director had said a word since they'd gotten into the car. The heels of the Judge's black loafers were propped on the ledge of the jump seat before him. His chin was down on his chest, brooding. Clearly, the man was troubled. Well, screw it, Bennington thought, I'm troubled too, and I didn't make a CIA career by keeping my mouth shut in front of directors.

"That was quite a scene, wasn't it?" His was a tentative opening, like a fly fisherman's cast or a boxer's left jab, a move designed to see the reaction it produced. The Judge shook his head slowly two or three times, the way a man will emerging from a catnap or when he's been disturbed while engrossed in an all-absorbing problem.

"You know," he said, "I've known him, what? Ten years. Maybe twelve. I've never seen him work himself up into a state quite like he has on this one."

"I never knew he had such a temper."

"Oh, he's got a temper, all right. Always has. Believe me, he can be mean and nasty when he wants to. All this Old New England prep school aura they've built around him, the real suburban gentleman in his dungarees and Shetland sweater, out there raking the leaves, never an angry word. That's just a facade. The way these things always are. But I've never seen him angry like this. There was almost a touch of hysteria in there, do you know what I mean?"

"Yes. I know exactly what you mean."

The Judge turned his head to Art, his eyes slightly narrowed. The way Bennington had pronounced those words made the director understand his deputy had deliberately maneuvered their conversation to this point.

"The way he had that napkin. It made me think of Captain Queeg in *The Caine Mutiny* with his steel balls," Bennington continued.

"All right, Art, what are you driving at? Spell it out for me. You're the man who went to medical school."

Art contemplated this veteran head of the Central Intelligence Agency. Are you ready for this? his eyes were asking his superior.

"The fact that we may have a President who's suffering from some kind of mental disability on our hands."

The Judge shriveled a bit at the implications of Bennington's words. He studied his fingernails in silence for a moment or two. The thought, Bennington realized, had already troubled the director's spirits.

"I don't believe it."

"You don't believe it, Judge? Or you don't want to believe it?"

The Judge let his eyes wander out the limousine window. "Do you understand, do you begin to understand the Constitutional implications of what you're suggesting?"

"What I understand, Judge, is the unmitigated disaster dropping a four-kiloton weapon on Qom would be for this country."

"He won't go through with that. He'll calm down."

"You hope."

The Judge gave a reaffirming shake to his head and tried to retreat into the sanctuary of silence. Bennington, however, wasn't going to let him escape into that preserve. "You know how our system works. The only person who's authorized to order a nuclear weapon fired is the President."

"The Secretary of Defense and General Schumacher would never let him do it. He just caught them off balance in there today."

"Maybe. But don't forget, legally, once he's got that missile set up, he doesn't need anybody's concurrence or approval to fire. Not General Schumacher's. Not Congress's. Nobody's."

"It could never happen."

"Certainly not with an intelligent President in command of his faculties. I've spent my life studying human behavior, Judge, and I'm convinced there was an edge of irrationality to his behavior in there today. He was in the grip of an uncontrolled rage. There were a few moments when he was spinning right out of control."

"You're right. I saw it. It frightened me, too. But what the hell are we supposed to do about it, Art? Say, 'Look, Mr. President, why don't you just forget about those kids in Wiesbaden for a while and go sit down with a friendly shrink'?"

"You remember that young officer named Witter that

got busted in Moscow? When we lost that colonel we had parked in the Kremlin?''

"What in God's name does that have to do with this?''

"I was convinced and I still am that the Russians got the colonel's ID out of him with a magnetoencephalograph.''

"So you said.''

"When the President had his last physical out at Bethesda, his physician said he'd had a magnetoencephalogram made.''

"So what?''

"Magnetoencephalography is fundamentally a research tool. Right now, it's only very rarely used for diagnostic work. So if they used it on the President, there had to be some very major medical reason for using it. A magnetoencephalogram is no electrocardiogram, Judge. They weren't taking his pulse in there.''

The Judge groaned. Why was he letting Bennington skate him out here to the middle of the lake where the ice was thinnest? Because he, too, had seen that haunting glimmer of irrationality in the President's behavior. "So what would they have been looking for?''

"I was training to be a neurosurgeon before I joined the Agency, but I'm not up to speed on the latest in neurology. Maybe they were looking for a tumor that might somehow be affecting his behavior.''

"Well, they couldn't have found anything, because they gave him a clean bill of health, didn't they?''

"Maybe it was inoperable.''

The director stirred and let his feet drop off the jump seat with a thud. "Art, for God's sake, we're way out of our depth here. I know where you're heading. I know exactly where you're heading. You want to tiptoe around to that doctor and whisper, 'Hey, is there any possibility, any physical evidence that might indicate the President is a little bit nuts?' ''

Bennington said nothing, because that was exactly what he intended to do.

"Can you see what will happen when Bob Woodward throws that all over the front page of *The Washington*

Post? The CIA running its own private investigation of the President's mental health?"

"Can you imagine what will happen if a President in a momentary fit of irrational behavior commits an act of irreparable harm to this country? Don't we owe it to the country, to the other men in that situation room, to see if that danger exists?"

"Art, the man is the President. We're his servants, not his custodians."

"And the country? What the hell is the CIA for if it isn't to protect the country from something like this?"

They were heading up to the Agency. The director indicated to his driver and the blue blazer security guard beside him to take them to the main entrance.

"One word, one whisper, gets out," he said, pointing to Nathan Hale's statue, "and I'll put the rope around your neck myself."

"Don't worry, Judge." Art chuckled grimly. "When you've been doing things outside of channels as long as I have, it comes naturally."

"Would you just repeat your story again to this man in here, Willi?"

Louis Doria looked up from the paperwork on his desk at Tegel Airport's security office to see his German counterpart and a scruffy-looking German civilian approaching his desk.

"Willi's a taxi driver," the German policeman explained.

That's obvious enough, Doria thought. Willi wore his hair shoulder-length in a vague resemblance of curls that appeared to have an even vaguer acquaintance with soap and water. He had on a gray ski parka and was smoking, his cigarette dangling from the corner of his lips, the way tough guys smoked in Hollywood movies fifty years ago. Your typical Berlin cab driver—shrewd, caustic, convinced he's forgotten more about human behavior than most people learn in a lifetime.

"So, Willi, what's the story?"

"Saturday night, I was at the top of the rank when the Pan Am came in from Frankfurt. Four Arabs got into my cab."

"Ah!" Doria's interest was now turned on to high. "How did you know they were Arabs, not Turks, say?"

"They were speaking Arabic." Willi gave Doria a pitying glance. After all, Frenchmen couldn't be expected to enjoy the international *savoir faire* of Berlin cab drivers.

"You speak Arabic, do you?"

"Some. The guys in the back started chattering in Arabic. The guy up front beside me turned around and told them to shut up. Not to speak Arabic. *'Maa't kalemsh Araby,'* " Willi said, in what Doria assumed was good Arabic. Willi probably moved a few drugs for the brothers in Kreuzberg from time to time.

He opened his drawer and took out the four CIA Artist photos. "Recognize any of these guys?" he asked.

"Aren't you going to ask me where I took them?" Willi demanded, unable to understand the amateurishness of the Frenchman's approach.

"I always like to save the bad news for last."

"Him," Willi said, pointing to Sayed's photo. "He was the guy sitting next to me."

"The others?"

He shrugged.

"And you took them to Zoo Station, right?"

"Yeah! How did you know?"

"Lucky guess." Doria extended his hand. "Thanks, Willi. We appreciate your help."

As Willi and the policeman left, Doria picked up his phone to call Schmidt. Their investigation was over. Just as both of them had suspected at the beginning, the terrorists were gone. Still, they hadn't done badly in forty-eight hours: positive IDs on the four of them, the cars, the apartments they used. Everything except the arrest. That, unfortunately, was Berlin.

• • •

At the KGB *rezident*'s request, his weekly dinner with Major Abdul Hamid Hatem, the head of the Havarat, the Syrian intelligence service, had been moved exceptionally this week from Thursday to Monday. The weather was turning cool, so they had chosen to eat in the ornate Oriental dining room of the Sheraton Hotel in downtown Damascus. Before going in to dinner, they decided to have a drink at the bar. Hatem indicated to the headwaiter the place he wanted to sit, a quiet corner from which he could survey everyone in the establishment. A waiter rushed over with bowls of green and black olives, iced raw carrots, pistachio nuts, a bottle of Chivas Regal, ice and soda.

Hatem served a generous ration to himself and his guest, then raised his glass to the *rezident*. "*Saa'htain*— health," he proposed. For a moment, he gazed contemptuously at his countrymen in the bar puffing on their nargilehs, concocting their deals. Then he leaned to the *rezident*. "What do you think about this bomb against the Americans in Germany?"

"I think it is very, very dangerous."

The Syrian sipped his scotch, reflecting on the Russian's words. "Do you suppose they'll retaliate?"

"I'm sure they will. Look at what they did to Qadaffi after the bomb in Berlin. For one dead American soldier." The Russian picked up his glass. Like most of his countrymen, he did not sip alcohol. He drank it, and he swallowed a quarter of the contents of his drink before setting it back on the table. He picked up a pistachio nut, split it open, and tossed the meat into his mouth. As he chewed, he studied Hatem, his face registering no more expression than that of a dentist looking at his tenth set of X-rays for the day. "I just hope that when they decide to retaliate, they retaliate against the right people."

The Syrian started. He pushed closer to the KGB officer and dropped his voice to a whisper. "We had nothing to do with it. We knew nothing about it until we saw the Reuters report. Believe me."

"I believe you had nothing to do with it, Abdul Hamid.

In fact, I know you had nothing to do with it. The question is, what are the Americans going to believe?"

The Russian paused to let the full impact of his words register. As he had intended, their effect was far from pleasant. He stretched out his hand and gave the Syrian's forearm a reassuring squeeze, the sort of gesture a coach makes to an aspiring athlete who's fallen just short of a much-desired goal. "Fortunately, you do not need to worry about the Americans attacking you as they did Qaddafi. They would have to contend with us, and they're quite aware of that."

"Yes," avowed Hatem, who had not believed a single word of the KGB officer's unctuous assurances. "I know that. We are all of us aware of the importance of Soviet-Syrian solidarity." He stopped to peck at his drink. "But why would the Americans think we were involved?"

"Because the people who did it came from the Bekaa Valley."

Now the Syrian was truly startled. He had not known that, and his ignorance was a major failing. He had already suggested to his country's ruler, Hafez al-Assad, that the bomb was the work of the German Red Army Faction. The Russian's disclosure was as worrying as it was embarrassing.

"You know the Americans," the *rezident* continued. "They assume that everything that happens in the Bekaa Valley is your doing."

He plucked another pistachio from the bowl and snapped open its shell. "Who knows?" he asked, cupping the nut to his mouth. "It may be in the interests of other parties to encourage the Americans in their beliefs. To be sure it is you, not they, who pay the price of their actions."

Had he put a gun to Hatem's chest, the *rezident* could not have commanded his attention more fully. "The Israelis!" he exploded. "Would they dare to do something like that?" Abdul Hamid Hatem believed in the omnipresence of the Israelis' malevolent hands as firmly as a Brahman monk believes in reincarnation.

The Russian demeaned Hatem's reply with a scornful little smile.

"Who then?"

First his Soviet colleague turned his attention to his glass of scotch. Then he leaned to Hatem and began to whisper.

"What I am about to tell you you must never, never tell anyone."

"I swear, my friend, believe me."

"Absolutely no one."

"I swear on the head of my firstborn son."

"The four people who did the bomb flew to East Berlin on Interflug. Our people knew two of them. They were from Ali Montazeri's group in Qom." He finished the rest of his scotch. "You know how we feel about them. So we put them under surveillance in East Berlin."

Hatem nodded. He was not about to interrupt this precious flow of information with some inane phrase.

"Forty-eight hours before the explosion, we saw them go into the Iranian embassy in Pankow, in East Berlin. They went in empty-handed."

"Yes," Hatem whispered.

"They came out carrying two heavy suitcases apiece."

"Explosives!" gasped the Syrian.

"I doubt very much that it was caviar."

A few minutes later, the maître d'hôtel informed them their dinner was ready. When their dinner was finished, Hatem announced that to his regret he would have to forgo watching Nimet Fouad, the Egyptian belly dancer in the hotel lounge. The pressure of work waiting in his office. The *rezident* nodded his understanding.

As always, he stood by the curb while Hatem left, as respectful as an old sergeant watching his commanding officer depart. Hatem he knew would be on his way to inform Assad of the startling disclosure he'd made before dinner. Then Hatem would summon his principal subordinates and rip them apart for their failure to obtain the information the KGB had given him. Hatem's intelligence service was one of the more thoroughly penetrated organizations in the world. How long, the *rezident* wondered, would it take for his information to reach Tel Aviv? Twenty-four hours? Less?

The headquarters of the Joint Strategic Target Planning Staff, the JSTPS, was in an underground command post fifty feet below the neatly trimmed lawn of the Strategic Air Command's headquarters building at Offut Air Base in Omaha, Nebraska. The officers assigned to the command were mostly Air Force, former missile silo commanders or SAC B-52 pilots, together with a minority of Navy submariners. Their job was to assign targets to the warheads in the U.S. nuclear arsenal, to be sure that threatening Soviet targets were adequately covered, to coordinate missile launch and flight plans, so that one strike didn't interfere with another, to keep launch-to-arrival times accurate, estimates of fallout, destruction, and casualties for each warhead up to date. Theirs was a task of extraordinary complexity, the sort of challenge that delighted people who enjoyed playing chess or Mastermind or designing intricate computer programs—except that in this case, what was involved was not a game but the near destruction of the planet.

The vast majority of the warheads in the nuclear arsenal they controlled, including all those on submarines and in missile silos, were committed to what was called the SIOP—the Single Integrated Operational Plan. The plan was not, in fact, a single plan but a range of just under a dozen options for nuclear strikes on the USSR. One option, for example, programmed strikes designed to target the Soviets' command and control facilities, another their silo-based thermonuclear missiles. A much smaller number of missiles with much less destructive capacity, most of them short-range land-based missiles in West Germany or air-and-sea-borne cruise missiles, were trained on preplanned theater targets by the commanders of U.S. area commands, but those targeting actions had all been supervised and coordinated by the JSTPS. A still smaller number of warheads had no preassigned target.

As soon as the order to program a missile on Qom had

been received from the Pentagon, the JSTPS duty officer had selected a missile from his inventory for the assignment. It was officially designated CDPN376W60 which meant it was a Tomahawk cruise missile of the most recent production series assigned to the Navy, with dual warheads, a conventional warhead, or, for a nuclear strike, a W60 variable-yield warhead.

Once all the information from the satellite was in, a targeting team of three Air Force officers sat down at their computers to lay out in precise detail the flight plan that would be stored in the missile's guidance cone. Essentially, what they did was to provide the missile's guidance system with a stored memory bank of the configuration of the ground over which it was going to fly. Based on that information, the missile could drone in to its target, adjusting its course whenever necessary along the route.

The task required six hours of hard, tedious work before the plan had been drawn up, verified, and cleared by the JSTPS commander. Once their map work was done, they drew up the Emergency Action Message which would control the actual launch of the missile on Qom should that order ever be given. Preformatted and short, it contained three vital pieces of information, all of which would have to be received by the captain of the *Valley Forge* before, in normal circumstances, he could consider an order to fire the missile valid and operational. The first was the code for the operation itself, Hemlock. The second was the authenticating code which would confirm to the captain that the order releasing the operation code had come from an authorized source. It was a number, 301427. Finally there was the enabling code authorizing the captain and the executive officer to initiate the launch-to-completion sequence which would set the missile flying. It was a complex and demanding process, but it reflected the extremely rigorous procedures with which the U.S. military surrounded any potential use of nuclear weapons.

The coded plan and message were sent to the *Valley Forge* over the Defense Satellite Communications System, the military's worldwide high-data-rate voice and data communication system. A second copy went by secure land line to the Pentagon office of General Schumacher, the chairman of the Joint Chiefs.

The Berlin Wall forms the eastern frontier of Kreuzberg. There the wall runs behind the grounds of an old monastery converted by the city into a warren of artists' studios. Years ago, the artists in residence discovered the wall's forbidding cement made a perfect showcase for their talents. They converted it into a kind of hallucinogenic kaleidoscope, a free-form comic strip of dancing bears and fire-belching dragons, leering ghouls, high-breasted nudes adorned with the defiant slogans of their creators: "Move your body," "Life is a trip," "All cops are bastards."

Every time Dante Russo walked down that strip of cement—and he passed it at least three times a week—he delighted in its colorful challenge to the world beyond the wall. Hell for Walter Ulbricht, the humorless East German Communist who built it, Russo thought, would be to have to spend eternity contemplating what the artists had done to his creation.

He unlocked the front door of 19 Bethanie Damm, a five-story building whose facade was barely three yards from the wall, and climbed to his fifth-floor apartment. His sitting-room window looked out over the plowed and mined dirt track behind the wall into the East Berlin neighborhood across the way. He took a pair of binoculars, the most powerful Zeiss made, from his desk. Standing well back from the window so the wall's border guards in the mirador couldn't see him, he focused quickly onto his target. It was the left-hand corner of the second kitchen window of the third-floor apartment at 7 Herbertstrasse. A message was waiting there for Russo. It was a blue cylinder of salt placed on the window ledge. So, Russo thought, laying down his binoculars, he's got something.

The occupant of 7 Herbertstrasse was a registry clerk

at STASI, East Germany's State Security Service. He was also an asset of Russo's employers, the CIA. Maybe, Russo mused, locking his binoculars away, he's got something for us on the Wiesbaden bomb. Not much happened in East Berlin that STASI didn't know about.

General Harold Schumacher, the chairman of the Joint Chiefs, had given orders that he was to oversee personally the insertion of Operation Hemlock, the firing of the cruise missile on Qom, into the U.S. nuclear options array. He remained philosophically opposed to the whole notion. Even programming the missile he considered a reckless and unwarranted action. Nonetheless, the order to do it had come directly from the President; it was a legal order. Hal Schumacher hadn't risen to the top of the U.S. military hierarchy by slighting legitimate orders. Still, he was determined to sit on this one as tightly as he could until this crisis had passed and he could stand the missile down.

Schumacher had first to send the emergency-action message and codes to the director of the White House's Military Office. That was the office responsible for the "Black Football," which was not a football at all but a black leather briefcase closed with a combination lock. Nor did the warrant officer responsible for it spend his day dogging the President's footsteps as popular legend insisted. He sat in a basement bomb shelter in the East Wing of the White House, watching TV game shows and reading paperback novels.

The "football" did not contain a magic red button which the President could push to send the nuclear missiles flying. No such red button existed. What it did contain was a seventy-five-page loose-leaf binder, the Black Book, which detailed, in all their infinite complexity, the nuclear strike options available to the President. It was what the military with their felicitous choice of phrasing liked to call the President's nuclear "menu," the proposals for what would surely be the most indigestible meal mankind would ever be called upon to stomach.

Also in the "football" were three-by-five file cards like Bingo cards with authentication codes to identify all the senior members of the U.S. command structure with a role to play in a nuclear emergency from the President down. A duplicate of that card, changed regularly, was also supposed to be in the President's wallet.

Early Tuesday the procedures for Operation Hemlock were hand-carried to the White House by armed messenger. A second set was taken to the National Military Command Center next to the chairman's office in the Pentagon, where they would be available to the flag officer commanding the nerve center from which the U.S. military forces around the world were controlled.

A painted ship upon a painted ocean, thought Captain Hobart Edmonds, the commander of the USS *Valley Forge*, looking out from the bridge of his vessel over the waters of the southern fringe of the Sea of Oman. For a brief instant the reflection of a setting sun was turning those still waters into a garish palette of scarlets, reds, and pinks. His meditation on Coleridge's "Ancient Mariner" was interrupted by the arrival of a yeoman from the communications center.

"Sir," he said, "there's an eyes-only coming down from the satellite."

Edmonds got up and walked along the passageway to the communications center, set just aft of his ship's ultramodern combat information center with its twenty-five radar Aegis sonar weapons and communications system.

"It's a double, Captain," the communications officer said as Edmonds entered the cabin, "for you and the exec. He's on the way."

Edmonds's eyebrows shot up. A "double" for him and his number two would by definition involve a nuclear matter. When the exec arrived, the two men repaired to the decoding room and, employing their personal codes, decrypted the JSTPS targeting message.

"Christ!" Edmonds said, rereading it. "What do you suppose that's about?"

The exec, a commander seven years Edmonds's junior, thought a moment. "Maybe that's where the people who blew up the gym in Wiesbaden came from."

"Four kilotons? For that?" Edmonds asked.

"I'll tell you something, Captain. I've got two teenage kids. If those bastards did it, twenty kilotons wouldn't be too much as far as I'm concerned."

Edmonds and his exec set about preparing the missile immediately. The gunnery officer cut the tape from the coded data forwarded by JSTPS, then ran the tape into the missile's guidance cone. An armament team went down to the ship's nuclear arms safe, guarded by armed marines, and withdrew the warhead for the missile from the *Valley Forge* stockpile. A chief petty officer set the "dial-a-yield" mechanism to the stipulated four kilotons, a relatively straightforward procedure, and the warhead was brought on deck and bolted into place in the missile's nose. When that was done, the *Valley Forge*'s captain radioed the commander of the Atlantic Fleet, on whom he depended via the rear admiral commanding the Persian Gulf Task Force, that Operation Hemlock was now an available nuclear option.

Captain Edmonds was uneasy. He did not like having that missile out there on his gunnery deck ready to go. But at least he knew that even in the almost inconceivable event of an accidental launch, there could be no nuclear explosion. Like all U.S. warheads, the warhead on the *Valley Forge*'s cruise was "one point safe." It could not trigger a nuclear detonation until its Permissive Action links had been unlocked, and only he and the exec, acting in concert, could do that.

"Dr. White? Dr. Arthur Bennington from the Behavioral Science Division out at Langley."

"Good morning, Doctor." The President's personal physician had never met Bennington, but he'd recognized his name as soon as his secretary had identified his caller. At its senior levels, Washington's bureaucracy was an old boys' net, an insiders' cabinet of contacts and acquaintances. "What can I do for you?"

"I need some help. As you probably know, Doctor, one of the things we're following closely out here is the development of the magnetoencephalograph."

"Remarkable machine, isn't it?" White answered. "One day it's going to revolutionize our approach to the brain."

"You're right. When I think back to how little we knew about the brain when I was interning at Columbia Presbyterian in the fifties, I—"

"Columbia?" White interrupted. "We're practically contemporaries. I did my residency at Bellevue about the same time."

"Really?" Bennington feigned surprise as best he could. He'd studied White's Navy file in detail before making his call and knew perfectly well where he had done his residency. "I don't suppose you ever crossed swords with old Pinckney Arledge? He practiced over there from time to time."

"No, but I certainly was aware of his reputation."

"Anyway, Doctor," Bennington continued, satisfied that he'd relaxed White, "I was both fascinated and curious to see you'd used the magnetoencephalograph as a diagnostical tool in a general physical with the President. I've only really been aware of its employment up until now as a research tool."

White paused a moment. "There were some special circumstances involved. I'm speaking, you understand, as one colleague to another."

"Of course, Doctor."

"The President was concerned he might be suffering from a brain tumor. He had some generalized symptoms, and he'd been indulging in a bit of self-diagnosis. I wanted to give him the best medical reassurance possible and at the same time be absolutely certain his fears weren't justified."

"Poor man. I trust his fears were baseless."

"Completely. His scan was perfect. His problems, we

discovered, were being caused by a liquid buildup in the inner canal of his left ear. Ménière's syndrome.''

"Ah, yes," Bennington answered knowingly. "We've had some success in our lab work pinning down the areas in the brain associated with certain emotional disorders such as schizophrenia through magnetoencephalograms, but we haven't really looked into medical applications.''

"Schizophrenia?" White intoned. "How interesting. Of course, the President's physiological state was not my concern as his medical adviser. And, in any event, he's never had any need for psychiatric care or counseling at any stage of his life. Despite," White laughed, "what some of his political opponents may say. Interesting, though. I didn't know this technology may one day have psychiatric applications.''

"Well, it's still very much uncharted territory," Bennington said. "Our Soviet friends have shown a great interest in it.''

There was a long and totally unexpected pause from White. He coughed. "Really?" he asked, then coughed again. "Then there's something that happened out here you should perhaps be aware of.''

"What's that?" Bennington's tone was as gentle as a lover's caress.

"Someone apparently stole two backup disks from the computer that stores our magnetoencephalographic data about a month after we conducted the President's examination.''

"And the record of his exam, his magnetoencephalogram, was on the stolen disk?''

"Yes. Coded, of course. Along with hundreds of others, all coded. I think it would be practically impossible for anyone to determine which one was his.''

"Sure," Art said. "But why would anybody want to steal those disks?''

"Take them home, erase them. Save a few bucks. Unfortunately, we've had trouble with petty thievery of this kind for some time.''

"Your investigators never turned anything up?''

"Not that I know of. To tell you the truth, I don't think anybody paid much attention to it."

Art Bennington waited for his fellow members of the CIA's Wiesbaden bomb committee to start drifting out of the director's office. Once they were well on their way, he raised an eyebrow to get the director's attention.

"Got something?" the Judge asked, positioning himself between Bennington and his departing colleagues.

"I ran that little check we talked about last night. He came out clear as a bell. No sign of any problem anywhere."

The director pulled his handkerchief out of his hip pocket and loudly blew his nose. What's he doing? Bennington wondered. Trying to avoid having to acknowledge my extracurricular forays? Finally, the director made eye contact. He winked. "Thank God."

"That was the good news, Judge."

"Damn you, Bennington. You really do jerk people around like yo-yos. And what's worse, you enjoy it." He looked over his shoulder. The others had left his office. "Okay, come over here and give me the rest of it.

"Art, my first reaction is, so what?" the Judge said after Bennington had told him the story of the missing disks. "It just shows some petty officers can be petty crooks."

"Could be. But those disks cost nine ninety-five at a Radio Shack. Why run the risk of stealing them?"

"So you're going to try to convince me the KGB went after them?"

"We went after Khrushchev's piss. Those so-called codes on there are a joke. The disk files give the time and date each exam begins. Any damn fool who can read the paper knows when the President had his. And nobody reads the American press more closely than the KGB."

"Suppose they had them, which I think is a wild supposition. What the hell would they do with them?"

"I don't know."

"Well, that's very helpful."

445

"What I do know is the Russians are way ahead of us in using this technology. The Witter case proved it."

"Proved it to you."

Bennington shrugged. This was not the moment to get into an updated version of that argument about how many angels can dance on a pinhead. "Okay, it's a supposition. But just for the moment, assume it's true. That machine is designed to read, ultimately, the signals that are being thrown off by the core of the brain where emotional responses are generated. If you can figure out what those signals are, could you find some way to duplicate them and generate an emotional response from outside the body's nervous system? That's the sixty-four-thousand-dollar question."

"And the Russians have got the answer and some KGB agent is out there with a Buck Rogers X-ray zap gun turning it on and off and getting the President mad? Art, that's crazy. That's weirdo science. I mean that's so far out—"

"Judge," Bennington interrupted, "the annals of science are filled with men and women announcing, 'It could never happen.' And then waking up one morning to find out it did. This is far out. Right there at the outer edge of the envelope ready to fall off, I agree."

"I'm glad we see eye to eye on something."

"But why else would the KGB want to get hold of those disks if it wasn't to do something like that?"

"Art, there you go again. Who says the KGB has those disks?"

"Assume, for the point of argument, they do. Why else would they want them?"

The director pinched his nostrils between his thumb and forefinger as though his nose were itching. Would you buy a used car from a guy who employed psychics to find submarines? he asked himself. Yet, you had to admit, Bennington might be a loose cannon, but he was also a very clever guy. "Okay," he sighed. "Give me your good news. What is it you want me to do?"

"Tickle the FBI. This is a theft of federal government property on a government reservation, right? Let them go over to Bethesda and see if they can turn anything up on who stole the disks."

"That's easy enough. All you have to do is say 'President's exam' and they'll be out there like a shot."

"And let me slide out of the situation room for forty-five minutes and have a chat with the guys that run the White House's electronic surveillance system. They're pals of mine. Let me just see if they're picking up anything that looks suspicious."

"You'd better be sure they're good pals. Because if the Secret Service catches you intruding on their turf over there, you'll be up for Nathan's rope again."

Once a year Art Bennington gave a Top Secret briefing at the Thunder Mountain underground security facility on Soviet electromagnetic capabilities. Among his regular listeners were the four Army officers who ran the White House's electromagnetic countermeasures program. So when he walked into their two-room suite in the Executive Office Building, his was both a familiar and a respected face.

The man on duty, a warrant officer, greeted him effusively, pulled out a chair, and offered him the latest fruits of his Mr. Coffee machine. The room looked like an overworked TV repair shop. It was banked high with monitors blipping out their gray-green lines of passing frequencies, of decks of tuners, oscillators, amplifiers designed to collect and record every electromagnetic signal coming into or going out of the White House. The aim was to thwart any Soviet efforts at electronic espionage at the seat of the U.S. government.

The ways in which a building like the White House could be bugged were legion: a classic telephone tap, or "Charlie Brown" in the eavesdroppers' tongue; a laser beam focused on windowpanes to pick up vibrations of a conversation in a room; a microphone planted by a workman in a wall's plaster or a doorknob; a transmitter as small as a hat pin stuck into a chair's upholstery; a device planted in a light socket when the bulb was changed which could then transmit the conversations in the room whenever the light was on over the building's power lines.

"So how's business?" Bennington asked as he sipped his coffee. The two men swapped stories for a while before the warrant officer came to the inevitable "What can I do for you?"

Bennington had noted the times on Sunday and Monday when the President had gone into his uncontrolled rages. "Did you pick up anything out of the ordinary coming in Sunday or Monday between twelve-thirty and two in the afternoon?"

"I don't think so." The warrant officer began punching up one of his computer consoles. "But we'll have a look."

Fundamentally, the equipment the office employed was a battery of audio countermeasures receiver systems. Each scanned a specific frequency range. Its computers recorded, analyzed, and stored the footprint of every electromagnetic signal coming in on the frequencies it scanned. They were then identified. Whenever an unusual signal was picked up the alarm bells would jangle until it was identified.

"You won't believe the shit we pick up with these things," the warrant officer said. "Ham radios, cop cars, radar pulses from speed traps. Some guy starting his car on Pennsylvania Avenue. A cement mixer over on 15th. We even get navigational signals from the lighthouse down in Chesapeake Bay."

The idea, of course, was either to detect a bug hidden in the White House while it was in the act of transmitting or a signal coming in to activate a bug. In addition, all the power cables coming into the White House were equipped with special filters looking for parasitic transmitters like the device in the light-bulb socket that could send messages out on the power line.

The warrant officer studied his displays slowly and carefully. Art watched over his shoulders, but the wiggling lines were a foreign language to him.

"I don't see any jangles in here, Art," he said. "We

had a lot of junk coming in Sunday from RFK for the Skins game, but all normal stuff.''

"Where do you start scanning?"

"One hundred hertz."

If something was really going on, Bennington thought, it would be way below that. They wouldn't have picked it up anyway.

"You know, we've got a scanner out at Langley that covers the zero-to-one-hundred-hertz range, which is a hole under the fence for you guys. Why don't we set it up here for forty-eight hours just to see if there are any major signals coming through that hole?"

"Yeah," said the admiring warrant officer, "that's a good idea. Be interesting to see what happens." Then almost as an afterthought, he added, "I guess I'd better just run it by the Secret Service."

"Oh, don't worry," Art assured him. "I'll cover you on that. Some of our stuff is pretty highly classified." No words, Art thought, stir quite so much respect in an old warrant officer as "highly classified."

"Oh, right, okay," his friend concurred.

"I'll be next door in the NSC most of the time anyway," Art added, "so I'll pop in from time to time and see if we're getting anything."

Brooding on what he had done, he walked back to the White House. I'd better catch something in that electronic mousetrap of mine, he thought. If I don't, it's my ass that's going to get caught in there the day the Secret Service finds out what I've done.

The big blue bus bore the words "U.S. Air Force—Tempelhof Air Base" painted in white along its flanks. It looked more than a little bit out of place nosing into a parking lot already filled with tour buses from Moscow, Kiev, Leningrad, Bucharest, Warsaw. The USO's regular guided tour of East Berlin had reached the high point of its visit, Treptower Park, the Red Army's imposing monument to the two million men and women who died in combat on the road to Berlin during World War II.

Just over forty people, U.S. officers and enlisted men from the Army and Air Force and their wives and offspring, spilled out of the bus and crossed the broad, linden-lined avenue, the only thoroughfare in East Berlin that required a traffic light, into the park. Trailing along at the back of the group in the uniform of an Air Force major, a camera slung around his neck, was the CIA's Dante Russo. He followed the party through a triumphal arch down a broad walk to a bronze statue of a kneeling woman. No act of the imagination was required to understand this was Mother Russia mourning her fallen sons. The statue was cast in the heroic Soviet poster style of the thirties, a style that seemed ludicrous elsewhere but here had a touching grandeur to it.

Following the toy-soldier pace of their East German guide, they marched up to the broad esplanade overlooking the memorial. Below them was a mass grave larger than a football field in which were buried the Red Army soldiers killed in the battle of Berlin. At the far end of the memorial on a high hillock was a miniature Roman temple, the monument to the Unknown Soviet Soldier.

The East German guide launched into her set-piece speech, ringing out her denunciation of the Fascist conspiracy and praise for the heroic workers' resistance with a passion of which a party observer would have approved. The only thing missing were the encomiums to the chieftain whose name was so prominently, frequently, and, unfortunately, ineradicably chiseled into the marble everywhere in the memorial, J. Stalin. Russo, of course, had heard the speech several times. The disguise, the USO tour, provided an ideal and relatively safe cover for his forays across the wall, and he used it frequently.

Twenty-five yards away, another group of visitors identified as a trade union delegation from the Kiev Locomotive Assembly Works followed the same discourse in Russian with poignant attention. No wonder, Russo thought. There was probably not a person among them who had not lost at least one close family member on the road to Berlin.

The visit finished, the group wandered back to the parking lot. A pair of concession stands adjoined it. The first sold souvenirs, the second coffee, bratwurst on a bun, schnapps, rum, and apple juice. Russo got a bratwurst and coffee from the surly white-smocked woman running the concession. Service with a smile was not an art much practiced in East Germany. Munching his bratwurst at one of the stand's tables, he saw the man with the dark blue Helmut Schmidt Hamburg cap disappear along the dirt path through the patch of woods leading to the Schönefeld S-Bahn line.

He finished his bratwurst, waited a minute or two, then headed to the toilets. They were in what looked like a Toonerville Trolley on blocks, its wheels removed, one end for boys, the other for girls. A grim elderly woman sat in the middle of the car, defining, apparently, the frontier between the sexes.

At the urinal Russo smiled as he always did at the sign taped to the toilet wall. "To Pee: 10 Pfennig" it read in German. "To Wash Hands: 20 Pfennig." What extraordinary burst of Marxist-Leninist logic, he wondered, had ordered those priorities? Finishing, he shifted his body slightly to screen his fingers from the woman's view as he flushed the toilet.

In a quick movement he plucked the message waiting for him out of its hiding place in a crevice behind the urinal. Then he washed his hands and with a cheerful smile deposited his tip in the old lady's cup.

There was an ebb and flow to these crisis meetings, Bennington thought, a swift peaking of tensions when a startling piece of information reached the gathering or the President pounded on the table demanding action. In between was a lot of meaningless spinning of the wheels, and upon such a tideless sea were they now afloat. The Judge was reviewing the latest information the Agency had received from Berlin, the taxi driver's report to Louis Doria. About half the people in the room were listening, the other half were working their telephone or whispering to each other.

"He took them directly to Zoo Station, which means they were headed into East Berlin," the Judge concluded.

"Jack," General Trowbridge said, "what are the chances of the East Germans picking them up for us? Assuming, of course, they're still over there?"

"Zero," said the Secretary of State, Jack Taylor.

"Even in these chummy new *glasnost* days?"

"Kent, we don't talk to the East Germans about East Berlin. Ever. That's an Allied policy written in stone. Talk to them and we acknowledge their authority in East Berlin. The English, the West Germans, the French would go bananas if we did that."

"Well, what the hell do we do in a case like this?"

"Talk to the Russians. Go on pouring our complaints into their presumably deaf ears."

"That's it?"

"That's it. Oh, once in a while, a few weeks after one of our complaints, we may find some Libyan diplomat's had his socks jerked up." The Secretary of State offered the National Security Adviser a little chuckle as a balm for his manifest frustration. State had long ago become inured to the difficulties created by Berlin's special status. "I've got an update on Mideast reactions. Radio Tripoli came out with denunciations of the bombing last night. Better late than never.

"One of those howling-mad mullahs was on the box half the night ranting away about how this was Allah's vengeance on us for shooting down the Airbus in the Persian Gulf."

"Have we had any back-channel communications from Tehran?" Trowbridge asked.

"Not a word. But they gave that mullah a hell of a lot of airtime on their state TV, which is not exactly a sign of official disapproval, is it?"

Trowbridge grimaced and turned to the representative of the National Security Agency, the nation's electronic eavesdroppers. "Have you people got anything for us yet? You're being awfully slow on this one."

"This isn't like Libya, where we had the two dozen phone numbers we knew Qaddafi's security people used. Then our computers could break out the calls we wanted to monitor. Beirut's a rat's nest. We have to go through our tapes of almost everything coming out of there. It's put a tremendous burden on our Arabic speakers."

"How about Iran?"

"We're working through our Tehran checklists. And the Agency's delivered us the tapes of their West Berlin wiretaps for the last two weeks. Our people are going through them this morning."

As he was concluding, the CIA phone rang. Art picked it up. It was Mott of Counterintelligence. "Give me the director," he said. The Judge listened to him in silence, then turned to Trowbridge. "General," he said, "we have something I think the President should hear immediately."

Art grinned at his boss's bureaucratic ploy. Certainly it was the President's prerogative to get the juicy morsels first, but it was also a very subtle way of marking points for the Agency.

"Mr. President," the Judge said as soon as the chief executive had come down from the Oval Office, "we've just received an urgent communication from the Mossad."

"Ah!" A smile, one of the first Bennington had seen there, enlivened the President's face. Such was the reputation of Israeli intelligence.

"One of their penetration sources in Damascus—they give their sources five reliability ratings, beginning with A down to E—and they rate this one a B."

"I'll bet their B's beat the hell out of anyone else's A's," the President commented.

The Judge let the slight pass unremarked. "Anyway, Syrian intelligence has been reliably informed that two of these four people we're looking for, apparently the two that were trained in Montazeri's center in Qom, were under surveillance in East Berlin. They were seen going into the Iranian embassy and coming out with two heavy suitcases just forty-eight hours before the bombing.''

"That's it!'' said the President. "The Iranians gave them the explosives.''

"Mr. President,'' said the Secretary of State, "we may have a presumption of Iranian guilt here, but it's certainly no proof. They might have had the collected works of the Ayatollah in there.''

"It's proof enough to me.''

"It would never stand up in a court of law.''

"This is not a court of law, Jack. It's the U.S. government trying to decide who was responsible for an outrage against some of its citizens.''

"Mr. President, can you imagine going to the French, the Germans, the British—to say nothing of the Russians —to justify beating up on the Iranians because someone saw a couple of terrorists coming out of an Iranian embassy carrying suitcases? They'd think we were nuts.''

"Well, I have no intention of going to them or anyone else. We don't need their goddam airspace this time.''

The President looked down the table to the chairman of the Joint Chiefs. He was angry, it seemed to Bennington, frustrated, but the glimmer of irrationality he'd noticed yesterday wasn't there today. "General,'' he asked, "is the option we discussed yesterday ready?''

"Yes, sir. The relevant material has been turned over to your staff for incorporation in your Black Book.''

"Mr. President.'' It was the Secretary of Defense. "The chairman and I have been looking for viable military alternatives to Operation . . .'' He paused and glanced at General Schumacher.

"Hemlock.''

"Right. For Operation Hemlock. Something you might want to use instead in the event we make a final determination that the Iranians were responsible for this outrage.''

"I'm listening.''

"We suggest we augment the Persian Gulf Task Force with a couple of carrier groups from Diego Garcia and the Pacific to give us some more muscle up there.''

"How long will that take?"

"We can have them on station in ten days."

"Ten days!" The President's eyes bulged wide in their sockets, and he knotted his eyebrows. "You've got to be kidding! I'm not going to wait ten days to take action here. Haven't you guys learned that the first rule in these things is, if you're going to strike back, strike back fast and strike back hard?"

"Perhaps," the Secretary of Defense cut in, throwing a warning look down the table to General Schumacher, "we can tighten that timetable up a bit—"

"A bit is not enough. What do you propose to do with those two carrier groups once you have them on station?"

"With the aircraft we'll have available from those two platforms, Mr. President, we'll be able to mount a devastating air strike on Qom. Devastating."

"I don't seem to be getting through to you guys," the President replied testily. "I told you what I thought about air strikes yesterday. Now you're going to level Qom for me with one. You know what's going to happen? They're going to shoot down three or four of our planes. Some more Americans are going to lose their lives."

"Mr. President, these will be members of our Armed Forces, aware of the risks they've agreed to run in uniform, not civilians—"

"Dammit!" For the first time Bennington saw something similar to the anger he'd witnessed in the President the day before surging through him. "Nobody takes the fate of naval aviators lightly in front of me, of all people. A couple of those kids will be captured. We'll see them being tried, tortured, beaten in color television right in front of our eyes. Well, not while I'm President, let me tell you. We're going to clobber the people who did this and we're going to do it without risking one single American flier's life."

"Right," growled Bill Brennan, the President's burly Chief of Staff. "We've got to show some American muscle on this one. It's just about time we stood up and were counted. We've been pushed and shoved around by these crackpots out there long enough."

The scraping of the President's chair announced he was preparing to leave. "In any event, gentlemen, we're not there yet. Keep all the burners going on this until we've found our smoking gun. I'll look in again at two before my meeting with the Wildlife Foundation this afternoon."

As soon as the President left, Trowbridge called a brief adjournment of their meeting. The Judge edged Bennington off into a corner of the situation room. "What do you think?" he asked.

"He looked better, didn't he?" Bennington acknowledged. "That irrational edge wasn't there today."

"No. He must have been overtired yesterday. Under the strain of his first real presidential crisis."

Bennington shrugged. "Let's hope so. I'm going over to the EOB and see if there's anything in those electronic lobster pots of mine."

"Forget about those things, Art," the director warned. "It was a wild goose chase. The man's fine, and I don't want us caught poaching off the reservation, okay? Get that damn thing, whatever it is, out of there before somebody finds out about it."

It was the kind of press conference that turns presidential press secretaries prematurely gray. The White House press corps was a pack of hounds tearing into a cornered fox, all of them shouting at once, stepping on each other's questions, cutting off the press secretary halfway through his answers.

"Here we are being humiliated in front of the whole world again. Every President comes into office telling us how tough he's going to be on terrorists. And then he turns into a pussycat the first time something happens." Britt Hume of ABC was using the polite smirk he reserved for cornered government officials. "How much longer is this going to go on?"

"Gentlemen, I can tell you the President's on top of this, he's been on top of it since the news came in—"

"Then why hasn't he done something?" the CBS correspondent shouted.

"He has. He's had the Executive Committee in session almost around the clock—"

"Talk, talk, talk," someone screamed out from the back row. "The people out there want to know when we're going to stop talking and do something, for God's sake!"

"We're trying with all the resources available to us, with the help of our allies, to determine who was behind this outrage. When we have the answer to that, we'll determine what course of action to take."

"Is the President going to hold a press conference?"

"I'm sure at some point in time he will."

"How about today?"

"I doubt it. He's due back in session with the Executive Committee at two. At three, he's meeting with the directors of the Wildlife Foundation—"

A chorus of jeers erupted at the last two words.

"Gentlemen, gentlemen," the press secretary pleaded, "that meeting was scheduled over a month ago."

CNN was on the air with the press secretary's briefing minutes after it ended. Valentin Tobulko watched the undisciplined circus with fascinated contempt. That disorderly, shouting, confused performance represented everything he loathed in Western society. And to think that there were actually some of these advocates of *glasnost* who wanted to allow spectacles like that in the Soviet Union. He turned to Captain Vaninya.

"So. They're meeting again at two. I think we'll plan to generate around two-fifteen."

"What is it exactly we're doing?" she replied. "It has something to do with the President, doesn't it?"

"You know better than to ask questions like that."

"How much longer is this operation supposed to go on?"

"I can't answer that. I don't know. We will receive orders, either from the satellite or that." He indicated the special receiver which had been delivered along with the van, its antennas set to pick up the transmissions of one of the pencil-sized senders Ivan Sergeivich had shown him in Moscow. "The important thing is to be ready to get out that door in seconds if the order comes. Keep your money and papers on you at all times."

Tobulko squeezed her shoulders affectionately. It was the first human gesture, the first acknowledgment of her femininity, her superior had made since they'd started living and working together. As he left the apartment and closed the door behind him, she understood why he'd made it. Her guess had been right. What they were doing was directed against the President—in the face of *glasnost*, in the face of détente. The reasons for it had to be enormously important. And the magnitude of the risks they were running had just been expressed by those fingers pressing into her shoulders.

The man in the blue Helmut Schmidt Hamburg cap, Dante Russo's asset in the East German State Security Service, got off the S-Bahn at Frankfurter Allee in Lichtenberg and headed east along the divided highway leading to Wrocław and the Polish frontier. At Glaschkestrasse he turned left up a slight rise. On his left was a block of prewar working-class apartments, upgraded by the exigencies of the postwar world to middle-class housing. Identical woven lace curtains screened every window in the block.

He crossed the street to a newer series of buildings. The windows on the ground floor were covered with metal grilles. Those on the upper floors were barred. TV monitors protruded from the building at regular intervals. It was silent, sinister, and, like so much of East Berlin, strangely lifeless. In the case of this building, there was good reason for that appearance. It was the Normannenstrasse, the headquarters of the STASI and the man regarded by both friends and foe alike as the world's foremost practitioner of the art of espionage, Markus Johannes "Mischa" Wolff.

As the man in the blue cap entered the building, the two men who had been following him moved up beside him. They signed the sentry's forms, then escorted Jurgen Stohlmeyer to what had been his residence for the last eight months, a basement cell in the Normannenstrasse.

Upstairs, a buzzer sounded in Mischa Wolff's office. He picked up his phone, then smiled at the colonel. "He's back," he said. "His message has been delivered to your friends at the CIA."

The instrument Art Bennington had installed in the White House's electromagnetic countermeasures room was called a three-axis magnetometer. It was a bulky machine measuring two feet square and weighing fifty pounds. If it was considered as the center of a circle, it was designed to pick up any low frequency electromagnetic signal coming into it from any point around the circumference of the surrounding circle. It could also pick up signals coming in from the vertical plane.

It recorded what each signal's frequency was, the time it blinked on and off, and its intensity. In addition, its amplifier was able to resolve the angle on which the incoming signal was arriving so that its operator could determine the compass bearing, or bearings, from which it was being sent. In the case of a tightly focused signal the operator could get that information with a high degree of accuracy. With more diffuse signals he would be able to define the arc inside which the transmission's point of origin lay. Bennington had hooked its inbuilt computer to a printer so he could have a readout of the information it had recorded in his absence.

"So, Art," said the curious warrant officer on duty as Bennington threaded his way through the morning's tape. "What have we got there?"

"Garbage," Bennington sighed. "A lot of garbage." The signals the device had picked up were, without exception, weak and brief. There was nothing that even vaguely met the definition he had in mind of the signal he was looking for. "You really aren't missing much by not screening down here."

"Yeah," the warrant officer agreed. "That's what the people who make this stuff"—he gestured to his banks of electronic equipment—"all tell us. You want to take your toy back to Langley?"

"I guess so." Bennington was very much aware of the Judge's order in the NSC situation room. He might take a certain pride in his reputation as the Agency's maverick, but there were limits to what was good for your health and well-being, and going against a direct order from the boss was one of them. And yet, he told himself, there had been an ingredient missing in the President's anger this morning, that intimation of the irrational, the obsessive, he'd seen the previous day. Why? Maybe it really was the pressure, the strain. God knew that in the presidency the strains were enough to unhinge any man. Maybe Art himself was the nut, gone paranoid from a lifetime around this electromagnetic circus he'd been involved with. Or maybe, Art thought, I am right and someone decided not to turn the signal on this morning.

"We've got one more session over here at two," he told the warrant officer. "Why don't we leave it humming until we wrap it up and I'll take it back to Langley with me then?"

The afternoon session of the Executive Committee was not quite fifteen minutes old when the muted buzz of the director's telephone went off. It was Bob Arnold from the Operations side of the house. The Judge listened for a few seconds, then spun to Bennington, gesturing for a notepad. This is major, Art thought, as he watched the director frantically scribbling his notes on the pad. When he'd finished, he coughed for attention and proceeded to interrupt the White House Chief of Staff in midsentence. "Mr. President."

Bennington shifted his attention to the chief executive.

His eyes seemed to have swollen in their sockets. His jaw muscles were constricting again. My God, Bennington thought, the man is building up to another monumental outburst of anger. You could sense that old New England training, that puritan heritage that said you never showed emotions, warring with the tides of anger bubbling up inside him, threatening to explode any second.

"Our principal asset in East Berlin has just passed out to his control officer a communication of extreme importance to this meeting," the Judge was saying. "I don't usually like to say anything about our assets at all, and I will limit myself here to stating that the asset in question does have access to the STASI, the East German State Security Service. This is what he says." The Judge glanced down at his notes.

Bennington, meanwhile, was watching the President. A slick of sweat was breaking out on his temples. The veins there were exposed and full. You could bet his systolic blood pressure would make the mercury jump if you put the pressure cuff on his arm right now. He glanced at his watch. It was eighteen minutes after two.

"Two of the terrorists we've identified as being involved in this, the two that trained in Qom, were identified by STASI when they arrived at Schönefeld Airport."

"Why were they watching them?" asked Trowbridge.

"They were on one of their watch lists. The Soviets don't much care for these Islamic extremists either, you know. They passed through the East Berlin border control at Friedrichstrasse last Monday into West Berlin. They returned to East Berlin from West Berlin at Friedrichstrasse at eleven thirty-five last Saturday night and left Schönefeld for Beirut on an Interflug flight on Sunday morning." The Judge paused to look at the other men at the table, allowing his brief interruption to underscore the importance of what he was about to say. "The immigration officer who checked out their documents at Schönefeld noted in his file that they were using Iran Air tickets with a connecting flight to Tehran."

A moment of silence as poignant as one devoted to

remembering the dead followed his words. Then a thunderous shout from the President tore through the room. "Damn!"

That's it, Bennington thought. Vesuvius has just erupted.

The President brought both his fists into the air, then slammed them onto the table like a spoiled child in a temper tantrum. "That's the proof! There's our smoking gun! Now we've got the bastards!"

His face was flushed, and Bennington could see, his chest was heaving. Yet this was a man in superb physical condition. His rage had to be tremendous to produce that shortness of breath. Suddenly, everything became clear to Bennington. The President had not erupted into this burst of anger because of the CIA's revelations. They had had nothing to do with it at all. His outbursts had built up before the phone rang, when they'd been discussing extradition procedures, when not a word had been uttered to justify an eruption like the one gripping him now. As discreetly as he could, Bennington rose and eased his way out of the room.

"Your meeting over already, Art?" the surprised warrant officer running the White House's electromagnetic countermeasures office queried as Bennington burst into his room.

"No, no. I've got to see that machine of mine." Art grabbed the accumulated coil of tape, went back to two o'clock, and began to work his way slowly forward, scrutinizing each incoming signal that had impinged on the machine's delicate sensors. There it was, at 2:14:19, a booming signal that had overwhelmed everything else, hammering its way into the depths of the White House at a frequency that was right in the heart of the spectrum where he'd suspected it would be.

Fingers trembling, Art pulled the tape through his fingers. The signal burst had lasted forty-five seconds. Then something else, a startling indication that this was not a random chance occurrence, leaped at him from those swirling lines and numbers on his printout. There was not one signal. There were two absolutely identical signals, and they had intersected on the White House.

"Quick," he shouted to the warrant officer, "have you got a good map of Washington?"

"Not a military target?" The President roared down the NSC conference table at his Joint Chiefs chairman, General Schumacher. The general had just protested attacking Qom, urging instead they select an Iranian military installation for a reprisal action. "They teach people to kill and murder there. To take hostages. To make car bombs. To blow up airplanes. It's a factory for terrorists. And you're trying to tell me it's not a military target?"

"Mr. President." It was the Secretary of Defense. "I'd like to appeal for a little calm here. A little quiet reflection. The military, which after all General Schumacher represents, is extremely reluctant to use force when the consequences of its use have not been well thought out. And that's multiplied by a factor of a hundred when you're talking a nuclear weapon. Nobody agonizes more about the consequences of nuclear weapons than our military people who may have to use them."

"Not well thought out?" The President's voice rasped with anger. "Putting an end to this savage terrorist era isn't a well-thought-out consequence of this?"

"Mr. President, you don't have the authority to do this in any event. This is an act of war, by definition. You've got to declare war before you can contemplate such a thing. You've got to consult the Congress."

"The hell I do. Read your laws. Read the Atomic Energy Act. I and I alone have the authority to order a nuclear weapon used. This isn't a war I'm launching. I'm not mobilizing the Armed Forces. I'm not going to land five divisions in the Persian Gulf. It's a defensive action to save the world from terrorists. We've been attacked and I'm responding now to prevent more of this."

The President's breathing cycle had become so short and intense he seemed to be snorting. He unbuttoned his shirt collar and loosened his tie. As he did, the Attorney General leaned forward to address the Secretary of Defense. "The law is very clear on this point. The President is right. It's the President's responsibility to make a decision to use nuclear weapons. It's not yours. It's not Congress's."

"Oh, for God's sake!" the Defense Secretary exploded. "You know perfectly well the intent of the framers of that law was to allow for swift action in case the Soviets' missiles were already flying against us. It has no bearing on a situation like this at all."

"I go by what the law says, Mr. Secretary, not what it 'intends.'" The Attorney General's voice was steeped in the entrenched self-righteousness of the Harvard law professor he had once been. "If the President is convinced we must make an example in this case and using a small nuclear weapon will put paid to terrorism once and for all, then I for one am not prepared to say its use is unjustified."

"Well, there's something else," the Secretary of Defense said. He'd made millions drilling for offshore oil around the world and had been brought to Washington to harness the Pentagon's spending with his entrepreneurial skills. "It's called the National Command Authority. Orders to use nuclear weapons go from the President through me to the unified area commander who's supposed to use them. And any order for the reckless, unjustified use of these things is going to stop right here with me."

Some of those across from him could see the color rise in the President's face at the challenge in the Defense Secretary's words. He slapped the table with his hand and pointed his finger at his subordinate. "Let me tell you something. I hired you. And I can fire you. In the time it takes to say 'You're out.' Remember what Harry Truman said. If you can't stand the heat, get out of the kitchen. If you can't handle the heat on this one, then get out."

* * *

The blue Honda of Dimitri "Antsy" Yashvili, the KGB officer operating undercover in the embassy's Cultural Affairs Section, rolled out the black steel gates on Tunlaw Road and turned south toward Wisconsin. His appearance was immediately noted by the FBI surveillance team in the apartment building opposite the embassy. Since he'd ditched his FBI baby-sitters a fortnight earlier, Antsy had become an object of considerable fascination to the Bureau. This morning he rated not one but three tail cars.

Antsy took his FBI colleagues on what could best be described as an unofficial tour of their capital. He went down Wisconsin through Georgetown. Around the Reflecting Pool, the Tidal Basin, and the Mall, down Independence to Capitol Hill, all the way to RFK Stadium, then back on Florida to Rhode Island to 17th, up 17th to Church Street, across Church and on to New Hampshire, then over to Kalorama Heights through Rock Creek and back to the embassy.

Chick O'Neill was in the surveillance post when he turned back into the embassy gates. "I swear to God," he growled to nobody in particular, "he's got that shiteating grin of his all over that dumb face of his again. If his Honda wasn't six years old, you'd think he was breaking it in."

Art Bennington studied the lines he'd laid out on his map of Washington. The signals his three-axis magnetometer had picked up were highly focused. That, plus the fact his device was able to resolve the angle between the coil and the direction from which the signal was coming, had allowed him to trace those two plot lines along his map. The first ran almost north on a bearing of 352 degrees angling away from 16th Street up toward the National Zoological Park. The second ran southeast across the Mall toward L'Enfant Plaza on a bearing of 132 degrees.

He now knew one thing with certainty: the transmitters that had generated the two signals that had intersected on the White House had to lie somewhere along those lines.

He followed up with an assumption: the transmitters being used had to be small enough to be carried into a house, an apartment, or a garage. Therefore, given the intensity of the signals his device had picked up, transmitters that could be carried into a house or an apartment and send out a signal that strong had to be no more than a mile or a mile and a half away from the Executive Mansion.

Now he had to find them. There was only one way he could do that. The people, whoever they were, who were using these things would have to turn their transmitters on just one more time. They had to give him another forty-five seconds to track them down. Without that it was hopeless. But if he could get this device of his to the other end of the White House and catch one more transmission from those transmitters, he could lay out a second set of plot lines on his map. Then he would have them. The transmitters he was looking for would be at the points where his new set of plot lines intersected the old, caught inside a circle fifty feet in diameter around the point of intersection.

Right now, he needed help and he needed help fast. Should I tell the Judge what I'm doing? he wondered. If I do, he's going to have to tell the other people in the room and set off a real crisis. And suppose I'm wrong? Suppose this is a fluke occurrence, some electrical machinery noise intersecting here by chance? And I've turned the White House upside down for that, cast shadows on the President himself?

He picked up the telephone. It was not to call the Judge. There were times to run with the pack and times to go it alone, and this was one of the latter. He dialed the number of the Agency's FBI liaison officer, Mike Pettee, whose offices were over in the F Street annex. If a second signal came up and he got his plot, they would have to knock down some doors, make some arrests, and that was not a task Uncle Sugar assigned to CIA.

. . .

"Mr. President."

It was the lieutenant general who ran the NSA, the government's electronic ears. The fact he was addressing the President directly instead of the National Security Adviser told everybody in the room that what he was about to say was worth listening to.

"I've been informed that our people have just finished going through the tapes of the Berlin wiretaps which the Agency handed over to us this morning. I want to preface what I'm about to say with this: Third World diplomats in East Berlin all know the East Germans tap their telephone communications. So when they have something important to say, they come over to West Berlin and say it through a West Berlin pay phone.

"The Agency watch teams"—he gave a deferential bow of his head in the Judge's direction—"observed that a lot of those people, particularly the Libyans and the Iranians, tended to get a little bit lazy. They'd cross over at Checkpoint Charlie in their CD cars, then head around the corner to Kochstrasse, where there's a bank of three phones right in front of a furniture store, and make their calls from there. So . . ." he gave a deprecatory wave of his hands.

"On went the taps," General Trowbridge laughed.

"Right. Now at seven thirty-two on Friday evening a call was placed to Iran from one of those boxes. The person who answered spoke Farsi. The caller spoke Arabic with a Palestinian or a Lebanese accent. He said, 'Tell the boss the package has been prepared and will be delivered tomorrow.' Then he hung up.

"The following night, Saturday, or to be precise, at oh-oh-twenty-three Sunday morning," the NSA officer continued, "a second call was made to the same Iranian number from the same phone booth. The caller was the same individual as the night before. His message was: 'Your package has been delivered. The messengers have all returned safely.'

"Gentlemen." His eyes seemed to have a kind of institutional sadness to them, like those of a police officer sent out to notify a housewife her husband has been seriously injured in an automobile accident. "We were able to re-constitute the number the caller dialed from the electronic impulses his call registered. It was 00 98 34 2716."

The lieutenant general stopped a second and leaned back in his chair. "That telephone number has been identified as belonging to the terrorist training center of Hussein Ali Montazeri in Qom."

The President leaped to his feet and started pacing up and down the narrow confines of the NSC situation room, his tie askew, gesticulating with his arms to underline each of his angry words.

"I say fire that missile," he roared. "It's ready. Let it go. What the hell more proof do you people need? They did it, and now, by God, they're going to pay for it!"

"Mr. President," protested the Secretary of Defense. "Whatever the provocation, whatever the guilt of those people, this is a catastrophic, reckless, wholly unjustified overreaction. What about the Soviets? Do you think they're just going to sit there and let us do this and not do anything about it?"

"What the hell are they going to do? Start a war with us because we clobbered a bunch of people they hate as much as we do? Talk sense, man."

"Gorbachev will be on a plane to the United Nations tomorrow morning. He'll excoriate us in front of the whole world. We'll become the pariah among nations. We'll be alone, isolated, hated by the entire globe."

"So what? We'll be respected, and let me tell you, I'd rather this country be respected than liked. We're a superpower, not some candidate in a global popularity contest."

"There is no military justification for such an order, Mr. President." General Schumacher had realized to his horror that this man really wanted to fire that missile. Why, he asked himself, did I ever allow it to be programmed in the first place? Because it was a direct order, and you don't disobey a direct order. And what the hell do we do if he issues a direct order to fire it?

"No justification, General?" the President shouted back. "Go ask the parents of those kids that were killed in Wiesbaden about justification! Your people, your servicemen, whose kids were killed in your military school."

"It's not justification for this, Mr. President. You're acting like a water-cooler commando. You order that weapon fired and you'll do it without me as the chairman of your Joint Chiefs."

"Then I'll do it without you!" the President barked. "You're not in the chain of command anyway."

Now Jack Taylor, Secretary of State, the President's closest political ally for years, spoke up. "You and I have been down a long, hard road together. We've had our differences, but we've always worked our way through them. You can't do this. You can't. The Soviets are having terrible problems with their Moslem populations. This will unite them to a man. Our position in the Persian Gulf with all its oil reserves will be destroyed. The Moslems of the world will be on a Jihad against Americans for fifty years. Our embassies, our people in every Moslem country in the world, will be put at risk."

"Oh, come on, Jack," Bill Brennan, the Chief of Staff, retorted. "After this, those embassies will be the safest places to be in the world. Nobody will touch them. That missile will get the word out once and for all: keep your cotton-picking hands off innocent Americans and American interests. Why the hell do you think the British ran this planet for three hundred years? Because somebody laid a hand on them, they sent out a gunboat and kicked the shit out of him."

The Secretary of State ignored his political rival. "Mr. President," he said, "this would be an act of moral bankruptcy. It would destroy everything this nation stands for, you stand for, I stand for. Insist on this, and you'll do it without me."

The President felt terrible. He was nauseous. His head was pounding as though someone had put it in a vise and was tightening the screws. He could feel the sweat at his temples and his hands trembling when he wasn't gesturing with them to conceal the fact that they were. My ear problem, he thought, I'm going to have an attack. I can't have it here. Not now. Not in front of these people. He leaned over and placed his hands on the conference table. "I've got an appointment upstairs," he said. "But I'll be back. And I'm going to see that that missile is fired."

As Antsy Yashvili's Honda had driven down Church Street a light had blinked on the radio receiver placed on the bookshelf in the basement flat at 1750. Dulia Vaninya noticed it a few minutes later. She took the brief message off the machine and, hoping it would relate to their exit procedures, decoded it.

The message had nothing to do with their departure, however. It indicated a time at which the Center wanted their generators switched on, three o'clock that afternoon. She immediately called Tobulko in his van.

The Moscow terminal of the U.S.–Soviet hotline was in a heavily guarded room on the ground floor of the Presidium of the Supreme Soviet, the massive building just inside the Kremlin's wall beyond the Savior Tower. Unlike its U.S. terminal, which was a facility reserved exclusively for the President, the Moscow terminal was regarded as an entity serving the Politburo in a collective sense—although, in point of fact, virtually all the communications which went out over it bore the signature of the Secretary General.

It was unusual, therefore, but not altogether unprecedented, that Ivan Sergeivich Feodorov should present himself to the Kremlin guards protecting the facility with a brief communication for Washington bearing the stamp of the Politburo's secretariat. He instructed the duty officer at the terminal to return the original of the message to KGB headquarters after it had been sent. It was eleven thirty-five at night Moscow time, two thirty-five in the afternoon in Washington. Feodorov had carefully analyzed the hotline procedures. His message, translated into English, would be in the President's hands in about twenty-five minutes.

With their insatiable appetite for acronyms, the U.S. military had baptized the Moscow-Washington hotline the MOLINK. Its Washington terminal was a couple of dormitory-sized rooms in the Pentagon, inside the sealed-off National Military Command Center. Its door, which bore a seal showing a U.S. eagle clutching a pair of lightning bolts rimmed by the words "Washington-Moscow Hotline," was always locked to the military world outside, a way of underscoring the fact that those two rooms were the preserve of the President of the United States and not the military.

The anteroom was lined with banks of Russian-English dictionaries and travel posters of basilicas, icons, and the Kremlin to aid, perhaps, its occupants to envisage the world at the other end of their circuits. The link room itself wasn't much larger than a big walk-in closet. Everything in it was redundant. All hotline messages were transmitted simultaneously over three circuits: an underseas cable to London and hence to Moscow by land line and two Intelsat satellite circuits. The Americans and the Soviets employed identical IBM computers to transmit, two in each terminal. Their screens were blue, bordered in red when they were transmitting in the clear, black when they were transmitting in code. Beside them were a pair of cocoa-colored Siemens coding machines, roughly the shape and size of cash registers. The settings, which governed the code, were determined on alternate weeks by Washington and Moscow.

Those machines pumped out their messages at a laborious sixty-six words per minute, but since they had to be translated as they came in by the duty translator, the machine's sluggish output was not a problem. Neither side wanted to contemplate machine translations for fear of losing the nuances of language of a President or a Secretary General whose idiom was as highly flavored as Lyndon Johnson's or Nikita Khrushchev's.

On Tuesday afternoon, the communications director and translator on duty were bored. Throughout their shift they had had nothing to do except send and receive hourly test texts, inane homilies on pharaonic funeral rites or Australian sheep breeding. They were delighted to hear the alert buzzer indicating an incoming message at two forty-nine. As procedure demanded, the communications director summoned the NMCC's deputy duty officer. His responsibility was to be sure everything was done according to standard procedures. Neither he nor the communications director were allowed to look at the text, however. Messages were the personal property of the President. No one except the President was allowed to read them. Not even the chairman of the Joint Chiefs or the Secretary of Defense could enter this room and ask to see them.

When the message from Moscow had cleared the decoder, the translator ordered the other two men out of the link room and began his translation. In one corner of his desk was a black telephone, a tie line to the White House switchboard. The instant his translation was finished, he would read it directly to the President over that phone.

The President was alone in the Oval Office, his head clasped in his hands. He was emotionally exhausted, as spent and as empty as he had once felt as a child after screaming out his rage at his father during one of the older man's drunken rampages. I've got to get hold of myself, he thought. I'm flying off the handle these days. He glanced at his office clock. It was a couple of minutes to three, almost time for the Wildlife Foundation. At that moment, his phone rang.

"Sir," a voice announced, "this is Lieutenant Esterling, the MOLINK duty translator. We've just received a communication from Moscow. Shall I read it?"

"By all means, young man."

The President grunted in satisfaction as the words began to come over the phone. Those guys downstairs might not understand his position, but in Moscow they did. There was not going to be any Soviet retaliation for a strike on Qom. "We understand you cannot let this outrage go unchallenged," the message stated. "It will not be our position to assail or attack you for the consequences of your retaliatory action whatever it may be."

The President hung up and began to pace the floor. Suddenly, his anger, that burning rage he'd felt so often lately, overwhelmed him again. The Russians understood what these well-meaning advisers of his didn't want to understand. They saw what had to be done. He clenched his fists in fury and bit down so hard he winced. He wanted to shout out his rage. The only argument his advisers downstairs had made that made sense concerned the Russians' reaction. Well, this message killed their argument. The way was clear now to hammer those savages behind the outrage in Wiesbaden. Why not? he thought. Why wait? Why get into any more of those never-ending debates downstairs?

"I sure as hell hope you know what you're doing, Bennington," rasped Mike Pettee, the FBI liaison officer to the CIA.

"Of course I don't know, Michael," Bennington laughed. "What fun would that be?"

Bennington had installed his magnetometer in what was nothing more than a large closet in the eastern end of the White House basement where the electromagnetic countermeasures people had set up some of their own equipment. Here he felt certain the magnetometer would be within the narrow focus of the incoming signal he'd picked up earlier. Yet at the same time, he was far enough away from the Executive Office Building site from which he'd picked it up to get a fix that would allow him to determine where the transmissions were coming from. Now all the operators had to do was turn their signal on just one more time.

"Suppose somebody out at Langley's trying to get hold of me?" Pettee sighed. The FBI man, Bennington knew, was the kind of guy who loved to agonize over little, inconsequential things, the sort of man who had to have each object on his desk from his wife's photo to his pencil stand aligned at a precise angle before he was able to work.

"They'll think you're over at the Hay Adams spending the afternoon in the sack with some bimbo."

"I suppose you think that's funny."

"Funny? No, but I sure as hell think it would be fun." As they talked, Art's eyes were focused on the monitor for his magnetometer. A series of figures blinked on and off, a cascade of numbers in shades of rose and pink. It was like the readout of one of the random-number generators he'd fooled around with in parapsychological labs. One thing was clear: the ambient electromagnetic noise they were picking up was an indiscriminate blur. None of the signals impinging on his magnetometer's sensors had any intensity to them at all.

"Listen, Michael, what's the best medal they give out over there at the Bureau?"

"How would I know?"

"If this goes right, you'll get one, believe me."

"I'll be lucky not to be named Special Agent in Charge in Lockjaw, Alaska, just for hanging around a guy like you. You know what they said about—"

"Wait!" Bennington leaped up. Four numbers were glowing like hot coals from the screen of his monitor. "That's it! They're transmitting again!" he shouted. He leaned over the magnetometer to be sure it was recording properly. "We've got them!"

"Got who?"

Bennington shrugged. "We'll find that out when we knock on their door."

Forty-five seconds after the signal came on, it blinked off.

Bennington grabbed the U.S. Army Engineers' one-to-one-thousand map of Washington, D.C., on which he'd traced the readouts from his machine. He realized immediately that something was very wrong. The signal that had come in from the southeast across the Mall on his first reception had swung almost eighty degrees to the southwest. He sickened. That meant the signal generator was mobile. They were transmitting from trucks or vans.

He turned to the reading for the second transmitter. Relief and exultation swept through him as he realized this one had not shifted location. Slowly, determined not to make an error or a miscalculation, he laid his new plot line onto his map. It intersected his first line on the southern side of Church Street. Church Street was 1,015 feet long. He measured out the distance. The lines intersected 485 feet from 17th. Therefore the transmitter was within a circle fifty feet in diameter around that spot.

Upstairs in the Oval Office, the President had rushed to his desk and grabbed his phone. "Put me through to the NMCC," he ordered the White House switchboard.

Within seconds, he had an Air Force brigadier general, the NMCC duty officer, on the phone. "Patch me through to the captain of the *Valley Forge*," he ordered.

"Yes, sir," the brigadier replied, startled but not shocked. Presidents had on occasion talked directly to military commanders in the field. Both Richard Nixon and Lyndon Johnson had done it during the Vietnam War. Since then, an informal procedure had been established for such circumstances at the NMCC. It was not formally authorized or a procedure written down in black and white, but it was understood. The brigadier set a tape rolling to record the conversation, then called up the *Valley Forge* on a limited-access secure voice network.

"Stand by for the President," he ordered a surprised Captain Edmonds on the *Valley Forge*, then informed the President, "You're through, sir."

The President had taken his authentication code card from his wallet and held it before him. "Captain," he said, "this is your commander in chief." He then gave the authentication code for the day, which confirmed beyond any question who he was to the captain.

"Yes, sir," Edmonds replied, although he had had no doubt who was on the line.

"You are aware of Operation Hemlock programmed for your ship?"

"Yes, sir."

"Launch the operation."

Edmonds was stunned. "Launch, sir?"

"Fire the missile. That's an order."

Edmonds was so thunderstruck, he could only gasp, "Yes, sir." Before he was able to formulate another word, he heard the click of the President setting down his telephone in the White House, and the NMCC duty officer coming on the line informing him the circuit was closed.

The officer of the deck and exec had both been with Edmonds in the combat information center, where he'd taken the President's call. "So now those bastards are finally going to get what they deserve," the exec said in a soft but satisfied growl.

"This is unprecedented!" Edmonds blurted.

"It may be unprecedented, Captain, but that was the President and that was a legal order," the exec replied.

"Legal order or not, we have an approved chain-of-command procedure, and my orders are never to launch a nuclear missile without an enabling code from a second channel with equal knowledge of the weapons system and the message system. There's a certain procedure I have to follow, and I can't deviate from that."

"You also can't ignore a direct order from the President of the United States, Captain."

"No," Edmonds acknowledged grimly. "I can't and I'm not going to. Put the ship into the Operation Hemlock firing position and initiate launch procedures," he ordered the exec.

Minutes later, the President stormed into the National Security situation room unannounced. Without waiting for General Trowbridge or anyone else to acknowledge his presence, he strode to his place at the head of the table. Instead of sitting down, however, he jammed his foot against the rung of his chair and grasped its back with both hands. So tightly did he grab it, his knuckles glowed white under his skin. "I've done it!" he snarled. "I've ordered that missile fired. Now those bastards are going to pay for what they did."

"Mr. President," the Secretary of Defense protested. "That's not a valid order."

"The hell it isn't!" the President shouted back.

"You've ignored the National Command Authority chain of command."

"Where is it written in stone I'm obliged to follow it?" the President retorted. "Nowhere." Then he turned and strode back out of the room, up to the Oval Office and his visitors from the Wildlife Foundation.

General Trowbridge recovered first. He turned to his deputy. "Get the Vice President. Wherever he is. Get him here immediately." He stood up and rapped on the table. "Gentlemen," he ordered, "I want the room vacated by everybody except principals. Right now."

The rear admiral commanding the Persian Gulf Task Force stumbled sleepily toward his telephone to take the urgent call from the captain of the *Valley Forge*. It was past midnight in the Gulf. Captain Edmonds's announcement of the President's order woke him up fast enough. The admiral was a shrewd man. He understood one thing right away: he was not going to go on record as having ordered Edmonds to disregard or ignore a direct order from the President.

On the other hand, he wanted to make damn certain Edmonds didn't fire the cruise missile until he'd been able to find out what the hell was going on. "I am not aware of the existence of that order, Captain. It has not been relayed through proper chain-of-command channels." That was meant to flash a red warning light to Edmonds, telling him to delay executing the order without actually coming out and saying so. "Prepare to execute the order while I secure confirmation of its validity from the proper authority." Since the cruise missile could be on its way to Qom in less than sixty seconds, those words told Edmonds, as clearly as anything could, to wait. The admiral knew Edmonds couldn't sit on that order forever. But now he was covered for the next fifteen or twenty minutes at least. He ran out of his stateroom and along the passageway to his communications center wearing nothing but his T-shirt and skivvy shorts.

"Get me the commander of Atlantic Fleet," he shouted to the astonished duty signalman. "I don't give a damn if he's in the head, the sack, or where the hell he is. Get him! Right now!"

Having notified his immediate commander, Captain Edmonds now took the step that was required both to comply with the President's order and follow the rigorous procedures laid down to govern the use of any U.S. nuclear weapon. He called the Air Force brigadier on duty at the NMCC.

"General," he said, "I have received a telephone call from the President of the United States. We have had a correct exchange of the authentication procedures for today. I have been given a direct order by the President to fire a cruise missile with a four-kiloton warhead on Qom. I now require the enabling code for today to release my weapon and launch."

"I do not have the authority to issue the code," the brigadier replied. That was a lie—in a nuclear emergency, he did have the authority, but he was damned if he was going to use it in this situation. He'd already listened to the tape of the President's call. Once Edmonds had the code, that missile was going to fly. It would have to. Edmonds wouldn't have any choice. "I will request release of the code from the Secretary of Defense, Captain, and be back to you as fast as I can."

As soon as the last assistant had left the room, Trowbridge got up and locked the door. Moving back to his seat, he took a small pamphlet from the inside pocket of his uniform jacket, opened it, and pressed it onto the table before him. It was a copy of the Constitution. Trowbridge had slipped it into his pocket twenty-four hours earlier when he'd first sensed a streak of irrationality in the President's behavior. He glanced at it for just a second as though somehow the sight of what was printed on its pages would give him the courage to pronounce the words he now had to utter.

"Gentlemen," he began, "I have sent an urgent message to the Vice President asking him to join us just as fast as he can get here. I feel we have a terrible and tragic problem on our hands. To issue an order like that, in violation of the established chain of command, against the nearly unanimous advice of his advisers, can only mean that the President has temporarily lost command of his intellectual faculties. I want to recommend to this group that we invoke the Twenty-fifth Amendment and relieve the President of his office on the grounds that he is temporarily disabled."

The enormity of what Trowbridge was suggesting was so overwhelming that for a few seconds no one could articulate a sound. Bill Brennan, the White House Chief of Staff, leaned to the National Security Adviser, but before he could speak, Trowbridge raised a hand. "Let me first read to you all the opening paragraph of Section Four of the Twenty-fifth Amendment.

" 'Whenever the Vice President and a majority of either the principal officers of the executive department or of such body as Congress may by law provide, transmit to the President pro tempore of the Senate and the Speaker of the House of Representatives their written declaration that the President is unable to discharge the powers and duties of his office, the Vice President shall immediately assume the powers and duties of the office as Acting President.' "

Trowbridge closed the pamphlet with a hand shaking both with sadness and horror at what he was proposing. "That, gentlemen, is what I'm convinced we must do. Pronounce the President unable to discharge the duties of his office by reason of temporary loss of mental balance. And right away. That missile has got to be stopped. Firing it would be a catastrophe for this nation. It would do us incalculable and perhaps irreversible harm.''

"You can't be serious, Kent," Brennan shouted. "You're asking us to mount a coup d'état against the legitimately elected President of the United States!"

The Attorney General was on his feet. "General Trowbridge." He pronounced the words like a prosecuting attorney beginning a summary to the jury. "As the first legal officer of this nation, I have a responsibility to address the legal aspects of the point you've raised. First let me say that I have seen no evidence that it was the intention of the framers of this amendment to have it invoked in a situation such as this. This is the so-called Wilson Amendment, designed to cover the case of a President like Woodrow Wilson, who was disabled by a stroke. Ronald Reagan invoked it voluntarily to cover the time when he would be under anesthesia during his operations.''

"You yourself said yesterday intent didn't count, it's what the text says that matters," Trowbridge rejoined. "That text provides us a perfect legal remedy to this appalling dilemma we're in.''

"General Trowbridge, just exactly what is illegal about the President's order? Nothing. It may be a bad order. It may even be an unutterably stupid order. It may be a wholly unjustified overreaction to a provocation. But it is still a legal order. That amendment gives you no authority whatsoever to depose a sitting President because he issued an order you don't like.''

"Well, dammit, I believe it does," retorted the Secretary of Defense, "to save this country from the horrific consequences of a wildly irrational order of a President who issued it in a manner so irrational it can only indicate he was mentally unbalanced when he gave it.''

"You're going to pronounce the President mentally unbalanced for us, are you?" the Attorney General sneered. "Where did you get the medical qualifications to justify that? Drilling for oil in Indonesia?''

The Attorney General turned and pointed a warning finger at Trowbridge. "However well intended, your proposal is wrong. The issue here is not the President's sanity or his ability to discharge his office. It's his judgment. The Constitution provides a remedy for grave Presidential errors of judgment—impeachment.''

"Impeachment!" Trowbridge stormed. "Are you mad, too? By the time we get around to impeachment we will have fried forty thousand people, destroyed this man, his presidency, and two centuries of American history!''

Now Bill Brennan was on his feet. "I'm absolutely unalterably opposed to the idea.'' The Chief of Staff was not given to understating his views. "What the hell do you propose to do? Call the President down here and say, 'Hey, we think you've gone off your rocker, and we're asking the Vice President to take over'?

"He'll say, 'You're the guys who are nuts.' He'll grab the phone and call the Speaker and say, 'There's a bunch of guys down here trying to stage a coup d'état.' How do you think you're going to stop that? Lock the President of the United States in a broom closet, for Christ's sake?''

As Brennan had been declaiming his views, the Secretary of Defense's phone had buzzed. "Yes,'' he whispered. It was the duty officer at the NMCC relaying Captain Edmonds's request for the release of the enabling code. "I'll call you back,'' whispered the Secretary of Defense. It was a laughably lame reply, but for the moment, it was the only one he could think of. At least it could buy a few minutes' time until the pressure from the NMCC built up. The important thing was that nobody realize that the President had forgotten to provide the enabling code along with his order. If Brennan or the Attorney General whispered that to him, all the President would have to do was pick up the phone, get the NMCC, tell the brigadier to release the code, and sure as hell that missile was going to fly.

Now it was the turn of the Secretary of State to spring to his feet. "I'm sorry, Bill, the answer to your point is, yes, we may have to restrain him, we may have to sedate him, but I'm with Kent. We cannot let that order be executed.''

"Jesus!" Brennan exploded. "You're going to turn the United States into a banana republic, do violence to the Constitution, and for what? To spare a bunch of thugs in Qom who deserve what they're going to get anyway."

"No," said Taylor, trying to be as calm and measured as he could be, "to save him as a person, his presidency as an institution, and this country, from an order that should never have been given. I know the President better than anyone else in this room. I love him like a brother. And I firmly believe he has been, for some reason, a sick and troubled man for the last forty-eight hours. If we're going to stop this we either have to authorize the Secretary of Defense to countermand the President's order—"

"Out of the question," barked the Attorney General. "He doesn't have that authority. Only the Vice President has."

"—or vote to invoke the Twenty-fifth," the Secretary of State concluded.

"And then persuade the Vice President to go along with it," said the Attorney General. "Because without him as your point man, this is going nowhere."

The Judge had taken no part in the discussions. He did not feel it was his or the Agency's role to intervene in such an argument. Where the hell was Bennington? If he could get him in here maybe he could explain the President's behavior to the group, even suggest some of those wild theories of his. But where was he?

A sharp knock on the door interrupted their deliberations. It was the Vice President. "I got here as fast as I could," he said, offering the gathering his charmingly boyish grin. "Is there a problem?"

Art Bennington and Mike Pettee were careening up 16th, squirting their siren to open a lane in the traffic, Pettee's revolving blue warning light fixed to the roof of the car with its suction cup.

"Makes you feel like *Miami Vice,* doesn't it, Michael?" Bennington laughed.

The FBI agent was taut, concentrating on spinning the car through traffic, in no mood for Bennington's jokes.

"What are we going to be looking at up here?"

"Who would be interested in trying to manipulate the emotions of the President? I trust you're carrying."

"Maybe we ought to call for help?"

"Maybe we'd better be sure I'm right first. Suppose this turns out to be some aspiring Edison's workshop? Do you think the director would appreciate surrounding this place with fifty agents and the District's SWAT team?"

They were passing Massachusetts, approaching P. Pettee reached up and pulled his blue light back into the car. "Better not announce our arrival."

At the corner, Art jumped out. "Park halfway up the street," he said. "I'll measure off the distance." His hand-held distance calculator set him right in front of 1750 at 485 feet from the corner of 17th. The house was identical to most of the others on the street, three stories high with a bulge running down its facade that held a stack of bay windows. Its brickwork was painted beige, its wood trim mahogany. Pettee led the way to the front door. The nameplate read Houlihan.

A rather distinguished elderly woman answered the bell.

"Mrs. Houlihan? I'm Special Agent Mike Pettee of the Federal Bureau of Investigation."

"Oh, my!" Mrs. Houlihan said. "Do come in. Would you like a nice cup of tea?" Mrs. Houlihan clearly came from a generation and background which looked on a visit from the FBI in a rather different light than did most of the people Pettee called on.

"No thank you, ma'am. I'd just like to ask you how long you've been living here."

"Going on forty-five years now. Since my late husband came home from the Pacific after the war."

"I see. You live here alone, do you?"

"Oh no, my daughter's here with me."

"And no one else in the house?"

"Just that nice couple who rent the basement flat. Doing some sort of work for IBM, they are."

"Been there long, have they?"

"Oh no, they just moved in." Pettee and Bennington exchanged a quick glance. "Before that I had a science professor from the American University down there."

"Perhaps we'll have a word with them," Pettee announced, tipping his hat in thanks to Mrs. Houlihan. The two men tripped quickly down to the door of the downstairs flat. Bennington could hear a set of high heels rapping over a hard wooden surface in response to Pettee's knock.

"Yes?" a female voice said.

"Federal Bureau of Investigation, ma'am. Could we have a word with you?"

The woman did not reply. Pettee knocked again. "Ma'am?" he asked. Bennington leaned his ear to the door. He thought he heard another door opening. Mrs. Houlihan, her face radiant with excitement, was leaning over their porch railing, absorbing every gesture.

"Is there a back door to this flat?" Bennington asked.

"Oh yes. To the garden."

"She's bugging out!" he shouted. He leaned back and slammed his shoulders into the door with a savagery he'd once reserved for Penn running backs. The door shook. Upstairs, Mrs. Houlihan, not yet fully appreciative of what Bennington's gesture was costing her, emitted a squeal of delight at seeing television come alive before her eyes.

"Jesus, Art, we haven't got a warrant!" Pettee gasped.

Bennington had pulled back for another hit. This one tore the door from its hinges. They burst into a small sitting room. At its far end, a glass panel looked into a little garden. Beside it a door was ajar. They could see a woman at the far end of the garden grabbing hold of the trellis to scale a six-foot-high brick wall into the neighboring garden.

"Get her!" Bennington shouted.

Pettee sprinted through the room to the door, pulling his .357 Magnum service revolver from his shoulder holster as he ran. "Stop! FBI!" he yelled as he reached the door.

The woman's forearms were now at the top of the wall, and she had hooked one heel onto its surface.

"Stop or I'll shoot," Pettee shouted, jumping through the door into the garden. The woman didn't stop. She was twenty-five feet away and rolling her body up to the top of the wall with an athlete's quick agility.

Pettee fired. The woman stopped. It had been a warning shot, but its effect on her gave Pettee the time he needed to reach the garden wall. Now he trained the handgun right on her head. "Okay," he said, "why don't you just come back down from there like a good girl now?"

In the apartment, Bennington had spotted the signal generator. He knew instantly what it was. With a yank, he pulled its electric cord from the wall socket. Outside in the garden, he could hear Pettee beginning to recite Miranda: "You have the right to remain silent . . ."

Art went out to join them. She was leaning against the wall which had almost been her passage to freedom, Pettee's body blocking Art's view until he came abreast of them both. And, of course, it was her. He'd known from the instant he'd heard that voice say "Yes?" behind the door. As he had said yes to her from behind his door that wonderful night not so long ago. He had wondered what he would feel if it came to this: angry? betrayed? horrified? fearful she would talk and destroy him? He felt none of these things as he looked at her now, her hair disheveled from her flight, the despair of the newly arrested stenciled on her features. He felt sadness, a terrible, poignant sadness.

She looked at him a second. Her eyes recognized his, and a wan smile confirmed their unspoken message. She turned back to Pettee. "I choose to exercise my rights to silence until I'm in the presence of my lawyer," she announced.

They train them well, Art thought.

Outside, Valentin Tobulko rolled along Church Street in his van. He saw the curious cluster of neighbors in the front of the flat and the shattered door. He continued straight down the street to 18th and set off for Dulles International Airport.

Three of the men in the room, Trowbridge, the Secretary of State, and the Secretary of Defense, were ready to invoke the Twenty-fifth Amendment, the Judge estimated. Two, the Attorney General and the White House Chief of Staff, were adamantly opposed. The Vice President was wavering. And why not? The responsibility being thrust upon him was awesome for a man as young and relatively inexperienced as he was. The Judge had been agreeably surprised by the maturity with which he was facing the crisis. The buzzer on his phone hissed.

"Bennington!" he whispered. "Where the hell are you?"

For thirty seconds, the Judge listened unbelieving, then stunned and finally outraged as Bennington described the events of the last half hour.

"Wait a minute!" He shouted the words across the table at General Trowbridge, who was preparing to call for a vote on the motion to use the Twenty-fifth Amendment to depose, temporarily, the President. "We don't have to do that!"

"What the hell do you mean?" A furious Trowbridge sensed the Judge's intervention was going to upset the delicate balance in the room in favor of removing the President from office.

"The President's been manipulated. He's been subjected to a very sophisticated form of mind control." The Judge waved the telephone in his hand as a prosecuting attorney might brandish before a jury the one piece of evidence certain to clinch his case. "I've got the head of my Behavioral Sciences Division on the phone. He and an FBI agent have just captured one of the people who did it and the equipment they used."

"What in hell are you talking about?" Disbelief was writ as large on the face of the Secretary of State as a TV logo momentarily frozen onto the face of a TV screen.

"They employed a form of electromagnetic emanation to interfere with his emotions. To artificially set off his rage responses."

"I can't believe such a thing is possible."

The Judge was cut off before he could get out an answer to the Secretary of State.

"What I want to know," shouted Brennan, the President's Chief of Staff, "is who the hell are they?"

"We don't have the proof yet, but it has to be the KGB. No one else in the world would have the sophistication to pull off something like this."

"Those bastards!" Brennan's face reddened in rage. "I never trusted that goddam *glasnost* business."

"Bill, there's a power struggle going on in the Kremlin these days," the Secretary of State retorted. "Maybe the KGB's wandered off the reservation."

"Wait a minute!" The Vice President's palm thumped onto the table to counterpoint the commanding tone of his voice, a tone the men in the room were hearing for the first time. He pointed his index finger at the Judge. "Are you absolutely unequivocally convinced of the accuracy of what your man's told you and what you just told us?"

"I am."

"Then let's get our priorities straight. We'll find out who did this later. Right now, what we've got to do is stop that nuclear missile from flying. Mr. Secretary." He looked across the table to the Secretary of Defense. "I'm formally countermanding the President's order. Instruct the NMCC to stand down that cruise missile immediately."

In just a second, as the Secretary reached for his telephone, the Vice President seemed to shrivel slightly at the enormity of what he had done. "You'd better be damn sure of your grounds, young man!" warned the Attorney General.

The Vice President ignored him. He was on his feet, composed and sure of himself again. "General," he told Trowbridge, "you and I and the Judge have got to go up to the Oval Office and explain to the President what I've done and why. The rest of you"—his eyes took an inventory of the room—"are not to utter one word, one breath, about what's happened here. Do that and we'll ruin this man. And let me personally promise you that if even a hint of this gets to the press, every pair of balls in this room is going into the nutcracker."

The President was staring dully out the window of the Oval Office, his hands clasped behind his back, emotionally exhausted by the events of the last few moments. In the paroxysm of rage he'd experienced after his hotline message, he had expected that a sense of vindication, a kind of emotional catharsis, would follow his action in ordering the cruise missile launched on Qom. Instead, he felt drained and shaken, assailed by doubts and misgivings about what he had done.

He turned as the door opened to admit the Vice President and his delegation. "Dick!" he said at the sight of his second. "I didn't know we'd roped you into this."

"Briefly, sir," the Vice President said. "We've just turned up some information we think you've got to have right away."

"Shoot."

"I think you'd better sit down for this, Mr. President."

A sudden flicker of anger flared inside the President once again as he settled into the chair behind his desk. What are these bastards up to? he thought. Trying to undo what I've done?

"Judge, go ahead," the Vice President ordered.

The President listened, first irritated, then incredulous, then dismayed, to the Judge's recital.

"Mr. President," the Vice President said when the CIA director had finished, "in view of this information, I took the liberty of standing down the cruise missile."

For a second, it seemed to the three men before his desk that the President was about to challenge that usurpation of his authority. In fact, his mind was spinning through a rigorous examination of his feelings and emotions of the last seventy-two hours, of the sudden and often inexplicable rages that had gone coursing through him. His shoulders sagged.

"Thank God you did," he said softly. "Now find out who did this and why."

Valentin Tobulko went to a pay phone at Dulles Airport and dialed the *resident* at the Washington embassy. He identified himself with the code word he'd been given in Moscow and told the *resident*, "Inform my superior Situation Six is in effect." That was the code he'd agreed to with Feodorov for a failed mission with the arrest of one of the KGB participants. Then he left to board his flight to London and the beginning of his journey home.

As it often did to men of his calling and character, sleep came easily to Ivan Sergeivich Feodorov. In fact, he was so soundly asleep his telephone's imperious summons did not disturb his rest. It was the presence of Xenia Petrovna's fingertips on his shoulders, her hoarse whisper, that finally aroused him.

He sat upright and blinked in the total darkness enshrouding his bedroom. Light was always sealed out of Feodorov's bedrooms, whether in his Moscow apartment or here in his hunting lodge. Policemen sleep at strange hours; total darkness helps their senses confuse time and mute the body's circadian rhythms.

His eyes finally focused on the flashing red light on his bedside console. It was the duty colonel at the KGB's modern office complex off the Moscow Beltway. "Sir," he announced as soon as Feodorov picked up the phone, "I have a 'special treatment' for you which just came in from the Washington *resident*."

Feodorov was now alert, awake and worried. "Read it," he ordered.

" '*Resident* to chairman CRTOL reports Situation Six,' end message," said the colonel.

"*Spasibo* —thank you."

"Will there be a reply, Comrade Chairman?" asked the duty colonel.

"No, colonel, not from me."

Feodorov hung up and laid his head back against his pillow. He settled it there with the deliberate slowness of a man caught in the stupor of a high fever. Situation Six. Tobulko had sent the cable, so the female captain had been caught by the FBI. Perhaps she would talk. Or defect. Perhaps not. Did it matter? Her cover would collapse once the FBI and the CIA started to pick at it. She might as well have the letters "KGB" tattooed under her armpits. And they would understand quickly enough what had happened. Feodorov never underestimated his foes.

This would shatter the Americans' faith in Soviet-American détente. They would inform the Secretary General of that immediately, with that naive sense of outrage that so characterized them. Their outrage, however, would be nothing compared to the towering rage of the Secretary General. There would be only one way for him to repair the enormity of what had been done, only one gesture that might save the cornerstone on which his foreign policy rested. He would have to propitiate the gods of the Potomac with a fitting sacrifice.

Beside him, Xenia Petrovna was sleeping soundly once again. He reached down and slowly drew his fingertips along her inner thigh, his gesture infused with an infinity of sadness and longing. "*Moya sladkaya*—my sweetheart—wake," he called.

Xenia Petrovna stirred. "What time is it?" she mumbled.

"Four."

"Ivanchik, why do you wake me?"

"I have news from Washington."

He felt her stiffen.

"We failed. They captured one of our people."

Xenia Petrovna had never been informed of the full details of Feodorov's plan. She was totally ignorant of the fact that her lover had deliberately staged the bombing outrage in Wiesbaden. However, knowing what she did of Feodorov's urgent need to manipulate the President's aggressive reaction, she had quickly sensed the possibility the Organs were involved in the attack. "Is it bad?" she asked.

"Very, I fear. I think you must dress and go as quickly as you can."

"They are coming for you?"

"Sooner or later. And it will do no good to your case to have them find you here. Not that the guard post's logs won't tell them everything they need to know."

"What will happen to you, Vaniusha?"

"It's you I'm concerned with, Xenia. Reveal everything you know, everything you did. Hold back nothing. Everything you did, you did on my orders, for the Organs, for socialist science."

"Vaniusha—" she started to protest, but he pressed his index finger to her lips.

"The Americans will understand quickly enough what happened. But they won't understand why it happened. That will demonstrate how important you are. You are a precious asset of Soviet science, Xenia, and that will allow you to overcome the difficult days ahead."

"And you, *moya doushka*?" she whispered.

"These are not Stalinist times. It will not be easy. I do not think we will meet in surroundings like these again." He had switched on the bedroom light. There was no sparkle in his dark Georgian eyes as he looked down on her now. "I have survived other problems. I will survive this one." A sad smile creased his face. "I will survive in less pleasant circumstances, but I will be all right. Come, it's time for you to go."

He brought her to the door of the lodge when she'd dressed. They stood there for a moment regarding each other in silence. "Remember me fondly, Xenia," he whispered as he took her in his arms. Drawing away from their long embrace, he saw tears glistening on her cheeks. "Don't worry," he said, squeezing her forearm. "I'll be all right."

He watched her start across the driveway to her car, then he turned into the lodge. He walked back through his living room toward the big stone fireplace and the trophies of thirty years of hunting. There was one thing he could do: reveal the tapes of his talk in this room with Chebrikov and Ligachev. But what good would that do? Save him? Certainly not. It would only destroy any last hope of a return to the path from which socialism had strayed. He opened his concealed taping device. The tapes had automatically rewound after their conversation. He reached up and activated the erase button. Then he closed the taping compartment and looked up to his matched Purdey shotguns in their gun cabinet above him.

Xenia Petrovna had started her Citroën and was driving out the gate when she heard the reverberation of the shotgun's blast shattering the silence of Zavidovo.

"Have they given you your medal yet, Michael?"

Mike Pettee looked up from his desk at the F Street annex and smiled at Art Bennington.

"How's the shoulder?" he asked.

"Sore." Bennington grimaced. "I should know better than to get up to stunts like that." He dropped himself into the chair in front of Pettee's desk with one of those wood-splintering thuds of his. "So what's up?"

"She's agreed to see you. And without her lawyer. In view of the way she's been behaving, that's more than a little surprising."

"How so?"

"We haven't gotten a peep out of her besides 'I refuse to answer on the grounds,' et cetera. She hasn't even opened up to her lawyer. He's tearing his hair out, which, when you consider he's almost bald, isn't that easy."

"What are you charging her with?"

"Word came down from on high this morning that nothing, and I mean nothing, is going to get into the courtroom about the electromagnetic manipulation of the President."

"So what does that leave you with?"

"Illegal entry with intent to commit espionage. Her

legend is already falling apart, and she had a fake passport on her when we picked her up in the garden."

"And you can make it stick?"

"Oh yeah, easy. Her lawyer's already indicating that with the lack of cooperation he's getting from her he's going to have to plead nolo contendere. If we can get her in front of the right judge, she's looking at ten to fifteen in Atlanta. Except"—Pettee offered Bennington the resigned smile of a poker player who's just called a full house with a straight—"you know how that's going to work out in the real world."

Prison interrogation rooms resemble operating theaters, Bennington thought. There is that same sterile coldness to both places, that same sense of life in a state of suspended animation, dangling between freedom and incarceration, health and illness. This one at the Federal District Jail was particularly drab. It was windowless, its furnishings limited to two chairs and a table salvaged from some government office being closed down in an economy move. The recessed lighting was so strong you had to squint for a moment or two before you could see properly.

An enormous black prison matron brought Nina in. She uncuffed her and flung a surly look at Art as though anyone spending even a few minutes with an enemy agent risked contamination by some deadly virus. Nina sat down and, as prisoners always will, began to massage her wrists where the cuffs had pressed against her flesh. Since she had not yet been tried, she was still in her own clothes, her red hair neatly coiffed, her lipstick and makeup fresh. She shook herself and looked at Art with a coquettish smile on her lips.

"You're smoking again. That's not good. I thought we'd dealt with that problem."

"You got me off them, Nina, but you sure as hell got me back on them."

"Sorry." Her look was almost mischievous. "Some things are unavoidable in our line of work."

"How are they treating you?"

"In the circumstances, I can't complain. Although I don't think as a steady diet I'll like it very much."

Perhaps, Art thought, she's opening the door. "I suppose you know why I'm here?"

"I think I could make an educated guess."

Art smiled and extended his hands, palms up, across the table almost as though he meant to take her hands into his. "Let me just lay out for you very frankly your situation. I think I can do it more candidly than your lawyer might. As you know, you've been denied bail."

"I know. I hadn't expected it."

"Nor is there any likelihood you'll get it in the future."

Nina acknowledged that reality with the gentlest of nods.

"You're being charged with illegal entry with intent to commit espionage. Your legend is falling apart like a timber eaten up by termites."

She gave a reluctant sigh. "Our legends really don't stand up under close scrutiny. We both know that."

"The very minimum that you are going to be looking at, Nina, is ten years in a federal penitentiary. I don't know what they tell you about federal penitentiaries at the Center before they send you over here, but they're pretty awful places."

This time he could sense just how hard it was for her to put a semblance of a smile on her face. "They prepare us well, Art. Even for that."

"It doesn't have to happen. We can handle this." Art had made this pitch twice before in his career, in Germany in the early sixties to East Bloc scientists in whom the Agency had had an interest. Both had come. "Come over to us, Nina. We take very good care of people who come over. You'll be well paid. You'll be able to do interesting work. If you choose to, you can quit and go your own way. You can put that shingle up again at Tysons Corner if you want to. And you'll be protected. You'll be safe from KGB vengeance. I'll see to that personally."

Nina sat still, terribly fragile in the harsh glare of the room's lighting, as vulnerable to what he was proposing as she could ever be. Art saw her shoulders sag and her chin, that pert, proud chin of hers, sink toward her chest. She remained frozen in that position for almost a minute. Then she stirred and looked up at him as someone will coming out of a trance.

"Art," she said softly, "I'm a professional. You're a professional. Yes, I know I'm going to jail. But not for ten years. A year. Maybe two. And then something will be arranged. The Center takes care of its own."

"Nina, even two years in a federal penitentiary is a long time. Believe me when I tell you we really will take good care of you. People like you are very valuable to us. We want the world to know it."

"I don't doubt your word, Art. But I don't doubt the Center's word, either."

Art took a copy of *The Washington Post* from his pocket. He spread it on the table between them, facing Nina. Feodorov's picture was on the front page, together with a headline announcing his suicide. Moscow, the paper's correspondent reported, was swept by rumors of a massive shake-up in the KGB. "The reception they'll have waiting for you at the Center when you get back, Nina, may not be the one you expect."

She read the article carefully, then pushed the paper to him. "It's not the same over there, you know. Things have changed."

"That much? For someone involved in a failed operation against the President of the United States?"

"Art, it's no. I have my service, you have yours. I have my ideology, you have yours. I have my motherland, you have yours. I will go back."

This kind of conversation was like a love affair, Art thought. There is a moment at which anything can happen but which, once passed, is lost forever.

"You can always change your mind. Anytime." He passed her his card.

"Thank you, Art. But I won't change my mind."

No, he thought, settling back in his chair, I don't think you will. "Nina," he said, "tell me one thing."

"If I can."

"How did you find out I was CIA?"

"When you were in regression. I played the role of your wife. You kept refusing to say where you'd been, who you'd seen. That seemed odd for an oilman." She gave a malicious twist to her smile. "So I looked in your wallet and found out you'd given me a wrong name. I sent your name to the Center, and, of course, they knew who you were and what you do."

"And you found out about the woman in New York who looked for submarines?"

"Yes."

Jesus, Art thought, how do I live with that? The matron was knocking at the door. He stood. Nina looked up at him. "That night, Art," she whispered as the matron entered. "It was ours, just ours."

Then she rose in turn, offered her hands to be cuffed, and let the matron lead her from the room.

The Executive Protection Service guard verified their papers and waved the Judge's limousine through the West Gate and into the White House, where the President's appointments secretary was waiting to greet them. "Red-carpet treatment," the Judge said, smiling, "and I don't think it's for me."

Bennington felt strangely ill at ease with the notoriety that had burst over him in the last forty-eight hours. The hero's mantle hung very uneasily on his shoulders after what he'd learned about Ann Robbins's death. Babbling effusively, the appointments secretary led them to the Oval Office anteroom. The President, he informed them, would be ready in a moment.

Bennington and the Judge stood off in a corner under an oil of Lincoln painted in one of the darkest hours of the Civil War. "Judge," Art said, "would you reckon I've earned one in the last couple of days?"

"I most certainly would."

"Witter. That kid whose clearances we pulled. He really was innocent, you know. This proved that. Bring him back upstairs."

The Judge grinned. "Never let go, do you? Okay, you got him."

"Gentlemen." The appointments secretary beckoned at the Oval Office door. The President, smiling broadly, walked from behind his desk. "Judge," he said shaking the director's hand. "And this, I gather, is your remarkable Mr. Bennington."

He waved them to a sofa and settled himself into an old New England rocking chair he'd brought down from his family's summer home in Maine's Boothbay Harbor. He liked the old chair, and besides, it evoked memories of John F. Kennedy in this office.

"Judge," he said, "I've had the most remarkable series of messages in from the Secretary General on the hotline. He's using this to really crack down on the KGB and set up accountability procedures over there similar to those we've fettered you with. He's distressed and furious about Wiesbaden. He's assured us he's going to root out all the people involved over there and see that they're severely punished. Quite frankly, I'm inclined to keep this whole business secret. Since it really doesn't represent Soviet mainstream thinking, I don't want it to put Soviet-American relations in jeopardy."

"I would agree with that assessment, Mr. President," the Judge said.

"Well, Mr. Bennington," the President continued, turning toward Art, "I've got to say you did a great job. Really terrific."

"Thank you, Mr. President." Bennington was in no mood to launch into one of those "just doing my duty" speeches.

The President arched his toes and set his chair into a slow rocking motion. For a second he stared off into the distance as though he might have been on the veranda in Boothbay Harbor watching an Atlantic sunset. "I still can't get over it, though. It's scary, really scary.

Where are we going if science can come up with stuff like this?''

The creak of the rocker's ancient wood provided a coda to his question. Bennington provided the answer.

''Welcome to the twenty-first century, Mr. President,'' he said.